Years ago,
she buried the memories
of a horrifying ordeal.

Today,
the nightmare has returned.

"By destiny appointed; so 'tis will'd,
Where will and power are one."

Too late she sensed the presence behind her; too late she whirled, raising the shotgun; too late she felt the weapon being knocked upward; too late the gun went off with a powerful blast, blowing a hole in the ceiling, falling from her grasp; too late she felt the pressure of acrid-smelling cloth over her mouth, the painful grip of iron arms over hers; too late she fought not to breathe in the terrible sickening fumes soaking the cloth; too late she fought.

The last thing she heard was the ringing of the telephone.

Too late. Too late.

Don't miss the terrifying novel DARK ROOM, also by D.F. Mills:

"A SPINE-TINGLING TALE OF SUSPENSE!"
—JUDITH KELMAN, author of
While Angels Sleep and *Hush Little Darlings*

Books by D. F. Mills

DARKROOM
SPELLBOUND

DEADLINE
(Coming in October)

SPELL BOUND

D.F. MILLS

DIAMOND BOOKS, NEW YORK

The excerpts used in this novel from *The Divine Comedy* by Dante
Alighieri were taken from the Doubleday edition published in 1946.

SPELLBOUND

A Diamond Book / published by arrangement with
the author

PRINTING HISTORY
Diamond edition / March 1991

ISBN: 1-55773-472-0

Diamond Books are published by The Berkley Publishing Group,
200 Madison Avenue, New York, New York 10016.
The name "DIAMOND" and its logo
are trademarks belonging to Charter Communications, Inc.

PRINTED IN THE UNITED STATES OF AMERICA

10 9 8 7 6 5 4 3 2 1

This book is dedicated to Corporal Donna "D.K." Lowe,
Dallas Police Department, formerly the Central Division,
now the DPD's first woman "motorcycle jockey,"
who took me behind the Blue Shield
and put me
"back in the highlife again."

Acknowledgments〰〰

When I first began researching satanic cults and ritualistic crimes, I had a hard time finding current information. Law enforcement was wary of the label, and library research tended to yield material more of a historical nature than a criminal one. As luck would have it, not long after I began my research, television talk shows began having as their guests individuals claiming to have survived violent cult rituals.

There followed a virtual tidal wave of mass hysteria on the subject. There was no dearth of information after that, but not all of the information was necessarily accurate or even true. As a researcher, it was my job to sift through everything I could find in a painstaking search for documented facts, or information which was reasonably well substantiated.

Although this story is strictly fictional, and not based on any single individual, the background material is the result of this research. I am deeply grateful to a number of people who made this realism possible.

First, I'd like to thank my editor at the Berkley Publishing Group, Ginjer Buchanan, for sending me two excellent books so hot off the presses they weren't even available yet in the bookstores: *Cults That Kill: Probing the Underworld of Occult Crime*, by Larry Kahaner, and *Satan Wants You: The Cult of Devil Worship in America*, by Arthur Lyons. These books provided viewpoints differing widely enough as to strike a nice balance.

While I'm at it, I'd like to thank Maury Terry for his

superb book, *The Ultimate Evil,* which concerned alleged cult connections to the Son of Sam slayings.

I am deeply grateful to Larry Jones and the Cult Crime Impact Network for sending me up-to-date information on open cases of ritualistic crime currently under investigation by various law enforcement agencies around this country.

Thanks, also, to the Central Texas Council of Governments for inviting me to attend an intense law enforcement seminar on ritualistic crime; the information and contacts I gathered there were invaluable.

I'd like to thank Dr. Robert Dobyns, Medical Director, Children's Unit, Charter Lane Hospital in Austin, Texas, for shedding insight into the psychological trauma of ritualistically abused children, and for coining the phrase "psychological murder."

Many thanks, as well, to Gail Trenberth and Teresa Phillips, of the Attachment Disorder Parents Network, for their valuable information on long-term results on children who have suffered serious preschool, or even infant, abuse, including those who were later adopted into loving homes or no longer remember the abuse.

As always, I owe a debt of gratitude to my friends: Ray Robbins, Professor of Criminal Justice at Western Texas College, author of *The Texas Peace Officer,* and coauthor of *Introduction to Criminal Evidence and Court Procedure,* for his encouragement, his wealth of information, and his friendship; and Lieutenant Steve Warren, of the Snyder, Texas, Police Department, for reading the manuscript in progress, offering valuable technical assistance, making excellent suggestions for the story, and being a loyal friend.

I couldn't write one word without the wholehearted background support, cheerleading, and sheer patience of my husband, Kent (my love, my life), and my two beautiful children, Dustin and Jessica.

One last note: I will never forget the support and encouragement this brash new upstart received from the following unparalleled authors: Dean Koontz, Judith Kelman, and Mary Higgins Clark. It's the stuff mentors are made of.

Know then, O waiting and compassionate soul,
that is to fear which has the power to harm,
and nothing else is fearful even in Hell.

DANTE ALIGHIERI,
The Divine Comedy: Inferno

Chapter 1 ~~~~~~~~

What is this comes o'er thee then?
Why, why dost thou hang back?
Why in thy breast harbor vile fear?
Why hast not courage there,
And noble daring?

Why, indeed, thought Faith "Dani" Daniels, as she slipped Diane Schuur's blues tape *Talkin' 'Bout You* into the tape deck of her red Chrysler LeBaron convertible and leaned back, willing the tension to drain from her body as Schuur's smooth, sensual voice filled the air with "Funny, But I Still Love You."

There was nothing particularly ominous about the warm afternoon. Early October in the "Deep East Piney Woods" of Texas was still top-down weather, and Thoreau grinned happily from the backseat, holding up his handsome German-shepherd head to the wind, oblivious to the vague anxiety which possessed his owner. There was no reason she shouldn't be able to shake that verse from Dante's *Inferno* from her mind.

At least, that's what she told herself as she steered the convertible toward the outskirts of town. The car was Dani's first, and only, extravagance to herself in all of her twenty-seven years of life. In spite of scholarships, getting through college hadn't been easy, and she'd saved bits and pieces of her schoolteacher's salary for years in order to buy the car she'd dreamed of since high school. In a sense, the car was a symbol, even a talisman, that the Dark Years were

1

behind her, and that she was on her way to strength and independence.

Moving to Maplewood for her first teaching job and buying the car had seemed a promising start. The town of Maplewood, population 63,491, had won national awards for being the kind of place in which most people in the United States wanted to live. It was a historical town. Spanish explorers had camped the surrounding woods, and neighboring towns, forests, and universities were all named after political or Alamo heroes: Davy Crockett National Forest, Sam Houston State University, Stephen F. Austin State University, Sam Rayburn Reservoir, Rusk, Tyler, Jefferson. One couldn't even drive down a Texas highway without being reminded of its history.

In some ways, it seemed almost to have been frozen in a simpler time at least a generation ago. The convertible passed down broad, clean streets underneath tunnels of huge magnificent trees, oaks and maples and hickory, pecan and walnut and birch, guarded throughout by tall stately pines. The fall frost had not yet made its stealthy visit in the night, but when it did, the trees would flame into crimson, copper, russet, gold, and harvest-moon orange—all to the background of deep piney evergreen.

Yet in spite of the beauty surrounding her, Dani focused inward, turning her day over and over in her mind, trying to soothe the disquiet which had settled over her since her exchange with Adam Prescott in her sixth-period lit class.

Dani sighed, braking for a traffic light, moving ahead like an automaton when the light changed. Sixth period was the dread "Dummy Class," the remedials, the losers, the misfits, the flunkies nobody wanted. Some of them took her class two and three times before they passed, because they could not graduate without it. Others simply dropped out: of the class, of school, and of life.

A careful check of their school records indicated that some of the students had above-average IQs, had even done well in the early years, but somewhere, somehow, they'd simply stopped giving a damn. Sometimes it took everything she could muster not to follow in their footsteps.

Dani lifted her face to the warm autumn sun, while the crisp air ruffled her hair. Maybe she was expecting too much of them, she worried. Some of these kids could barely make it through a comic book, much less Dante's *Inferno*. But she liked to think that maybe, just maybe . . . nobody had ever really challenged them before. If Jaime Escalante could teach calculus to East L.A. barrio kids, then why couldn't she teach Dante to East Texas country kids?

It would be easier, she mused, if it weren't for Adam. That passage, especially the part "Why in thy breast harbor vile fear? Why hast not courage there . . . ?" had set him off.

She'd asked Adam to explain the verse because half the class was asleep, writing love notes, or doodling, and the rest hadn't even brought their books. Adam alone had paid almost uncomfortable attention to her discussion of the great poem.

Adam Prescott, seventeen, had an IQ of 140. He'd been a straight-A student until two years ago, when his grades had begun to take a sharp slide. He was popular, even charismatic, but had gradually begun isolating himself from extracurricular activities. Other teachers blamed drugs. Dani knew it went far deeper than that, but Adam was a closed book who kept counsel with no one.

She remembered how their eyes met, how sure she'd been that he knew the answer; and that he knew she knew it. The question was: Would he give her a break and go along with things, just to keep the class moving? Would he pretend ignorance? Even worse, would he throw back at her one of his deliberately opaque questions, designed to make her feel stupid and look even worse?

But he'd stretched gracefully and Dani had relaxed. No embarrassing questions today. With the wisp of a smile on his classically handsome face, he said, "The writer is afraid to enter the gates of Hell, and his guide, the poet Virgil, is giving him a little pep talk, explaining that he shouldn't be afraid because they have the protection of Heaven itself. He's kind of a hypocrite, though."

"Oh?" she'd responded. "Who's a hypocrite, and why?"

She could still feel the familiar stirrings of excitement that had trilled through her, that little twinge she always felt when a child was touched by literature, when he understood it, when he identified with it.

"Well, this angel or whatever she is, Beatrice, had to come down from Heaven just to convince Virgil not to be afraid himself. He said . . . over on page 265, that sometimes fear . . . let's see . . . 'so overcasts a man' that he recoils, even from doing the right thing, like an animal who's afraid of stuff in the dark."

"But he also says that 'from this terror thou mayest free thyself,' and goes on to explain to the writer how this can be done," said Dani. "He wants the writer to have courage." The class had fallen silent. Most of the kids stared at Adam as if he'd sprouted wings right there at his desk.

As for Dani, it was these glimpses of brilliance that made her want to grab the boy and shake him, just for so deliberately squandering his potential.

"I don't know, though," Adam mused. "I don't think Heaven ever protected anybody from anything."

"Why do you say that?"

"Well, if it did, Dante wouldn't have had to include the seventh circle."

Dani leaned forward. "The seventh circle? That's in Canto Eleven. I only assigned the first two cantos of the *Inferno*."

He shrugged luxuriantly, confident in his own intelligence, and his own control over the use of it. "I read the whole thing."

Dani hadn't been able to hide her surprise. "You mean, the entire poem?"

"Yep. Even the Paradise shit. Uh . . . excuse me." The apology was insincere, and all the kids who'd broken into giggles knew it.

She'd struggled to retain her composure. Naturally she'd taught this before, but teachers were used to the tunnel vision of only preparing one week's—or even one night's—lessons at a time. For some maddening reason, her mind had gone blank and she couldn't recall which wretched sinners the poet had condemned to the seventh circle of Hell.

The ghost of his sardonic grin haunted her still. She wasn't fooling him at all. "I'll quote it for you," he said lazily. "I memorized my favorite part." He fixed her with that mesmerizing gaze that had brought down more than one teenaged girl. In clear, ringing tones, he quoted,

> *"Death, violent death, and painful wounds*
> *Upon his neighbor he inflicts; and wastes,*
> *By devastation, pillage, and the flames,*
> *His substance . . . Man can do violence*
> *To himself and his own blessings: and for this,*
> *He in the second round must aye deplore*
> *With unavailing penitence his crime."*

The room was hushed. Adam, who'd portrayed the lead in several school plays, knew how to hold an audience. But it wasn't his voice that caused the hairs on the back of Dani's neck to rise, nor was it the peculiar choice of verse he'd learned. It was his eyes. Already brown, they'd darkened to near black as his pupils widened. They seemed sparked with . . . excitement? Surely not.

With effort, she had drawn her attention to the text he'd quoted. "You're referring to the punishment reserved for those who'd committed violent crimes," Dani said. "Either upon their neighbor, their neighbor's goods, or upon themselves. The poet says they will regret what they've done forever."

"Right. And I'm saying that if Heaven really protected people, there wouldn't *be* any violent crimes in the first place. And I'm also saying that there's people who commit violence who don't regret it at all." A disarming smile spread across his face.

A sickening sense of impending disaster had settled over Dani then, as sure as if she'd walked into a corner cobweb in a shadowy attic, but before she could talk herself out of it, or even respond to the boy's disturbing comments, the bell sounded.

Everybody—including Dani—jumped.

And now here she was, cruising away from it all into the wind in her red convertible, dressed in comfy running clothes, as if somehow she could leave all the, well, *weirdness* behind, but the cobweb still clung.

On the outskirts of town, Dani turned down a bumpy, little-used road which dead-ended at the gates of a huge estate. The owner, Lillian Palmer, an elderly reclusive widow who'd recently died, had willed the estate to the city, on the grounds that the house be preserved as a historical monument and the small lake and surrounding meadow be used as an educational summer day camp for underprivileged children. There'd been a rather complicated rezoning election, and the city limits had been redrawn to include the estate as a result. Renovation work was scheduled to begin shortly.

Dani pulled down a road which amounted to two dried-mud tire ruts in the grass, almost hidden in the thick trees, and parked her car. Thoreau bounded out and she pocketed his leash in her running suit. She was going to miss this place. As soon as work began on it, she would no longer be able to claim it as her own private domain. In fact, she wouldn't be allowed on it at all.

Dani followed the plume of Thoreau's tail as he plunged through the trees and down a short hill, where they both emerged, panting, took a furtive glance around, then squirmed through a hole in the bottom of one section of the high, chain link fence. It was nearly six P.M., and already the afternoon had taken on a golden glow. They waded through honey-colored wild grasses to a well-worn path at the edge of the little lake. There Dani did a few stretching exercises while Thoreau waited impatiently, then set off at a slow jog.

For a little while, she let the accumulated stresses of the day wash over her; even little things like that stupid reception she had to attend for some rich guy—what was his name? Blake Jordan? Or was it Jordan Blake? He'd donated a wing to her high school library. The reception was to celebrate the grand opening. Dani, painfully shy, hated empty-talking social events like that and she was dreading it.

But eventually her mind cleared and she gave herself up to the pure pleasure of running and the healthy sensation of her muscles purring smoothly beneath her skin. It was very still; the lake a mirror reflecting towering pines and crowded hardwoods. Mosquitoes dogged Dani in the muggy air and she swatted at them and picked up the pace a bit. The circumference of the lake was a little over two miles. Dani ran it with Thoreau three or four times a week after school, depending on whether she spotted anyone else on the grounds. She'd been doing it for about a month, and she was really going to miss the solitude, the peace, and the spectacular beauty. Perhaps, she mused, she could start coming out very early in the morning, before the workmen arrived, and continue for a few more months.

She passed the wooden dock which would probably be thronged with kids and canoes in summer, and took a sharp jog to the right where the lake jutted inward for a ways. With practiced legs she hopped over the gnarled tree root that had tripped her headlong on the first run. Thoreau disappeared into the underbrush. She could hear him barking furiously, probably at a squirrel, and she whistled him back. Reluctantly he returned.

Breathing was somewhat difficult in the warm and humid East Texas air, and Dani was coated with a fine film of sweat. She rounded the east end of the lake and began working her way down the opposite side, passing the waterlogged but picturesque gray wooden rowboat which must have been tied in that same spot on the lake for years. Dani was now running directly into the sun on a stretch of pathway flanked by open meadow, which offered no shade from its low-set rays. She'd forgotten her cap and she cursed herself.

Panting a little, Dani finally entered the cool shade of the trees, growing even darker as the sun settled lower in the horizon. Her skin suddenly crawled with goose bumps. Thoreau had stopped ahead of her, blocking the path completely to sniff and paw at something. Her eyes still blinded by the sun, Dani slowed to a walk and squinted at the dog.

"What did you find, Thoreau, an armadillo hole?" Smiling, she walked up to the shepherd and leaned forward.

He was nosing at a woman's leg.

Dani's heart slammed against her rib cage and she sucked in her breath as if she'd been punched. Pushing the dog aside, she scrambled closer, and what she saw caused her to recoil as if she'd been shot, the image a frozen-frame in her mind.

The nude woman was soaked in blood. Her throat was slit from ear to ear, both breasts appeared to have been removed from her body, and there was something protruding from her vagina.

"Oh God, oh God . . ." Dani crossed her arms over her belly as her stomach heaved. She stumbled against a tree and threw up. Trembling violently, she felt dangerously light-headed, and squatted near another tree, her head cradled on her knees. Thoreau stood worried vigilance over her.

"*No no no, it can't be!*" Dani rocked back and forth on her heels. She had to get control of herself. Maybe she was mistaken. Maybe she hadn't seen anything. Sun in her eyes. Dim forest, all that. Heart hammering, she forced herself to stand and sidled back to the body.

It was still there.

An overwhelming desire to scream, to scream and keep screaming, welled up from within, but Dani suppressed it. She would have to get help, but for a long, dumb moment, she couldn't stop staring at the body.

"This is real," she murmured. "I'm not crazy. I'm not crazy."

The object protruding from the woman's vagina was a crucifix.

Dani's throat began to close, and for a few hysterical moments she was certain that she would be unable to breathe. Dusk was falling fast; the woods were getting darker. She whirled around, halfway expecting to find someone standing behind her, and reached for Thoreau, pulling him close to her side. He looked up at her as if to ask, What's going on?

She began to run.

It was the primal flight response to physical terror, and Dani ran as she had never run before, her feet flying along the soft sand pathway around the lake. Panic dislodged her mind from her body, as if she were watching herself in a slow-motion horror movie. Trees blurred. All she could see was the path in front of her; all she could hear was her own ragged gasping for breath; all she could feel was her heart banging against her rib cage, bruising her chest.

Even after she emerged from the trees, the hill leading to the fence seemed perpetually out of reach, bobbing with each strike of her white sneaker to the ground. As she lumbered up the last stretch, her weary legs gave out on her and she scrambled along, crab-like, clawing at the tufts of grass with her hands, digging her toes into the dirt. The tall chain link fence was her friend. In her mind, it separated her from the terrible. She leaned against it for a moment, gulping for air.

Thoreau, sensing urgency, bounded into the car without waiting for her to open the door. Her hands were shaking so hard it took both of them to fit the key in the ignition, and for one horrifying moment, she thought the car was stuck in the sand, but they bumped backward to the road and raced toward the nearest phone like Andretti toward the finish line.

And all the time, all Dani could think, all she could think over and over in her mind was, *It's starting again.*

Chapter 2 ~~~~~~~~~~

Detective Sergeant Nathan Kendall followed the black-and-white to the 7-Eleven store from where the call reporting the homicide had come. The woman had said she'd meet the officers there and lead them to the body. He hoped she would still be there.

They pulled into the parking lot. Over by the pay phone, he saw a snazzy red Chrysler LeBaron convertible. A woman sat in the front seat, her arm around a huge German shepherd. It was the only occupied vehicle and they drove straight to it. Kendall recognized the uniformed officers. The rookie, Taylor, he didn't know too well; but he remembered training the other officer, Randy Jackson, himself. Jackson had been a sharp rookie and had made a good cop. Jackson allowed Taylor to approach the car, as per his training, and followed behind at a discreet distance. The dog set up a cacophony of barking. Kendall hung back, sizing up the situation.

The woman appeared to be petite, dressed in a pink running suit, her thick blond hair pulled back in a device his sisters called a banana clip. Her cheeks were flushed as she told her story to the officers, her words tumbling out so fast they could hardly follow her. Taylor shot Jackson a bewildered look.

Kendall went up to the car door, and the dog set up a new racket.

"Thoreau! Hush!" The dog obeyed immediately. The woman turned bold blue eyes to Kendall, and his mouth went dry. She was exquisitely beautiful.

11

"I'm Sergeant Nathan Kendall. And you're . . . ?"

"Faith Daniels. Please call me Dani."

"Well, Dani, it's getting darker by the minute. Why don't we take a ride out to the Palmer estate and you can show us the body? There'll be plenty of time later for you to tell us how you found it."

"May I bring Thoreau? I promise he'll behave."

"No problem." Kendall gestured to the officers, who got back into their squad car. The woman snapped a leash to the shepherd's collar and stepped out of the car. Kendall was average height—five ten—but the top of her head would fit neatly underneath his chin. He stifled the thought and headed for his beige sedan.

The dog jumped into the backseat and the woman gave him a sharp command. He lay down quietly. Kendall was impressed. On the drive out to the estate, she told him about finding the body. He would make notes on her story later. Right now, he was just as interested in *how* she spoke as in *what* she said. Though she was soft-spoken and very lady-like, even dainty, she twisted her hands together in her lap the whole time she talked.

Kendall never got home from work before midnight, but he was usually keyed up for hours afterward. Sometimes he watched late-night reruns of the *Magnum, P.I.* show. Thomas Magnum liked to talk about the "little voice" he had at the back of his mind which gave him guidance on cases. Kendall didn't have a little voice, but like most cops, he had a built-in alarm system which he had learned to obey through the years. Call it instinct. Call it gut reaction. Whatever it was, it worked.

Right now it was telling him something wasn't right, and Kendall couldn't name it. Well, he *could* name part of it, and it made him feel stupid. All during the short drive, he kept stealing glances at Faith Daniels, glances that had nothing to do with professional procedure. First he looked at her left hand. No rings. After that, he couldn't seem to keep his eyes off her face. Blond tendrils had pulled loose from the clip and sprung out around her cheeks and forehead. She had tiny, even white teeth and high, chiseled cheekbones. She reminded him of the actress Michelle Pfeiffer. She had that same vulnerable, haunting beauty.

He wrapped both hands around the steering wheel and concentrated on the bumpy track, parking where she'd said she had parked. The sun had gone down but it was still light. He grabbed his flashlight from its on-board recharger and got out. The dog scrambled to his feet.

"Thoreau. *Stay*." The shepherd ducked his head and whined, but he obeyed.

They slipped their way down the hill to the fence. He glanced sideways at her. "I guess you know you were trespassing."

"Yes, sir."

"Please . . . don't call me 'sir.'" He grinned at her. She couldn't be that much younger than he was. Could she?

Her face was pinched with anxiety. They made their way through the hole in the fence and Kendall instructed one of the officers to obtain the estate keys from the city later.

"We'll take the short way," said Dani, plunging down a trail through the trees at a fast, determined pace. Kendall followed, his gaze moving from her petite waist, past her small, tight ass, and down her slender legs. He'd never seen a running suit look so good.

It was utterly still and quiet, colors lost in the evening gloom. The air was heavy, like a suffocating cloak. Clouds on the horizon, which was no longer visible through the trees, promised rain. Something felt hinky. Kendall looked behind him and all around.

Jackson and Taylor were right there. Kendall was sweating profusely in his sport jacket, but he always wore it to cover the .357 Magnum he carried in a small, tidy hip holster. Its heaviness against him was a comfort now. Silly thoughts, really. They'd all seen dead bodies before. So he kept telling himself.

They emerged into a small clearing and the woman headed straight for a large tree, the base of which was lost in the brush. He heard a sharp intake of breath, followed by a long, eerie moan.

Kendall hurried to her and put his hands on her arms. Her

knees buckled and she leaned heavily against him. Her whole body shook so hard it felt like convulsions. He looked down.

There was nothing there.

She turned and put her palms against his chest. "It was here! I swear to God it was here! You have to believe me!"

The other officers were poking around in the brush. Kendall met Jackson's eyes over the top of her head. Jackson lifted his hands, palms up, and raised his eyebrows.

"Are you sure this is the place?" Kendall asked her. "Maybe it was somewhere near here."

Great tears glimmered at the edges of her lashes. "I'm sure it was here, Sergeant Kendall. I run this path almost every day."

Keeping his face impassive, as he'd learned to do through the years, Kendall led her to an overturned log and sat her gently down. "You stay right here. I'm just going to check around."

It was conceivable that she had stumbled onto a fresh murder, with the killer still lurking in the woods. Why he hadn't killed her too was anybody's guess. He could have moved the body before they got here, but not without leaving behind all sorts of calling cards.

Gathering dusk was his greatest enemy. He went back to the base of the tree and shone the powerful flashlight. A badly mutilated body would leave pools of blood behind. Squatting down close to the earth, Kendall searched all around the general area.

Not only were there no pools of blood, there wasn't even a drop of it.

He looked over at the woman. She was sobbing into her hands. Would this be the normal reaction of someone who had discovered a body and then couldn't find it again? Then again, *was* there a "normal" reaction to such a thing?

He walked over to her and knelt down on one knee. After digging around in his pocket, he handed her his handkerchief, which she took with a tremulous, grateful smile.

"Could you explain to me, now, exactly what you saw?" he asked.

She stood, handed him his handkerchief, and walked stoop-shouldered over to the large tree. He saw her straighten her shoulders and take a deep breath. He joined her.

While she described what she had seen and patiently answered his detailed questions concerning such things as the height of the victim, he focused his attention on the woman. All the time he'd been scribbling notes, he'd been watching her, too. Her story never wavered, yet there was nothing rehearsed about it. She gave every indication that she was telling the truth. Kendall could usually spot a liar fast. It had to do with the drop of an eyelid, a sideways glance, a lift of the eyebrow, a twitch of the mouth. Faith Daniels's gaze was steadfast, intelligent.

Her face was drawn and pale. He paused a moment, thinking. "Ms. Daniels, how did your dog behave?"

Her forehead wrinkled. "My dog?"

"Yeah. Did he bark at anything? Did he act as if anyone was close at hand?"

"No. Not then. But . . . earlier . . ." Her blue eyes opened wide. "On the other side of the lake. Over there." She pointed. "I thought . . ." Horror crossed her face. "I thought he was barking at a squirrel. I called him back."

Jackson was standing within hearing range. Kendall nodded at him. "Go check it out."

Jackson nodded and left, unsnapping his holster as he did.

She looked up at him helplessly. He couldn't resist reaching out to squeeze her elbow. "You're doing fine." Up close, she emitted a musky scent, a combination of physical exertion and fear, yet it mingled pleasantly with a light, fresh perfume. With effort, he drew his attention back to his job. She was visibly trembling, her face white as a ghost's in the murky woods. He stopped writing and stared at her for a long moment in the gathering gloom.

"Sergeant Kendall." Officer Taylor had materialized from the dusk at Kendall's elbow. He almost jumped. Kendall nodded to Taylor. "Stay back out of the trees for now," he told him. If there was any evidence, he didn't want them stomping all over it.

If there *was* evidence.

If there was a body.

The woman raised her face and looked him directly in the eye. Her words would haunt him for a long time.

"Sergeant Kendall . . . no matter how this looks . . . I want you to know . . . I'm not crazy."

Thunder rumbled long past midnight, and Nathan Kendall was driving aimlessly, his police radio turned off, thinking. It was a habit he often indulged when he was off duty and having trouble unwinding. It didn't bother him that he was using a company car and company gas. It was his little way of getting back at City Hall for underpaying police officers in the first place.

He'd hung around out in the woods for a long time after the other officers took the Daniels lady home. Some things just didn't add up. The soft red East Texas sand of the clearing was full of dog tracks and running-shoe tracks that would fit her small foot. But right up to the base of the tree where the body was supposed to have lain, the sand was brushed clean, as with a tree branch.

Some of the brush was pressed flat, but that could have been caused by any one of them. He'd photographed the scene, anyway, just in case. Force of habit prevented him walking away without doing so, and now, with the rain building, he was glad he had.

Still, there was no visible trace of blood anywhere. Yet, on his last flashlight inspection, Kendall had found a tuft of blond hair snagged underneath a bush. He'd put it into an evidence bag. Thought he'd sent it off to the Southwest Institute of Forensic Sciences in Dallas, just for the hell of it. All he needed now was some of *her* hair, for comparison.

Of course, he knew that even if the hair wasn't hers, that didn't prove that a body had lain there. Then again, maybe there *had* been a body, and now it rested peacefully at the bottom of the lake. Either way, as of now—unless a body surfaced one way or the other, or a missing person was reported—the case was closed because there was no evidence that a crime had been committed. Just the unsupported testimony of a terrified witness.

Kendall turned down Redbud Lane, driving slowly. He tried to pretend that it didn't make any difference where he was, but he managed to drive slowly enough to read house numbers. In the end, her house wasn't hard to find; every light in every window shone forth. Kendall glanced at his watch: ten minutes to one.

He pulled up in front of the house and waited, drumming his fingers along the top of the steering wheel. This was the dumbest thing he'd ever done. Even worse, that persistent little alarm in the back of his head was positively clanging.

Why would a schoolteacher have every light in the house on at one A.M. on a school night? He should leave. He didn't have any business being there. On the other hand, maybe something was wrong. Wouldn't hurt to check it out.

He got out and walked up to the door, where he hesitated again, arguing with himself, his natural cop's curiosity wrestling with his very personal attraction to this woman.

He knocked. Immediate dog barks sounded forth from within.

"Who is it?" Her voice was shaky. She must have been standing right by the door to answer so quickly.

"Sergeant Kendall. I . . . I thought I'd come check on you. See how you were doing." *Stupid*.

There were fumbling noises and the door opened. Faith Daniels stood in a shaft of light, clutching a baseball bat. He stepped back. Her face lit up in a large smile and she leaned the bat against the wall. "Please come in. *Thoreau! Hush!*"

He stepped inside the door, trying not to look like a pimple-faced teenager with his first crush. Her hair tumbled around her shoulders. She wore a robe with tiny blue flowers that brought out her eyes, and God, even without makeup, she was drop-dead gorgeous.

He glanced around the room, tastefully decorated with chrome-frame art posters, overstuffed couches, and glass-topped coffee table. There was a blanket and pillow on one of the couches, and Thoreau sat warily nearby.

Why would she be sleeping on the couch? Maybe she had a live-in lover and they'd had a fight. Kendall's face felt hot. He should have known a woman this attractive would not be available. He turned toward her, about to make his embarrassed excuses and leave, when he stopped, dumbstruck.

Kendall had been a cop long enough to know sheer terror when he saw it. He'd seen hatred and disgust, anger and shock, but fear . . . fear was something a cop learned to *smell*. He touched her sleeve. "Are you all right?"

She bit her lip. "I'm just so glad you're here."

"What's going on here, Ms. Daniels?"

"Please call me Dani. Would . . . would you like a beer, Sergeant, or are you still on duty?"

"A beer would be perfect. And no, I'm off duty now." He flushed. Now she would know he'd come for reasons other than business. It didn't seem to bother her, and she headed for the kitchen. He followed. The shepherd padded along behind. "Nice house."

"It belongs to my roommate. She got it in a divorce settlement, but she needed help with the mortgage payments. Otherwise I never could have afforded such a nice place."

Kendall relaxed. She'd said *she*. "How can she sleep with all these lights on?"

She rummaged around in the refrigerator. "Do you mind light beer?"

"Anything's fine, thanks."

She handed him a Miller Lite and a mug which came from the freezer. He smiled. This lady had class.

"Beth had a chance to teach overseas for a year and she jumped at it. She's been gone a month and I really miss her." She got a beer for herself and he followed her into a large, handsome den with a fireplace. She motioned him into a chintz-covered wing-back chair and sat in a matching one opposite him, tucking her small feet underneath her.

The cold beer in the frosted mug was just the ticket. He took a long swig and looked over at her. She was watching him.

"I'm sorry I got so upset today," she said.

"It's okay. Anybody would."

"Did you find . . . anything?" Her face was pitifully eager. She leaned forward in her chair.

"Let's just say we're still investigating."

Her shoulders slumped. Thoreau, who'd flopped down onto the floor next to her, sighed.

"It's the blood thing, Ms. . . . Dani." His voice was gentle. "There's no way a body as badly mutilated as you said it was could have lain there, could have been moved, without leaving a trail of blood behind. It would have pooled or dripped or splattered or *something*."

She nodded miserably. "I guess you think I'm crazy."

There it was again. That word. He took another drink of beer and said nothing. Finally he said, "I wouldn't be here now if I really thought that."

"Why *are* you here?"

Because I can't get you out of my mind. "Because I need a hair sample."

"What?"

"Just a little snip of it."

"At this time of night?" She was smiling at him with a teasing glance, and he ducked his head into his beer mug again, feeling foolish. This was ridiculous. He never should have come, and yet he was glad he had.

"I'm so glad you're here," she said, as if on cue. There were hollow shadows underneath her eyes. He looked at her for a long time, thinking.

"What are you so afraid of?" he asked finally.

She looked away, got up, walked to the hearth, leaned against it. Wordlessly she shook her head.

There was that feeling again. This time it was more than just a little alarm; it was hairs on the back of his neck, bristling. Uncomfortably he glanced behind him. "You were sleeping on the couch with a baseball bat, weren't you? And you've got all the lights on in the house because you are afraid of something. Or someone. If you want me to help you, you're going to have to tell me what it is."

"Let me get you that hair sample," she said abruptly, and left the room.

Kendall got up and roamed the den nervously. He never should have come. Hell, he didn't know anything about this woman. She could accuse him of rape if she wanted to. For all he knew, she was a screaming schizo nutcase. It was time to go.

She came back into the room holding a pair of scissors, and he stood back, watching her suspiciously while she snipped off a small strand of her hair and handed it to him. It curled softly around his fingers like a live thing. He dug around in his pockets for an evidence bag, carefully labeled it, and stuffed the bag into another pocket.

She was hugging her elbows to her chest like a scared child. She seemed so alone. Suddenly he hated to leave her like this. "Would you like me to check around, make sure everything's all right?"

She nodded, visibly relieved. "I'd appreciate that a lot."

As if she were a kid afraid of monsters, he searched all the closets and underneath all the beds, then went outside and checked around the shrubbery and in the garage. Together they locked all the windows and doors.

"You should be able to go to bed now," he said. She rewarded him with one of her lovely smiles and he knew he was sunk. He patted his pocket. "I'll let you know if we find anything." At the door, he hesitated. Huge drops of rain began to splat against the porch. "Call me if . . . if you want to talk, or anything. And . . . stay away from the Palmer place."

She took his hand in her small, warm one. "I can't thank you enough. I guess I was being silly to be afraid." And she smiled again, but Kendall had seen that look before.

He'd seen it in the eyes of a rabbit that he'd found once, caught in a snare, with no way out.

Chapter 3 ～～～～～～～

Dani closed the door behind Sergeant Kendall, bolted, locked, and chained it, then leaned against it for a moment. What a lifesaver he had been. He exuded such a calm, assured presence that was just what she needed. It helped her put the whole thing in perspective. She was not a kid anymore. There was really nothing to be afraid of.

She moved through the house, turning out lights, thinking about Kendall. He was not what she would call handsome, but he was not unattractive, either. His dark hair was crisply short, but his eyes were unfathomable, something she'd noticed about police officers. Though he was broad-shouldered and barrel-chested for his height, he seemed flat-stomached and fit for his age, which she guessed at about thirty-five or thirty-six. Apparently he kept in shape. His hands were large, but not beefy or clumsy. Capable hands. She wondered if he was single, because the way he looked at her was not the way a well-married man looked at a pretty woman.

She found herself hoping he was unattached, and marveling at that. It had been a very long time since she'd been interested in *any* man.

Dani entered the dressing room by the bath and began brushing her hair. Mirrors don't lie. Dani was aware of her looks, but unlike many attractive women, she considered them a curse. It hadn't taken her long as a teenager to figure out that boys only wanted to show her off to their friends, rack up some sort of macho locker-room points. At one point she had even begun to suspect that there was a contest

21

going to see who could take her virginity and win the prize, whatever that was.

None of them ever seemed to care about *her*, her person-hood, her soul. Only possessing her.

During the time she called the Dark Years, after all the trouble, after the things she didn't like to think about, she'd gone through a period of promiscuity. She knew now it was a desperate bid for love, hoping that, if a man felt he *did* possess her, maybe then he would love her.

It was during that disastrous time in her life, the self-hatred and emptiness and suicidal thoughts, that she was selected for a full college scholarship for troubled but promising kids. She hadn't even applied for it, but had been recommended by an English teacher.

It turned her life around, gave her goals to strive for, direction, a renewed sense of self-worth. At college she distanced herself from men altogether, concentrating on her studies, and graduated *magna cum laude*. She discovered a natural ability for teaching, and had actually requested the Dummy Class, which had been shunned by every other teacher at her school. Maybe she could make a difference with the Adam Prescotts of this world, just as a teacher had made a difference with her.

Dani left the dressing room and dropped her robe on the edge of the bed. She reached for hand lotion and began rubbing it into her hands. A gentle East Texas rain was falling, drumming softly against the roof. Occasionally muted thunder would sound from somewhere far off, like a memory. She kept thinking about Sergeant Kendall.

Since college, Dani had dated a few times, mostly other teachers or men her friends insisted on fixing her up with. The years hadn't changed much, Dani found. There was still the front-door wrestling match, only grown men tended to be more demanding than adolescent boys. She was accused of being a prude, a tease, frigid, an "ice maiden."

She sighed. Maybe they were right. Or maybe she just hadn't found a man yet who was willing to treat her like a lady. Dani yawned. Maybe that was a hopelessly old-fashioned idea. She snuggled under the covers and turned out the light. Thoreau curled up on the floor at the foot of the bed. She smiled. Maybe she'd been born a few decades too late.

"You shouldn't have been born at all."

"*What?*" Dani sat bolt upright in bed, her heart hammering against her rib cage. "Who said that?"

There were sounds of whispering in the hallway. Dani's mouth was so dry she couldn't even swallow. Summoning all her courage, she snapped on the light.

Nothing happened. Had the electricity gone out in the storm?

"Thoreau." Her voice came out cracked, barely audible even to her own ears.

He didn't come. Maybe he hadn't even heard her. She slipped from bed and groped around blindly on the floor, hoping to stumble over him. He was not in the room.

She crouched on the floor, paralyzed, her fear balled up in her throat like a fist. Soft yellow light glanced off the hallway walls; moving, flickering light. Crouching low to the floor, Dani moved down the hall toward the lights, which were coming from the den.

Dani could barely breathe, as if her lungs were no longer capable of expanding to full capacity. Sometimes she didn't breathe at all.

She reached the door leading to the den and peeked around it. Dark, faceless figures moved around a table in the middle of the floor, holding candles. There was something large on the table but she couldn't see what it was. She stood up.

The whispers were uniting in a singsong cadence that she couldn't follow. The chanting grew louder and louder, and suddenly Dani knew she should run but she couldn't; her legs were rooted to the floor. One of the figures stepped back from the table and turned toward her and began to laugh, but all Dani could see was the limp, dead figure on the table, and the blood, so much blood; it was everywhere and everyone began to laugh and dip their fingers in it, but all Dani knew was the grief that tore through her heart, and she tried to call out, *"My dog! What have you done to my dog!"* but she couldn't talk, couldn't cry out.

Suddenly she was able to move. She turned and stumbled away, but she couldn't run fast enough. She could hear them say, "You can run, Faith, but you cannot hide! You can run, Faith, but you cannot hide! You can run, Faith, but . . ."

Escape. Escape. It was all she could think or do. They were coming after her. They were coming after her and she knew what they would do to her when they caught her. Escape. She couldn't escape. She'd have to hide. Here. Here. She'd have to hide here. It was like a little hole. They'd never find her. She'd stay here forever and they'd never find her.

Someone was crying and it wasn't her. Someone was crying in the hole with her. They were pressing something against her face, rubbing something against her face, something wet and rough. Dani tried to scream but she couldn't. She opened her mouth and strained against her vocal cords with all her might, crying, *"No! No! No-o-o—"*

Dani opened her eyes, jerked awake by the sounds of her own cries. Her heart was clamoring wildly; she was drenched in sweat, panting loudly as if after a very long run. Thoreau was licking her face and whining. She caught herself struggling, pushing him away. Something slick and cool batted against Dani and she screamed, thrashing at it with her hands.

It was a dry-cleaning bag.

Dani was curled up on the floor of her own closet.

Gray, damp, cold light seeped through the drapes which Dani had pulled tightly across the den windows. She sat swathed in an old quilt in one of the wing chairs, facing a dead fireplace. Thoreau sat patiently by the back door, waiting to be let out. The poor thing was so well trained that Dani knew he'd die of kidney failure before he'd mess up the floor. Yet she was afraid to let him out of her sight and afraid to go outside alone.

It was the effect these dreams always had on her. Poisoning her life with paranoia, making her doubt her own sanity.

"Dammit! Dammit! Dammit!" She pounded the arm of the chair. Thoreau ducked his head and fidgeted nervously. It had been so long since she'd had a dream like this. What was happening to her?

Thoreau whined softly. Dani sighed and crossed the floor to him, dragging the quilt with her. She opened the door and watched him bound out to the backyard, but she didn't close the door. She waited, watching him relieve himself in various places and sniff busily along the ground for squirrels or birds or cats or some other intruder he could challenge. Finally, she closed and locked it, pressing her back against it.

It was that woman's body.

Dani squeezed her eyes shut for the hundredth time, picturing the scene. Could she have imagined it? Could she have made a mistake?

Maybe she should talk to somebody. A psychiatrist or something.

No. No. Never again. Never would she ever put her mind in somebody else's hands. Forget it.

She hadn't imagined it. She *hadn't*.

Just like the other time.

Dani's head was beginning to ache. She was exhausted and tempted to call in for a substitute teacher. It was cold and wet and raw outside. She started a pot of coffee, mixing it strong, using some of Beth's. Beth would never touch Dani's instant decaf.

Living with Beth had almost made Dani forget just how alone she was in life. She'd been distant from her parents ever since the Dark Years, aloof from men, shy at making friends. Only at work did she ever have a sense of real *competence,* a belief that she really could make a difference with her life. She was a prodigious worker, putting in long hours at home or in her room after school, planning careful lessons designed to make the English language and its literature come alive for her students. In her fourth year of teaching, she'd won Teacher of the Year from her state's education association, even though she was still considered a rookie by many more experienced teachers.

Beth was so different from Dani, living on impulse. It had only taken her two weeks to make her decision to go overseas, pack up, get her visa, and leave. The house was so empty without her.

It was Beth's house, anyway, and now, more than ever, Dani felt like a guest.

Sometimes she felt like she was just visiting life altogether.

She sat down at the table, still wrapped in the quilt, and put her head in her hands. Steam from her coffee cup warmed her face.

If the dreams come back in full force, she found herself thinking, *I know I'll go mad.*

Shaking her head, she got up, carrying her coffee mug into the bathroom, where she turned on the shower as hot as she could stand it. "I can't think like that," she said to herself. "I'll get through this somehow." She stared at her wan, sad face in the mirror until steam hid it from her.

The coffee and hot shower were somewhat revivifying. Dani applied makeup carefully, trying to hide the ravages of the night before. As usual, she pulled her hair smoothly back at the nap of her neck, then dressed in a loose-fitting skirt and blazer, rolled up the sleeves, and put on a large pair of glasses in blue plastic "preppie" frames. The effect was no-nonsense; all business.

She didn't need the glasses. The lenses were not prescription. She wore them to teach in so that her young adolescent male students would take her more seriously. Her face was much younger-looking than twenty-seven and her petite size caused her to look more like a student than a teacher, anyway. She didn't want to give them anything to daydream about.

By the time Dani was dressed, her thinking was geared to the classroom, and the marauding midnight dreams were buried in the recesses of her mind. Even so, she whistled Thoreau back into the house. He came reluctantly. She knew that he preferred to stay outdoors all day, even in cold weather, but the dream had made her just nervous enough that she wanted to keep him in. She would come straight home after school and let him out.

After stuffing ungraded papers into her tote bag, she gathered up her car keys, and headed for the front door.

An envelope had been dropped into the mail slot. FAITH DANIELS was typed on the front.

The envelope was not sealed. Dani pulled out a card, upon which were two words written in bright red block printing:

RED RUM

Little spots of light began to swarm in front of Dani's left eye. She felt dizzy and nauseated. Her cheeks were flushed. A cold sweat broke out all over her body.

Clutching the card, she lay down her tote bag and keys. It was hard to breathe. There was a tightness in her chest. Trembling, Dani managed to make her way to the bedroom. Later, she would not remember that she had called her principal and requested a substitute.

Her left eye was practically blind and the vision in her right eye was blurred. Sharp points of pain stabbed at the left side of her head. Somehow she got her clothes off, but she would not remember doing that, either. Her stomach heaved, but she knew she'd never make it to the bathroom without passing out. Perhaps, if she could just lie flat . . .

The card lay on the dresser, where she had dropped it, the ugly crimson letters clearly reflected backward in the mirror.

Chapter 4 ~~~~~~~~~~

Kendall was late for briefing. He'd seen his ex-wife, Roxanne, before work and it had flung him into a foul mood. He mumbled "Sorry" to the lieutenant and took his seat next to Seth at the scarred, cigarette-burned table.

"Glad to see you could join us, Sergeant." Lieutenant Thomas Ward was a humorless, by-the-book officer who'd risen rapidly through the ranks and made it clear he was still in transition, on his way to bigger and better things. His iron-gray eyes brooked no nonsense, and he had no fear of older, more experienced officers under his command. His thick hair had begun to turn gray while he was still in his twenties, and now flowed back from a relatively unlined face, giving him a look—in spite of a close departmental trim—of a fierce iron lion. New detectives, recently transferred from the ranks of patrol officers, were terrified of him. Kendall, and his good friend Seth Rollins, simply stayed out of his way.

Rollins was a former collegiate basketball star who might have made the pros if an injury hadn't sidelined him his senior year. But that was long ago. At forty-five, he towered over Kendall at six feet six inches. His skin was the color of burnished mahogany, his grizzled black hair gray at the temples, his mustache salt-and-pepper.

In spite of his size, Rollins was a chameleon, superb undercover. With his sad brown eyes and gentle voice, he could coax statements from the most reluctant witnesses, and tame the most hostile suspects, but when needed, he could turn his size into a frightening advantage on the streets.

Under the table, Rollins bumped his knee against Kendall's. He glanced over. Rollins raised his eyebrows. Kendall took his pad and jotted the word "Roxanne." Rollins rolled his eyes heavenward. That was about all the communication thèy ever needed.

With effort, Kendall brought his attention to the case under discussion. Something to do with a knifing at the Black Cat Bar.

"The suspect is in custody now," Manuel "Manny" Garcia was saying. "We've got the bloody knife with his fingerprints all over it, the statements of four witnesses, *a-a-and* . . ." He paused, as though waiting for a drum-roll. "This is a clear parole violation. He was doing time in Huntsville on aggravated assault charges."

"Very well done, Sergeant," said Lieutenant Ward. Garcia beamed, his young, handsome face alight. "Thank you, sir."

Kendall glanced at Rollins. Rollins mouthed the words "Suck up." Kendall smothered a grin.

"Sergeant Davis, you have an update on the shooting over in the Projects?" Lieutenant Ward never called his officers by their first names or nicknames, and they wouldn't dare call him even the affectionate "LT" used in many departments.

Fred Davis was coasting toward retirement. His bloodhound face hung in folds underneath his eyes and around his mouth; his ears were huge saucers. He'd burned out on the job years before and he drank too much. His philosophy was, never interview more than one or two witnesses if you could help it, and never follow any leads that were more than a day or two old.

While Davis droned through his report, Rollins was reading over the suspect's statement. He pushed it over to Kendall and tapped the first sentence with his pen. It read, "I boke da winda." Kendall glanced over at Davis. Davis yawned.

"Excellent, then, Sergeant Garcia, Sergeant Davis.

Now . . . Sergeant Kendall. While checking over the blotter from yesterday, I noticed you answered a homicide call at the Palmer estate, but reported no body found?"

"Uh . . . er, yes . . . sir."

"So it was a prank call."

"Not at all. The witness seemed very sincere and pretty scared. I decided to do a little follow-up, just in case there *was* a body which had been moved by the time we got there."

"What sort of follow-up?"

There was something about the lieutenant's manner and tone of voice that was making Kendall uncomfortable. "Well . . . I found some blond hairs where the witness claimed to have seen the body. I decided to send those hairs, plus some from the witness's own head, to the forensics institute in Dallas for analysis."

Lieutenant Ward, who always stood during the briefings, forcing the other officers to look up at him, now placed his hands on the table and leaned forward. "I don't need to remind you, Sergeant Kendall, just how short-handed we are. As you very well know, two of our best investigators left this year for better-paying jobs elsewhere. We are spread so thin now that you are no longer working with partners. You are each working a full caseload. I suggest that *your* time would be better spent working *real* cases instead of wasting time chasing after phantom bodies."

Kendall locked gazes with the lieutenant. He'd seen many a young officer wither under that icy glare, but he'd made up his mind long ago never to blink first. "I assure you that I will not neglect my ongoing cases," he said.

"See that you don't," returned the lieutenant crisply, then closed the meeting as if he were in a hurry.

Seth hung around until after the others left. "What's this all about, Bulldog?" he asked, using a nickname Kendall had acquired as a collegiate wrestler.

Kendall told him.

"You know, this reminds me of a call I made once as a rookie on patrol. This woman was screaming, told me her little boy had been kidnapped, gave me every stitch of information, right down to the fact that his shoelaces were a different color from his shoes. Just cried and carried on. I went hurrying back to the department, gonna round up a *posse*, know what I'm sayin'?"

He paused, shaking his head slowly at the memory. "Captain called me aside, and told me that this woman, turned out she was crazy, man. Crazy as a bedbug. See, thing is, she had a little boy, all right, but twenty years before that day, he'd run out in the street and got hit by a car and killed."

Kendall felt his mouth go dry.

"Time, see, had stopped for this poor lady. It stopped that day. From then on, every now and then, she'd live it over in her mind. But she couldn't bear the thought of that child being dead, so she'd call the cops and say he'd been kidnapped instead."

Seth put an enormous hand on Kendall's shoulder. "I'd go real easy on this one, Bulldog. It sounds like one of those things that can't do anything but get you into trouble. I mean, when crazy people see things, it's *real* to them, like it just happened."

He tapped a long finger against his temple. "But it's all right up here."

Chapter 5 ~~~~~~~~

The natives were restless.

"Okay, guys, what is happening in this canto?" Dani let her gaze check the room; a mine sweep for the slightest show of interest. Jason Tankersly, still a senior at nineteen, was picking his nose and wiping it on his jeans. Jennifer Dawson sat sideways in her chair, so that her swollen belly could fit. Jorge Garza was sound asleep, his face cradled in his arms on his desk (the result of the night job he held to pay for his souped-up car).

"This poem is boring, Ms. Daniels," opined Jason.

"It's depressing," said Jennifer shyly. "I mean, if you believe this guy, if you even *think* a bad thought, you'll be tortured in Hell forever and ever."

"It's too hard. Can't we read something easy?" whined another student.

"Mrs. Johnson used to let us read *Mad Magazine*. She said it was a good example of satire. Can we read *Mad*?" piped up a voice from the back of the room.

"How 'bout we don't read at all," said Jason.

"Yeah. It's pure *Hell*, reading this poem." The class giggled.

"I like it," said Adam Prescott. Silence descended upon the room like a sudden fog. Some of the kids looked uncomfortable. Most averted their eyes.

Dani would have expected them to groan, roll their eyes, throw spit wads at him. She could have sworn that a couple of the kids even looked scared.

She sighed. Even though she'd slept most of the day

before, and even though the migraine was gone, she felt washed out. It had been one of those endless days when she found herself watching the clock more than the kids did. Unfortunately her most difficult class was the last period of the day, and today she was no match for Adam Prescott.

"In Canto Five," he went on, "it says, 'Look how thou enter here, beware in whom thou place thy trust.'" His eyes had that electrified quality again, an inner excitement she couldn't begin to understand. "I'd say Dante knew the score pretty well. Basically you can't trust anybody in this world."

If she hadn't been so exhausted, she'd have given him a small lecture on not selecting verse out of context, of understanding what the poet intended as it related to the rest of the poem. She'd have turned to Canto Five and explained the reference in greater detail.

Instead, she chose to ignore him. "Jennifer, you were talking about the severe punishments Dante reserved in Hell for various sinners. Granted, they were harsh, but you have to understand that the poem was written in the fourteenth century and fit in with the predominant religious beliefs of the day, and of the times themselves, which were harsh."

Jennifer glanced nervously at Adam and nodded.

"Do you believe in the existence of Satan?" asked Adam suddenly, his gaze fixed on Dani.

Without warning, her hands broke into a sweat and she could feel the pounding of her heart in her throat. She swallowed. Her mouth was dry. The kids were watching. "This poem is an allegory, Adam. M-most modern scholars don't take it literally."

"But do you?"

"Do I what?"

"Do you take Satan . . . literally?"

She could hear the students shifting around in their seats and shuffling papers. Everyone seemed unnerved by his question.

It was a perfectly reasonable question. She should be able to answer it. So why . . . *why* . . . did she have to fight the impulse to turn and run for her life?

Adam's eyes were mesmerizing.

She couldn't respond.

With effort, she pulled her attention away from his eyes, turned away, in fact, from the class, and fumbled for the chalk. She managed to say, "Let's discuss the word *allegory*."

And then she completely forgot what it meant.

"Um . . . it's almost time for the bell. We'll discuss allegories tomorrow. Please read the next three cantos." She glanced at her watch.

There was a half hour remaining of class time.

She glanced up. Nobody was moving to gather up books. They were all staring at her. Adam was smiling.

When Dani was mercifully released by the bell from her little classroom prison, she'd have sprouted wings and flown home if she could have, safe in the sanctuary, with her dog at her feet by the fireplace. It was still cold and damp outside, an East Texas cold that seeps into the bones and possesses a body until spring.

She would have, that is, if all teachers hadn't been "encouraged" to attend the after-school reception honoring Jordan Blake, the wealthy local businessman and philanthropist who had just donated another wing to the school library. English teachers, of course, were encouraged with special enthusiasm.

Resentfully Dani stashed papers into her tote, reflecting on the many chores teachers had which were never mentioned in their contracts, things like lunchroom duty, parent-teacher conferences, faculty meetings, selling tickets at ball games, sponsoring clubs and talent shows and bonfires. Not to mention grading papers and planning lessons until late at night.

She was tired. Normally she loved her job, loved the kids . . . she even loved the *smell* of a school. When she was a little girl, the school was the only place she ever felt really comfortable . . . or safe. Usually she drew energy from the restless young people, but today she felt as if she'd

taught a classroom full of vampires who'd sucked the life
from her body.

A reception. Great. Just what she needed.

On the way to the library, she stopped off at the faculty
ladies' room to take her hair down, brush it, and pin it back
up. Her face was pale, but she wasn't in the habit of
carrying makeup with her and didn't like lipstick. She
squeezed a little petroleum jelly on her dry lips from a small
tube in her tote bag, stuck her glasses back on her nose, and
headed for the reception, trying not to drag her feet.

The exchange with Adam was still gnawing at her. Ever
since finding the body, she'd been off center somehow,
every nerve poised for impending crises. She should have
been able to answer his question. Why hadn't she been able
to?

What was *wrong* with her?

The library door was propped back. The large room was
already bustling with people, dressed in conservative, easy-
care clothes. Some of the older women teachers were dressed
exactly as Dani remembered seeing her *own* teachers dress:
longish skirt, white blouse buttoned to the throat, and a
cardigan sweater with a gold pin. It comforted her, somehow.

In the center of the room, one of the library tables was
covered with a white tablecloth, a flower arrangement, a
punch bowl, and several plates of cookies. Along one
window-lined wall, the new wing jutted back in an "L"
formation, smelling of new carpet, new furniture, new
books. Crepe-paper garlands in the school colors had been
stretched across it.

Activity in the room centered on a man who seemed to
stand in bas-relief to the rest of the crowd: from his tailored
pinstripe Italian suit to his silver hair, brushed to a soft
gleam, to his tanned face.

Had to be Jordan Blake.

Dani was not about to flutter around Mr. Blake like some
kind of faculty groupie. She shifted her weight from one
foot to the other and glanced around. Dani hadn't made
many friends among the other teachers, because she seldom
frequented the teachers' lounge. She didn't like the negative

comments the others often made about various students, wasn't comfortable with the time-wasting aspects of spending her conference periods there, and cynically rejected the little social cliques.

She liked the kids better than the teachers.

Still, she wasn't entirely without a friend, and she scanned the crowds for John Raymond, who taught history, and Carol Crandall, another English teacher. She spotted Carol in the group around Blake, but she couldn't find John. Dani smiled. *He'd* had the courage not to show up.

She moved past the cloth-covered table, nodding a "hello" to her principal, Bruce Weams (thus serving notice that she had, indeed, made an appearance), and decided to wander around the new wing for a few minutes before making an early exit.

Everything there seemed to have a soft gleam. The librarians had ordered some excellent up-to-date reference materials. She wandered up and down the aisles, breathing in the smells, letting the calm sink in. It was a dandy new wing, indeed. Of all the charities which must clamor for money from an individual like Jordan Blake, he'd taken this project on voluntarily. Dani was impressed. She pulled a book down from the shelves.

"What do you think of your new addition?"

Dani whirled. There stood Jordan Blake himself, watching her from between the stacks. How had he managed to slip away from his crowd of admirers?

She considered her answer. It wasn't her style to gush. Finally she said, "I think it's the kind of gift that can't be measured. What the kids will learn from these materials will serve them the rest of their lives."

He sketched a bow. "Precisely." He walked toward her. There was a handsome sophistication about him. His voice had a deep, ringing quality to it, like an American Richard Burton. He stopped next to her and looked up at the books, his hands behind his back. "I was watching to see which of the teachers would be more interested in the books than in me. So far, you are the only one."

Glancing at the book she held in her hand, he said,

"Dante. The greatest poet who ever lived." He took it from her and flipped through the pages. "*The Divine Comedy* is one of the most exquisite allegories in literature, I think. In it can be found many truths about the human condition."

She smiled wryly. "Try teaching that to a roomful of adolescents."

He returned the book. "My dear, I expect that if anybody can, you can." His blue eyes, striking against a tan face and silver hair, held her own, and Dani found herself speechless, awkward as a teenager. She knew there was something she should say, but she couldn't think what. It was as if she had forgotten something very important that he needed to know.

Something he would understand.

"*There* you are, Mr. Blake! We've been looking all over for you!" It was the school secretary, Gladys Kopeckny, who *was* a gusher. A floral tent dress stretched over her five-foot-four-inch, 225-pound frame. Bright blue eye shadow coated her eyelids like paint on garage doors, and sticky red lipstick clung to her teeth.

"I see you've met one of our teachers, Faith Daniels. Faith teaches *English*, don't you, dear? She'll *love* the new wing, won't you, dear?" Gladys clamped crimson claws on Blake's arm. "Now, if you'll just come along, Mr. Blake, we've got a nice little presentation for you that you're just going to love, won't you, dear?"

He lifted aristocratic eyebrows at Dani in amusement but allowed himself to be towed along by the lady the kids claimed was *the* student body.

For a long moment, Dani stood holding *The Divine Comedy,* wondering why she felt suddenly so confused.

Midnight. It was the same as every other night since she'd found the body. Dani was unable to sleep because she was afraid to sleep. Flinging back the hot covers, she reached for her robe and padded into the kitchen, turning on the lights as she went, setting the kettle on for herb tea. Maybe *that* would relax her.

Thoreau flopped his tail and grinned at her as she walked

past him and plunked down at a kitchen chair. The house was too quiet. She jumped up again, restlessly wandering the den. Finally she put on some Carlos Reyes and let the sound of his electronic harp wash over her.

Headlights flashed in the front windows and Dani could hear a car door slam. With her bottom lip caught between her teeth, she peeked through a slice in the drapes and smiled when she saw who it was. She had the door open before he could knock.

"Sergeant Kendall, what a surprise! Please come in."

"I can't stay long," he said, his gaze lingering on her face. "I just thought . . . I was wondering . . . how you are, I mean, how you've been doing."

"How nice of you to ask, Sergeant Kendall. I'm doing better, thank you. Would you like a cup of coffee? I've got the kettle on, if you don't mind instant."

"Well . . . sure . . . I mean, I don't mind instant at all."

"Great." Dani headed for the kitchen. She was delighted to see him.

Kendall was sitting, stroking Thoreau's head, when she returned. "He's a great dog," he said. "All I've got is mutts."

"You have dogs?"

"Dogs. Cats. Whatever."

She smiled at him. She'd never have pegged him an animal lover. For a moment, there was silence between them.

"I probably shouldn't have come by," he said finally, "this late and all."

She found his awkward manner endearing. As a professional, he seemed to have nerves of steel, but when it came to relating to her as a woman, he didn't seem to know how to act. It was refreshing. "I can't tell you how glad I am that you stopped by," she told him. He grinned boyishly. She decided that she liked him immensely.

"Sergeant Kendall . . ."

"Please, you don't have to call me that."

"Okay."

"My friends call me Bulldog." He grinned. "But my mother calls me Nathan."

"Nathan is a beautiful name. It means 'a gift, given of God.'"

"It *does*? I never knew that. Are you sure?"

"It's an interest of mine. At the beginning of each school year, I do the names of all the students. It's a good way to get acquainted."

He shook his head, and soon he was laughing.

"What's so funny?"

"I was just thinking what my ex-wife would say if she knew that."

"What's *her* name?"

He made a face. "Roxanne."

She crossed the room to a bookshelf, took out a book, a paperback with a smiling infant on the cover, and flipped the pages. "It means . . . 'brilliant one.'"

"Oh, God, *never* tell her that!"

They laughed together. Dani couldn't remember when she had felt more comfortable with an individual. There was something about this man's presence that made her feel . . . protected.

He stood up. "I gotta get going."

She tried to hide her disappointment.

He hesitated. "I'm off tomorrow. Well, technically I'm on call, but I don't have to go in." He looked at her as if he wasn't sure what to say next.

"I'd love it if you came to dinner," Dani said impulsively.

His face cracked into a grin. "You mean, a chance to eat something besides my own culinary delights?"

"I guarantee it."

"What time?"

"Seven?"

"Sounds great." They smiled at each other. "See you then."

She walked him to the door, and that night the demons didn't stalk her sleep.

They lurked in the shadows instead, poised to pounce.

Chapter 6 ᵕᵕᵕᵕᵕᵕ

A setting sun singed autumn trees with fire as Nathan Kendall maneuvered his battered old jeep down a narrow country lane toward home. It seemed that he never had a day off that he didn't spend running fourteen errands in town and this was no different. Although he was cutting it close, he estimated he had just enough time to get cleaned up before his date with Dani.

A date with Dani. He rolled the sound of that around on his tongue and pronounced it delicious. Any alarms he might have heard in the back of his mind had long since been muffled by the little thrill he felt at just the thought of seeing her again.

And it wasn't only because he was lonesome, or she was beautiful, though that certainly had something to do with it. It was more than that. There was a certain . . . *mystery* about her that made him want to know more. She was warm and yet . . . aloof. And she had a secret little smile that he loved to see.

No doubt about it. He was hooked.

The jeep clunked into a hole, splashing mud onto its filthy sides. Nathan hummed an off-key tune without missing a beat. But his detective's eye caught sight of something that didn't seem right. He slammed on the brakes and threw the jeep into reverse.

He backed up, rolling down the window as he went, stopped, and peered over the side. A rain-soaked cardboard box had been tossed onto the side of the road. Its sides heaved back and forth, and Kendall could hear tiny squealing noises. He got out and approached the box cautiously.

"Aw, geez! This is sick! I hate when people do this." He crouched beside the box, reached inside, and pulled out three starving, squalling kittens, who clawed at him frantically for milk. Cradling the squirming animals to his chest, Kendall looked around the isolated road. Trees crowded almost to the edge. There was no sign of anyone. "They didn't even have the balls to shoot you or nothin', did they?" he murmured as one tiny creature made a loud, contented rumbling noise and curled up within the warmth of the palm of his hand. "Just left you out here to starve, they did. Or to be some critter's dinner." They shivered in his hands and rooted around for warm spots. "Poor little buggers."

With a sigh of resignation, he headed back toward the jeep, juggling kittens. All the way home they clung to various parts of his body, mewing loudly.

He talked to them. "This is just a reprieve, you know. I mean, you can't live with me. I got my hands full as it is. I'll just feed you up, and then find you a nice home, you hear?"

The jeep crunched into a gravelly yard fronting a small, rustic, log A-frame cabin that Kendall had built with his own hands during the long and lonely days and nights after Roxanne left. All that physical labor, sawing and hammering, lifting and carrying, sweating and panting, had been better therapy, he figured, than any shrink could have provided. And the end result was much more productive.

He was greeted by a cacophony of barking, from both within and without the house. Three large mixed-breed dogs bounded up to him as he struggled up the front steps carrying dry-cleaning bags, a grocery sack, and three frantic kittens.

The dogs stopped barking to sniff energetically at the kittens. One kitten swiped a nose, and the largest dog, who looked most like a black Lab, yelped.

"That's what you get for being nosy, Columbo . . . Magnum, you're stepping on my clothes." Miraculously he managed to get the door unlocked and step inside, where he was greeted by two small dogs of debatable lineage and, standing further back in dignified disinterest, three large cats.

The house was a bachelor's place, cluttered, lived-in, and masculine. The logs lent warmth and coziness. Navaho rugs were scattered over the plank flooring. Full, round logs beamed the ceiling beneath the upper-floor bedroom. Kendall had hand-collected the rocks that made up the fireplace wall.

The living area opened into a serviceable kitchen and eating area. Kendall headed straight for it with the kittens, which he deposited gently on the floor, where they wandered, mewing pitifully. The three cats-in-residence looked on with contemptuous disdain, while the dogs sniffed and wagged in open curiosity. One little black kitten with a white throat and paws staggered over to a sleek yellow tom and was rewarded with a hiss and a slap.

"Hey, Sherlock! Watch your manners. Have you forgotten how *you* came to live here? I saved all your asses off the streets, and don't you forget it." From the sack, Kendall pulled a carton of milk, then he carefully diluted some with water in a shallow dish, and popped it into the microwave for half a minute. After testing it with his finger, he placed it on the floor and arranged the kittens around it, pushing one sneaky gray cat away with his foot. "Back, Agatha. Go eat your own dinner."

The kittens attacked the formula. The black kitten climbed all the way into the dish and settled in for a feast. Kendall laughed, glanced at his watch, yelped, and bounded up the stairs toward the shower, two steps at a time.

"So Seth and I knock on the complainant's door, see, and we notice that every single window in the house is covered with aluminum foil, from the inside. Even the little peephole window in the door.

"The lady hollers, 'Who is it?' and we tell her it's the police, and she opens the door just a crack. She's got her hair rolled up in curlers, but *every single curler is covered with aluminum foil!* Just a sweet little old white-haired lady.

We show her our ID, and she opens the door and practically *hauls* us into the house, slamming the door behind us.

"Talk about weird. All the tables, lamps, and the TV were covered with foil. She sits us down on the couch and says, 'It's my neighbor. He's trying to kill me.'

"So we get out our notebooks, real serious, you know, and get the guy's name and address and stuff, and we ask her why she thinks he's trying to kill her, and she says, 'He's bombarding my house with radio waves. Can't you tell? I can't take it anymore. He's going to kill me!'

"And Seth, you should have seen him. He puts his hand on her arm, real kind, and says, 'Well, now, ma'am, we just can't allow that. It's against the law. We'll go right over there and take down every piece of radio equipment he's got.'

"And she says, 'Can the police do that?' And he answers, 'Absolutely. He's violating Code 5420'—or some such number he made up—'which specifically states that using airwaves for destructive purposes is illegal.'

"And she gets big tears in her eyes and tells us how grateful she is, bless her heart. So we go next door and talk to the neighbor. Turns out he's never even seen the lady. We told him what was going on. He promised to keep an eye on her for us and never to take his portable radio outside! A real nice guy. We don't often get to see such nice people in our business."

Dani laughed, and Kendall smiled, watching her. She'd put a small table in front of the fireplace and set it with linen, candles, and good china. He didn't even taste the food, so busy was he, watching the way the firelight shone off her soft, stylishly disheveled hair and sparkled in her eyes.

"You must meet a lot of interesting people in your work," she said.

"Every day is different. It's never boring. Sometimes I can't believe I get paid to do what I do. Other days I can't believe anybody would want this job." He shrugged. "Once you're in it, though, you're hooked. You can't imagine doing anything else."

"That's the way I feel about teaching. Oh, the bureaucracy and the paperwork and little tedious chores get to you, but it's the kids . . . the kids keep each day alive and full of hope."

He nodded. "It's the same with police work. Except for maybe the hope part. Well, that's not entirely true. When you close a case, you feel real hopeful that you've served justice. Then the legal system gets hold of it and next thing you know, some slimebag's out on the streets again. You get to start all over." He took a sip of wine. "Don't get me started."

They watched the dancing flames for a while in companionable silence. She was not a woman who felt she needed to chatter to keep things going. He liked that. "Let me ask you something."

"Sure."

"It seems like every date I've had since I got divorced two years ago, we've spent the night dissecting the carcass of either my dead marriage or my date's. You haven't asked me a thing about it. Why?"

She smiled her enigmatic little smile. "I think we're all entitled to our privacy, or to whatever secrets we don't care to share. I figure you'll tell me when and if you want to."

"She had an affair with another officer," he blurted. "And the worst thing about it was, I knew this guy real well. Liked him a lot. He was a nice guy and a good cop . . . but hell, cops don't screw each other . . . or each other's wives."

She nodded but said nothing.

"I thought that if I married another cop, we wouldn't have the kinds of problems some cops have in their marriages, where their wives just don't understand what they do and the kinds of things they see each day. I figured we'd understand each other perfectly and really *share* our lives."

"You're still hurting," she said.

"Yeah. I guess so." He looked away, and she said nothing more. She didn't assault him with questions or attempt a pop psychoanalysis of the situation. It was refreshing and he appreciated it.

He looked up. "I've been an ass. Talked about myself all night. So what about you? Did you ever find yourself close to the altar?"

She shook her head. "I was always too busy for romance, I guess. Or maybe I just didn't find anybody who interested me." She glanced away, a pretty flush on her cheeks.

He fervently hoped she found *him* interesting.

She stood then and began clearing the table. He helped. They worked together easily. She didn't urge him to get out of her way or flutter over him like he was some kind of king to be served. They simply cleaned up the clutter and when they were done, carried coffee to the sofa.

The firelight was dying and shadows gathered in the corners. They sat close together but not touching. Kendall's loins ached for this woman. He longed to tangle his hands in her thick, soft hair and bury his nose in her scent. He could only imagine how smooth her skin must be, how round her breasts would feel cupped in his hands.

But he sensed that she was not a woman to be manhandled. She would have to give him clear and unmistakable signals when, and if, she wanted to sleep with him. There was a certain . . . space . . . around her that he did not want to violate. He knew, instinctively, that if he did, she would never let him near again.

They were talking softly, getting further acquainted, when Dani suddenly sat straight up on the sofa, her back rigid, her face taut.

Kendall watched her look around for Thoreau, who slept soundly in front of the fire where their table had stood earlier. He touched her shoulder. "What is it?"

"Probably nothing." But he could feel the tension underneath the smooth fabric of her blouse. "Did you hear that sound?"

He moved forward, to the edge of the sofa. "What sound?"

She swallowed. "It . . . may have been the mail slot in the front door."

"The mail slot?" He stood up. "It's almost eleven. Who'd be putting things in your mail slot?" He left the room and walked to the front door. A plain white envelope rested on the floor in front of the door. Kendall pocketed the envelope, flung open the door, and hurried out, checking up and down the street. He saw no one.

It was cold, and he'd left his jacket inside. As he turned to go in, he saw Dani standing in the doorway, fear etched in her face. "Did you find anything?" she asked.

He went back into the house, shut the door, and showed her the envelope. She took it, and with trembling hands, tore it open. One page fluttered to the floor. Kendall picked it up. Neatly typed on the plain white sheet were the words "After long striving they will come to blood, and the wild party from the woods will chase the other with much injury forth."

He looked into her face. "What the hell is this?"

"It's from Dante's *Inferno*," she said, and turned away, grasping her elbows with her hands.

Taking hold of her arm, he turned her to face him. "What's this all about, Dani?" Her face was white, her eyes wide. She didn't answer.

From the back of Kendall's mind came that old familiar alarm.

He gave her a gentle shake. "What's going on here? Talk to me. Let me help."

There was indecision in her eyes. He'd seen it before, many times, just before getting a confession. "C'mon," he coaxed.

Loud, high-pitched beeping caused them both to jump. He touched the gadget attached to his belt. "Sorry. My beeper. I'll . . . I'll be right back. Here . . ." He led her into the den and sat her on the couch. "Sit here while I make a quick call." She didn't move.

He hurried into the kitchen and dialed his office.

"Davis."

"Hey, Fred. This is Bulldog. What's going on?"

"Vacation's over. They found a woman's body, cut all to

pieces and stuffed into a trash dumpster. Corner of Twenty-third and Buckeye."

"I'm on my way." Kendall slammed down the receiver and strode into the den, prepared to make his excuses and leave, already wearing his cop-face, already geared to business, already working, when he saw *her,* sitting on the couch, staring wide-eyed at him.

It was the same way she'd looked at him in the woods that day when he first met her, and she was trying to convince him that she'd seen a woman's mutilated body by the lake.

It was a sucker-punch to the gut, because now a woman really *was* dead, and he had to wonder . . . was Faith Daniels somehow involved?

Lieutenant Ward was already at the scene. "I've secured the area and posted guards. I'm putting you in charge of the preliminary investigation. The rookie over there found the body." He pointed toward a clean-cut, pinched-face young man in uniform, leaning against a squad car, smoking. "Name of Baxter. JP's on the way, but we'll ship this one on to Dallas for autopsy."

Kendall nodded. Just once, it would be nice, he thought, if they could have a medical examiner or coroner right there on the scene. Instead, every small town in Texas shipped its autopsy cases on to one of the large metropolitan areas and waited their turn behind all the big-city stiffs. In the meantime, they had to depend on a justice of the peace to make an official pronouncement of death, render a guess as to the cause, and even make the decision as to whether an autopsy was required—a thorn in the sides of many detectives, since JPs were elected to their positions and not required to have any medical or criminal justice training. Kendall had butted heads more than once with Maplewood's JP, Sam Wilson.

"Garcia and Rollins are on their way to assist in the investigation," continued Lieutenant Ward. "I'll coordinate from headquarters. Any questions?"

Kendall shook his head, and the lieutenant left.

The first thing Kendall did was crouch down next to the body, which was eerily lit by a few flares the patrol units had set around to supplement the alleyway's poor lighting. The nude woman, who appeared to be in her mid to late twenties, had that look of shock on her face that he'd seen on many victims of homicide, as if to say, "You can't mean that it's really going to end *now*!"

She lay curled—almost *wadded,* he thought, into a fetal position. One brown plastic garbage bag had been pulled over her head, one up over her feet, and they'd been tied together with a narrow nylon rope. The bags had been cut open and the rope as well, without damaging the knot. He'd have to commend the rookie on a job well done.

He asked for a flashlight and somebody handed him one. Under the harsh glare of its light he inspected the savage slice on her throat, the abrasion on her cheek, and the split at the side of her skull just above her ear. Moving the light downward, Kendall recoiled for a moment. "Aw, Jesus," he whispered.

"Sick, isn't it?" said a cop from over his shoulder. "It's hard to believe there's people like that loose in the world."

Kendall nodded, staring into the flickering crimson lights of the flares for a moment, collecting himself.

Her breasts had been sliced off.

After a moment, he continued his inspection of the body without touching it. There was a smear of blood across one inner thigh. No doubt she'd been raped as well. The autopsy would tell for sure.

"God in heaven." Kendall heard Seth's voice. The tall man folded himself into a crouch, stork fashion, next to Kendall. Kendall gave him a moment. It was only fair.

The he said, "Seth, I want you to be in charge of photographing the crime scene. I want to be able to reconstruct the whole thing, like a puzzle, when you're done."

Seth nodded. "Right."

"Manny?"

Garcia materialized at his elbow. "You're in charge of searching every inch of that dumpster and the alleyway.

Label anything blood-spattered or that could be connected in any way to the crime. Wait—before you get started, I want the dumpster and everything else handy to be dusted for fingerprints. Where's Fred?"

"Um . . . back at the department."

"Well, call him. We need him here. Let him do the fingerprinting. While you're waiting, measure every square inch of the scene and draw up a diagram with measurements listed. I want a clear picture of how everything is related to everything else, something we can't show with photography. And don't *touch* anything." Manny headed for a squad car to call Fred Davis.

Kendall walked over to the young rookie, still leaning against the car, not casually, but as if he needed it for support.

"I'm Sergeant Kendall. I'm in charge of the investigation." They shook hands.

"This is only my second day out of training, sir," said the recruit. "Man, I never saw anything like that."

"Well, if it'll make you feel any better, neither have I. Tell me what you did see."

"I was making my rounds. I got out of the car to check and see if the back door to the pharmacy was securely locked. My sergeant said pharmacies get burglarized a lot. For the drugs."

"Go on."

"Well, this dumpster is right by the door. I was kind of flashing my Kel-Lite around and I saw little drops of blood along the side of the dumpster. That just didn't look right. When I looked in, I saw those garbage bags tied up and . . . I guess I screwed up, wallering around to get those bags out. It wasn't easy, and there's probably my fingerprints all over the place, and I guess I should have called for help—"

"It's all right, Baxter. Go on."

"Anyway, I remembered that sometimes the way something is tied helps us figure out who tied it, so I cut the rope, and the bags, and . . . Oh, God, I've never seen anything like it!"

"Don't worry about it. You did a good job. Tough initiation for a rookie. You ought to be able to handle anything now."

"Yeah?" The young officer smiled nervously.

"I'd like a full report on everything, exactly as you found it. Search your mind and see if you can remember seeing *anybody* around here earlier this evening, even a car pulling out of the alley."

"Well, I can't think of anything off hand, Sergeant, but I'll let you know right away if I do."

Kendall returned to the body. The JP was there. Sam Wilson was a pudgy-faced family man who took his job seriously. He was a forensics buff and considered himself a bit of an expert, after reading up on the subject somewhat and attending a few seminars. Sometimes he liked to pretend that a murder scene didn't bother him, but Kendall knew better. It was one of the things that annoyed him about the man.

The truth was, such situations bothered them all.

"Whew!" exclaimed Wilson. "She's really dead, huh? Guess we need to ship this one off to Dallas."

" 'Fraid so."

"Well, anyway, I'd say this blow to the head, here, rendered her unconscious. Somebody literally whacked her upside the head with some blunt object. Lacerated her skin. Probably fractured the skull. My guess is that the throat-cutting was a sort of overkill. The lab will tell us whether the mutilations occurred before or after death."

Wilson's talk was glib, but Kendall noticed that he didn't look back at the body. He shifted his weight uncomfortably.

"See, here on the right side of her body, the skin is purplish," said Wilson, forcing himself to look back.

"Lividity," said Kendall. "I read, too."

Wilson ignored the sarcasm. "That's right. Body's lain on its right side long enough for the blood to collect there. But rigor mortis has not set in, and the body is not very cold to the touch, even though it's a cold night, so . . ."

"So she hasn't been dead all that long."

"That's what I'd say. Of course, I'm no *expert*," he said

with false modesty, "but it could be no more than four or five hours. Be sure and let me read the autopsy report when it comes in."

Sure, Kendall thought. *Be a nice bedtime story for you.*

Wilson leaned closer, inspecting the woman's head. Taking the Kel-Lite from Kendall's hand, he shone its full beam on the head. "Hm-m-m. Interesting."

"What?"

"See here, in her hair? Pine needles and dirt."

Matted in with the bloody hair, which acted like sticky glue, were a number of pine needles, little bits of dirt, and something that resembled dried grass.

"It looks as though she was killed outdoors somewhere and deposited like so much garbage in this dumpster," he said. Kendall met the man's gaze, but he already knew what he was going to say.

"What with the pine needles and all," Wilson went on, "she might have even been killed in the woods."

Chapter 7 〜〜〜〜〜〜

They were coming to get her. She knew that now for sure. What could she do? Where could she hide?

It wasn't like the other time. No. This was much, much worse.

She wanted so badly to tell that nice man. But she couldn't! She didn't dare!

All she could hear was the ticking of the clock. She was used to it, though. She liked to be alone. They couldn't hurt her then.

It was cold and dark outside. Where could she go?

All those houses on either side and across the street, filled with happy families watching TV. How she longed to be in one of those houses now!

Soon they would be here.

She had to find a place where they could never, never find her. Where could that be?

If only King could be with her. But he was too big. She could never hide him. It was too late anyhow. Too late!

She began to whimper, thinking of King. They wanted her to sleep in her bed but she never did! She wouldn't, ever again! Not after that . . . *thing* . . . they put underneath her pillow. Poor, poor King. She missed him so much!

Standing in the middle of the hallway, she started to cry.

She put her fist in her mouth and bit down. Hard. *Stop it! Stop it!* She couldn't cry. *She wouldn't let them see her cry! Never, never again!*

She had to hurry, anyway! She had to hide!

The bathroom. In the linen closet, behind the towels! She

could make herself into a little tiny ball and they would never guess where she was.

She headed for the bathroom. *Wait a minute. What about Bear?* She couldn't hide with Bear. Think what they might do to him!

Running now, she pushed open her bedroom door and looked around. Where was he? Flinging open the closet, she kicked over shoe boxes and shoved aside garments. No sign of him.

She fell to the floor and searched underneath the bed. No Bear.

Panicky, she grabbed a pillow and threw it to the floor.

There it was. She screamed and covered her face with her hands, but it was too late. She'd seen it, the thing she tried not to think about, tried not to ever think about, *Oh, King!*

She couldn't help it. Her eyes wanted to cry and she couldn't stop them.

This is what we'll do to your ear if you say one word to that social worker when he comes to visit, they'd said to her. *You mention that dog, or our meetings, or one damn thing . . . this is what we'll do to you.*

She was sobbing now. She couldn't find Bear and it was too late; she had to hide *now*.

Dashing into the bathroom, she began dragging out towels and washcloths until she could see a space. Crouching low, she started to crawl into the cabinet and found, to her surprise, that she could barely fit in her head and shoulders.

What was wrong? She should be able to fit.

Panting, she gave up and sat back on the bathroom floor, where, to her shock, she saw reflected in the full-length mirror bolted to the bathroom door a distraught, weeping, disheveled adult looking directly into a child's eyes.

Dani touched her hands to her face, then looked away at the towel-cluttered bathroom floor. After easing herself to her feet, she forced herself, step by step, back into her bedroom.

Catching her bottom lip in her teeth, Dani made herself look straight at the bed.

It was a wreck. There where the pillow once rested was a wadded-up knee-high stocking.

She picked it up. There was nothing sinister about it. Just a stocking she'd kicked off while getting ready for . . .

Moving slowly down the hall, Dani entered the den.

Thoreau lay there, sleeping peacefully right in front of the fire, where he'd been all night. She sank onto the couch. Next to her lay an envelope with a jagged tear. There was nothing in it.

Of course. Nathan took the note. He'd been called out. A woman had been murdered.

Dani began chewing on the end of a fingernail, something she hadn't done since her teen years. She felt drained of all energy. Why in hell had she tried to cram herself into the linen cabinet?

Try to remember.

There was the note that said something about blood, and injuring someone in the woods. Then there was the phone call about the murdered woman. Somehow it must have triggered some kind of flashback to her childhood . . . to the things she couldn't remember . . . didn't *want* to remember.

That note. *Why did they send the note to her?*

Methodically Dani began rocking back and forth, gnawing on her fingernail, shredding it. All she knew was that she was drowning beneath a great overwhelming wave of terror.

What she didn't know was *why*.

Dani plodded heavily down the corridor toward her classroom, willing her brain and body to work in sync at eight-thirty in the morning without the benefit of sleep. Her mind felt as if it had blown a fuse from emotional overload.

No way could she handle teaching today. She planned to give them all free library passes and turn them loose.

Someone tapped on her shoulder and she started violently, dropping books, papers, and tote bag in a flurry of skidding chaos.

"My goodness, Ms. Daniels, I didn't mean to scare you."

Her principal, a wiry, energetic, and thoroughly annoying little man, stooped to help her pick up her things.

"It's all right, Mr. Weams. Here, I'll get that."

He squinted at her behind thick-lensed horn-rimmed glasses. "Are you all right?"

"Just a little tired." She stuffed everything into her overloaded tote and scrambled to her feet. Too late, he offered his hand.

"What I came to ask you about," he said briskly, his words nearly drowned by the sounding of the bell, "is if you have completed your recommendation for the Select Student Scholarship. It's due today, you know."

"Scholarship?"

"Yes, you remember. In fact, you yourself would not have been able to partake of the fruits of a college education if you had not received the assistance of this very same scholarship."

Three tardy students brushed past them breathlessly and dodged into Dani's room. The corridor stretched empty from one end to the other. Overhead lights gleamed off Weams's bald head. He frowned at her from behind his glasses. "The deadline is today," he repeated.

The strap of Dani's tote bag dug into her shoulder. A hot flush crept up her cheeks. "I . . . I don't quite have that recommendation prepared, Mr. Weams."

"You've had a month!"

"Mr. Weams . . . I haven't had time to sufficiently get to know these kids yet. I'm not sure who would be the best candidate."

His lips smiled at her; his eyes did not. "It shouldn't be that difficult. You are to select the most promising student from among our more troubled youth. Someone who shows potential in ways other than the traditional academic measurements of grades."

She shifted the weight of the tote bag. "I'm aware of that."

"Well, I should think the selection would be obvious."

"Choices like this are never *obvious*, Mr. Weams. There are a number of students who would receive tremendous benefit from an honor such as this that goes beyond a college education."

"Cut the crap, Daniels."

She sucked in her breath.

"You know good and well that Adam Prescott is the obvious choice for this scholarship recommendation."

"*Adam Prescott!*" Dani glanced into the room to see if anyone had heard her. The kids were giggling and talking noisily. No one had heard her. She looked back at the principal.

"You have a problem with Adam?"

I have a lot of problems with Adam. "I just . . . I just don't like his attitude. I'm not sure he would appreciate the spirit of the scholarship. I was thinking more of Jennifer Dawson—"

"*Jennifer Dawson!* Are you *crazy*? She's *pregnant*! I even heard she's planning on *keeping* the kid!"

Dani narrowed her eyes at the man. How dare he accost her on this subject in the middle of the hallway, where students could overhear. "I think we should discuss this matter in your office, Mr. Weams. During my conference period."

He ignored her. Crossing his arms over his chest, he said, "Jennifer Dawson has set a miserable example for the other kids. She hardly deserves to be rewarded for it."

"She works harder than any other student I have, trying to bring up her grades. They really fell when she first learned about the baby. She wants desperately to go to college. This would be a wonderful opportunity for her."

He shook his head and chuckled. "Well, she should have thought of that before she jumped into the backseat with that fellow, now, shouldn't she?"

Grinding her teeth together, Dani whirled away from him and headed for class.

"*Daniels!*"

She stopped, but kept her back turned to him. His voice was so low she could hardly hear. "Whichever student you refer for the scholarship has to have a joint recommendation

from the principal. The deadline is today. I expect to find
the paperwork on my desk by four o'clock."

"My God, girl, you look like death warmed over! I say
that because we just got through studying similes and that
was the best one the class could come up with." Carol
Crandall, her face crinkled into her usual generous smile,
sailed into Dani's room during her fifth-period conference
time.

Dani sat alone, staring dumbly at a stack of themes she'd
intended to have graded for her sixth-period class. The
difficult class. Adam Prescott and Jennifer Dawson's class.
Lying next to the themes was the Select Student Scholarship
recommendation sheet. Neither the themes nor the sheet had
been completed.

Carol was a big-boned, hearty-voiced woman ten years
Dani's senior, with short-cropped dark hair and warm,
mischievous brown eyes. Popular with the students, she had
a house full of her own kids and boasted a long, happy
marriage to an instructor at the local community college.
She was a woman of common sense, great humor, and a
willingness to take a chance on shy types like Dani.

She perched her ample rear end on the edge of Dani's
desk. "What gives?"

"Weams wants me to recommend Adam Prescott for the
Select Student Scholarship," blurted Dani.

The smile faded from Carol's face. "You've got to be
kidding."

Dani met her gaze.

Carol got up and began to pace, a habit she had when she
was agitated. "Weams is out of his mind. Doesn't he *know*
anything about Adam?"

"Just that he has potential."

"Which he'll never use. At least, not for anything good."
She leaned against Dani's desk, chewing on the inside of
her cheek. "The other kids are afraid of Adam. Have you
noticed that?"

Dani nodded.

"Do you know why?"

She wasn't sure she wanted to know.

Glancing toward the open door, Carol said, "They say he's a devil worshipper."

Dani could feel a pressure against her ears, as if her brain were swelling in its skull. She could hear a ringing. She swallowed.

"The kids say he drinks blood in front of them. And they don't know where he gets it." She leaned closer and lowered her voice. "He tells them that he gets *power* from the blood."

"Kids . . . t-talk," Dani faltered.

Carol shook her head. "There's something *weird* about that boy, Dani. Don't you feel it?"

She nodded miserably.

"What are you going to do about the scholarship?"

Dani sighed heavily. "I'm going to recommend Jennifer Dawson for it."

A big grin split Carol's face. "*That's* the spirit! Jenny deserves it, and besides, it'll make Weams crazy!" She giggled.

Dani shook her head. "He'll never approve it, Carol."

"As long as you don't cave in where Adam Prescott's concerned, it doesn't matter."

"It does matter," said Dani. "It matters to Jennifer Dawson." She got up and wandered over to the row of windows, driven by a sudden restlessness, the almost irresistible urge to flee that had been dogging her heels more and more in recent days.

Carol joined her at the window and they stood together silently for a few moments. "Dani . . . sometimes I think I should do something about Adam."

"What do you mean?"

"I mean . . . this satanism. It frightens me. Some of these kids who get involved in this stuff . . . they can be dangerous. I've read that some of them have murdered their own parents. Violence, to them, seems to be some sort of badge of courage." She bit her lip. "Maybe I should talk to someone about it. His parents, or . . ."

Dani suddenly backed away from Carol, her voice rising

to a high pitch, a cry wrenched from deep within her. "No . . . No . . ."

Carol's face wrinkled into a frown of concern.

Dani held her hands out in front of her, palms up, as if to ward off some hidden adversary, and her voice dropped to a near whisper. "You can run, but you cannot hide," she murmured. "You can run, but you cannot hide."

Turning away from her bewildered friend, Dani ran from the room, down the hall, around the corner; flashing past open doorways with their surprised faces, stumbling into the faculty ladies' room where, finally, she hid herself, trembling, in a cubicle.

Chapter 8 ⌇⌇⌇⌇⌇⌇⌇⌇⌇⌇⌇

The first misty-gold shafts of morning light were beginning to reach through the thick trees and pine boughs surrounding the log cabin when Kendall hauled his exhausted body up the front steps and across the leaf-littered plank porch. Frosty cold didn't prevent birdsong from drifting through the dawn hush.

For a moment he stood, sucking woodsy air into his lungs, clearing his mind of blood and the sad aftereffects of violent death. He would see the woman's poor mutilated body in his mind's eye for a long time, an occupational hazard for homicide investigators.

It wasn't true that you got used to it. It *was* true that you either learned to live with it or you got out of the business.

As he let himself into the house, he was nearly mowed down by the loving greetings of his furry roommates. In the kitchen, three yowling kittens came scrambling out from under the refrigerator. It had been a long time since their last meal. He fixed them another dish of milk and dumped dry dog food and cat food into various pans set out near the back door for the other pets. Scooping from a fifty-pound sack, he added more dog food to a tub on the back porch for the three big dogs. It was easier for Kendall to leave dry food out at all times so the animals could eat whenever they needed, rather than expecting them to wait on him for some sort of schedule. To a messy chalkboard nailed to the wall, he scribbled, "Buy kitten chow."

Kendall wasn't hungry. Digging around a pile of junk mail and other clutter on the kitchen table, he retrieved a yellow legal pad and felt-tip pen. From the refrigerator he took a long-neck beer. Both he carried into the den, where he settled onto the sofa. He took a long, satisfying swig of beer and sat for a moment, listening to the tick-tick of his grandmother's old clock, watching dust motes float through the sunlight which slanted through the window, willing his shoulder muscles to uncoil and his mind to settle down.

One of the first, unwritten rules that a homicide investigator learned was that, if you couldn't name the victim, your chance of naming a suspect was almost nil. Most homicides fell into the "crimes of passion" category . . . a jealous boyfriend, a battering husband, fury out of control. Other homicides were a matter of a victim getting in the way of another crime, like a robbery or a drug deal gone bad.

But this was like nothing Kendall had ever encountered. He'd seen women who'd been murdered by their rapists, mostly so that they could not be used later as courtroom witnesses. But this was a calculated sexual mutilation, carried out in an intelligent manner that left, at least in the preliminary investigation, no physical evidence, nothing that could give them a direction.

They couldn't even start with the victim. Even with the rude intrusion of TV cameras and excited late-news announcements of the murder, they'd had no leads as to the woman's identity.

Kendall took another swallow of beer and closed his eyes, running through a mental list of possible suspects from the criminal element he'd encountered on the job. A shy sheltie-looking dog he'd named Joe Friday crept forward and pushed his nose into Kendall's hand. He stroked the dog's head absently. He knew men who had killed women; he knew men who had killed and felt no remorse. But he did not know anybody who was capable of the almost scientific slicing off of a woman's breasts.

And then there was Dani.

A black cloak of fatigue and depression settled on Kendall. The victim's mutilations matched the description Dani had given him of the body she had supposedly discovered on the Palmer estate. Yet it could not be the same woman, because *this* woman appeared to have died only hours before the patrolman found her.

Automatically he glanced at the date displayed on his watch. It had been a full week since Dani reported finding the body. It was hard to believe he had only known her that long. Still, if Dani had, indeed, seen a body a week ago which resembled the one found just last night, then where was it?

And what about the note which had been slipped into her mail slot? Kendall took the note from his pocket, carefully unfolded it, and laid it across his lap. It had long since been ruined for fingerprints, but he studied it now, examining the typeface and the paper. Was it connected to the murder? And if so, how was Dani involved?

She had to be involved somehow. He'd already decided that. It had to do with her reaction to the note, among other things. Any other person would have been baffled by the message and the way in which it had arrived. Curious. Maybe a little intrigued.

Not Dani. Dani was terrified of it.

She knew something she wasn't telling him.

But that wasn't what was driving him nuts. Cops were used to people not telling them the whole story. Witnesses who didn't want to get involved. Suspects who had good reason to keep quiet. Defense attorneys who knew good and damn well their clients were guilty but whose only goal in life was to win at all costs, even if justice was the stake.

What was *really* making him crazy was the simple fact that he liked the hell out of her. Okay, maybe he wanted to take her to bed. True enough. But it was *more* than that. There was something about her that made him want to take care of her, to shield her from whatever demons were tormenting her.

And it was even more than that.

There was no way he could explain this to a living soul, maybe not even to himself, but the truth of the matter, the gut-level bottom line . . . was that he *believed* her. If

there was any way she *was* involved in all this, Kendall
believed that it was against her will.

But why?

Even more important, did she know anything that could
lead them to the killer?

He would talk to her again. First, he had a few other
things to check out. Kendall folded the note and put it back
into his pocket. No need to show it to the lieutenant just yet.

During the three-hour drive back to Maplewood from the
Southwest Institute of Forensic Sciences, through lovely
wooded hills and valleys of East Texas, Kendall hardly
noticed the patchwork quilt of color on either side of the
highway. The trees were not yet wearing their full regalia of
autumn colors, but the fields were heavy with harvest. Yet
all Kendall could see was the puzzle of the case at hand. He
kept turning over the little jigsaw pieces of information he'd
picked up in Dallas at the autopsy, none of which seemed to
fit together.

The ME explained that the blade used in the mutilations
was very sharp, because there weren't any bruises on the
edges of the cuts; nor were there any hesitation marks—
smaller, superficial cuts around the fatal wounds—cuts that
a person would make in order to work up the courage before
the final act. Which meant that the killer knew what he was
going to do and just did it. The lack of forcefulness and
savagery—something which would be expected in a ven-
detta or crime of passion—indicated that the butchery had
been done with almost surgical precision, a fact which
chilled Nathan.

Pursing his lips as a lumbering logger's truck forced him
to slow down on the two-lane road, he thought about the
blood smear across the victim's thigh, which probably
meant brutal sexual entry, possibly with an inanimate
object.

The only source of relief in the whole gruesome scene
was the ME's certainty that the victim was never aware of
what was being done to her. The absence of defense wounds
on her hands and arms and the blow on the side of the head

indicated that she'd been rendered unconscious before the mutilation.

What happened next haunted Nathan. The ME had been pointing out the lack of defense wounds, and as he began to lay the woman's arm back on the gurney, Kendall stopped him. "Wait. What's that on the underside of her upper arm?" He leaned forward. "It's a tattoo!"

"Indeed it is," said the doctor.

"Please take pictures of it," ordered Kendall. "It might help me identify her."

Every now and then, as Kendall drove, he'd pick up the Polaroid snapshot from the seat beside him and examine it. The characters were arranged in a row: a lightning bolt, followed by a triangle, an upside-down cross, another triangle, and finally, another lightning bolt. They formed a pinnacle, like an over-all triangle, with the line of the cross making up the triangle's apex.

He'd never seen anything like it.

Even more puzzling were the blond hairs he'd found at the Palmer estate where Dani said she had seen a woman's body. They did not match the hairs from Dani's head. In fact, they weren't human hairs at all, but were synthetic. A cheap wig?

As for the *real* homicide, the clinical method of mutilation seemed consistent with the almost sterile lack of physical evidence on or near the body. The only fingerprints and clothing fibers found on the garbage bag belonged to the young rookie.

The red sandy dirt and pine needles in the woman's hair could have come from almost anywhere in the woods around Maplewood.

Kendall drove straight to the Maplewood Police Department and headed directly for the nearest available computer, scarcely speaking to Seth, whom he passed in the hall. Seth wouldn't mind. They didn't call Kendall "Bulldog" for nothing.

In fact, nobody bothered him much, possibly because his clothes still reeked of formaldehyde.

For the next couple of hours, Kendall worked to register

the woman's description—including the tattoo—with the FBI's National Crime Information Center and the Texas Crime Information Center, and prepared a packet to submit with her file, photograph, and a copy of the photograph of her tattoo, to the Texas Department of Public Safety's Crime Analysis Center for publication in its Missing Persons Clearinghouse Bulletin. If she was reported missing from another county, or had ever had a run-in with the law, or if there were any other crimes in the state with a similar MO, he could hope to hear from another law enforcement agency about her.

For dinner he had a candy bar, a package of cheese and peanut butter crackers, and a Coke, alone at his desk.

After that he stopped by the lieutenant's office to ask about the possibility of dragging the lake at the Palmer estate, on the off chance that Dani's report was accurate and that the body had been dumped there. The lieutenant was out of the office. Kendall made a note to speak to him about it during briefing the next day.

By the time Kendall cruised down Redbud Lane toward the house with all the lights on, most Maplewood residents were snug in their homes, watching prime-time TV lead into the late-night news. Sharp barks from Thoreau greeted his knock, followed by a shy "Who is it?"

"Serg—Nathan," he answered, surprised at his own emotional rush at the sound of her voice.

The door swung open, silhouetting her slender form against all those lights. As he stepped in and looked down at her, he almost gasped. She was wearing a robe and her hair was swept up in a bath towel; she must have been in the shower; but it was her face that shocked him.

Purple shadows underscored her eyes. Her complexion was so pale as to be almost translucent; he could see delicate blue veins in her forehead. Her eyes were bloodshot with fatigue. Her chin thrust a sharp shadow against her throat, and he wondered if she had lost weight. It had only been a couple of days since he'd seen her, but it looked as though she hadn't eaten or slept in that time. Tears welled up in her eyes and she blinked them away. "I thought maybe you weren't ever coming back," she said.

"Why would you think that?"

She shrugged, her thin shoulders stooped. "Just the way you took the note, and ran off into the night," she said vaguely.

"I was working."

"The woman. I saw it on TV." She tilted her face up to him.

He didn't mean for it to happen. Lord knows he hadn't planned on it. He didn't even stop to think about the formaldehyde. All he knew was that in the next moment she was in his arms, trembling against his chest like a little bird.

At first, he only meant to comfort her, and he held her for a long moment in just that way, but then when he pulled back his face to say something, his lips brushed her temple, and before he knew what had hit him, he was pressing her soft lips against his in a kiss so sweet it made his head reel.

She returned his kiss with a surprising passion, but when he moved his hand to cradle her head, the cumbersome towel fell to the floor and her mouth turned up into a infectious laugh that broke the moment. Chuckling, he stooped to retrieve the towel.

"Let me go dry my hair. I'll be right back," she said, her smile transforming her face. Bending over, she deftly wrapped the towel around her hair, then stood, reaching up to hold it in place. As she did so, the loose sleeve of her robe slid back on her arm.

And there, on the soft underside of Dani's arm, standing out boldly against her creamy skin, Kendall could see, as if in a clear Polaroid snapshot, the same tattoo he'd seen earlier that day, in a morgue, on the arm of a dead woman.

Chapter 9 ~~~~~~~~~

Nathan's face changed before Dani's eyes into an expression she'd never seen before, cold-eyed and stern. He grasped her small wrist, his big fingers clamped like a vise, and yanked her close to him, gesturing toward the tattoo with his other hand.

"Where did you get that?" It was a demand, not a question.

She cried out. "You're hurting me."

He didn't let go. "Tell me where you got that tattoo."

Needles of fear pricked her skin. She bit her lip and tasted salt.

"*Talk to me, goddamm it!*" Nathan took hold of her other arm and shook her.

"*I don't know!*" The guttural shout was wrenched from deep within her soul, and they both knew it was the truth. He let go of Dani and whirled away from her, clawing his fingers over his scalp in a gesture of intense frustration. She rubbed her wrist and tried to get control of the deep trembling which had overtaken her body.

After a moment, Nathan turned back to her. She couldn't read his expression, but his voice was kind. He took gentle hold of her wrist and checked it for bruises. "I'm sorry," he said. "I didn't mean to hurt you." He held her gaze with his own. "Dani, you've got to talk to me. The woman who was murdered—she had a tattoo just like yours, in exactly the same place on her arm. You are involved in this in some way and you've got to tell me how."

She tried to swallow and found it difficult.

"Dani . . . how can you *not know* where you got a tattoo?"

Tears sprang unbidden to her eyes and she tried to blink them away. A misery so deep-seated, so inbred in her psyche that no psychiatrist had ever been able to touch it, spread outward from her chest to the very bottom of her soul. In that same moment, she knew that if she'd been alone right then, she might have tried to kill herself.

Nathan's strict cop-face seemed to melt before her eyes. "Dear God," he whispered. "What happened to you?" He gathered her in his arms and held her so tightly that she could barely breathe, but it was exactly what she needed and she clung to him. After a moment, he said, "Let's go find some coffee and talk." She nodded and let herself be led into the den, where he settled her on the couch and went to make the coffee himself.

While he was out of the room, Dani collected herself. She blew her nose and wiped her eyes and pressed her hair back. She breathed deeply and told herself to calm down. Thoreau, who always seemed to know her moods, came to her and put his head in her lap. She stroked him. By the time Nathan brought the coffee, black and hot, she was ready for him.

He didn't sit next to her, as she'd expected, but in a chair close by, facing her. Then he waited.

"I don't know where to start," she said.

"Try the beginning."

"You'll think I'm crazy."

"What makes you think I don't already?"

She glanced sharply at him, saw he was smiling, and relaxed. "Okay. I don't know where I got the tattoo. I've always had it."

"Always?"

"For as long as I can remember."

"You mean . . . your *parents* gave it to you?"

"I don't remember my parents. I was adopted when I was seven. I've had it since before then."

"Where did you live before that, an orphanage?"

"A foster home, in California."

"Did you get along well with your adoptive family?"

"Well enough. They were good to me. I just never . . . fit in."

"What about your foster family?"

Dani's fingers went cold and the coffee cup slid right out of them. She watched it tumble to the carpet as if in slow motion, slewing coffee all over the place, but she didn't move. It was Nathan who sprang to his feet, vaulted into the kitchen for a dish towel, and returned to mop up the mess. Slowly she rose on numbed feet and stumbled into the kitchen for a damp sponge, and together they managed to repair the damage. They took the towel and sponge back to the kitchen, where Nathan reached for a clean cup. Dani waved him away and groped in the refrigerator for a bottle of wine. She poured herself a glass, drank it, poured herself another one, and carried it into the den, leaving the bottle open on the cabinet.

Nathan settled back into his chair and watched her in silence. "Your foster family?" he repeated patiently.

She took another sip of wine and ran her hand along the top of Thoreau's fine head. "When I was little, I had a dog just like Thoreau," she said. "His name was King." She tugged gently at Thoreau's ear. He turned his head and licked her hand. "They killed him."

"Who killed him?"

"They did. All of them."

"Your foster parents?"

"Not just them."

Nathan shifted his weight in his chair. "Who?"

"The others. The ones who came late at night. They dipped their fingers in his blood. They cut off his ear and put it under my pillow."

Dani felt as though a giant pit had been excavated in the middle of her soul. To speak of King now was the biggest risk she could possibly take with another living human being. It would have been easier to leap to her feet and strip herself naked in front of this man. For a timeless moment, she was afraid to look up, so very afraid of what she would see in his eyes, because if she looked up and saw . . . then she would not be able to tell him another thing.

It took all of her courage, but she did it. She hazarded a look.

And it was there. God, no, not *this* time! She had thought, if there was anyone, anyone in the whole world she could tell . . . but there it was. Just like the other times. The look she dreaded more than any other.

Disbelief.

Oh, he tried to hide it, but she *knew*. He didn't believe her. Therefore, he wouldn't believe any of the rest of it.

She lost her footing, the pit opened up, and Dani fell in.

She felt her face become a porcelain mask, the mask that had served her well through all the Dark Years. "You don't believe me." It was a statement. A fact.

"I didn't say that," he objected. "It's just . . . hard to absorb. Why would these people cut off your dog's ear? I never heard of anything like that."

She stood and carried her empty wineglass into the kitchen, where she poured herself another glass. Nathan followed her. "It's late and I'm very tired," she said woodenly. "There's nothing else I can tell you."

His eyes were bewildered, but they didn't touch her. Nothing could touch her in the pit. "Dani . . ." He reached out.

She turned away and his hand fell limp. "Good luck with your investigation," she said, and found that she simply could not keep the bitterness out of her voice.

While steering the car with his left hand, Nathan removed his sunglasses with his right and lay them on the car seat beside him. Then he reached into the plastic cup filled with the ice water he liked to carry with him on trips, took out a piece of ice, and rubbed it over his eyes, which were grainy and burning from fatigue. It was a three-hour drive from Maplewood to Austin, and it had been no easy feat.

First, he'd had to track down the name and address of Dani's adoptive mother (her father had died some years before). Then he'd had to lie to the lieutenant in order to get away for the drive to Austin. He'd told him that he was tracking down a lead on the identity of the murdered woman. In a way, that was true, so he didn't feel very guilty about the ruse.

Ever since the strange scene in Dani's house the night before, Nathan had been obsessed with unraveling the mystery of her past. Her tale about the bloody murder of her pet had been shocking enough, but even worse was her reaction when she thought he hadn't believed her.

He'd wanted to tell her that cops are naturally skeptical, that they hear such a litany of lies in their day-to-day lives that they see the lie so many people live in their white-bread, middle-class existence; that nothing can ever be taken at face value anymore. He'd wanted to tell her that, but she'd slammed shut the book of her face so fast it had taken his breath away.

But, he had to admit to himself, here he was now, looking for proof. If he could verify her story in some way to his satisfaction, then maybe they *would* be on their way toward solving the mutilation murder.

But at what cost? Nathan feared, deep in his gut, that he had already lost Dani.

He worked his way through the labyrinth of Austin highways, past the pink marble capitol, glowing softly in the autumn hill-country sun, and into the city itself, where, with the help of a map, he maneuvered his way through thick traffic to a street near the University of Texas campus.

Austin was a beautiful city. Dani's mother lived in a pretty neighborhood with nice, if older, homes, the kind which offered a room, kitchen privileges, and cheap rent for college students. Some of the houses sported signs advertising businesses within, the product of Austin's complicated and unusual city zoning laws. Tall trees were sprinkled throughout. Mrs. Daniels lived in a white frame home with green shutters and a profusion of flowers. A Toyota Celica was parked in the drive. He parked behind the Toyota, made his way up wooden steps, and pressed the bell, looking around him. After a moment, he pressed it again. A fluff-tailed squirrel dashed across the grass and up a tree trunk.

When no one answered the door, Nathan walked around the side of the house and peered over a white fence into the backyard. A woman was hunched over a flower bed. Birds jabbered noisily above her. "Excuse me . . . Mrs. Daniels?"

The woman stood up and regarded him, shading her eyes with her hands. She was tanned nut-brown from hours of yard work, with black hair gone salt-and-pepper. *No wonder Dani felt left out,* Nathan thought with a smile. He flashed his badge. "I'm Sergeant Nathan Kendall, Maplewood Police Department."

The woman clutched her chest. "Oh, God, has anything happened to Dani?"

"No, no. Dani's fine. To tell you the truth, Mrs. Daniels, this is a personal visit, not a professional one. We can talk outside, if you'll feel more comfortable."

"Nonsense," she said. "You look trustworthy enough. Come on in." She held open a green gate and Nathan followed her into a large kitchen.

"So you've fallen in love with Dani," said the woman as she handed him a tall glass of iced tea.

"I, er . . . not exactly . . . I mean, I don't know . . ." Nathan felt a hot flush spread across his face and knew he'd already lost control of the interview. He drank the tea down in one gulp and she refilled his glass without question.

She smiled and her dark eyes twinkled. "I doubt a man like you would drive all the way from Maplewood to Austin to talk to a girl's mother if you hadn't fallen for her."

"I hardly know her, Mrs. Daniels."

"Join the club." A shadow crossed her eyes.

What a peculiar thing for a mother to say. He cleared his throat. "I'm conducting a murder investigation. I am afraid that the victim may have had some connection with Dani. I've tried to talk to her, but . . ."

"She ran away."

"In a manner of speaking."

"What do you mean, a connection?" Mrs. Daniels took

her bottom lip between her teeth in a gesture Nathan had seen Dani do as well.

"The victim had a tattoo, on the underside of her arm, just like the one Dani has. She says she's always had it. Is that true?"

Mrs. Daniels got up from the table and roamed the kitchen. She took a dishcloth and began wiping up imaginary crumbs on the spotless white cabinet. After a moment, she said, "Yes. She had it when she came to us. She used to try to scrub it off in the bath. I'd find her little arm scraped to the bleeding point where she'd rubbed it with the washcloth. Once she even tried to slice it off with a razor blade."

Nathan felt the hairs on the back of his neck rise.

Mrs. Daniels began working on the clean stovetop. "It was the same thing with her name," she said finally.

"Her name?"

"Her name is Faith. A beautiful name. From the beginning, she made us call her Dani. She despised her real name and would get completely hysterical if anyone called her by it." She glanced at him guiltily. "My other children—the ones I had naturally—always knew they could get to her that way. She was a difficult child, Sergeant Kendall. You can't imagine."

"Difficult? In what way?"

She began scrubbing off the shining sink. "We had three beautiful children of our own. We wanted more. My last birth was very hard, and they'd given me a hysterectomy. Anyway, when my youngest was ten, we learned about this little girl who had been removed from a foster home. We knew she had been abused, but the agency didn't give us many details. We were sure that if we just gave that child a secure, happy, loving home, why . . . she'd be fine." She stopped and stared off into the past. "We were so naive, Sergeant Kendall. We thought that love was all we needed." She sighed and looked back at him. "She was the most beautiful child I ever laid eyes on in my life. Clouds of white-blond hair, cornflower-blue eyes, cheeks of roses . . . Like an angel she was. An angel named Faith. We thought it was a good omen."

Abruptly she left the dishrag and sank into the chair opposite Nathan, as if her legs would no longer hold her. "As soon as the adoption was final we moved to Texas. My husband had been transferred and anyway, we thought it would be a nice new start for Dani." She sighed deeply. "It was a nightmare. From the beginning. She wet the bed, woke up screaming night after night after night. Had a violent, uncontrollable temper. Moody. Sad. *Haunted,* I guess, would be a better word. And I don't even want to talk about her behavior in school." She paused. "Our family life was torn asunder. The other children resented her. Sometimes, during a fight, she would threaten to kill one or the other." She sighed. "My husband and I quarreled all the time about how to handle Dani."

Nathan shook his head.

"There's more," she said. Nathan wasn't sure he wanted to hear any more.

Mrs. Daniels swirled ice cubes around in her tea glass. "Dani . . . told lies, Sergeant Kendall. She could lie as easily as tell the truth and no one could know the difference. Sometimes she would steal things that she didn't even need."

"What kind of things? You mean shoplifting?"

"No, no. I mean things from us. Like, she'd hide food in her room, when she was offered plenty at mealtimes, and I always allowed after-school snacks. Or she would steal money from my purse even though I gave her an allowance. Occasionally she'd steal toys from the other children and hide them." She plunked the glass down with a *clink,* glanced up at Nathan, and then down, as if unwilling to meet his gaze. "I guess I may as well tell you all of it, since I've gone this far."

"I'd appreciate that."

"Please, don't misunderstand me, Sergeant Kendall." Her eyes, when she looked at him, were agonized. "I would never tell you these things if I didn't believe you cared for Dani, if I didn't think you were trying to help her. I mean,

I don't know anything about this . . . murder investigation . . . but I'm a pretty good judge of character, and I don't think you'd have made the drive to speak to me if you weren't concerned for Dani's welfare. Am I right?"

He couldn't deny it. He nodded.

"Okay." She hesitated.

"What is it?"

"I just don't want you to take this the wrong way, Sergeant. You have to understand that she was a child, a very disturbed child. But she's better now. Surely you can see that. She's made a success out of her life; she's a teacher, and a good one. These things happened a long time ago."

"All right. Please go on."

She gave him a long, steady look, then said, "There was a doll."

Something in the look in Dani's mother's eye caused Nathan to squirm inside, though he kept his expression steady.

"I found it one day. She was, oh, about ten, I think. The doll was under her bed, stashed against the wall. It was slashed to pieces."

For a beat, time seemed suspended. Nathan let out a slow, pent-up breath. He didn't think it could get any worse, but he was wrong.

"Did you get her any . . . help?" Nathan asked.

She rubbed her hands over her eyes, almost black now from painful memories. "This was twenty years ago, Sergeant Kendall. Back then, nobody ever thought about hiring a psychiatrist for a *child*. At least, nobody in our income bracket. We contacted the social worker in California who'd helped us with the adoption, but he couldn't—or wouldn't—give us any more information on Dani's background. He insisted that we knew everything, but I always thought there had to be more. But in those days adoption records were tightly sealed." She looked away and her voice grew quiet. "I don't know. Maybe we should have tried harder."

Nathan made a dismissing gesture with his hand. She

lifted her chin—just as he'd seen Dani do once or twice—and went on. "When we realized that Dani needed serious help, we looked into it, but you can't imagine how expensive that kind of care is. We're talking thousands and thousands of dollars. We just didn't have it. We tried to get aid from the state, but they told us that, as the adoptive parents, we were responsible for her. There didn't seem to be anything we could do but keep working with her at home, keep loving her."

For a moment, they were both silent, remembering their own private Danis.

"It took years to calm that child down. Win her trust. The nightmares went away, for the most part. She wasn't quite so moody. She stopped stealing and didn't seem to feel the need to lie anymore. She even began to get along better with her brothers and sisters and they were kinder to her. I thought everything was going to be all right." She smiled sadly to herself. "Once in a while, she would even crawl into my lap for a hug. It was like a rare, precious gift." Her voice broke, and she cleared her throat.

She twisted her wedding ring around on her finger. "When puberty came along, Dani became even more beautiful. She lost her baby roundness and began to develop a lovely figure. We thought we were going to have to chase the boys off with a shotgun." She chuckled, a brief, hollow laughter that did not reach her eyes.

Flashing a look of agony at Nathan, she said, "And then we lost it all. We lost our beautiful girl and we never really got her back." Tears glimmered under sooty lashes.

Nathan swallowed, trying to ignore the alarm sounding loud and clear at the back of his mind again. He knew that what this woman was about to tell him was the reason he had come. And he knew that, more than anything in the world, he did not want to hear it. "What happened?" he asked, willing her not to answer.

"We were living in another neighborhood here in Austin. Behind the house was a ravine where the kids liked to play. Dani was about fourteen then, and she liked to ride her bike out by the ravine. She'd take a book, and kind of hide away

and read sometimes." Mrs. Daniels stopped for a moment
to replenish Nathan's glass with ice. With growing impatience, he waited.

"One afternoon, Dani had been out at the ravine, and she
came tearing back on her bike, running *screaming* into the
house. Absolutely hysterical. It was all we could do to
understand her. She told us she had found a woman's body,
that it had been horribly cut up . . ." She shook her head
and shrugged.

Nathan's mouth turned to cotton. Her voice droned on as
if from a very great distance.

"Naturally we called the police. They *combed* that area,
Sergeant Kendall. With a fine-tooth comb."

Nathan felt his body go cold, then hot.

She got to her feet and began to roam agitatedly. "Dani
wouldn't believe them when they told her there was
nothing—no woman's body, no blood—*nothing*."

He swallowed.

Dani's mother turned to him with supplication in her
eyes. "She was out of control! We didn't know how to
handle her!"

He heard himself ask, in a very small voice that did not
sound like himself, "What did you do?"

A single tear slid from the corner of her eye. Her voice
broke, but her answer would echo in his mind forever.
"God forgive us, Sergeant Kendall . . . *We had her
committed to a mental institution*."

Chapter 10 ~~~~~~~~

Dani couldn't feel her left arm. She couldn't feel much of anything but the steady, plodding ache in her head. Her tongue was thick. She couldn't move. *Must be the Thorazine,* she thought. *Makes me slow and stupid.*

She opened her eyes. Tiny flowers.

Confused, she shut them again. Hallucinations? *Hold it together. Don't let them get to you.*

Drugs. The straitjacket of the mind. It was how they controlled you. But they weren't going to control her. Say it again: *I'm not crazy.*

If they didn't want to believe her, that was their problem. Oh, she could play their game. The shrinks thought she was delusional. All she had to do was admit it and ask for help. *No!*

She had to be careful, though. They'd already upped her dose once. If she didn't settle down they'd make a zombie out of her like some of the other patients. The *real* crazies.

As if she didn't have enough problems, she'd seen the way that sleaze orderly Ted Manderly had been watching her. She had to be sharp, or else he'd catch her underneath some stairwell and jump her—who'd know the difference? What's one more delusion, right?

By sheer force of will, she opened her eyes again and sat up all at once. Her left arm lay like a dead thing in her lap, red and wrinkled from where her face was imprinted upon it. She'd been asleep on her stomach, her left arm a bent pillow beneath. The tiny flowers were the pattern of the couch.

Thoreau whined nearby, backing his ears in a silent plea for her to hurry over and let him out.

So it wasn't the hospital. Not anymore.

An empty wine bottle lay on the floor beside the couch. Dani couldn't find the glass, but the search caused her to wince. She glanced at the clock. It was eight-fifteen.

She dove for the phone, knocking the receiver onto the floor in her haste, willing herself to think and sound sharp, awake, and not hung over. Pleading car trouble, she promised Gladys Kopeckny that she'd be there in time for the second-period class, which began at nine-twenty. Then she bolted for the back door to let Thoreau out, groaned, and sank into a kitchen chair to keep from passing out.

Ten years. That's how long it had been since Dani had faced a morning hung over. And it had been a helluva lot easier then.

While coffee brewed, she lingered too long in the shower, then flew through the house half dressed, flinging things into her tote. At the last minute she hesitated over the stack of themes from last period, then left them on the table in the den beside her chair. No way she'd get to them at work today.

And all that time, she would not let herself think of Nathan.

At the school, every single parking space for a three-block radius was filled, so she parked at a yellow curb. She made it to her classroom by nine-fifteen. Too rattled to teach, she gave time-filling writing assignments to each of the classes and used the opportunity to get caught up on paperwork. Too late, she realized that she could have completed grading the themes in time for the last period if she hadn't left them at home.

By two-thirty in the afternoon, Dani had a bad case of the shakes and was fighting nausea. It seemed that her life was a kaleidoscope, and no matter which way she twisted or turned it, trying desperately to line up the pieces into some kind of *order*, they would simply disintegrate into another pattern. Only this time, it seemed to Dani that she had made

such a violent twist that the entire structure had collapsed
and lay in shambles at her feet.

"Ms. Daniels?"

Dani jumped so badly she knocked over a jar of pencils.

"I'd help you pick them up," said Jennifer Dawson, "but
I'm afraid I might get stuck down there." She giggled.

"It's okay," said Dani, scrambling up a number of
pencils and shoving them quickly back into the jar so that
Jennifer couldn't see how badly she was trembling.

"Are you all right? You look ill." Jennifer's sweet face
was creased with concern.

"Just a little upset stomach." Dani forced a smile.

"I sure know how *that* feels." Jennifer grinned. "I'll be
going on home-study pretty soon, until the baby's born and
all, but I'll be back full-time in January. My mom's going
to help me."

Dani thought of the Select Student Scholarship, and Mr.
Weams, and Adam Prescott, and her heart ached for
Jennifer. "Let me know if there's anything I can do to
help," she said, feeling an acute sense of having failed a
deserving student.

Jennifer went back to her desk. Dani sensed the unease of
being stared at, and looked across to where Adam sat
defiant, his paper unmarked before him, no pen in sight.
His eyes burned into her. For a moment they locked gazes,
but Dani said nothing about his insolent refusal to do the
make-work assignment she'd given the class. She couldn't
face him down. She lacked the strength.

Restlessly Dani roamed around the room, watching
students write, then turned away and busied herself erasing
the chalkboard. To her blissful relief, the bell rang, and she
waited until the last footfall cleared the hall before she sank
gratefully down into her chair.

A copy of her teacher's guide to the *Inferno* was open on
her desk. A passage was circled in red. From Canto
Nineteen, it read, ". . . thou fearedst not in guile to take
the lovely lady, and then mangle her?"

The page blurred before her.

Adam. It had to be Adam.

But why? What did it have to do with her?

The notes in her door. *He* must have been putting the notes in her mail slot.

Unless . . .

No! She couldn't think that. Wouldn't think it. Not for one minute.

Stumbling, dream-like, Dani clutched her tote to her and staggered down the endless corridor, ignoring other teachers, students, or anyone who crossed her path; out the door, straight across the grass to her car, where she got in without removing the parking ticket from her windshield; then shocked a dozen onlookers by driving up and over the curb in order to avoid waiting for an opportunity to back out; and sped blindly home with only the barest notice of traffic signals.

It couldn't be.

She let herself in the front door. Her head was pounding and her stomach churning. The phone rang. She let it ring. Thoreau barked. She left him out.

"Did you ever stop to think why it is that the whole world is out of step but you? How can it be that everyone else is wrong and only you are right?" Her mother's words from . . . how long ago?

The psychiatrists had preferred more expensive words. Words like *hallucinatory, delusional, paranoid, cognitive distortions.*

Nobody believed her. Not even Nathan.

A small, infant cry escaped her. "I'm not crazy," she murmured.

Then her gaze fell to the table by her chair. The last-period themes were gone.

The first thought to cross Dani's mind was a flash of memory, improbable at first, of a scene she'd watched once on the evening news. An abandoned skyscraper in a busy downtown area had been destroyed by a process known as *implosion,* a skillful blast that collapsed the building from the outside in, rather than the inside out, so that surrounding structures were not damaged.

Instinctively she sensed that an emotional implosion was

bringing about her own collapse, so subtly that others watching her were hardly aware of what was going on. Always before, she'd had a sort of psychological infrastructure of steel that withstood pressures that would crumble another individual.

But now, for the first time . . . self-doubt was weakening that inner structure, and the hideous thought that had taken shape in her mind at the school threatened to cave in every ounce of sanity remaining to Dani.

She had to face it. She *had* to consider it.

Had she really seen the body in the ravine, or the body by the lake?

Even more horrible . . . *What was her connection to the woman with the tattoo?*

Sinking onto the floor, Dani clasped her arms about her knees and buried her face there. Squeezing her eyes shut did not blind her to the questions that demanded answers:

Am I sending these notes to myself?

"We couldn't afford expensive private care, so we had to put her in a state-supported institution," said Mrs. Daniels wearily. "After two years, when she was sixteen, our insurance money ran out, and they let her out. Her father and I objected to it, but they did it, anyway. We tried therapy for a while, but it was so expensive and Dani was so unresponsive that we finally just gave up."

Still reeling from the first revelation, Nathan struggled to follow the thread of Mrs. Daniels's story. The thought that Dani could be seriously mentally ill or emotionally disturbed was something he had never considered, though it was true his instincts had warned him. "Why didn't you want her released?" he asked. "Other than the money, of course."

"We were afraid she'd kill herself. Or even somebody else. Sometimes, on bad days, I found myself almost wishing she would. Kill herself, I mean."

"Why?"

Mrs. Daniels sighed, cleared her throat, looked away. Nathan had been a cop long enough to know guilt when he saw it. He waited, a job-taught virtue. Finally she said, "Dani was almost unrecognizable to us when she came home. I don't know what they did to her in there, but she looked like a concentration camp survivor. That part I could have handled. I could have fattened her up, rested her up, you know? It was the other part I couldn't deal with."

"What other part?"

"Her personality. It was completely altered." She thought a moment. "When Dani first came to us as a child, she was like a damaged little bird. Wounded, vulnerable. Bleeding almost before our eyes. We heaped on the love and it seemed to be working." She stopped a moment, took a long sip of iced tea. "But when she came back from that place, she was a caged wild animal. I never saw so much rage packed into one person. She completely ignored our house rules—stayed out all hours, drank herself into a stupor, and I'm certain she was promiscuous. Whenever we tried to control her, she would run away. We'd track her down, or the police would bring her back."

"What about school?" asked Nathan. "I mean, she's obviously college-educated. How did that come about?"

Mrs. Daniels's face lit up, and Nathan saw that she had been a dark beauty at one time. "It was a miracle, Sergeant Kendall, a miracle from heaven. That's all I can call it." She leaned forward, more animated now. "Dani was always smart. She always liked to read. Well, a *saint*, I meant a *saint*, not just a teacher, mind you, must have seen the potential in Dani because she submitted Dani as a candidate for a special full-tuition scholarship for troubled but promising kids. Dani got it. It changed her life, Sergeant Kendall, and I'm not kidding. She took all that energy she'd been putting into hating and rebelling and channeled it into studying. Graduated college at the top of her class." Mrs. Daniels smiled, as if she had just relayed a particularly satisfying fairy tale where everyone lives happily ever after.

Nathan wished he could look at life with such a neat and tidy attitude. He was full of questions, but he was a wise student of human behavior. If he bombarded her with all the questions he had, it would only rip away at the fabric of her carefully constructed little world. She would resist. Fight back. He had to go carefully.

"Only . . ."

He prompted her with his facial expression to go on.

"Only, sometimes I worry that the same problems are still there, only now they're buried under workaholism and overachievement. I mean, her work is her life, and I don't think she'll ever be willing to even attempt a meaningful relationship with a man." She smiled apologetically. "I thought you'd want to know that."

Nathan stood up and wandered into the den, where family pictures crowded every available surface. Struggling to collect his thoughts, he studied the photographs. One portrait, dimming with age, caught his eye. There was a younger Mrs. Daniels, a man who had to be Mr. Daniels—a basic blue-suit, white-shirt, thinning-hair guy; he had a pleasant enough face—three dark-haired kids with mischievous grins (two older girls and a younger boy); and standing just a smidgeon apart from the rest of the family, not touching the others, solemn-faced and big-eyed, stood a blond little beauty. The lonesome sadness in that child's face tugged at Nathan's heart.

"Mrs. Daniels, did Dani ever tell you anything about her foster family?"

She came up behind him. "Not us, no. But she told the psychiatrists at the hospital things that were so bizarre they wouldn't even tell *us*."

"What did the doctors think?"

"They told us that it was obvious that she had been brutally abused in some way—even sexually—and that those tales she was telling was her way of dealing with it."

"But they didn't think the stories were real."

"Delusions, they said. Or maybe even lies."

"What about the woman's body—the one in the ravine? What did the doctors think about that?"

"They said that her burgeoning sexuality, brought on by puberty, was frightening to her, you know, because of all the abuse she'd had in that foster home. The woman with her breasts sliced off was a hallucination that symbolized Dani's fears."

"So that wasn't real, either."

"No."

Nathan roamed the room, fidgeting with figurines, looking at more photographs of a pretty young girl with haunted eyes. Finally he sat on the sofa and gestured for the woman to sit down next to him. She did. He chose his words carefully. "What would you say if I told you Dani saw another body which the police never found?"

She shook her head. "My poor baby." Glancing sideways at him, she added, "Maybe she's falling in love, and it frightens her the same way puberty did, so . . ."

He smiled gently. "Good theory. But I didn't meet her until she reported finding the body."

"Oh, that's right. You're a homicide detective."

"There's only one problem with all these theories, Mrs. Daniels."

She raised her eyebrows questioningly.

"This time there is a body for real. And it looks exactly like the other two Dani reported finding. And there's a tattoo on its arm, just like the one on Dani's arm."

For a long moment they sat in silence, each in their own thoughts. Nathan kept seeing Dani's face when she told him about her dog King, kept hearing the bitterness and despair in her voice when he questioned her story.

That was what really kept tearing at him. It was the *truth* in her eyes.

Then he remembered Seth's words: *When crazy people see things, it's real to them, like it just happened. But it's all in their heads.*

And then the seed-thought of an idea took hold in his mind . . . an idea so horrifying he could barely face it.

Could Dani herself be capable of murdering and mutilating another human being?

Chapter 11 ~~~~~~~~

Slowly Dani raised her head from her arms and got to her feet. *The tattoo*. Everything came back to the tattoo.

Digging around inside her tote bag, she pulled out some paper and a pen. Brow furrowed in concentration, she walked down the hall and into the bathroom, snapping on the overhead light. With startling clarity she saw the dark shadows underneath her eyes, the translucent white skin stretched skull-like over her face. But it was not her face she had come to examine.

Quickly now, fumbling, she unbuttoned her blouse and dropped it to the floor. Then she raised her arm and, for the first time in years, examined the bloodred mark forever branded in the soft flesh on the underside of her left arm. As she had grown, the tattoo had spread out somewhat, but it was still clear. There were scars, too. White slice marks she had put there herself with a razor blade when she was eight years old.

Why?

Even now, she couldn't look at the markings without feelings of revulsion. And that old impulse to run.

But this time she didn't run. This time she took the pen and painstakingly reproduced the tattoo on paper. For most of her life, Dani had shut her past away into a dark inner closet and kept it hidden from everyone—even herself. She'd ignored that closet successfully, for to open the door was too terrifying and painful even to consider. But now the door had swung open on its own, tormenting her with ghostly, diabolical images from its shadowy recesses, images she could only partially see, but which horrified her by their mere presence. The hated and long-avoided tattoo was the only key within Dani's reach with the power to release those demons. And Dani now realized that she *had* to free those dark memories . . . or they would destroy her.

After changing out of her school clothes and into some comfortable sweats, Dani carried the paper into the den, plopped down into a chair, and studied it under a light.

A lightning bolt, reaching from the left toward the center. A triangle, the right side vertical. An upside-down cross. A triangle, the left side vertical. A lightning bolt, reaching from the right toward the center. The cross came to a pinnacle in the center of the mark, creating an overall triangular shape for the design.

What did it mean?

She stared at it until her eyes burned, but it meant nothing to her. The feelings of dread and revulsion provoked by the design only asked questions that the markings couldn't answer.

At least, Dani couldn't answer them. But she knew a place where she might find some answers. With a resurgence of energy, Dani bounded up, struggled quickly into her socks and running shoes, grabbed her tote and the paper with the design, and hurried out the door.

The Maplewood Public Library was housed in a quaint old rock building that seemed perpetually too warm. Huge shaggy oak and maple trees hugged the building. Inside, the smell of books and furniture polish always brought back one of Dani's few happy childhood memories—lounging in the library on hot summer afternoons.

But there was nothing happy about her visit today, and she set about her worrisome business with singular determination. The lightning bolt was fairly easy to find among common Nazi insignia. Some things, she figured, didn't bear thinking about too much, just yet.

She found the center symbol in a book on ancient occult practices. It was meant to be an upside-down cross, a blaspheme of the Christian God. The same book mentioned the triangle, another aged symbol. The three sides stood for earth, sky, and water.

The occult.

Feeling suddenly chilled, Dani hurried to collect some more books on the subject, some of which dealt with satanism.

Satanic cults. The *Inferno*. it was all starting to come together. It made a certain macabre sense. Dani didn't know whether she should feel relief . . . or horror.

She was cold. She'd lit a fire and turned up the central heating, but still she couldn't feel warm. Every light in the house blazed, and Thoreau dozed at her feet, but she didn't feel safe. She sat cross-legged on the couch, wrapped in a quilt, with books piled around her.

There were books on witchcraft and demonology, cults and the occult. White Magick and Black Magick. And Satan.

Dani read as long as she could stand it, then she got up, poked the fire, freshened her coffee. Simply reading about such subjects provoked a strange restlessness within her, an almost overpowering desire to be anywhere else, like a bad case of stage fright on the night of a performance. No matter that she told herself she was prepared for it; she still wanted to run away and hide.

She forced herself to go on. Public fascination with the occult tended to travel in cycles, but one of the most potent influences on American satanism was from a Britisher who liked to call himself "The Great Beast 666," Aleister Crowley, whose German Secret Society, known as the Ordo Templi Orientis, or OTO, concentrated on various "sexual magic" rites in the early 1900s. The man's photograph, with his shaved head and wild, piercing eyes, sent trembles through Dani's body. Quickly she turned the page.

The watershed years for American satanism seemed to be the 1960s, concentrating particularly in the hedonistic Haight-Ashbury district of San Francisco, reaching tentacles even to such criminal luminaries as Charles Manson.

Anton Szandor LaVey founded the first official Church of Satan in 1966, also in San Francisco.

San Francisco. Dani sat up straight, rubbed her burning eyes, and stared at the page which had blurred before her. *I was born in San Francisco,* she thought. *In 1963.* She stood for a moment, the old restlessness returning, then made herself keep reading.

The Satanic Bible, written by LaVey, was published in 1968, and included various satanic rituals and the famous "Nine Satanic Statements." Other satanic "churches" followed LaVey's, some splintering off on their own. But for every organized, legitimate satanic "church," complete with mailing lists and tax breaks, there were hundreds, maybe thousands, of underground cult groups which performed their own secret rites and rituals for their own illicit purposes. Some were known to have committed murder and mutilation.

She couldn't stand it anymore. Heading for the kitchen, she found another bottle of wine and started searching for a corkscrew. Suddenly she stopped herself. *This isn't the way,* she thought. *Keep your head clear.* She put away the wine bottle and prepared herself hot chocolate instead. Something about hot chocolate seemed soothing. Back in the den, the wall clock chimed three times.

The old song about going to San Francisco and wearing flowers in your hair came into her mind. Yeah. Right. She couldn't stop herself from pacing. Whatever it was, it had something to do with her foster family, back in San Francisco, in the sixties.

Finally she wearied of the pacing, which was getting her nowhere mentally as well as physically, and sat back onto the couch, where she thumbed through a book on "diabolism." A phrase leapt at her: "*the devil's badges.*" Converts to diabolism received a mark of identity or badge of servitude, which could be *in the form of a brand or tattoo.*

Dani began to shake in earnest. The paper with the sketch of her tattoo rested on the coffee table in front of her. The lightning bolt, the triangle, the upside-down cross, the triangle, the lightning bolt. Resting at an angle, some distance from her, the insignia, the *brand* stood out in a new way, a way in which it had never stood out before. She was unaware that she was holding her breath.

They weren't just symbols. They were *letters*.

The lightning bolt. *N*. The triangle. *A*. The upside-down cross. *T*. The triangle. *A*. The lightning bolt. *S*.

NATAS.

Say it backward.

"*Satan*," she whispered.

Chapter 12 ~~~~~~~~

"Lieutenant Ward . . . I'd like to have a word with you." Briefing was breaking up. Seth raised his eyebrows at Nathan but said nothing as he gathered his things and left the room. Ward turned stern eyes toward Nathan. He always had a way of behaving as if he had far better things to do than wasting time talking with his officers. He waited, glancing alternately toward the door and at his watch.

"I think the reported body out by the Palmer estate and the dumpster body may be related," said Nathan. "I'd like permission to drag the lake."

"Listen," said Ward, fixing Nathan with one of his famous withering looks. "As far as I'm concerned, this particular victim must have been a hooker who picked up a john somewhere who liked rough sex. Which got a little too rough. We'll probably never know who she is. If it was a local do-gooder citizen and the press was breathing hot air down our necks, we'd pull out all the stops to get an indictment on *somebody* for her murder. But it's not. As far as I'm concerned, you can stash that file in the 'unsolved' bin and get on with your *real* cases." With that, he pushed out the door. Interview over.

Nathan stared after him, openmouthed. A woman was dead, horribly mutilated and probably raped. Somebody's daughter or sister or lover. Dumped like so much garbage in *their* jurisdiction. And this guy didn't give a shit. At least, not as long as the case didn't generate any career-making (or career-breaking) publicity.

He'd been told, in so many words, to drop the case in the cold file. Which meant he'd have to do most of his investigating on his off time. Welcome to the wonderful world of law enforcement, he thought.

As he headed for his office, shaking his head, a fresh-faced rookie in a crisp uniform stopped him. "There's a lady here to see you," he said. He gave Nathan a sidewise leer. "A good-lookin' babe if I ever saw one. She's one cool blond."

Dani.

Nathan was annoyed at the little leap of his heart at the thought of seeing her. Hell, all he knew about her so far was that she was possibly nuts. "I'll be waiting at my desk," he said, annoyed at the young officer. He didn't want any brash new cops putting the make on Dani. Even if she *was* crazy.

Nathan shared an office with three other scarred, military-type desks. Seth, Manny, and Fred occupied the others. Unfortunately everyone had just finished briefing. None of them had left yet. He hated for them to see her. He'd never hear the end of it.

When she walked hesitantly into the room, looking shyly around, he hardly recognized her. Her hair was pulled back from her face at the nape of her neck and held in a gold clasp, and she was wearing glasses and a conservative blazer. Even so, she was a knockout. All conversation came to an abrupt and obvious halt. She spotted him and approached his desk. All eyes followed.

"Nathan, could I talk to you in private?"

He winced. She'd called him *Nathan*. That meant he couldn't claim that he'd been interviewing her as a witness. "Nathan" was *personal*. Not only that, but she wanted to talk to him "in private." God, he'd *never* hear the end of it!

"Sure," he said, getting to his feet awkwardly and taking her elbow. As they left the room, they could hear a couple of low whistles. "Ignore them," he mumbled. "Their growth was stunted at the age of twelve."

"Don't worry," she said. "It's not the first time I've been whistled at." She gave him an impish grin.

His heart stumbled a beat. Could a lunatic be such a little

doll? He showed her into an interrogation room and sat down opposite her at a small wooden table which thumped back and forth because of one short leg.

There was something different about her. She was still pale and exhausted-looking, but her eyes were different. The whole set of her expression was one of determination. Remembering his last visit with her, and her cold rejection of him and his skepticism following her bizarre tale of animal mutilation and child abuse, he wondered what she could be up to now. And how he should react.

Reaching into her tote bag, she pulled out a crumpled piece of paper and spread it out on the table between them. It was a drawing of the tattoo. "I know what this means now," she said, tilting her chin defiantly.

"You mean you remembered?"

"No. I did some research. At the library. I worked on it all weekend."

He nodded. Good idea. Why hadn't he thought of that?

"These symbols are consistent with the occult," she said, sounding schoolteachery. "Some are ancient symbols of the Antichrist. Put together, they are meant to represent letters of the alphabet. They spell the word *natas*."

He shook his head. "Never heard of it."

"It's a term used by some satanists. You're supposed to say it backward." She waited.

He read the word backward in his mind. "Satan?"

"That's right."

He sat back, letting air slowly out of his lungs, careful not to make a sighing sound. "What are you telling me, Dani?"

"I'm telling you that I was *branded*, Nathan, by a satanic cult, when I was a little girl. I think maybe that woman who was murdered was branded by the same cult—maybe when she was a child, too. I don't know. And I think . . ." She faltered a moment. "I think they murdered her."

She looked at him searchingly. He knew better than to show doubt. He thought rapidly. "You think your foster parents were involved in that cult?"

"Yes, I do."

He raised his hands, palms up. "Then why don't you remember what happened to you? Like when you got the tattoo?"

She sighed wearily. "I remember bits and pieces. Like King. But my mind played a trick on me and blocked other things out." She leaned forward earnestly, sending the table into another *thump*. "But I've been having nightmares, Nathan. And flashbacks. Migraines . . ."

The boy couldn't have been more than sixteen. Somebody's son or brother. But the AK-47 in his hands was grown-up enough. It glinted in the shadows of jungle foliage. And Nathan didn't have to think. All he had to do was pull the trigger and brace himself against the staccato bursts of his M-16. They cut the kid's head off.

Nobody had to tell Nathan Kendall about flashbacks and nightmares.

Something in his eyes must have encouraged her. "There's more," she said, reaching into that bottomless bag. She handed him a sheet of white paper with the words *Red Rum* blocked out in red marker ink.

"Murder," he read aloud.

She nodded. "This was dropped into my mail slot after I found the body in the park."

The mail slot. He groped his pockets, then remembered he'd left at home the note that had been dropped into her mail slot the night the dumpster body was found. It had said something about much harm coming to somebody in the woods. Like mutilation and murder?

"I think the cult is trying to contact me again," she said. "What I can't imagine is why."

Nathan sat back in his chair once again, thinking, keeping his face carefully impassive. There were officers on the force who believed that satanic cults were actively committing crimes in the area, but so far all they'd been able to produce were a few mangled cats. He'd heard them talk about conspiracies, and about hiding or destroying evidence so that the cops would never find it. He'd always thought such talk was just cop paranoia run rampant. Most of the cult fiends were members of staunch fundamentalist churches, and Nathan believed their judgment was clouded.

It was all so hard to believe.

Now here he was, hearing it from a woman who had seen a nonexistent mutilated body in her youth, had reported finding another one as an adult, and whose parents had committed her once to a mental institution. Could he believe her?

"I don't expect you to believe all this right now," said Dani, as if she had read his mind. "I just want you to keep an open mind, be aware of it when you investigate this murder. And if it happens again . . ."

"What makes you think it will happen again?" he said sharply, remembering his own earlier suspicions that Dani herself could be involved in the murders.

"Because," she said, "they won't leave me alone."

Now, *that* sounded crazy. Was this another delusion? He scrutinized her face. He'd picked up a few street people in his time who were plumb wacko. Hallucinating. Talking to invisible people. Praying to the television. There were absolutely no such signs in Dani.

Then he thought about all the things he'd read about the sociopathic personality. How charming and *normal* they appeared to the world, and how completely without remorse they could be when they destroyed the lives of innocent people. Ted Bundy, for example.

Could Dani be one of those people? He remembered what her mother said: *When she came to us from that place, she was a caged wild animal. I never saw so much rage packed into one person.*

A new thought popped into his mind. *I'd be pissed off, too, if somebody threw me into a loony bin when I wasn't crazy.* He'd acted pretty nuts himself, after Vietnam.

The thought took root, began to flower. *What if I couldn't remember that I'd been in a war? What if the shrinks didn't know it, either? Wouldn't they have reason to believe I was a certifiable nutcase?*

She was watching him quietly, her hands folded demurely over the paper. He had a sudden urge to yank those glasses off her face, pull the pins from her hair, let it tumble down into his hands, and make love to her right there on the floor.

Watch it, Kendall. He was losing it again. Something about this woman . . .

"Okay," he said finally. "I'll admit that this does sound somewhat crazy." *Woops. Maybe he shouldn't have said that word.* But she only nodded solemnly. "I have to check this out," he added apologetically. "I can't take this all at face value. It's my job."

To his surprise, her eyes lit up. "Oh, thank you, Nathan," she said. "That's all I ask of you. An open mind. Take it under consideration. Believe me, I *know* how crazy it sounds." Her cheeks were flushed. He thought, *Her skin is so soft* . . . With effort, he redirected his thoughts. "Would you leave these things with me?"

She agreed, and handed them over.

Would you have dinner with me? Would you make love to me? I don't even care if you're nuts. Thoughts clamored, but he said nothing. They got to their feet. She looked as if she were about to say something, then changed her mind.

He wanted to be with her so badly he could hardly think straight, but something held him back. *Not until I find out what the hell is going on here,* he thought.

She held out her hand to him; he took it, then drew her to him and held her for a long moment. "It's going to be all right," he whispered over her head. She nodded, then pulled away. He opened the door for her. All three detectives were lounging about the hallway with studied casualness. They all smiled, ducked their heads, and parted to make way for her as she left. Nathan rolled his eyes heavenward.

When she'd left, he said, "What is this, gym class?"

"We wish," said Manny. "With a hole in the locker room wall." They all giggled.

"Oh, grow up!" Nathan growled, stomping into the office. Seth followed. He stood for a while, watching Nathan slam things around on his desk.

"That was the lady who reported the Palmer body, wasn't it?" he said.

Nathan glanced up, nodded, and wadded up a piece of paper loudly, slam-dunking it into the wastebasket.

"You really like her, don't you?"

"Of course not. She's just a witness."

"Methinks thou dost protest too much."

"I've gotta go," he said, brushing past his friend, avoiding those soulful brown eyes.

"Hey—Bulldog."

Nathan turned and looked reluctantly at Seth.

"Be careful, my friend," Seth warned.

Nathan nodded and left, stuffing Dani's design of the tattoo into his breast pocket as he went. The design that was supposed to be satanic. Funny that it didn't burn his hand.

Chapter 13 ⌇⌇⌇⌇

"In the name of Satan, Lucifer, Belial, Leviathan, and all the demons, named and nameless, walkers in the velvet darkness, harken to us, O dim and shadowy things, wraith-like, twisted, half-seen creatures, glimpsed beyond the foggy veil of time and spaceless night."

Flickering shadow-light. Black-hooded figures. Cold. So cold. She wanted to move, to get away, but when she tried to move her legs and arms, nothing happened. She was naked. That's why she was so cold. She wanted to cover herself. Her legs were spread apart and at the end of the hard concrete slab on which she lay stood the figure who chanted the words in clear, ringing tones. He lifted a chalice over his head; it gleamed silver in the candlelight. Over the upraised chalice, emblazoned on the wall in crimson, was a lightning bolt, a triangle, an upside-down cross, a triangle, a lightning bolt.

"Draw near, attend us on this night of fledgling sovereignty. Welcome a new and worthy sister, creature of exquisite magic light. Join us in our welcome. With us say: welcome to you, child of joy, sweet passion's daughter, product of the dark and musk-filled night, ecstasy's delight. Welcome to you, sorcerer most natural and true magickian."

Voices from all the hooded figures joined the chant in a rhythmic, sexual beat. The figure between her legs bent down and poured warm liquid from the chalice onto her body. It was sticky and foul-smelling. Then he leaned over and kissed her, his tongue forcing its way between her clenched teeth, filling her mouth until she gagged. She bit down hard—it was her only weapon—and he pulled back quickly, peered at her from the black hidden folds of his cloak, then threw back his head and laughed, a wild, wicked, evil laugh that seemed to roll on and on until they were all laughing; high, wild laughter that echoed and echoed in her mind and she wanted to scream *Stop it!* but she couldn't; she couldn't speak, all she could do was sob and sob and sob . . .

Dani opened her eyes. Her hair was damp, her body soaked in sweat. Chest heaving, she struggled to her elbows and found that she was spread-eagled atop the covers. Her mouth was bone-dry, but she was afraid to get up and make her way through the dark hallway to the bathroom for a drink. Instead, she burrowed underneath the blankets and curled into the fetal position, shivering convulsively.

Warmth was slow in coming. Suddenly an idea occurred to her: *Write it down.* Snapping on the bedside light, she fumbled in a nightstand drawer for some stationery and a fading felt-tip pen. It would have to do. Then, still shivering, her handwriting barely legible, she recorded the dream in as much detail as she could remember.

All except for her tormentor's face. She could smell his breath, feel his grip on her body, taste his mouth still, but she could not *see* him. *Him*. With the clarity of dream-revealed insight, Dani realized that, although she may be endangered by a cult, that cult had a leader, and it was the leader who hated her—for whatever reason—the most. Therefore, he was the one she had most to fear. He was the one she had to defeat.

After she wrote down what she could remember of the dream, she felt calmer. She switched off the light and curled underneath the covers again. Gradually warmth set in and the shivering stopped.

"I'm going to get control of this thing," she whispered to the darkness. "I'm going to remember. And when I do . . ." Her voice grew stronger, gaining courage, flinging the challenge to the night. "When I do . . . I'm going to find the son of a bitch who tried to destroy me."

Sleep came quickly after that, and the dreams fled.

"Ah me! O Satan! Satan!" loud exclaim'd
Plutus, in accent hoarse of wild alarm:
. . . "Let not thy fear
Harm thee, for power in him, be sure is none
To hinder down this rock thy
safe descent."

Dani looked around the room, and her eyes rested on Adam. "What the poet is saying," she said, "is that Satan himself does not have power over us. In fact, the poet and Virgil actually *rode* the Great Beast down the mountain. Symbolically I think that says that we have nothing to fear from evil—in fact, we can overcome it—as long as we have courage and . . . and faith."

Adam met her gaze with a cynical little smile which might have unnerved her earlier, but not now. She stared at him with a hard coolness that, to her surprise, caused him to glance away. *I'll take little victories where I can get them,* she thought.

"Read the next three cantos for tomorrow," she said. Ignoring the groans of the class, she continued to watch Adam. There would be no more secret messages underlined in her copy of the *Inferno*.

When the bell rang, she called to him. "I want to speak to you after class." As the rest of the students filed out, he slouched before her, gazing at her in a brazenly suggestive way, up and down. She refused to let it get to her. "Someone has been dropping little notes in my mail slot, late at night. Would you know anything about that?"

He shrugged. "Things go bump in the night. Who can know whence they came?" He smiled down at her; her short stature was a disadvantage.

"Sit down, Adam." She gestured toward one of the front desks. He did so, and she remained standing. *Advantage, Daniels.* She handed him her textbook. "Do you see the lines which have been marked? I want to know if you did it."

"Gosh, Miss Daniels," he said in a little-boy voice, "I don't know *how* that happened."

She yanked the book from him, then bent over, her face level with his, her voice like steel. "You listen to me, and you listen good. I don't know what the hell you're up to, and I don't care. But you leave me out of it, you understand?" She stood up, crossed her arms over her chest, and glowered down at him. "And you can pass that little message on to your leader."

Adam's face went pale. Sweat broke out on his forehead. He licked his lips. Gone was the cockiness. "Wh-what do you mean?"

Dani was disturbed. She'd thrown that last part out just to see how he would respond. She hadn't expected to see the kid dissolve into abject terror. "Adam . . ." Her voice softened. "You're in way over your head. These . . . things . . . you've been fooling around with are not a game. It's serious. Deadly serious. You've got to get out before . . . before it destroys you." She leaned forward slightly. "Let me help you."

He looked as if he were about to throw up. "I can't," he said. "It's too late." With that, he grabbed his books and bolted from the room.

The baffling conversation with Adam had almost faded from Dani's mind later that afternoon as she pulled up in front of the police department barely ten minutes from when she'd left her house. Bounding up the steps two at a time, Dani slammed into the entranceway, turning heads as she went.

A trim young female officer, with short-cropped dark hair, approached her warily. "May I help you?"

"I'd like to see Sergeant Kendall, please. It's important." Dani could feel the heat in her face. Rage had a way of doing that to her. "Tell him it's personal."

The officer gave her a quizzical look, told her to wait a moment, and left.

Dani squirmed inside her sweater and avoided the glances of other officers, who had turned to stare. She recognized some from her earlier visit. A couple were openly smiling. Obviously they thought it was pretty funny. She turned away and studied a bulletin board, which was covered with pictures of missing children and Most Wanted criminals. While she waited, the phone conversation she'd had with her mother after work burned in her mind.

"Let's get out of here." Nathan had somehow materialized at her elbow. She nodded and led the way out of the building, not waiting for him to hold the door open.

He confronted her on the steps. "What's this all about?" An officer climbed the steps and greeted Nathan. He nodded.

She looked around. "Not here." One of the detectives who shared an office with Nathan, a tall black man, exited the building, ducked his head at her, and said to Nathan, "I'll be in the Projects, snooping around about that stabbing last night."

Nathan took a step forward. "I should go with you."

The man shook his head. "No problem. Tell the truth, I can get more done in that neighborhood without you, white boy." He grinned.

Nathan nodded. "Keep in touch." The man headed down the steps, and Nathan looked at Dani.

She said, "I shouldn't have come. You're working. It was . . . an impulsive thing."

He shook his head. "Don't worry about it. My car's down here. Let's take a ride around the block."

Dani followed him down to a nondescript, cream-colored sedan. A radio squawked underneath the dash. He turned it down. Dani was beginning to feel sheepish. As they headed down the road, he looked sideways at her, but she didn't speak. After a couple of turns, he pulled into a secluded spot behind an abandoned warehouse and shut off the engine. The radio stayed on, speaking quiet mumbo jumbo in the background.

"You went to see my mother," she blurted, staring straight ahead. "How could you?"

"Is *that* what this is all about? I thought something terrible had happened."

"It *was* terrible! To *me* it was! My private life is my *own*, do you hear?" She got out of the car and slammed the door, too angry to sit still. After a moment, he followed, leaning quietly against the car. She whirled to face him. "You can do all the snooping you want to, but you *leave my family out of it!*"

"Look, *you're* the one who reported a body *nobody could find,*" he said. "*You're* the one supposedly getting cryptic messages in your mail slot the night a *real* woman is murdered. I'm an investigator. It's what I do: *investigate.* I had to find out whether you were—"

She crossed her arms over her chest. "Go ahead, Nathan. Say it."

He turned away, shaking his head.

"You had to find out if I was crazy, right? Tell me, what did you find out from my mother? Huh? Did you find out about the *mental institution*? I'm sure that was your favorite clue to this whole mystery." His face was turned away from her. She could see the muscles working in his jaw. "No doubt you just *loved* what I was telling you the other day. I'm sure all that talk about demons and devils was very entertaining." She looked away.

He sighed. "You just won't give a person a chance, will you? If anybody tries to help you, you push them away."

"I don't need any help, Nathan," she said quietly. "I found that out long ago." She climbed into the car, slamming the door, and muttered to herself, "Certainly not from you."

Chapter 14 ～～～～～

Dani's visit had given Nathan a lot to think about, but unfortunately his job didn't offer much time for brooding. Not long before he was supposed to go off duty, less than an hour before the late-night news, another mutilated woman's body turned up.

A teenaged couple, looking for a suitable isolated spot to park and make out, had caught her in the sweep of their headlights, dumped unceremoniously at the dead end of the two-lane track leading to the Palmer estate. No attempt had been made to cover or hide the body, and this time there were no garbage bags shrouding it. The poor kids shook and cried as they spoke to police.

A TV news crew had arisen, bat-like, from whatever caves housed them at night, and had actually beaten Nathan to the scene. He cursed them, drove them back, and assigned more patrol officers to herd them into roped-off corrals out of the way. Even as he assigned Seth and the others to photograph and diagram the scene, Nathan knew, with despair weighing down his soul, that they would find no evidence.

When he was asked to give a statement to the press, he spoke carefully. "We have discovered the body of a white female, in her late twenties, on a private drive leading to the Palmer estate, which is not currently occupied. She was apparently the victim of foul play. We will not release her identity until the family has been notified. Officers are investigating the crime scene and will be doing so all night." He took no questions. He had too much work to do.

• • •

Sometime between three and four A.M., Kendall sat at his desk, drinking stale coffee and filling out an interminably long report on this latest pathetic loss of life. He was depressed and angry, as though it were somehow his fault that the killings were continuing, that he couldn't find some way to stop them. Somewhere out there a madman stalked, who got his jollies out of carving up women like so much Thanksgiving turkey ("Who'll have a breast?") and then dumping the carcass out with the trash.

It was happening in *his* town, on *his* turf.

Maybe he even passed the killer while walking into a grocery store or sitting at a traffic light. Maybe the killer knew it, and laughed.

"Bulldog! Lieutenant Ward wants you in interrogation quick!" Manny Garcia was so excited it was all he could do not to lapse into Spanish. "We got the guy, and he wants to *confess*!"

John MacIntire was a man of average everything. Average height, weight, and appearance. Brown hair, brown eyes, complexion which was now as sick-pale as a tuberculosis sufferer. He smoked continuously, lighting one cigarette with the butt of another, his hands shaking so hard that sometimes an officer had to hold the cigarette for him while he lit it. He always said, "Thank you."

He did not look like a cold-blooded savager of women.

Not long after the evening news, he had called in to report his wife missing. Officers had taken him to view the woman's body, and after giving them a positive ID, he'd broken down and confessed.

"I did it. I killed my wife and the other one. I did it. Now can I go to jail?" he said as soon as Nathan entered the room. Lieutenant Ward, who had accompanied Nathan to the interview, had a little grin on his face which the man was too distraught to see, but Nathan saw it, and he didn't like it.

"Mr. MacIntire," he began.

"Please, call me M-Mac."

"Okay . . . Mac . . . You are aware that you have

every right to have an attorney present at this questioning, aren't you?"

"No lawyers! No. I don't want any lawyers."

Nathan noticed that a video camera had been set up and was running. A very unusual move for this small town. "All right. That is your choice, but I am going to read your rights to you as spelled out in the Miranda decision of the Supreme Court," he said, taking the white card from his breast pocket. Of course, he knew the statement by heart, but he didn't want anything to mess this up when the DA got ahold of it.

He examined the man's face and general behavior to see if he could spot any evidence of drug use. There was none visible.

While he read the trembling man his rights, Nathan took mental note of his nervousness and impatience. "Do you understand these rights as I have explained them to you?" he asked finally.

"Yes, yes, can we get on with it now?" Mac dropped his cigarette and picked it up again with trembling hands.

Lieutenant Ward smiled.

Nathan spoke for the camera's benefit: "This is a statement taken voluntarily of Mr. John MacIntire, at the Maplewood Police Department, on Saturday, October 20, 1990, at three-thirty A.M., concerning the murder of Mrs. John MacIntire and of an unidentified female. Present at the interview are Detective Sergeant Nathan Kendall and Detective Lieutenant Thomas Ward; questioning by Detective Kendall."

During the preliminary questioning, the man gave his age as thirty, and his occupation as shipping and receiving manager for ChemCo, Inc., a company owned by Jordan Blake. He had two small children. Once, when Nathan mentioned them, the man broke down.

"Okay, Mr. MacIntire—"

"*Please*, call me Mac."

"All right, then, Mac. Would you trace for us your actions earlier this evening, on the night of October 19?"

Mac's voice assumed the quality of a monotone. "My

wife, Sally, and I were making love, and . . . I got this . . . compulsion . . . It's something I can't control. I just wanted to *hurt her*. I couldn't help it. I didn't know what I was doing. I grabbed her and hit her head on the bedstead, and when she was unconscious, I, I . . . cut . . . her . . ." He broke down again and wept, ragged, torn sobs wrenched from deep within.

Ward nodded smugly.

"Then I, um, realized what I had done and I took her away and dumped her at the Palmer estate."

"Where were the children, Mac?" interrupted Nathan as he scribbled notes to himself. *Check sheets. Check car.*

"In bed. They never knew." Mac tried to light another cigarette, failed, accepted help from Nathan. "Please . . . please, leave them out of it. They're so young . . . " With this, he sobbed some more.

"Mac, what time was all this taking place?"

"I don't know. Nine, maybe ten."

Check neighbors for witnesses of suspect's movements. "I have to ask you this. What did you do with the . . . body parts?"

Mac stared at him. "Body parts?"

"The breast tissue matter."

"Breast tissue . . ." He put his face in his hands. "I don't remember. Oh, God . . ." He put his head on the table and wept. It thumped forward on its one short leg.

"Mac, *Mac* . . . where did you put the knife?"

"Knife?" The man was stupefied from emotional overload.

"What did you cut her with, Mac?"

"Cut her with? I . . . ." He glanced over at Lieutenant Ward. "I don't remember. I threw it away."

"Where, Mac?"

"I don't know. The side of the road someplace, I guess."

Check roadsides, garbage, and dumpsters. Get search warrant or consent form.

Trying to light still another cigarette, the man trembled so violently and fumbled so distractedly that he wound up putting both cigarettes in his mouth at once. If Nathan hadn't gently removed the shorter butt, the distraught man may not have even noticed.

For a long moment, Nathan sat watching him. He'd heard plenty of confessions in his day, and not all of them rang true. There was something about this one . . .

"Mac, we have to ask you some questions about the murder of the other young woman, on October 10 of this year."

"Fine. Yeah." Mac took a deep drag on his cigarette.

"Would you like some coffee? Water? A Soda?"

"Water, please."

Nathan signaled to the eager Manny, who stood just outside the door, and ordered a glass of water, which he fetched quicker than Nathan could say it.

"I killed her," volunteered Mac, after downing the water in a single gulp.

"Who was she?" Nathan leaned forward, pen poised.

"I don't know. I picked her up. She was hitchhiking."

"Are you in the habit of picking up young women from the side of the road?"

"*No!* It just . . . happened."

"What happened, Mac?"

"We went riding around. We stopped in the woods. We started to make love. I couldn't control myself. I cut her."

A block of wood would show more expression, thought Nathan.

"Where did this take place?"

"I don't remember." Mac took a deep drag on his cigarette and looked away.

"What did you do with the body?"

Mac rubbed his eyes. "Put it in a couple of plastic bags and put it in the dumpster. I thought nobody would notice."

Ask suspect to tie two pieces of rope together. Check the knot.

"Please, can I go now?" Mac begged.

"Are you asking that the interview be terminated?"

"Whatever. I don't care."

"Do you have anything else you'd like to tell us at this time?"

The man lunged across the table, into Nathan's face. Nathan pulled back and instinctively reached for his service revolver. "*Please,*" Mac whispered. "*Please, please* promise me that my children will be safe."

"Your kids are in the care of neighbors right now, Mr. MacIntire. They will eventually be placed in foster care, until this thing can be ironed out."

Nathan studied the man closely. Why was he so terrified for the safety of his children?

As officers led the defeated man away, Lieutenant Ward beamed and slapped Nathan on the shoulder. "Good work, Kendall! Killer caught, cases closed. One more slimebag nutcase off the streets. I'll call the chief myself," he added, and left the room.

Nathan glanced at his watch. Nearly five A.M. A new day was dawning. Exhaustion dragged at his body. Loose ends tugged at his mind.

He'd seen street bigshots crumble in jail and call their mommies for help. He'd seen defiant killers, regretful killers, and remorseless killers.

But he'd never seen a killer like John MacIntire.

As far as Nathan Kendall was concerned, this case was a long way from being closed. Heading wearily for his office, he dug around in his files for a search warrant form, trying, all the while, to shake the feeling that something was very, very wrong.

Chapter 15 ~~~~~~~

From somewhere deep within the lost well that is sleep, Dani heard something different from the gentle *whirr* of the ceiling fan over her bed, or the hum of the clock radio on the bedside table. The noise was neither loud nor alarming; nevertheless, she opened her eyes as if she'd never slept at all.

For a long moment she lay perfectly still, sorting through her jumbled dream-memory to see if she could figure out why she was wide awake at (she turned her head) three o'clock in the morning. Her thoughts carried on a dialogue in her mind.

Get up! Something is wrong!

Don't be silly. You're just being paranoid again.

Dani pushed herself into a sitting position and rubbed her face, glancing over at the clock again. Her eyes were getting adjusted to the dark, and the digital numbers cast an eerie red glow.

Dani switched on the light.

The ear of a German shepherd dog, bloody on one end, rested with evil innocence on the pillow beside her.

With a half-scream, half-cry, Dani recoiled violently, tumbling from the bed onto the floor. *Oh, God. Thoreau. "THOREAU!"*

Staggering to her feet, Dani stumbled down the hall, calling him, hoping insanely that he would come trotting up to her with concern on his face, eager to help.

He was lying on the den floor, his head, missing the left ear, bathed in blood. She dropped to her knees beside him.

God, please, please don't let him be dead.

She lifted his poor head. It wobbled like rubber on his neck.

"Please, *please* don't let him be dead."

She struggled to pull him into her arms, but he was dead weight. She couldn't tell if he was breathing. Prostrating herself over him, she pressed her ear against his chest. If she lay very still, she could faintly hear the *thump, thump* of his heart.

A vet. Got to get him to a vet.

There was no twenty-four hour animal clinic in a town the size of Maplewood, but one advantage of a small town was that vets often listed their home phone numbers in the telephone book.

Phone book. Phone book. *Where's the damn phone book?*

In a panic now, stumbling, dropping things, Dani scrambled for the phone book and found it buried underneath some newspapers in the kitchen. Her hands were shaking so hard she could barely turn the pages.

Thoreau's veterinarian was a country doctor of few words, who had been practicing longer than Dani had been alive. He answered the phone with a grunt on the third ring.

"Dr. Sanderson, this is Faith Daniels. My German shepherd, Thoreau, he . . ." Her voice trembled so that Dani could hardly be understood. "He's been p-poisoned, I think, and they c-cut off his ear, and I think he's going to d-die." She bit her lip, struggling mightily to get herself under control.

"All right. Bring him into the clinic. I'll meet you there." And he hung up. No questions, no recriminations. It was the old vet's way.

The calm, sane voice at the other end of the line helped to reassure Dani. *She was getting some help. Thoreau was going to be all right.*

Heedless of the gown she was still wearing, Dani stooped down beside the unconscious dog, gathered him in her arms, and lifted.

Nothing happened. *She couldn't lift him.* Struggling,

whimpering, Dani tried several different ways to raise the animal, but she was simply too small to manage it.

She desperately needed help, and there was only one person she could think of whom she could call at three-thirty A.M. for an emergency of this nature. Dashing for the phone, Dani rooted around for the white card still lying on the kitchen cabinet, turned it over, and dialed Nathan Kendall's home phone number.

Just the thought of calling Nathan gave Dani strength. One ring. He would come straightaway, she knew. Two rings. Please. *Please*. Three rings. *Where the hell could he be at three-thirty in the morning, for God's sake?* Four rings.

"Hello."

"Oh, God, Nathan, I'm so glad—"

"—come to the phone right now, but if you'll leave your name and number, I'll get right back to you." *Beep*.

She slammed down the receiver. Trembling, still in shock that Nathan wasn't home, angry that the one time she *did* ask for help, he wasn't there, Dani finally absorbed the knowledge that she was on her own again. Just like always.

She would have to drag the dog.

Flinging on a coat over her gown, shoving bare feet into a pair of cold boots, Dani retrieved her wallet out of her tote bag and stuffed it into her pocket. Then, stopping once again over the comatose animal, Dani slipped her arms underneath the big dog's elbow joints up near his chest and began backing toward the door.

His head smeared her unbuttoned coat, and the gown beneath, with blood.

Fumbling with the front door, she managed somehow to get him out of the house and over to the car. A cold, creepy fog had settled in. Streetlamps produced small halos of light, before being smothered by the fog. She could feel the dampness down the back of her neck and shivered.

With one great herculean hoist, Dani managed to load her near-dead friend into the front seat. The car was slow to start, and for one panicked moment, Dani thought she would be stranded, but it finally fired to life.

Due to the fog, she had to drive with frustrating slowness. All the way, she talked softly to Thoreau, stroking him with one hand, trying not to look at his beautiful, mutilated head.

As soon as her headlights pierced the murk in front of the clinic, Dr. Sanderson emerged. He was a huge man, barrel-chested and shaggy-browed, who'd spent a lifetime tangling with farm animals. Lifting the big dog easily in his powerful arms, he headed into the building. Dani held the door for him.

Stretched out under the cold glare of lights on the unforgiving white table, the dog looked for all the world to be dead. In his wordless way, Dr. Sanderson worked over him while Dani hovered on the other side of the table.

"Ear bled a lot, but he'll get over that," he mumbled as he stretched clean bandages over Thoreau's head.

"What about the p-poison?" Dani couldn't seem to stop shaking, or get her mouth to work properly.

"Not poison. Drugs."

"You mean, like . . . s-sedatives?"

He grunted agreement, and murmured, "Enough to kill a horse, looks like."

"But . . . how could they get near? He's very protective of me."

He shrugged. "Threw meat over the fence, I guess."

Dani stared at the doctor in cold shock. He was assuming that Thoreau had been *outside*. Instead, he'd been on the floor, where he slept every night, *at the foot of her bed*.

He looked up. "You all right?" Peering at her over Thoreau's inert form, he said, "Better sit down."

She shook her head. Blindly stroking the unconscious dog, she asked, "Is he going to be all right?"

The old vet hesitated. "Long as he sleeps off the effects of the drugs, yeah. His hearing might not be quite so keen in that ear, and his looks are ruined, of course . . ." His voice petered out and he turned away, busying himself with a hypodermic.

"What if . . . what if he doesn't get over the drugs?" Dani could feel her heart pounding in her chest.

Dr. Sanderson turned back and placed one big hand over her own. "He just might not wake up, hon. That's all I can tell you."

She nodded, a numbness so deep in her soul that she was incapable of even simple thought.

He patted her hand. "I'm gonna put him up now. Nothing to do but wait. I'll call you when . . . when we know something one way or the other."

"May I stay with him?"

He shook his head. "No point in that. Besides, it would upset the other dogs. It's Saturday. Why don't you go on home, get some sleep?"

Home. "Please." She didn't want to beg, but Dani could not, would not go home.

Something in her face and eyes must have moved him. Finally he shrugged. "Got a pen over here in this other room," he said. "Nobody in there." Lifting Thoreau easily again, he carried him into a bare room with a large pen in the corner of the cold concrete floor, where he deposited the dog. "I'll leave the cage open," he said kindly.

Dani settled herself on the floor in front of the cage.

Towering over her, Dr. Sanderson said, "Well, little lady, I don't open up here for another five hours. I'm goin' home, get some shut-eye. But I have to lock up. There's drugs and things in here . . ." He yawned.

"Do whatever you need to," said Dani. "I'll be fine." *Safer here than anywhere else,* she thought.

When the kindly old vet had left, Dani leaned her head against a cinder-block wall adjacent to the cage and tried not to be overwhelmed with loneliness. She'd rested Thoreau's head on her leg. It was swathed with bandages. His chest rose and fell shallowly with each breath.

Stroking his glossy fur, Dani spoke to him softly, nonsense words and babytalk, willing him with every fiber of her being not to leave her alone.

In the small, white-walled room lit by bright overhead lights, cocooned from sound by the cinder-block walls, she was kept awake by the harsh concrete floor, desperate and alone, and it occurred to Dani for the first time since

childhood that maybe . . . just maybe . . . it might help
to pray.

Though her parents had raised her a Catholic, Dani had
followed along with the rituals of that religion just to keep
from being scolded. The truth was that any thought of God
often filled her with an inexplicable revulsion and anger.
During the Dark Years, both in and out of the institution,
Dani had convinced herself that there was no God.

Now she wasn't so sure.

If there could be an Evil so incarnate that some people
felt moved to worship It, then could there not be, somewhere, a Goodness incarnate? A Spirit of love and peace?

Dani had never known such a spirit, but she realized now,
alone in the cold concrete womb, that she had always
longed to. But how to begin to find it?

"Um . . . I'm not sure how to go about this," she said,
almost surprised at the sound of her own voice aloud in the
empty room. "I don't even know if there is anybody
listening or not. All I know is that God . . . if You are
there, and if You are real . . . I need help, and I don't
know where else to turn."

She stopped for a moment, feeling slightly sheepish. "If
You are there, and if You are listening . . . I guess I just
need to know that I'm not all alone."

She waited. What was she waiting for? A blinding light?
An apparition? An emotional sense of overpowering peace?
A sign?

None of those things came.

Dr. Sanderson finally sent Dani home around noon, when
Thoreau was resting comfortably, though they were still
unsure as to how he was going to survive his ordeal.
Exhausted, she collapsed on the sofa in front of the TV in
a zombi-like trance, trying not to look at the small pool of
blood on the carpet and too tired to clean it up.

It was a Saturday, and when football games became too
noisy to sleep by, Dani switched to a talk show, a little local
community-service thing she sometimes listened to with
one ear while grading papers or cleaning. Soothed by the

relative quiet of the show, she was almost asleep when she heard the words *satanic cult*. Dani sat bolt upright.

The program was nearly over. The host sat talking to a pleasant-faced blond woman. "Cult crimes sound so bizarre," the woman was saying, "that we sometimes believe the victims to be lying . . . or crazy."

"What would you suggest a cult crime victim do?" asked the skeptical young reporter.

"Talk to someone who understands."

"Like you?"

She smiled warmly. "Like me. I'm listed in the phone book."

The reporter flashed a TV smile and shuffled his papers. "Well, thanks for joining us today, Ms. McCall." He beamed at the camera. "We've had as our guest today Ms. Kate McCall, noted cult crime expert."

As he spoke, the word *prerecorded* appeared beneath him.

"Please join us next Saturday, when we will have as our guest . . ."

But Dani wasn't listening. She was already fumbling through the phone book.

The house was unassuming and looked like all the others in an older area of town. It looked as if, with work and money, it could be restored to Victorian splendor, but now it was just an old house with fading paint and a sagging porch. Dani parked in a gravel driveway. The fog was worse than ever and completely blotted out any light from the sun. She made her way through a sort of netherworld of tangled trees and up the porch. It almost seemed as if it were a dream and she was merely an observer, not a participant. It was an unreal feeling: protective shock, maybe, after her horrible awakening. Only *this* was the nightmare, and she was no longer sleeping.

The front door was almost entirely made of leaded glass. There was a small bell with a chain. Dani pulled the chain and the bell chimed softly.

Almost immediately the door opened and a woman of

about thirty-five stood on the threshold. She was thick around the waist, solid-looking, with soft blond hair and a broad, smiling face which radiated warmth. "You must be Dani," she said. "I'm Kate McCall. Please come in."

Dani stepped into a parlor which completely negated the tired-looking exterior of the house. It was filled with antiques, flowers, books, and on the walls, old framed prints. A card table in the center of the room held a large jigsaw puzzle, unfinished.

"Let met get you some herb tea," said Kate. "Please sit down." She left through French doors with stained-glass windows. Dani sat down on an overstuffed chintz-covered couch. She felt instantly at home. Brahms, played by a string quartet, wafted from a stereo system somewhere that she couldn't see. Everything about this room spoke of peace, warmth, and solace. The nightmarish feeling slowly began to fade.

The woman came back, handing Dani a delicate blue china cup. "I raise the herbs myself," she said, "and dry them in my kitchen."

"I love this house," said Dani simply.

"Yes," said Kate. "The Lord has blessed."

Dani looked away and took a sip of tea, lightly sweetened with honey. The remark had made her uncomfortable.

"I'm so very sorry about your dog," said Kate. "I pray he will recover."

Dani nodded, unsure what to say.

"I'll tell you a little about myself, in a little while. First, I'd like to hear about you."

"Well, I teach English at Maplewood High School—"

Kate McCall shook her head. "I know all about that, Dani. I want to hear why a satanic cult would want to cut off your dog's ear."

"What makes you so sure it was a cult?" Years of protecting the secrecy of her past kept Dani from being frank.

"Some cults believe that the sacrifice or blood of a dog such as a German shepherd gives them power. The left ear signifies the 'left-handed way,' the way of Satan. I'm surprised they didn't kill your dog outright, or steal him. Did they take the ear, or leave it?"

"They l-left it." Dani set down the delicate cup.

The woman's face grew very serious. She reached out and touched Dani's hand. "If the cult just wanted a dog for a ritual, they'd have stolen him. Instead, they cut off his ear and left it. Where did you find it?"

"Beside my pillow. Thoreau . . . sleeps in the house."

"Oh, Dani. This is worse than I thought. These people are dangerous." She leaned forward, her brow furrowed. "Why has the cult started harassing *you*? They've come back into your life, haven't they?"

Dani stared at the woman. She could feel the color draining from her face. Slowly she stood up and removed the bloody coat. In slow motion, she pushed up the sleeve on her arm and showed Kate the tattoo. "They t-took me when I was a little girl," she mumbled. "I think they want me back." Something within her began to swell, bigger and bigger, a balloon in her chest, choking off her throat.

Kate took Dani's cold hands and drew her back onto the couch. "Well, we're not going to let them get you," she said quietly.

Then there was a great explosion inside, and the break was physical. With a powerful, guttural cry, Dani fell to her knees on the floor. Bone-cracking sobs racked her body. Strong arms went about her shoulders and held her firmly while a voice she scarcely recognized as her own—a voice child-like in its anguish—keened. When at last she wept, a geyser of emotion erupted, so long pent-up that Dani feared being swept away by it.

Kate McCall never spoke. She held Dani tightly until the tears had spent themselves out, and still Dani shuddered as with dry heaves. Finally, after an eternity, Dani looked up into eyes tear-filled with compassion and said simply, "This is the first time anyone has ever believed me."

Chapter 16 ~~~~~~~~~~

While Seth and Manny went over the suspect's car, Nathan paid a visit to the MacIntire home. He'd taken just enough time off that Saturday morning, after spending all night on the case, to shower, shave, take a short nap, feed the animals, and return to work. His whole body felt fuzzy.

He had a search warrant for any evidence related to the murder of either Mac's wife or the unidentified female. Mac had claimed to murder his wife in their bed in the grip of a strange, sick passion. The place should be drenched in evidence.

There was no tattoo on Sally MacIntire's body. Nathan had checked.

The house was new, recently built in a fashionable modern subdivision on the edge of town, carved in the brutal way of developments right out of the forest. There wasn't even grass on the lawn yet. Nathan let himself in with the key they'd gotten from Mac. The house even *smelled* new.

He stepped into a huge sunken living room, complete with chandelier, that was almost bare of furniture. Sheets hung over the bay window. The fireplace had never been lit. The brand-new kitchen was fully stocked. Here, at least, the family had done some living. Supper dishes soaked in the sink. A child's old teddy bear lay on the table in the breakfast nook. Nathan turned away from it, trying not to let the sadness of the sight get to him.

He looked out the curtainless window. A large concrete patio had been poured. There was a big gas grill, but no

lawn furniture, and no lawn. Down the hall, Nathan found
the kids' room. The furniture in it—colorful bunk beds with
matching dressers and desks—looked brand-new, but the
white walls were bare, which made the room appear stark.
Toys littered the floor. The bathroom nearby contained old
faded towels with strings hanging loose.

If the family had just moved in, it would account for the
lack of furnishings and decorating; Nathan would have to
check on that. Still, there was something about the house
which struck him as very odd. It was as if the people didn't
really belong in it.

Bracing himself, he opened another door. It was an
empty room. Down the hall was one more just like it. No
furniture, not even any packing boxes. They hadn't even
used the rooms as depositories of junk until they could get
settled. They'd just closed them off altogether.

The fourth bedroom had to be it. Nathan prepared himself
for the sight and overpowering odor of a room bathed in
blood.

But there was no blood. Not a drop of it.

"Car's soaked in blood," said Seth as soon as Nathan
appeared in the office. "There's no question in my mind that
the guy carried his wife's body out to the Palmer estate in
that car."

Nathan's head hurt. He took some aspirin with a cold cup
of coffee, grimaced, went to fetch another cup, and found
the pot empty. "Goddamn it! Can't you guys at least keep
some decent coffee around here? Do I have to do everything?" He slammed things around on the table, found a
can, took off the plastic lid. The can was empty. He gave
Seth a murderous look.

Seth stood, stretched his lanky body, grinned, and said,
"Let's go get some breakfast, partner."

It if was true that truckers knew the best places to eat,
there was no doubt about the food at Kelly's Truckstop on
State Highway 59 on the outskirts of town. Every cop,
trooper, and sheriff's deputy in town ate there. Seth and
Nathan greeted a few as they went in and took a back booth

where Seth could stretch his legs out in the aisle and they could talk privately. The place offered breakfast twenty-four hours a day, and nobody thought it odd that they ordered it at twelve noon—a dietician's nightmare—fried eggs, ham, hash browns, grits, and pancakes. Neither of them could remember when they'd last eaten.

"There wasn't one stitch of physical evidence in that house," said Nathan between mouthfuls.

"So he didn't kill her there, after all."

"Obviously not. But why would he lie about where he killed her? I mean, what difference does it make *where* he killed her, as long as he is guilty?"

Seth shrugged. "Maybe he's covering for an accomplice."

Nathan put down his fork. "You know, that would explain a lot of things."

"Like what?"

"Like why I don't think he even killed her in the first place. Or the other lady."

Seth gave him a lopsided grin and said sarcastically, "Ri-i-ght. He was just using his car as taxi service."

"I'm going to talk to him again, anyway. Without Ward around."

Seth raised his eyebrows and said in thick dialect, "Mas-sa won't like that a'tall."

Nathan grinned, then shook his head. "This whole thing is so weird. Why the *Palmer estate*?"

"Why not? It's secluded."

"Well, hell, it's still in the city limits, isn't it? Do you realize how many isolated loggers' roads there are in East Texas? Not to mention abandoned oil leases. He could have dumped her so that *nobody* would ever find the body."

"Maybe he's just stupid."

"Very funny."

They ate in silence for a while, then Nathan said, "I want to search the area again. Who knows, maybe we'll find that body Dani reported."

"Or maybe we'll find a little collection of boobs."

"That's disgusting even for you."

"Oh, I don't know. I can be a lot more disgusting than that."

Nathan laughed, but for the first time during the previous hectic hours, he'd started thinking about Dani again. And the more he thought about her, the more uncomfortable he felt, as if there were something important that he needed to know.

Lilith Douglas greeted Nathan in her large, attractively furnished office with her lovely smile, as if she had nothing better to do than visit with him. Cops never had to make an appointment to see Lilith. In return, they went out of their way to present her with solid cases. Working in tandem, they'd made a pretty safe and peaceful little town of Maplewood.

Lilith Douglas was a cop's prosecutor. She'd come into the DA's office as a scared young law school graduate and had shot up through the ranks. It wasn't easy, being a female prosecutor in the macho state of Texas. Lilith had had to prove herself and then some, but her conviction rate was excellent and she had ties to the governor's office going way back. She was already on track for a district judgeship, and talk around town was that she'd be moving to Austin before long, and maybe beyond.

Nathan had worked with her on many cases. She, too, was divorced, but he'd never had the nerve to ask her out. There was something about Lilith, an elegance and grace, that made him feel like a bumbling country boy. Still, there was no one he'd rather see in his corner in court.

Lilith Douglas reminded Nathan of Elizabeth Dole. She had that same Southern charm, the same dark beauty, the same incisive intelligence. Juries loved her. Defense lawyers never underestimated her more than once.

Nathan told Lilith everything. He told her about Dani's report of the body, the message in her mail slot the night of the first "real" murder, his instincts about MacIntire's confession. While he talked, Lilith made notes on a legal pad.

When he was through, she tapped her pen upon the pad

thoughtfully. "This . . . Faith Daniels . . . What do you know about her, Nathan?"

Nathan felt a hot flush creep up his neck, and it infuriated him. It wasn't only because he, well, cared for Dani . . . it was the business about the mental institution. It made her a very unreliable witness for court. "Well, she's a very well respected teacher at the high school . . ." he began, then melted in front of Lilith's probing, steady gaze. "She had some . . . emotional problems . . . in her youth and . . . was committed to a psychological treatment facility for a time."

Her dark eyebrows raised slightly.

"She's fine now," he insisted (maybe too quickly), "but I guess she'd get ripped apart on a witness stand."

"You'd better believe it, my friend." Lilith leaned back in her chair. She was dressed in a striking red blazer, a black silk blouse, and a tight black skirt with a wide belt. Nathan remembered some of the bawdy jokes that used to go around the department about her, before most of the cops had had the opportunity to see her rip to shreds one hapless defense attorney after another.

"Nathan, I can appreciate your doubts about this case, but I have to tell you, this has become a political situation. The media is having a field day, and our quiet little town is terrified. They want to see justice done and the matter put to rest so they can go about their everyday lives." She got up and wandered over to a shelf crammed with law books, leaning against it in a pose he'd seen her use in the courtroom. "If this guy was just a nut, and we had no evidence to back up his claims, then I'd be right there with you. But that car . . . it's pretty compelling stuff."

He nodded. "But . . . what about Faith Daniels?"

She pursed her lips together and shrugged. "I'm sorry, Nathan. I don't know what to tell you about that. I guess you're on your own there."

The neighbors next door to the MacIntires fit the stereotype of what Nathan imagined a Yuppie couple to be. They lived in the "right" neighborhood, the "right" car was parked in the drive, they wore the "right" clothes—and were absolutely unprepared for tragedy of any kind in their well-ordered world. They seemed more upset that murder had been committed on their street than that the two children now in their care had been left motherless.

"We haven't told them anything," stage-whispered Derek Spencer. "Their grandparents are on the way. We thought we'd let them take care of that." He pushed back a lock of well-moussed dark hair from his forehead.

Gutless Wonder, Nathan thought. He stood awkwardly, holding a cardboard box and a teddy bear.

"We couldn't believe it," added Mindy Spencer with a toss of her fashionably styled hair. "I mean, they all seemed so *normal.*"

"Did you have any reason to believe that there were any marital problems between them?" asked Nathan.

The Spencers shrugged at exactly the same moment. "We hardly ever saw them," said Mindy.

"They've only been here a couple of months," added Derek.

"What was your impression of them?"

"Like I said, we hardly ever saw them," sniffed Mindy.

"She was a real nice lady," said Derek, "but he was kind of weird. Didn't talk much. Kept to himself, you know, a loner."

Oh, God, groaned Nathan inwardly, *you've heard that so much on TV you think you have to say it.*

He asked to see the children.

Jennifer and Jason MacIntire were sprawled on the Spencers' bed, watching *Sesame Street.* Since they had not been told yet of their mother's death, or of their father's arrest, Nathan decided not to introduce himself as a police officer, but as "a friend of your grandpa's."

"Can we go home now?" asked Jennifer, a pretty, dimpled child of five with a quiet, matter-of-fact way about her.

"Not just yet," said Nathan. "Your grandma and grandpa are on their way to visit you. They'll take you home. They asked me to come and tell you."

Apparently the kids hadn't heard of that news, either, and responded with enthusiastic delight.

Nathan held out the bear he'd seen on the kitchen table. "Does this belong to anyone in this room?" he asked.

"*Oh, Bubba Bear*!" squealed Jason, grabbing the stuffed toy to his chest. "I missed you."

"Where's Mommy and Daddy?" asked Jennifer, fixing him with bright, alert eyes.

Nathan swallowed. "They can't be here right now," he said. "That's why Grandma and Grandpa are coming." He looked around the stylishly decorated master bedroom. "Are you having fun here?"

"It's boring," said Jennifer.

"They won't let us touch anything," added Jason.

"Crummy," said Nathan.

"Yeah," Jennifer agreed. "They won't even let us go over to our house and get some of our toys."

"I'll get them for you," Nathan offered. "You just tell me what you want." He proceeded to take down a detailed list, dictated by the two children. Then he pulled open the loosely folded lid of the cardboard box. A fluffy white kitten tumbled out onto the bed. Jennifer squealed and cuddled the kitten underneath her chin, turning shining eyes toward Nathan which melted his heart. He had always wanted children. Roxanne hadn't.

"Oh, can we keep him?" Jennifer begged appealingly.

He grinned. "I'll have to ask your grandma and grandpa," he answered, watching the happy child, dreading her future.

After a time, he asked, "How do you like your new house?"

"It's nice," said Jennifer, the self-appointed spokesperson for the two. "But we miss our friends from where we used to live."

Nathan made a note: *Check out old neighborhood*.

"Mommy doesn't like it," offered Jason.

"How come?" asked Nathan.

"She cries a lot."

"Is she sad?" Nathan asked.

"She doesn't like for Daddy to go away at night," said Jennifer, teasing the kitten with a hair ribbon. "I think she misses our old friends, too."

"I'm sure she does," said Nathan. "Does your daddy go away a lot at night?"

The children nodded. "Sometimes when he gets home," whispered Jason, "they yell at each other."

"Did they yell at each other last night?" he prodded gently.

"Daddy wasn't home last night," said Jennifer, still smiling at the kitten.

Nathan leaned forward. "He wasn't?"

She shook her head solemnly. "Some men came to visit Mommy."

"How do you know, sweetheart?"

"I wanted a drink of water. Mommy was talking to the men. She got me a drink and kissed me night-night. Then I was asleep."

Questions clanged in Nathan's mind. *What did the men look like? What time did they come? Was your mother friendly with them?* How far could he go with a five-year-old? Could a five-year-old even tell time?

"Did you know the men, honey?" he asked finally.

"No. But they were nice. There were two of them."

"What did they look like?" Nathan fondled the kitten. "Do you remember?"

She stared at him. "Were they young or old?" he persisted.

"Old. When is Grandma going to be here?"

"Soon, sweetie. I'll come visit you again and talk some more. Would you like that?" asked Nathan. The kids agreed energetically. "I'll take the kitty for now, but if your grandma doesn't mind, I'll bring him back to you."

"Oh, thank you, mister," said Jason.

His heart aching, Nathan smiled. He reached out and ruffled the boy's hair.

"You'll like Mommy," said Jennifer. "She can sing songs, and she's real pretty."

"And she gives noogie kisses, too," said Jason. The children giggled, but Nathan had to look away.

Whatever sunset there might have been was cloistered in fog, and a mist dampened the windshield too much to see through but not enough for windshield wipers as Nathan headed his car down Redbud Lane. His mind was a labyrinth. Every time he followed one train of thought, it would round a corner only to hit a wall. The more trains of thought he followed, the more walls he encountered.

His body was numb with exhaustion. All he had intended to do was go home and hit the bed, but something drew him to her house, an urgency that he couldn't explain. All he knew was that he had to see her, just to convince himself that he could go on home and sleep in peace.

He didn't see her car, but it could be in the garage. There were a couple of lights shining dimly from within. Nathan mounted the front porch, and froze.

The door was ajar.

He pushed it, and it swung inward. "*Dani?* he called.

No answer.

Unsnapping the holster, he rested his hand on the grip of his revolver and stepped into the house. He called again.

The den light was on. Moving cautiously, Nathan entered the room. There was a small pool of blood on the rug in front of the fireplace. Blood smeared toward the front door, and Nathan realized, too late, that he had stepped in some of it.

Fighting panic, Nathan hurried down the hall toward Dani's bedroom, from where the other light came, careless of the fact that an intruder could still be in the house. All he could think about was Dani.

He stumbled into the room and stopped stock-still.

A bloody dog's ear rested on the pillow of her bed.

"Dear God, what's going on here?"

Had she gone berserk and cut up her dog? Should he have paid more attention to what her mother told him? Nathan jogged down the hall, back into the den. Her tote bag rested on the coffee table.

He forced himself to calm down, to think. There was no way he could picture Dani harming Thoreau, certainly not in such a sadistic manner. He rummaged through her bag. Her wallet and car keys were gone. He checked the garage. No car.

Then, standing in the middle of Dani's den, next to a pool of blood, Jennifer MacIntire's sweet voice rang in his ear. *Some men came to visit Mommy.*

Nathan's knees felt weak and he sat down in one of the wing-back chairs in front of the fireplace. Dani had said that she thought a cult had murdered the first woman. *I think they're trying to contact me again,* she'd said.

Had some strange, bizarre cult "contacted" Sally MacIntire?

A cold fist took hold of Nathan's heart and began to squeeze. He forced himself to take a few deep breaths. Maybe *he* was going nuts. Maybe all this cult talk was nonsense. On the other hand . . . something terrible had happened in this house, and now Dani was gone.

And he hadn't done a damn thing to stop it.

With a dread worse than anything he had ever known in his life, not even in Vietnam . . . Nathan faced the prospect that, no matter whom they arrested and locked up, the very next mutilated body he stood over by the side of a road would be the sweet and beautiful Faith Daniels.

Chapter 17 ~~~~~~~

They didn't talk right away. Kate McCall bundled Dani off to a hot soaking bath in a real claw-footed bathtub. Kate ran the bathwater herself and sprinkled in it herbal bath salts that seemed to suck the tension straight out of Dani's body. The peppermint soap made her skin tingle.

Afterward, Kate handed her a roomy flannel gown through the door and pointed the way to a bed so soft Dani felt enveloped in it. An eiderdown quilt hugged her. Her sleep was deep, long, restorative, and dreamless.

When she awoke, her clothes lay across the foot of the bed. As she dressed, she looked around the bedroom. The bed was a four-poster; an antique quilt lay atop the cedar-lined cherrywood hope chest at the foot of the bed, and window seats pointed to a view of a backyard garden that looked as if it came straight out of an English village in its colorful orderly confusion, barely visible in the mist.

She left the bedroom and followed strains of Vivaldi down polished hardwood floors, past a huge grandfather clock with a crescent moon on its face (for some reason, it made her think of Captain Kangaroo), and into a wondrous kitchen that made her gasp. Dried flowers and herbs of all colors hung in bunches from the grooved wooden ceiling and filled the kitchen with their scent. Jars of homemade jellies lined the deep windowsills. A copper teakettle sang on the big old-fashioned range. There was an enormous herb chart on one wall and a lovely wreath on another. Dani went over to study the wreath.

"Oh! There you are. I thought I heard you get up." Kate

sailed into the room. "Thought you might like some tea and toast." She came to stand by Dani. "Like it? I'd be glad to make you one. See, it's made with sage, thyme, basil, garlic, yarrow, and peppers."

"It's beautiful. This whole house is wonderful. It even *smells* wonderful."

Kate laid a table with muslin place mats hand-embroidered with bunches of flowers in the corners. An old jelly jar held fresh flowers. The bread for the toast was homemade. The butter came from a small crockery tub. Kate told Dani she'd mixed into it garlic, parsley, thyme, sage, and basil. The honey, explained Kate, came from local beehives and was supposed to help allergies.

It was the most delicious meal Dani had ever eaten.

Over the table hung a delicate sampler which quoted Shakespeare: "There's rosemary, that's for remembrance: pray you love, remember."

An old-time Victorian print hung over a shelf crammed with cookbooks. It quoted Cicero: "A friend is, as it were, a second self."

When they were finished, Kate said, "Why don't you watch me bake banana bread? We can talk while I work." She began laying out bananas, walnuts, flour, cinnamon, and the like on a huge butcher-block table that dominated the center of the large kitchen. The movements seemed routine to her; she didn't even consult a cookbook, and as she worked, she talked. Kate's wide blue eyes were expressive, her mouth generous, her hands blunt-fingered and plain. There was a maternal quality about her that soothed Dani in spite of the bizarre nature of their conversation.

"The first thing I want you to remember is that you are a *survivor*, not a *victim*. It makes all the difference to your recovery and reentry into the real world."

"You mean . . . there are others?"

Kate looked up from the pan she was greasing. "You're looking at one."

Dani stared at her.

"We both survived what psychologists now term *ritualistic abuse*."

Dani nodded. "Yes. I've read about sexual abuse of children."

"No. You don't understand." Kate sprinkled flour into the pan. "Ritualistic abuse is not the same as sexual abuse. Sexual abuse is only a *part* of ritualistic abuse." She rinsed her hands in the sink and dried them. "Dani, the ritualistic abuse of a child amounts to psychological murder."

Dani sank back in her chair.

Kate gave her time to absorb what she was saying. She measured flour, baking soda, salt, cinnamon, nutmeg, and cloves into a big blue crockery bowl and mixed them with a wooden spoon. "Children who are the victims of ritualistic abuse are made to take part in rituals that strip them of every known form of security they have: their self-image, family values, religious beliefs, sexual identity—you name it." Gradually she whipped in butter and sugar until the mixture was light and fluffy. "Remember the day-care scandal out in California a few years back?" Slowly she added eggs and beat them into the mixture.

Dani nodded. "The kids claimed that small animals were tortured in their presence and they were threatened that the same thing would happen to their parents if they told."

"Right. Now, unfortunately, that kind of case is almost impossible to prove in a court of law, but if what those kids said was true, then they were victims of ritualistic abuse." Kate set the bowl aside and began mashing ripe bananas in another blue bowl.

"They killed my dog in front of me and dipped their fingers in his blood," blurted Dani. "Then they put his ear underneath my pillow and threatened to cut off mine if I told the social worker."

Kate set down the bowl. "You poor kid. I know how you feel. They hung my cat."

They stared at one another in mute sympathy for a long moment. For the first time in Dani's life, staring into the calm blue eyes of this woman, she felt as if she had rounded a corner in her life's journey, and had stumbled from a rocky desert into the most beautiful oasis she'd ever seen. She settled in, and poured herself another cup of rose-hip tea, sweetened with local honey.

Kate began mixing in the bananas. Dani watched curiously. She was surprised to see Kate add a little orange juice. They might be any two other women in the world, sipping tea in a warm, comfy kitchen, sharing recipes and chatting.

"The textbook definition of ritualistic abuse, if memory serves me," continued Kate, "is a bizarre, systematic, and continuing mental, physical, and sexual abuse of children for the purpose of implanting evil and giving a form of sacrifice to a force or deity." She shook her head. "It makes something so personal and terrible so . . . dry." She folded in the walnuts, then added vanilla.

Dani shook her head. "This is all so unreal to me. Like a dream. I'm going to wake up with a nice, warm, wonderful feeling, but it will fade away because . . ." To her great and embarrassed surprise, tears sprang to her eyes. "Because I've never been happy before in my whole life."

Kate smiled at her. "Well, my dear, that's all about to change."

That was almost too much to believe. "Why don't I remember *all* of it?" she asked in frustration. "Why do I feel as if I'm losing my mind most of the time?"

Kate poured the batter into the greased loaf pan. "Because very small preschool children are used in these rituals, usually more for the pornography than any worshipping ceremony. Your conscious mind has *protected* you all these years, blocking it out from your subconscious mind. Now something has triggered the subconscious. Like most victims of torture, you've had flashbacks and nightmares and things which begin to pierce through to the conscious mind, piecing together the jigsaw of your puzzled past. Only none of it makes sense. So you think you're going crazy."

"But how do you *know* this?" cried Dani. "We only just met, and you are telling me things about myself that my own *mother* doesn't know!"

Kate popped the pan into the oven, wiped her hands, and said, "Let's talk some more. We'll clean up this mess later."

While they sat in front of a huge and efficient wood-burning stove, while Kate worked yarn into a soft afghan of dusty rose and sky blue, and the house filled with the luscious scent of baking banana bread, Dani talked. She told her everything, from the adoption, through the mental institution, through the present.

When the oven timer went off, Dani followed Kate into the kitchen, still talking. After the bread had cooled, Kate cut big slabs for them and slathered them with with real butter, and nobody gave a damn about the calories. They carried the bread into the parlor and ate it in front of the stove. When Dani got to the part about her prayer in the veterinary clinic, Kate finally interrupted.

"It took a lot of courage for you to pray like that."

"Courage?"

"Yes. Most people don't realize that faith is a *choice*. I mean, nobody is ever going to find out all the answers to all of life's questions. So you either decide to believe in the Mystery, as it were, the Spirit of creation, or you decide not to. For a survivor of satanic abuse, this decision is even harder to make. You were taught in your childhood, not to *not believe* in God, but to actually *hate* God, and all things good. It takes courage to go against that type of brainwashing."

"No wonder I hated my name!"

"Exactly." Kate bent her head over the afghan.

They could hear the great clock in the next room ticking out the passing seconds. Dani had never felt such peace. Never had she imagined the powerful impact of simply being believed.

"Don't be too hard on your parents, or on Nathan either, for that matter," said Kate suddenly, as if following Dani's train of thought.

"What do you mean?"

"You know what I mean." She met Dani's eyes. "You have to realize, surely, how bizarre this all sounds to innocent people who cannot in their wildest imaginings see someone doing to a child what was done to you. Think, too, about your behavior after you found the body in the ravine when you were fourteen."

Dani took her bottom lip in her teeth. "I was hysterical. Out of control. In fact, I have to admit . . . I gave my parents a lot of grief almost from the day they adopted me.

It took years for me to settle down. Things had been going pretty well, though, until that day. I was a maniac."

"Exactly. What were they supposed to think? They had no idea the psychological explosion you were experiencing. And neither did the shrinks. Back then, they just assumed you were paranoid schizophrenic." She sighed. "Thank goodness they're making some strides about this. Now kids who've suffered early abuse and behave as you did later in life are labeled *attachment disordered*. It's a clinical name for the simple inability to love someone." She leaned forward. "Dani, you have to learn to love that little girl who was so terribly hurt. You have to be tender to her, reassure her that what happened to her was in no way *her* fault."

Dani jumped up and began to pace. "But what do I do with all this anger? Sometimes it frightens me."

"Well, therapy . . ."

"No. Absolutely not." At the look on Kate's face, she faltered. "At least . . . not just yet."

"Okay, then. *Channel* it. Use it as a driving force to free yourself from your past."

Dani liked that. It made instant sense. In fact, it energized her. A long, thoughtful silence stretched between them. Finally Dani said, "I guess I've got a lot of forgiving to do."

"Start with yourself."

Dani paused. "What about Nathan?"

Kate twinkled. "What about him?"

Dani sighed. "He thinks I'm crazy."

"Don't underestimate him. Give him time." She smiled. "You really care for this man, don't you?"

"I feel . . . safe . . . with him. And he's funny, and strong, and sensitive . . . What are you laughing at?"

"Nothing." Kate ducked her head over the afghan again. "You'll figure it out. Now, you're going to be here for a while, so first call that good vet and let him know how to reach you and then we'll talk as long as you want."

They talked most of the night with Mozart in the background, drinking something Kate called a "ruby cordial," made with cranberries and vodka. This time, Dani did most of the listening. In that warm home of classical music, flowers, books, herbs, and an old-fashioned kitchen which smelled of baking; in that safe heaven, Dani heard tales of horror that nobody but a fellow survivor would ever believe.

They went to bed sometime around three A.M. It had begun to rain, and the drops beat hypnotically against the roof. Dani fell blissfully asleep underneath the eiderdown quilt. But this time, her sleep was not dreamless. Hooded figures chased her, shouting filthy profanities, into a black and seamless alley, to a dead end, where she crouched, screaming, until Kate pulled her out. Somehow, she'd found her way into a closet.

"You've had a major breakthrough," explained Kate over a brunch of homemade chicken soup and garden salad. "Your subconscious is going to start pouring out the details your conscious mind has kept hidden all these years."

"I thought . . . after last night . . . that I'd never have another nightmare. That I'd gotten it all out."

"No. You've gotten out what you remember so far." She reached across the small table by the kitchen window where they sat, and patted Dani's hand. "You must be a warrior, my friend. The battle has only just begun."

The phone rang. Dani was almost surprised to hear such a modern sound in Kate's house. While Kate left the room, Dani tried not to feel defeated by what she had been told. The thought of encountering memories even more horrible was almost more than she could stand. She wondered, bleakly, if she would ever have anything approaching a normal life.

Kate hurried back into the room. "That was Dr. Sanderson. Your dog got up, took a long drink, and conked back out again! They think he's going to be all right."

Dani excused herself, went into the bathroom, sat on the edge of the high claw-footed tub, and wept.

"Your education begins," said Kate, handing Dani a book. It was entitled *The Satanic Rituals*, by Anton LaVey. "Flip through that and see if anything looks familiar."

Dani thumbed through the book of rituals. "Wait! I

recognize this." She began to read, " 'In the name of Satan, Lucifer, Belial, Leviathan, and all the demons, named and nameless, walkers in the velvet darkness . . .' " She looked up. "I remember this! From my dream. It says here it's the Satanic Baptism, a Children's Ceremony." She skimmed through the ceremony. "Whoever performed this ritual on me didn't follow it to the letter. I mean, my so-called *baptism* was sexual in nature."

Kate nodded. "LaVey couldn't publicly endorse acts which were illegal, certainly not and keep his tax-free status. But he couldn't control what offshoots of his cult did in secrecy and darkness."

"Such as human sacrifice."

"Such as anything depraved, immoral, or illegal."

Dani nodded, thinking. "LaVey founded the Church of Satan in San Francisco in 1966. I lived with foster parents there until, let's see . . . 1970. There were other cults active there during that time as well. So it could be that my foster parents belonged to a bizarre underground cult that was one of those offshoots of the satanic church."

"Very possible."

The big clock began to gong out the hour. Dani didn't stop to count. "Then, if this cult got its start in California in the sixties . . . what's it doing in Texas in the nineties?"

"It may not even be the same cult," Kate said. "It, too, may be an offshoot of an offshoot, so to speak. A cult very dangerous and very deadly." Kate's brow furrowed. "Dani, I'm very worried about you."

Dani sighed. "I know. It's like I'm a mouse, being tormented by this huge cat before it kills me."

At the sound of the word *kill,* they were both struck silent.

Kate walked over to the card table upon which rested the partially completed jigsaw puzzle. "The answer's here," she mused.

"In that puzzle?"

"No. In *your* puzzle. You've got to find the missing pieces, Dani. And you've got to find them very soon. Otherwise . . . I'm absolutely terrified at what could happen to you."

Chapter 18 〰〰〰

Discreet inquiries to a few friends on patrol were often an effective way to deal with a situation, thought Nathan. More than once he'd tracked down Fred that way at a bar and pulled him out before he got himself—and the department—in trouble. Police departments greatly preferred doing their own housekeeping to having the media do it for them.

It didn't take them long to spot Dani's snazzy red convertible parked in front of the white house with a wraparound porch, set back in the trees, in one of the older neighborhoods which had once been stately and dignified and now seemed increasingly crime-prone. Thus satisfied that her car wasn't abandoned on the side of a rural road or parked by a warehouse or stashed behind a sleazy nightclub, Nathan managed to get a few hours' sleep, but only a few. He was still very worried.

It was a soggy, messy Sunday afternoon when Nathan pulled up behind the Chrysler and parked. The damp cold made his joints ache, which depressed him. He didn't like the thought of getting older. As he mounted the steps to the sagging porch, he couldn't remember when he'd been so very tired.

There was a bell with a chain, but Nathan knocked instead, peering into the leaded-glass door, reflecting that it would be easy for someone to break into this house, when the door opened and he faced a smiling blond, somewhat plump, who seemed his age or a little older.

143

"You must be Sergeant Kendall," she said warmly. "I'd
know you in a minute. Please come in."

He didn't know what to think. But he did as he was told,
stepping over the threshold into a warm, inviting living
room, and there was Dani, crossing the room with a bounce
to her step, beaming at him.

He wouldn't have noticed anything else in the room,
anyway.

The transformation in her was unbelievable. Gone was
the hollow, haunted expression, the wan, thin look. There
was a pretty flush to her cheeks and a bold new glance to her
eye that caught him completely off guard.

He didn't even stop to think, just reached for her and
embraced her so tightly she squeaked. "God, woman, I've
been so worried about you," he whispered into her soft hair.
She felt damn good in his arms. Not until that moment did
the full impact hit him, of the loss he'd have felt if anything
had happened to her.

She pulled back and gave him a baffled look.

"I went by your house and the door was open," he
explained. "I saw blood, and the dog's ear . . . What in
heaven's name is going on, Dani? I was worried sick."

"Oh, Nathan, it was terrible. I tried to call you for help,
but you weren't home. It was three o'clock in the morning,
and you weren't there."

"There was another murder."

She stiffened in his arms. "Another murder?" she repeated.

"You haven't heard?" He looked over her shoulder at the
woman in the background. She, too, had a perplexed look
on her face. "Don't you have a TV?" he asked.

"I don't watch it much. What happened, Sergeant?"

He looked into Dani's eyes. "A woman, Dani. Just like
the one in the dumpster."

She shut her eyes and leaned against his chest. "Dear
God, when is this going to end?" she murmured.

"We've got to talk," he said.

"Please sit down," said the woman. "By the way, I'm

Kate McCall. I'm Dani's friend. Why don't you two get caught up on things. I'll go make some tea."

He nodded, and she left. He and Dani sat on a comfortable couch. While he held her hand, and sometimes stroked it, she explained about discovering her mutilated and drugged dog, hauling him to the vet, and meeting Kate.

He told her some of the details of the murder as Kate reentered the room, carrying a tray laden with tea things. Nathan withheld his doubts about the validity of John MacIntire's confession.

But Kate was already shaking her head. "He's a fall guy," she said. "Somebody expendable to take the blame for the whole group."

"What whole group?"

Kate leaned forward earnestly from her chair. "Sergeant, haven't you noticed that both times a murder victim was found, Dani received some kind of communication that seemed related? And what about the tattoo on the first victim's arm? And now, this time, they left a clear message to her when they cut off her dog's left ear."

"*What* message?"

She ignored his impatience. "They are warning her that these killings are cult-related. They are threatening her, preparing her for something, I don't know what. Somehow, they know her from her past, from when she first got the tattoo."

He shook his head. "This sounds like a B-movie plot."

"Believe me, Sergeant, this is all too real."

Images of crumpled, slashed-up women's bodies crossed his mind, and he said nothing. Nobody had to tell him how real it was.

Dani took his arm. "Nathan, Kate is . . . a survivor, like me. We were both horribly abused by cults in our childhood. Kate works with other survivors, too. She's done a lot of research and study into cult-related crimes. I think she can help us. Both of us."

"I've worked with other law enforcement agencies," said Kate.

"Which ones?" asked Nathan suspiciously.

"Just a moment, and I'll show you." Kate left the room. In a minute, she returned, handing him a stack of letterhead correspondences and business cards from various police agencies across the state.

"I do training seminars," she said as he looked through the cards. "Sometimes I assist on investigations. Sergeant, I understand your skepticism. I've seen much of it. This all sounds so bizarre the first time you hear it. I don't expect you to accept everything I say right off the bat. All I ask you to do is listen with an open mind, conduct your investigation, and see if the investigation begins to bear me out. If it doesn't, you haven't lost a thing. If it does . . . you may gain everything."

He nodded. "Fair enough, Ms. McCall."

"Oh, please, call me Kate."

"Okay, Kate . . . What the hell do *you* think is going on here?"

"I think Dani was brutally abused in cult rituals by her foster parents and others when she was a small child. Her conscious mind blocked out the abuse, but, now bear with me, Mr. Skeptic . . . I think the cult kept up with her through the years, for reasons only they can know. The body she found when she was fourteen was a plant, deliberately designed to throw her into a psychic trauma . . . again, I wouldn't presume to know why. Now, at the age of twenty-seven they've hit her again, this time with the body in the woods. And it worked. Look what happened to her." She got up and began to pace back and forth in front of them.

"But this is a particularly vicious cult. Usually such crimes are done in great secrecy. Bodies are never found. Stop to think, if you will, Sergeant Kendall, just how long the Matomoros cult may have continued their human sacrifice, if one upper-middle-class American white boy hadn't been snatched off the streets. Only then was an investigation launched of such proportions that he—and more than a dozen other victims—were found in a mass grave in Mexico."

He had to admit she had a good point.

"But here we have a situation where the victims are displayed in plain sight, or at least disposed of so that they will be found fairly soon. Why? Does this particular cult have no fear of getting caught?"

"Why women?" interjected Dani. "Why mutilate them?"

"My guess, since the bodies are so easily discovered, is that the cult is using these murders as a *warning* to its members. Shape up, or this is what could happen to you or to one of your loved ones."

"What's that got to do with *me*?" pressed Dani. "Why do they keep involving *me*?"

Kate stopped pacing and shook her head. "I wish to God I knew, my friend."

"You can't go back to that house," said Nathan to Dani. It was getting quite dark out. They had talked for a long time.

"I agree," said Kate. "Apparently they can get in there as easily as cutting soft butter."

"But I have to work tomorrow," protested Dani. "And Kate, I've imposed on your wonderful hospitality far too much as it is."

"Nonsense." Kate smiled, then pursed her lips. "But Dani, I'm known all over as an anticult activist. If they really want to find you, they just might come looking for you here."

"Look," said Nathan. "I don't know if there's a cult out there or not. All I know is that I can't walk up to Dani's door without Thoreau barking his head off. Somehow somebody got into her house without even the dog knowing, and did a sadistic act which tells me that some nut, somewhere, has got it in for Dani." He turned to her. "I don't want you sleeping in that house again. Come home with me. I'll sleep on the couch," he added hastily.

"It's a great idea," Kate agreed. "They'll never think to look for you at a cop's house."

Dani laughed. "Talk about a conspiracy!"

"So it's settled," said Kate, a mischievous look in her eyes. She extended her hand to Nathan. "It's been a pleasure, Sergeant Kendall. If I can do anything at all, call me anytime, day or night."

He took her hand. Her handshake was firm and direct, like a man's. Her look was clear-eyed and honest. He had to admit to himself that he liked her a great deal. "I want to thank you for looking after Dani," he said. "She really needed somebody like you."

She glanced over her shoulder. Dani was carrying the tea things out to the kitchen. "Oh, I don't know about that, Sergeant. I think what Dani really needs is *you*."

He blinked in surprise, embarrassed at the flush he felt creeping up his neck. He turned away. "Is this Dani's coat?" He fumbled for it.

"Yes. I tried to get the blood out."

Dani returned.

Suddenly there was a silence between the two women. Nathan looked at Dani and was surprised to see that she was struggling not to cry. "I just wanted to say that . . . if ever there was a God of peace and love and goodness . . . His spirit is present, right here, in this house." Her voice broke.

Kate smiled, and there were tears in her eyes, too. "Honey, how else do you think He answers prayer?" They embraced.

"I don't know how to thank you," said Dani.

"Thank *Him*," answered Kate, pointing upward.

Funny thing about women, mused Nathan. *One day they meet; the next day they're soulmates.* He kind of envied that quality.

He helped Dani on with her coat. They agreed to go by her house first to pick up some things, then she would follow him out to the cabin.

As they stepped into a bleak and starless night, Nathan realized that it had been a long time since he had felt this young.

There is something about bringing a woman home that makes a man look at his place with new eyes. As soon as they entered the A-frame, Nathan spotted empty beer bottles, scattered newspapers, clothes dropped here and there—and everywhere, the pungent aroma of litter boxes that desperately needed changing. He winced. "I've been so busy lately—" he began.

But she was on her knees, squealing with delight over the kittens. They were fat now, and lonesome for someone to play with. They tumbled around, putting on a show for her. In fact, every animal in the place seemed drawn to her. "Oh, Nathan! They're adorable!" She cuddled the black one underneath her chin and looked up at him, laughing.

"I can't believe how pretty you are," he blurted. What he meant was, *I can't believe anyone as pretty as you would be here with me*.

"Why . . . thank you."

"I guess you hear that a lot," he mumbled, picking up beer bottles behind his back.

"Nathan, when it comes from you, it's like I'm hearing it for the very first time." She ducked her head and baby-talked to the kittens.

Feeling foolishly delighted, he dumped the bottles into the trash and gathered up some newspapers. "I wasn't expecting company," he said.

"Don't worry about it."

He stumbled around in the kitchen, opening and closing cabinets. "I don't know what I've got in here for dinner. He peered into the refrigerator. "Let's see . . . I've got some eggs and cheese. How about an omelet?"

"Perfect."

"Ah-*ha!* A bottle of wine, even." He groped around for a corkscrew, opened the wine, and poured them each a glass.

"I'd like to toast," said Dani. "To new beginnings."

"I like that." They toasted. The wine was an inexpensive blush chablis, but it was ice-cold and good. While Nathan whipped together eggs and heated a skillet, Dani wandered around, exclaiming over the Navaho rugs and the rock hearth, introducing herself to the dogs, who all seemed to approve of her. He told her the agonies and ecstasies of building the house himself.

She found his jazz collection and put on some Dave Brubeck.

The omelet wasn't half bad.

They didn't talk about anything scary or worrisome. No murder, no mayhem. Instead, they discussed books, and music, and movies. She told him some funny stories about teaching. He told her what it was like growing up, the only boy with five sisters.

He lit a fire, and they sat down on the floor in front of it on a heap of pillows and polished off the wine. She was so incredibly beautiful by firelight that he settled himself back in the pillows and just watched her, listening to her dulcimer tones as she talked quietly, happy just to be with her, knowing that he could be with her just that way forever, and be as happy as he was right this moment. *Perhaps now would be a good time to make love,* he mused drowsily. *It seems right.*

But the next thing he knew, pearly daylight was seeping through the windows, and he was curled up on the pillows underneath a blanket, with one dog, and several cats, and Dani was gone.

Chapter 19 〰〰〰〰

      Dani had no fear of her home in the daytime. Somehow she knew that those who stalked her were creatures of the night who scattered, like cockroaches, into the shadows in the light of day. She left Nathan's cabin at the first suggestion of dawn, eager to crawl into her own shower, wander around nude in her own bedroom selecting her clothes, and tinker in her own kitchen for breakfast. While she appreciated the kindnesses of Kate and Nathan, she welcomed her own space to think.

      The house was hollow without Thoreau. She tackled the grim task of cleaning up his blood and disposing of his ear. She would not bring him back to this house, she decided, until the situation was settled one way or the other. She would ask Nathan if he would mind boarding the dog with his brood of canines. She didn't think he would notice one more.

      Poor Nathan. No sooner had they settled on the pillows in front of the fire than he was out cold. She'd found a blanket and tucked it around him tenderly, watching him sleep, wondering if they could ever have a real future together. Her past seemed to entangle itself around her feet, tripping her headlong whenever she tried to live a normal life. Perhaps it was a foolish fantasy to imagine that she ever could.

      Even worse, how could she ensnarl another human being in that Gordian knot? Would she be endangering Kate just by sleeping at her house? Kate had said they might look for her there. Could *Kate* wind up mutilated and dumped by the wayside, simply for offering help and shelter to Dani?

"I can't live like this," said Dani aloud to her image in the mirror as she dressed for work. It was like a game of checkers, in which she made no moves at all, but simply allowed all her pieces to be jumped, one after the other, and swept off the board. Soon there would be nothing left of her.

"Then there's the jigsaw puzzle," she mused, brushing her hair. She grinned wryly. "I can change metaphors if I want to. I'm an English teacher, after all." Kate had said, *You've got to find the missing pieces, Dani. And you've got to find them very soon.* Someone, somewhere, had the whole picture. Dani was piecing it together blind.

"But at least I can *try* to piece it together," she said, laying down the brush and giving herself a hard, scrutinizing look. "I can look for those missing pieces myself." A little thrill of excitement took hold of her, deep inside. If she could put the puzzle together herself, could see the picture in its entirety, then *maybe she could get them before they got her.*

"Checkmate," she said, then giggled at herself. "Wrong metaphor again, old girl." But already she was formulating a plan in her mind, a strategy, as it were.

She burned inside with a fire which fueled a tremendous pressure to *get at the truth*. Somehow, she knew that she would never have any hope for a normal life until she did.

Monday proved to be a busy day for Dani, so busy that the emotional flights of previous weeks had been replaced by a focus so telescopic that each task under scrutiny was dispatched with ruthless efficiency to make way for the next so that her plan could be implemented, step by step.

First she had to contact a locksmith to have all the locks in her house changed. Since there had never been any signs of breaking and entering, it was clear to Dani that someone had gotten hold of her house key and had a duplicate made. Because she tended to be careless with her tote bag at school, Dani had no doubt as to who that individual might be.

Next she spoke to her principal and had a substitute teacher lined up for the next couple of days, "for personal business." Since midterm exams loomed, he was not pleased with the request. They had been at odds ever since Dani's refusal to recommend Adam Prescott for the Select Student Scholarship. But she would not be intimidated by him and he had no choice but to relent.

Then she called the vet to check on Thoreau. He was doing fine but the doctor wanted to keep him a while longer.

During her brief lunch break she called Nathan.

"Long time no see," he said. "Where'd you go this morning?"

"I had to get ready for work."

"You never heard of leaving a guy a note?"

She smiled into the phone. "I'm sorry. I guess I had a lot on my mind."

"Listen, drop by the station after school today and I'll give you a key," he said. "I've cleaned the place up, believe it or not, and stocked the fridge. Keep the doors locked. I'll check on you from time to time, and I should be home around eleven-thirty tonight."

She hesitated. "Nathan . . . I'm not going to stay with you."

"Dani . . . if it's the sex thing, you don't have to worry about that. I'm not going to put any pressure on you."

"No, it's not that, Nathan. It's just . . . I can't keep hiding out, expecting other people to take care of me. I have to handle this my own way."

"*Are you nuts?*" he exploded. "Don't you realize that whoever it was who cut up your dog can get to you in that house anytime he wants to?"

"I'm having the locks changed."

"Great. I guess they never heard of busting out a window."

"Nathan—"

"Look, I don't know from cults, okay? I don't know if anything Kate McCall says is true or not. All I do know is that young women are getting sliced up in this town and that somehow, someway, you are connected to them. That tells me that you are probably next on the list. I can't put it to you any more clearly than that, Dani."

"I realize that."

"Then let me help you, for Chrissake!" He was yelling.

She waited for him to calm down, trying not to get angry herself. "I'm going out of town for the next couple of days," she said finally.

"Where to?" he asked sullenly.

None of your damn business, she wanted to respond, but didn't. He was only trying to protect her. "I'm going to visit my mother."

His sigh of relief was audible. "Good idea. Let her take care of you for a while."

I don't want anybody to take care of me, she almost shouted, but refrained. She had no desire to quarrel with Nathan at this point.

"She's a nice lady," he added.

"I know," said Dani. "We have a lot to talk about."

"When are you leaving?"

"Tomorrow morning."

There was a long silence. "Okay, let me ask you this. Would you at least let me come over tonight and stay at your place? I promise not to jump your bones. I just don't want you alone in that house."

How could she tell him that she *wanted* to be alone? How could she explain the psychic cataclysm that was going on in her mind? She'd spent a lifetime fighting for her sanity, and now she was fighting for her life.

It was something she had to do alone.

On the other hand, she was in no mood for a battle of wills with Nathan Kendall. She suspected that if she were ever locked in a power struggle with him, he would come out the victor. They didn't call him "Bulldog" for nothing. She sighed. "All right," she conceded. "For tonight."

"It'll be late . . ."

"I'll be up."

"Dani?"

"What?"

"Just . . . be careful, that's all. I'd hate for anything to happen to you."

She smiled into the phone. "I like you, too, Nathan."

Dani was ready for last period. She intended to confront Adam Prescott about the message behind her door, the mutilation of her dog, and anything else that came to mind. Adam, she knew, was a very important piece to her jigsaw puzzle.

But the stooped young man who shuffled into the door at the beginning of class was almost unrecognizable as the cocky, arrogant Adam Prescott. His hair was unkempt, his appearance disheveled, and his eyes so dull that Dani wondered if he was drugged.

Her gaze fell to his left hand, and every accusation was stillborn in her throat. Heavy bandages couldn't disguise the fact that somehow, Adam Prescott had lost the little finger on his left hand.

Chapter 20 〜〜〜〜〜

The midday phone conversation with Dani gnawed on the back of Nathan's mind as he found a parking space in front of the county jail which housed Maplewood's prisoners. It was that elusive quality about her that both attracted him and drove him mad. Every time he let himself feel close to her she skipped back out of his reach.

Like most Texas jails, this one was overcrowded. Nathan had no intention of meeting MacIntire in his cell, or even in the busy visitors' area. He'd requested a private meeting, and the sheriff had promised to make a room available.

A young deputy escorted Nathan into a room which must have been a closet once but was now being used as office space. A beat-up desk took up almost all of the area. When another deputy delivered MacIntire to the room, Nathan showed him into the chair and perched on the edge of the desk, looking down at him. It was an old power trick, but it worked most of the time.

Nathan had run a check on MacIntire and found his record to be clean. It was clear that he had never been in jail before; he had that shell-shocked look about him. He wasn't trembling this time, but he did request a cigarette, and Nathan, a nonsmoker, sent a deputy after a pack.

The first thing MacIntire said was, "Are my kids all right?"

"They're with your wife's folks. They're here to arrange the funeral and to petition the court to allow them custody until after the trial . . . Maybe permanent custody, Mac."

Mac put his elbow on the desk and leaned his head into

his hand. When he looked back up at Nathan, there were tears in his eyes. "That's probably best," he said. "Do you think . . . do you think they might let me see them?"

"Well, now, Mac, I think that might be open for negotiation."

"What do you mean?"

"I mean, I might be able to arrange for you to see your kids if you are willing to cooperate with me."

Mac took a drag on his cigarette. His hand was beginning to tremble. "What kind of cooperation?"

Nathan leaned forward, established eye contact. "This interview is strictly off the record, Mac. I'm not wired. There are no witnesses. Just you and me, pal, here in this little room. If you tell me what really happened to your wife and the other woman, I'll see what I can do about getting you together with your kids. And Mac . . . if the evidence bears you out, you might possibly get to take your kids home yourself."

Mac shook his head. "No. No, it will never happen. You don't understand . . ."

"Don't understand what?"

"Nothing." He lit another cigarette with the butt of the first.

"You didn't kill your wife and the other woman, did you?"

The cigarette fell to the floor. Mac picked it up, looked away. "Yes. I told you I did. I signed a statement. Just get . . ." His voice broke. "Get my kids out of this town, you understand? I don't have to see them, okay? *Just get them out!*" he shouted. He stood up. "Please let me go back to my cell. They'll find out I was talking to you. Please."

"Who'll find out, Mac?"

"You don't understand. You'll *never* understand!"

"*Who* are you talking about?"

"P-prisoners. Yeah, that's it. The other prisoners. They don't like it when one of us talks to the cops. Now can I go?"

Nathan stared for a long time into the eyes of a thoroughly terrified man, sighed, and said, "Yeah, you can go."

She had the door open before he rang the bell, threw her arms around him, and kissed him.

He never knew what to expect from Faith Daniels.

"What was that for?" he asked, smiling into her blue eyes.

"I'm glad to see you, that's all. It's kind of spooky around here without Thoreau."

It *was* strange without the big dog, and Nathan was glad he had come, too. He followed her into the den where David Letterman was interviewing some actor on TV.

"Hungry?" she asked.

"Starved." While Dani made him a sandwich and got him a beer, he sat at the kitchen table and told her a little about his day. It was a comfortable, domestic feeling, and it filled Nathan with a yearning he hadn't known in years.

She had a glass of wine while he ate, and talked about this weird student named Adam Prescott. "I'll run a check on him if you'd like," he said.

"It wouldn't make any difference," she said, which he thought was a peculiar remark. He studied her face. Every time he saw her, she seemed . . . stronger somehow. More self-assured. *Something*. He couldn't quite put his finger on it. There were so many facets to her that he could never get a grip on what it was that made her tick. For a while, she had seemed so unstable, so vulnerable. Now she was almost frighteningly independent.

That bothered him.

They talked for a while, then Dani yawned and said she needed to get some sleep so that she would be sharp for the drive to Austin. She showed Nathan to a guest room next to her own, and handled it so smoothly that neither of them felt awkward. But as usual, Nathan wasn't even remotely sleepy. For a long time he stared rigidly at the ceiling, trying not to think about Dani in bed in the next room, thinking instead about the whole jumbled case, turning it over in his mind, searching for *something* that would break it for him. Eventually he exhausted himself into sleep.

A muffled cry and a loud *thump* right against the wall above Nathan's head brought him wide awake sometime deep into the night. He flew from bed in his underwear, grabbed his gun from the bedside stand, and charged into Dani's room, his body prepared to do battle with an intruder even before his mind had fully focused.

In the split second it took his eyes to adjust to the dark and his mind to click into place, Nathan realized that Dani was not in her bed, but another cry sent him whirling for the closet, where he yanked back the clothes, poised for action.

Huddled against the back wall, whimpering, was Dani.

He pulled her to her feet. "Dani. *Dani!* What's happening?" She mumbled something incomprehensible. He sat her on the bed and proceeded to search the house, but all the locks were firm, and there was nobody but the two of them.

Once again, Nathan could feel the hairs rise on the back of his neck. All the old doubts came flooding back. *Had Dani written the notes to herself? Had Dani cut up her own dog?* She was crying when he returned to her. He sat down on the edge of the bed and pulled her into his arms.

"It's the dreams," she said. "I'm sorry I woke you up."

"Dreams?"

"I have recurring nightmares. They bring back things that happened when I was little. I used to hide in closets, and I guess I still do, only now I do it in my sleep."

In a flash, Nathan remembered a night soon after he returned from Vietnam, when he'd flung his mother's cat across the room after it brushed over his face in the night.

She sighed against him. "I keep thinking I'm doing so much better, getting so much stronger, and then the dreams. They just seem to *plague* me."

"They'll go away in time," he said. "Once you get your life in order."

"Oh, Nathan," she whispered. "I don't know what I'd do without you." She tightened her arm around his neck; he turned her face up to his and kissed her, and the power of it took his breath away. With an urgency he almost couldn't control, he lay her back on the bed, kissing her eyelids, her cheeks, her sweet soft lips. His hands moved over her body, underneath her gown, cupping her breasts. He could feel her heart pounding against his.

Slipping his arm underneath the small of her back, he moved her up on the bed in one fluid movement and rolled over, pressing himself against her. She gasped. Tangling his hands in her hair, he kissed her long and deep, searching her mouth with his tongue. His erection was painful. He took her hand and guided it there.

Suddenly she pulled away. "I c-can't, Nathan," she whispered. "We have to stop." She was panting.

He could hardly breathe. "Why not?" *Don't do this to me*, he thought. *I'll beg. I'll plead. Anything. Just don't leave me like this.*

She pulled herself out from under him, straightening her gown. "I want to come to you in joy and exuberance, not abject surrender." She stroked his cheek.

He sighed mightily. "I don't care about that," he said truthfully.

"Please give me a little more time, Nathan. I want to feel in *control* of my life. I'm tired of having to analyze every move I make, wondering if I'm crazy. I'm tired of letting my emotions get steamrollered."

He rubbed his hand over his eyes. "I'm not trying to steamroller you."

"I know. I don't expect you to understand. Those nightmares . . . I just don't want to feel so *helpless*."

"Look, Dani. I know you're having problems. It doesn't matter to me. I want to be with you. I've never in my life wanted a woman more."

"Would it make any difference if I told you I felt the same way?"

"Right now? No." But he laughed softly to take the sting out of his words. He got up, went around the bed, and took her face in his hands. "I've never forced a woman in my life, and I'm not going to start now. Just don't expect me to wait forever." He couldn't hide the frustration and anger from his voice. So much about Dani was difficult. Never had he worked so hard to be accepted by a woman. He honestly wondered if it was worth it. She reached for him but he pulled away.

Her hands dropped to her lap. "There are some things I have to do," she said simply. "Some things I have to find out about my past. When I do, when I find those missing puzzle pieces, I know I'll be strong enough to bring another person into my life. You, if you still want me."

Maybe she was right. Her past seemed to be a shadow that cast darkness over them every time they tried to build any semblance of a relationship. Trying to keep his voice casual, he asked, "What about in the meantime?"

She took one of his hands in her own. "I think I'm going to need some space."

Dreaded words. He'd heard them before. He pulled his hand away and headed for the door.

"Whatever you say, Dani-girl." Inside, his churning emotions battled with the bleak feeling that she would never be satisfied with the answers to all her questions, would never have room for him in her life.

Then he left her, and did something he'd never done before. He shut himself up in the bathroom and took, if not a cold shower, a very, very cool one.

Chapter 21 ~~~~~~~~

Nathan sat at the kitchen table in yesterday's clothes, looking rumpled and tired, when Dani padded in to start the coffee.

"I'm surprised you're up so early, considering the hours you work," she said. "Oh! You've made coffee. I can't remember when someone last made coffee for me." She reached for a cup, and glanced over her shoulder at the man who sat silent and morose, dipping a spoon aimlessly in and out of his coffee cup. "What's wrong?"

He didn't turn around to meet her gaze, but only said, "Us."

She felt a little stab of panic, deep inside. "What do you mean?" Her voice didn't sound as unconcerned as she wanted it to.

He shrugged.

Dani sat at the table, across from Nathan, and studied his face. It was closed to her, as unreadable as a Chinese newspaper. "Listen, if it's about last night . . ."

He shook his head, lips pursed, and waved his hand in a gesture of dismissal. "Last night was only a symptom," he said. "Not the whole sickness."

She sat back and crossed her arms over her chest. "I have no idea what you are talking about."

"I know. That's the problem." He got up and walked over to the sink, as if he didn't even want to be close to her.

A cold winter wind gusted over her heart. She swallowed. "You're not making any sense, Nathan."

"*We're* not making any sense! Don't you get it?" He

splashed the coffee out of his cup and into the sink, the staccato movements of a frustrated man. "Ever since I met you, I've been trying to get close to you. And every time I do, you push me away."

"You *are* talking about last night."

"No, goddamm it! *No*. That's not it, Dani."

"It *is* it. If I'd welcomed you into my bed last night, we wouldn't be having this conversation."

Anger darkened his face. "If you think that's all there is to me," he said, his voice deadly quiet, "then you don't know me at all. I've been wasting my time." He turned and left the room.

Dani leapt to her feet and hurried after him into the guest room, where he was strapping on his holster. His outburst had left her dazed and confused. Apparently he'd been thinking it over all night, whereas she had only just woken up. She watched him, frantically trying to think what to say. Somehow she knew that if he walked out the front door now, it would be the last time she ever saw him. The thought was unbearable.

But she seemed unable to express it.

In one hip pocket, he stuffed his wallet; in the other, another wallet containing his badge. A laminated card printed with the Miranda warnings went into his shirt pocket.

Dani stood, helplessly rooted to the carpet. Finally she managed, "I didn't mean to make you mad." It wasn't what she wanted to say.

He stopped for a moment and looked into her eyes. "I'm not mad," he said. "I'm just giving up."

She wanted to fling her arms around his neck, sob on his shoulder, beg him to stay, tell him . . . tell him what?

That she loved him.

Say it. Heart pounding, she swallowed and said, "I—"

But he turned away from her and headed down the hall.

Only a moment before, it seemed, she'd been splashing happily on the seashore, and in the next instant, she was smacked from behind and engulfed in a cold tidal wave of misery. She heard the front door open and close, and there she stood, all alone on a deserted beach, without even the sun to warm her.

It was strange, reflected Dani, how the little things could be the most distracting and worrisome in times of crises. A madman—or group of them—might be stalking her; the only man she had ever cared about might have just left her; but what bothered her the most for the time being was what to do with Thoreau, who was now ready to leave the vet's.

So Dani loaded him in the car for the trip to Austin. His whole demeanor changed immediately; his eyes sparked and he wiggled all over with excitement. His one ear and bandaged head gave him a cock-eyed, comical appearance that made Dani want to laugh and cry at the same time. She hugged him and was rewarded with a slurpy lick on her cheek, which helped to restore her own flagging spirits. Still, she could never look at him without being reminded of what she was up against.

All morning she argued with herself about Nathan. Part of her wanted to run after him, beg him not to leave, promise to include him more in her life, make passionate love to him and to hell with the consequences. Part of her was furious with him for leaving. *Men think with their gonads,* she'd mutter to herself, though she knew he had insisted that sex was not the problem. He'd said she pushed him away and maybe she did . . . for there was another part of her that did not desire the complications of trying to build and sustain a loving relationship with a man in the middle of the fear and turmoil which roiled inside her daily since finding the body at the lake. Something told her that it was going to take every fiber of her concentration to fit all the puzzle pieces together. She was going to have to have tunnel vision, exclude everything else, no matter how much it hurt. No matter how much she missed the support and company Nathan had given her.

Twenty years may have passed, but she was still in this alone.

With a deliberate effort to compartmentalize her problems, Dani pushed thoughts of Nathan to the back of her

mind and spent the drive to Austin chewing over what to say
to her mother. Their history was such a roller coaster of
emotional ups and downs that their present relationship,
while affectionate, was distanced. Neither one wanted to
trigger painful memories by a careless remark, so their
conversation was not easy and open. She could forgive her
parents for committing her to the mental institution. What
she could not forgive was their failure to believe her.

Start by forgiving yourself, Kate had said.

Forgive herself for what?

Had she blamed *herself* all these years for the abuse she'd
suffered at the hands of her foster parents?

The thought brought her up short. *Maybe she had.*

Dani knew, intellectually, that child abuse was never the
child's fault. She'd said so to more than a few troubled
students. But it wasn't so simple, she found, when it was
her own life. Even now, she wondered if her dog King's life
could have been spared if she had only said something to the
social worker in charge of her case.

Chewing the inside of her cheek, Dani thought, *If I'm
having trouble getting people to believe me now, as an
adult, who would have believed me then?* The thought was
tremendously comforting. She took it a step further, re-
minding herself that she *did,* eventually, speak out. Somebody, somewhere, must have listened, because she was
removed from the home and adopted by the Daniels family.

Which brought her thoughts full circle back to her
mother. How could she bring up the past without reopening
painful wounds? She had to convince her mother to cooperate with her, give her the information she needed.

All I have to do, she thought grimly, *is explain to her that
a satanic cult is behind all our grief, then and now. Yeah.
Sure. She'd probably have me committed again.*

But it wasn't even a funny thought. Not by half.

Austin, like most Texas cities, was like a family living in
a small house, suddenly invaded by a huge crowd of
out-of-town guests, having difficulty finding a place to put
everyone. Housing developments were springing up willy-

nilly on wooded hillsides, and environmentalists feuded constantly and furiously with developers. The University of Texas, alone, now had as many students as the entire population of Maplewood, and though Dani was fond of her hometown, she was glad she'd gotten out before all the company showed up.

Like most dutiful daughters, Dani went home each Christmas, but it had been nearly a year since that last visit, and her stomach fluttered as she turned the convertible down the familiar street. She loved her family deeply, but just as with Nathan earlier that day, she'd never been able to let them know. Making something of her life, after all the strife and trouble, seeing the pride in their eyes, seemed to be the only way she knew how to say, "I love you."

There didn't seem to be any way to say it to Nathan.

Her mother seemed to have ten green thumbs, and flowers flourished everywhere, even in the cool of October. Like the other family members, Dani took Thoreau and went directly around the back of the house.

"Mom?" she called through the screen door. In the distance, she could hear the murmur of the television. She glanced at her watch. Soap opera. Thoreau, delighted to be set free in such a grassy, shady place, trotted back and forth, nose to the ground, his one good ear perked to the sky. He would be fine in the fenced-in yard. Watching him, she made the decision on the spot to leave him behind with her mother until all the trouble blew over. Her sisters still lived in Austin, and their kids would send him into doggie paradise.

Smiling, she let herself in the screen door and called again to her mother. There were scurrying footsteps, then her mother entered the kitchen, shock and pleasure registered on her face. "Dani!" She enfolded Dani in her strong arms and squeezed the breath out of her. "What are you doing here on a Tuesday? It's a school day! It's so good to see you. Why didn't you tell me you were coming?"

"It's good to see you, too, Mom," Dani said, meaning it. Suddenly she was almost too weary to stand. She led the way into the den and flopped onto the couch. This comfy old house that spelled *home*, her mother's face creased into

a welcoming smile, even the familiar scents, enveloped her
and, for the moment, anyway, stole away her loneliness and
confusion and replaced them with a sense of rightness and
order. She thought of the quote "Home is where, when you
go there, they have to take you in."

Murder and madness seemed so very far away.

"What are you doing here on a school day?" her mother
repeated suspiciously, fretful furrows between her brows.

"I . . . I need to talk to you, Mom, but not right now.
Why don't you catch me up on family gossip first? When is
Cathy's baby due?"

Diverting her mother's attention to the grandchildren was
always easy and sometimes frustrating to the unmarried
daughter, but this time Dani welcomed her mother's prattle
about all the cute things little Beth, Jeremy, and Casey said
and did. Her sister's pregnancy was going well, but her
other sister was unhappy in her marriage, which worried her
mother a great deal. Her brother was facing his orals but it
looked as though he was finally going to get that Ph.D.,
after all. Imagine, a Dr. Daniels in the family.

Dani lay her head back on the couch and let her mother's
chatter wash over her. It seemed to be the first normal
conversation she'd had in ages. Her world was so very
removed from theirs, and it saddened her. Maybe that was
why she didn't like to come home too often.

After a while she realized her mother had grown silent
and was watching her. "Something is wrong."

Dani stared at the floor, struggling to find the right
words. "I have to find some answers, Mom. It's very, very
important."

"What kind of answers?" There it was, the strain she had
dreaded.

She gave her mother a level gaze. "About my past. I need
to know what happened to me before I was adopted."

Her mother was already shaking her head. "Let the past
bury the past, Dani. All it can do is cause you pain. It can't
possibly help."

Dani leaned forward, imploring her mother with her

whole body. "I have to know, Mom. Trust me on this, *please*. It's very important."

"Why?" Suspicion rang in her mother's voice.

"I'd rather not say."

"Then I'd rather not talk about it."

"*Mom* . . ." Dani hesitated, counted to three, tried to take the anger out of her voice. She decided to use the shock treatment. "The people who had me before . . . I think they are trying to contact me again."

"What do you mean, you *think*? Have they called you? Written you? What?" Clearly her mother was alarmed. "Oh, God, Dani . . . are you talking about that murder that Sergeant Kendall told me about?" Her voice sharpened.

Dani crossed the room and sat on the arm of her mother's chair, draping her arm over her mother's shoulders. "Mom, this is terribly serious or I wouldn't ask you. I need your help. Please."

The older woman's shoulders drooped. With a slow nod of resignation, she got up. Dani followed her to the bedroom, where her mother knelt on the floor in front of a huge chest of drawers, a piece of furniture she'd had as a bride. Pulling out the bottom drawer, she reached under a pile of sweaters and withdrew a slim manila file, which she handed over to Dani as if it were a Fabergé egg.

Sitting on the edge of the bed, Dani opened the file with trembling fingers. Inside was a single sheet of paper, an official-looking carbon copy of a report detailing the history of Faith Matthews, age seven.

Her father and mother had been killed in an automobile accident when Faith was two, at which time she had been placed in foster care. During her third year in foster care, the social worker had noticed certain "irregularities" in her home situation and had begun an investigation. She was taken from the home at the age of six and held as a ward of the court until her adoption one year later.

Dani raised her head. "Did you show this to Nathan?"

Her mother shook her head. "I was so rattled by his visit that, to tell you the truth, I didn't even think about it."

Dani studied the sheet. "*Irregularities? Are* you *sure* this is everything?"

"It's all they gave us, Dani."

Dani jumped up and began pacing the floor. "*Irregularities?* But you *had* to know something was dreadfully, terribly wrong, didn't you?"

"We asked them. We called the agency about six months after we got you, and all they told us was that you had been abused. We thought they meant you'd been beaten. We couldn't imagine what else—not then, anyway. That was twenty years ago."

"Mom, somebody has got to know!"

"I don't understand why it matters now, Dani!" her mother cried. "Why can't you just forget about it and get on with your life?"

"*Forget about it?*" shouted Dani. "How *can* I forget about it when it terrorizes my sleep and haunts my every waking moment?"

Her mother's jaw dropped.

Tears of frustration sprang unbidden to Dani's eyes. "If I don't find out what happened to me then . . . if I can't figure out what's happening to me now . . . then I know I'll lose my mind. Can't you understand that?"

Her mother glanced away.

Dani grabbed her arm, hard enough to make her wince. "I want to show you something." She yanked her mother toward the hallway, then let go and headed down the hall, her mother following. She was so angry and frustrated that she shook all over. She hadn't wanted it to come to this, but she found that she simply could not dredge up the past without losing control somewhere along the line. She pushed through the screen door, slamming it against the house.

Thoreau came bounding up on the porch, grinning like a pirate.

Her mother gasped behind her.

Slowly Dani turned to look at her. "Do you see what they did to him?"

Her mother's face was ashen.

"If you don't help me," Dani said evenly, "I don't know what they will do to me."

Her mother swallowed. "There was a lawyer." Her voice cracked. "He represented you in the adoption. I don't know if he is still practicing or not, but I have his old telephone number. Maybe he would have the answers you want."

"Mom, *why* didn't you call him before?" Dani hadn't intended for the question to sound accusatory, but she could tell from her mother's expression that it had.

Her mother turned away, but not before Dani glimpsed the misery of guilt on her face. "I've *told* you. The social worker told us that we had all the information there was."

"And you *believed* him?"

Her mother's back stiffened. "We didn't think we had any choice, Dani. You have to understand how *alone* we were in all this. We didn't know any other family who was going through what we were, or who had a child as troubled as you. We thought . . ." Her voice softened. "We thought it was our fault, somehow."

Dani stared at her mother. For that brief moment, she understood exactly how her mother must have felt.

Chapter 22 ~~~~~~~~~~

"Bulldog! Lieutenant Ward wants to see you in his office pronto. He looks really pissed." Manny Garcia's face was alight with curiosity. Seth glanced Nathan's way with arched brows. Nathan, who was on his way out, anyway, shrugged, then took his own sweet time taking leave of his desk and wandering down the hall to Ward's office. He owned and trained dogs; he was damned if he was going to behave like one, groveling with tail tucked between his legs.

Ward was standing ramrod straight in front of his desk. "Close the door, Sergeant," he ordered.

Nathan did so but remained standing; not exactly at attention, but he had no intention of sitting and being glowered at from on high. He had no idea what this was about, but kept all expression from his eyes as he faced the lieutenant.

"I've become aware of some most unprofessional behavior on your part, Sergeant," said Ward in his sternest voice.

Nathan waited.

When he said nothing, Ward went on. "We can't have our officers shacking up with material witnesses."

It was shock treatment, and it worked. Nathan stopped himself—just—from flinching, but nevertheless blinked his eyes. His mind raced. Seth, he knew, would never have said a word to anyone. Who else knew? Certainly Dani's visit to the department had caused some gossip, but nobody *knew*. How, then, did the lieutenant?

"I'm waiting for an explanation." Ward's gray eyes were cold as a snake's.

What could he say? They'd spent two nights together; who would believe they hadn't slept together? He'd gone by to see her after work, late at night, several times. She'd come to the police station twice to see him.

He'd even gone to Austin on her behalf.

Even worse, he'd kept things from the lieutenant which could prove to be evidence later. The note dropped in her front door mail slot on the night of the first murder. The tattoo on her arm which matched the one on the victim's. No matter what he could possibly say, it looked bad.

He swallowed. "No explanation, sir."

Ward's eyes glittered. "I don't have to tell you how bad this looks in the midst of an ongoing murder investigation."

"The witness's initial report has proven unfounded, Lieutenant, and it was my understanding that the two murder cases had been closed." He gave the lieutenant a level gaze, which said, *Your orders, you bastard.*

Ward's cheek blanched. He'd read Nathan's unspoken comment correctly. He turned and walked behind the desk. "No case is closed until the jury comes in with a verdict." He leaned forward, his fingertips splayed out on his desk. "If you want to keep your job, Sergeant, you'll stay away from that woman. Do I make myself clear?"

Nathan nodded slowly. "Perfectly."

The lieutenant sat down in a gesture of dismissal and began fussing with papers on his desk.

Nathan pivoted on his heel and walked out with studied casualness, but he was working the muscles in his jaw. Somehow it made him furious to think that Dani had made the lieutenant's order only too easy to keep.

Still, underneath, he was shaken. He had no doubt that if he was caught seeing her again, the lieutenant would call in Internal Affairs and put him on such a poor report that, even if he wasn't fired, he'd find himself stuck over in Dispatch or Records, shuffling papers at a desk until retirement. He could lose a rank, which would affect his pension, or he could even be put back in uniform, on patrol, handing out traffic tickets.

Hell, he thought, as he slid behind the wheel of the nondescript departmental sedan assigned to him, it was probably for the best. Dani didn't seem to want to be with him, anyway. Besides, she had so many emotional problems, and what with all this weird cult talk, he was better off without her.

Better off. Had to be.

That's what he told himself, over and over, as he backed out of the parking space in front of the police department and drove down the road toward his next interview, marveling that his own life had somehow become as complicated as this murder investigation.

ChemCo, Inc., was located on a state highway on the outskirts of the county. It looked as though it could have been designed by a protégé of Frank Lloyd Wright's, so well did it blend in with the wooded surroundings. The building was only three floors tall, but sprawled into several complexes joined by covered walkways. It was constructed of glass and natural stone, with redwood highlights and a cedar-shingled roof.

The glossy, four-color brochure Nathan picked up in the lobby said that ChemCo manufactured all sorts of chemical products for agricultural uses, including pesticides, liquid fertilizers, and weed killers. The brochure went to some length to defend the company's environmental integrity and use of "environmentally friendly" chemical compounds and "other natural ingredients." It claimed to adhere to strict EPA guidelines on air pollution and waste disposal.

A smiling, pretty young receptionist led Nathan to Jordan Blake's office. He wasn't kept waiting long. Blake came out into the waiting area, flashed Nathan a Hollywood smile, gave him a firm handshake, and led him into a handsomely furnished office with a splendid view of the compound and wooded hills beyond. Placed artfully around the room like museum exhibits were several large glass display cases containing stuffed wildlife; a covey of quail, a fox, and a raccoon, arranged in natural-looking habitats and looking disturbingly real.

"What can I do for you, Sergeant Kendall?" Blake's voice was smooth and well modulated, a wealthy, cultured voice. He settled gracefully into a large leather swivel chair. The clouds of previous days had cleared, and bright sunlight from the picture window directly behind him haloed his silver hair and shadowed his face, which left Nathan unable to read his expression.

"I'm here about a former employee of yours, Mr. Blake. Name of John MacIntire. He's been arrested for the murder of his wife."

"Oh, such a tragedy!" clucked Blake. "And such a shock to us all."

"I understand he worked for you in Shipping and Receiving."

"Yes. And an excellent job he did, too. One would have never guessed how troubled he was."

"I just wondered if you noticed any erratic behavior in his job performance—tardiness, absenteeism, threats to other employees?"

Blake cleared his throat. "Well, there was one thing. I feel rather hesitant to bring it up."

"Please. It could be very important."

"Well . . . I remember my secretary mentioning once, not long ago, that she believed Mr. MacIntire was having an affair, because his wife had mentioned to her something about his having to work late all the time, which wasn't true."

Nathan sat up straighter. "Did she know the woman's name?"

Blake shook his head. "I don't think so."

"Could I talk to your secretary?"

"Certainly."

Nathan started to rise.

"But she's not in today. She's on vacation. Be gone two weeks."

Nathan sat back down. "Can you remember anything more about the conversation?"

"Not really. It was office gossip. You know how it is."

"Can you think of anything else that might help us?"

Blake seemed to be pursing his lips, but Nathan was going half blind from looking into the bright light behind him, and couldn't tell for sure.

"No. I'm sorry. This whole thing has been so awful for company morale."

"I'm sure." Nathan withdrew a business card and slid it across the polished desk toward Blake. "If you can think of anything further . . ."

"I'll call right away, Sergeant."

Nathan got to his feet. "Mind if I look around?"

Blake came around from behind the desk. "Please. Let me give you a tour of the facilities." He was smiling again, and for some unfathomable reason, Nathan decided he did not like Jordan Blake. In fact, he didn't really want a tour, but couldn't see any polite way out of it.

Blake launched into a public relations monologue about ChemCo, in a syrupy political kind of voice. They walked through spotless laboratories and cavernous warehouses and assembly-line areas that gave off acrid odors. Workers there wore surgical masks, goggles, rubber gloves, and protective body clothing. Nathan wondered if farmers knew how dangerous some of these chemicals were. So much for protecting the environment.

On their way toward a set of double doors marked *Shipping and Receiving,* they passed another door with a red *No Admittance* sign. It was padlocked from the outside. "What's in there?" Nathan asked, gesturing. Blake had already opened one of the doors leading to the shipping area, and Nathan had to raise his voice over the noise of the conveyor belts.

Blake let the door swing shut. He gave Nathan one of his ingratiating smiles. "Ever hear of industrial spies?" he asked in a conspiratorial tone. Nathan nodded. Blake drew closer. "Often other companies will send out people on their payrolls to apply for jobs with competing companies," he explained unnecessarily. "They take back information on new products under development, which gives *their* companies the edge on the marketplace." Shaking his head, he chuckled. "It's worked for the Soviets for years."

Trying not to grind his teeth, Nathan waited.

"Anyway, that padlocked door is a lab where we develop new products. Our scientists are carefully screened, and they work varying hours. When they are out, the door is padlocked. When they are in, it's locked from within."

Nathan thought a padlock was pretty extreme, but Blake struck him as the perfect type to be paranoid.

"I'm the only one who has a key to that door," added Blake. "Keeps them from being able to have copies made."

Nathan started to ask if he could see the lab, but the tour had taken far too long as it was, he was in a hurry, and all he'd wanted to see in the first damn place was Shipping and Receiving, the area where MacIntire had worked. He'd have preferred to do it without the bossman at his sleeve, so that he could question MacIntire's coworkers and get more candid responses. Maybe some other time. Maybe when he came back to talk to the secretary.

He only half listened to Blake's rambling dissertation on the complexities of receiving chemicals and off-loading finished products directly onto "piggyback" cars—semitrailers perched atop railway cars on the tracks directly outside the huge sliding back doors, which would be hooked up to periodic freight trains. From there they would be delivered to some distant railway destination, where Mack trucks would then connect directly to the piggybacks and complete delivery to points all over the country.

Because Blake seemed to expect it, Nathan feigned a mild expression of being impressed, then pried himself away from his well-dressed, eager host and made his way out to his car. The walkways from building to building wound in and out of the pines as if the builder hadn't been able to part with a single one, but had simply plopped the company down in natural spaces between trees.

The entire layout looked expensive and attractive, like Jordan Blake himself. Maybe that was why Nathan didn't like it.

Chapter 23 ~~~~~~~~

Dani should have guessed that the twenty-year-old phone number would be disconnected. Nothing in life was ever that easy. She called San Francisco information and was given a number for Richard Miller, Attorney-at-Law, and with shaking fingers, she dialed it.

No answer.

Of course. California time was two hours earlier than Texas time; it was a working day; naturally the man would not be at home. Dani had waited all her life, it seemed, to find out what was at the other end of the line, but waiting a few more hours now seemed unbearable. Especially with her mother hovering about, anxiety etched all over her face.

"I just don't want you to get hurt," she kept saying to Dani.

"Mom," Dani would say, "I can't be hurt any worse than I already have been."

Finally, hesitantly, Dani began to tell her a little of what Kate had said about children with attachment disorder. "She said that all the problems you had with me were classic symptoms of the attachment-disordered child," said Dani. "Therapists are now realizing that severe abuse—even of babies—is retained in the subconscious and reveals itself in the child's acting out. The child may not even know why she is behaving in that way. She may not consciously remember any of the abuse. She desperately wants to be loved but doesn't trust anyone who tries to love her. She is constantly testing that love, because deep down inside she does not believe that she is deserving of it."

179

Her mother nodded slowly, thoughtfully. "Yes," she said. "Your daddy and I always thought we were being tested. And I have to tell you, Dani, in all honesty, we got sick to death of it. It was like . . . no matter what we did, it was never enough. We couldn't figure out where we had failed you."

"I know," said Dani in a soft voice. "I know where I first felt that you had failed me. Back when I was fourteen, and you didn't believe me."

There it was. Like opening a deep, dark closet and having a skeleton crash down on her in a rattle of bones. The subject never spoken about between parents and child. The subject long since buried.

Dani's mother got up abruptly and hurried out of the room.

Dani sighed, a long, worn-out sigh. Maybe some wounds were simply unhealable. For a long moment she sat, then thought, *No. I'm not shoving this back in the closet. We are confronting it, and we are confronting it now, or we will never, ever be able to speak without it resting between us.*

She got up off the couch and followed her mother into the laundry room, where she found her stuffing sheets into the washing machine with short, jabbing movements. Wordlessly Dani opened the dryer and removed warm fluffy towels, which she began folding. "Mom . . ." she began.

Her mother whirled toward her, her lips pursed, her eyes flashing with anger. "You tell me how you are supposed to *believe* a hysterical child, an uncontrollable child, a difficult child with a turbulent history, when half a dozen cops can't figure out what the hell she's talking about!" Long-buried anger assaulted Dani like a blow.

There was a time when they would have had an explosive quarrel, when Dani would have stormed from the house. But after being with Kate, Dani understood now; she understood a little something about pent-up emotion. She waited.

Her mother slammed shut the washer, turned it on, cursed, lifted the lid, added detergent, slammed it shut again. "No matter what we did with you, it was never the right thing. I suppose you are going to be throwing it up to me for the rest of my life." She turned and left the room.

Dani's cheeks were hot and she was breathing too fast. She took a deep breath, made herself finish folding the towels, carried them to the linen closet, and put them away. Then she went in search of her mother. She found her chopping carrots into smithereens in the kitchen.

"Mom." She approached her shyly, stood next to the woman's rigid body. "Please forgive me. I am so sorry for all the things I ever did to hurt you." Her voice broke. "I never meant to. But what these people did to me . . . *warped* me . . . I'm only just now fighting my way out of that damage. I've always appreciated everything you ever did for me . . . And . . . I've . . . I've always loved you."

Her mother lay down the knife carefully, as if it would break. She turned, wiping her hands on her apron, and held out her arms. They embraced, holding each other tightly, their tears wetting each other's cheeks.

"Hello?"

"Is—is this Richard Miller?"

"Speaking."

"Mr. Miller, um, my name is Faith Daniels. You represented my case in an adoption hearing back in 1970. My name was Faith Matthews then. I was seven years old."

"That wouldn't be me. I'm Richard Miller *Junior*. You want to speak to my father, Richard Miller Senior. But he's retired now, and his number is unlisted."

"Please, Mr. Miller. This is extremely important or I wouldn't be calling after twenty years."

"Is this about finding your birth parents or something?"

"No, I assure you. My birth parents are dead."

"Then what's it about?"

"I'd rather not say. I'd rather discuss that with your father, if I may."

"I don't know. We don't give out his number to just anybody."

"I'm not just anybody. I'm a former client, and I'm calling from Texas. I have a *right* to speak to him."

"Well . . . all right. I'll give it to you, I guess . . ."

And Dani took down the number with hands shaking so hard she could barely write.

She had to try five times, over the next two hours, before there was an answer.

"Miller's residence."

"Richard Miller, please."

"This is he."

Dani took a shaky breath. "Mr. Miller . . . my name is Faith Daniels. Twenty years ago I was seven years old and my name was Faith Matthews. You handled my adoption out of foster care."

A long, deep sigh sounded over the line. "Yes," said Miller.

"Mr. Miller, I'm calling about my files, the ones that detail my situation before I was put up for adoption. I . . . It is extremely important that I be allowed to see those files."

"Well, all I can say is that I am surprised it has taken you this long."

"*What?*" She wasn't sure she had heard him correctly.

"For years now, I've been expecting your parents to contact me about those records."

"The social worker insisted that there were no more files than the single page we were given."

"Good God. You don't have *any* of them?" The receiver vibrated with his shock.

"I guess it's like, a synopsis."

"I don't know what it is with social workers. I guess they were afraid if they dumped the whole file in the Danielses' lap, they'd refuse to adopt you."

Dani's chest was beginning to hurt. "Mr. Miller, I don't know what you are talking about."

"I'm talking about 124 pages, detailing some of the worst child abuse I've ever encountered in my entire career. I'm talking about some people who went to prison for it."

• • •

That night, all of Dani's brothers and sisters and their kids and spouses came for dinner, just to see Dani. It was the first time in years—maybe ever—that she felt like a real member of the family. Perhaps it was the encounter with her mother; or maybe they had always embraced her this warmly, and she'd never noticed, or had held herself back from it. She thought wistfully of her father, and wished that he could have been with them to share this new closeness. There was so much she could say to him now that she never could have said before.

They all wanted to know what had happened to Thoreau, and she told them it was a cruel prank played by one of her nastiest students. They seemed to accept that. There was food and wine and laughter, but through it all, Dani could think of nothing else but the file, which was due to arrive by overnight mail the next day. She tried to push it out of her mind, but it kept creeping back in. At one point, Dani looked around at all the familiar faces and was struck with the thought: *What would have happened to me without them?*

A sobering thought, indeed.

Long after the house was silent, company gone, her mother asleep, Dani lay wide-eyed, staring at the gently whirring ceiling fan above her bed. She wanted to see the file. She didn't want to see the file.

There would be answers, but there would also be questions.

People in prison.

She could hardly believe it. Her foster parents? The others?

If they'd gone to prison twenty years ago, they had to be out now. And that made more sense than anything anyone had said to her yet. Someone had gone to prison because *she* had spoken out to, who, a social worker? Probably. It had sparked an investigation. There must have been some evidence, enough for a conviction.

Prison can ruin a person's life.

Because she spoke out.

It was terrifying. But it was also exciting. It was another puzzle piece. One piece closer to the completed picture.

Sometime in the predawn hours, she finally slept.

The heavy package arrived, as promised, by midmorning. Dani's mother had to open it because Dani's hands were shaking too much. Together, they pored over its voluminous contents.

There were psychological reports, medical reports, caseworker's reports. There were transcripts of the adoption hearing. Interviews with the foster parents who had kept her after she'd been removed from the abusive home, before the adoption. There was a handwritten notation: her foster father had been sentenced to ten years for endangerment to a child and indecency with a minor; her foster mother, six years.

All names had been blacked out with a marker.

In another hand was written, "Pornography ring busted. Couldn't make charges stick, but could stick sexual assault on a child. Same ten-year sentence."

Pornography ring?

One caseworker's report read, "A surprise inspection of the house soon after child's outcry revealed a black room with religious artifacts arranged in a bizarre manner, including a pedestal which looked like a sacrificial altar. When questioned, foster parents claimed it was decorations for a Halloween party, though Halloween had passed a month before. On the next visit, the room was changed and the child refused to speak to caseworker."

There were a child's drawings, *her* drawings, which gave Dani chill bumps. The only color she had ever used was black or blood-red, and all the figures in them were frightening and threatening, surrounding a small figure who had no mouth and no arms. One drawing depicted a dog with one ear; red crayon marks jabbed over the dog and dripped off the page. Dani felt the hairs rise on the back of her neck.

"Drawings show the child's feeling of powerlessness and unhappiness," surmised the psychologist, who added,

"Sexual knowledge far advanced for a child of seven, which is indicative of sexual abuse, but her descriptions of black-robed monster-figures involved in the act may be delusional, resulting from the abuse." He suggested long-term therapy—something the Danielses had never been told.

The medical exam revealed the tattoo, which showed signs of having been infected at one point but untreated, clear indications of rape, and old scars.

Dani's mother put her face in her hands and wept.

After they plowed through all the material, Dani went to the dusty, little-used liquor cabinet and poured them both a stiff scotch and water. "Appetizer before lunch," she mumbled, and they both drank deeply.

"Nobody ever said a goddamn word to us," her mother said numbly, using a curse word Dani had never heard her utter before. "They told us you'd been abused. That's all. They said you were bright and beautiful and would make a wonderful daughter and that's all we heard once we laid eyes on you, anyway." She polished off her drink and poured herself another one.

"Tell me . . ." Dani fingered her glass, took a swig. "Would you have adopted me if you'd known all this?"

"Tough question," said her mother, taking another big gulp. "By the time we realized how troubled you were, we also realized we couldn't begin to afford to get you the kind of help you needed, and there wasn't any kind of state aid or anything for that kind of problem. But the thing is . . . we loved you. We couldn't have given you up for anything."

Dani drained her glass, fetched some more. "But would you have adopted me *then*, if you'd known?"

Her mother shrugged. "Who knows? We were naive. We probably still would have thought love could conquer all." She hiccupped and giggled. Dani giggled, too. She'd never seen her mother so relaxed.

"Well, it kind of did, in the long run, didn't it?" Dani asked. She'd never been a scotch drinker, but this stuff was really smooth.

"Yeah, but it was a major pain in the butt," said her mom, and they broke into gales of laughter.

They both had another drink, and toasted. "Like that hair color ad, though," quipped Dani, "I'm *worth* it."

This was hysterically funny to them both.

One of her brothers dropped in for lunch. He found his mother and his adopted sister rolling around on the couch, howling, an open scotch bottle (nearly empty) nearby, and a fat file folder on the coffee table, vomiting its putrid contents onto the floor.

Chapter 24 ~~~~~~~~~

Since the second watch—the four to midnight shift—was the busiest for law enforcement officers, all the other detectives were out on calls while Nathan finished up paperwork on calls he'd made himself earlier in the evening. The office was quiet. Nathan's pencil scribbling was punctuated by occasional distant rumbles of thunder, threatening more rain.

There was a movement at the door, and Nathan looked up to see Kate McCall standing at his desk, a fat file folder cradled in her arms. Scrambling to his feet, he shook her hand and indicated a seat.

"What brings you out on a nasty night like this?" he asked. "You should be home, snug in bed with the late-night news."

She grinned. "Like that would help me sleep? Actually"—she leaned forward and plopped the file down on Nathan's desk—"since I'm usually at work while you're asleep, and vice versa, I figured this would be a good time to catch you and bring these by."

"What are they?" He picked up the file.

"These are actual case files from other police departments, on ritual crimes which are currently under investigation."

He gave her a suspicious glance. "How'd *you* get hold of them?"

"I told you. I have contacts in law enforcement who understand and appreciate what I'm trying to do. Unlike some *other* people I know."

Quirking a corner of his mouth, Nathan flipped open the file uneasily and scan-read a case from one of the Florida Keys; it was a pair of mutilation murders. The hearts of two young women had been cut out. He looked up at Kate. Her face was serious.

Another case, this one from Oregon, involved the slaughter of an Arabian stallion. His genitals had been surgically removed and all the blood drained from his body.

One file yielded information on a grave-robbing case in Indiana. Some fifteen bodies were missing from various cemeteries.

The body of a dismembered eleven-year-old boy was discovered in Oklahoma.

A seven-year-old girl from Texas had vanished with her father. A private investigator found boxes of child pornography left behind, along with a handwritten sheet of instructions on how to dismember a human body.

An involuntary shiver crept down Nathan's spine. Kate had not taken her eyes off him as he read. "Gets to you, doesn't it?" she said.

Nathan eyed the thick file she had placed on the desk. He hadn't even dented it. "I've seen enough," he said.

Kate swept her hand over the file. "These cases haven't even received much media attention. Consider the ones which have, and I'm not talking about Matomoros, either. I'm talking about Richard Ramirez, the Night Stalker, in California. Henry Lee Lucas—"

"A serial killer."

"Yes. Who claimed membership in a satanic group. The Son of Sam in New York—"

"That hasn't been proven, Kate."

"Read Maury Terry's book *The Ultimate Evil*. Ten years' worth of investigation. Pretty convincing stuff."

"*Convincing,* maybe. *Proven,* no."

"All right. I'll give you that. I'll concede that most of these cases haven't even been solved, much less proven in a court of law. But for God's sake, Nathan, look at the sheer *number* of them."

Nathan's mouth was dry. He felt extremely uncomfortable. Kate had a point. The total volume of criminal cases which *appeared* to have links to cult rituals was staggering. But there was a question in his mind. "Let me ask you something," he said, leaning forward in his chair. He was thinking about Dani. The rituals she claimed to have been a part of had taken place twenty years ago. "How come all this is just now coming to light? I mean, if Dani is to be believed, then this has been going on for years and years. How come we haven't heard anything about it before? Why *now*? I mean, are you sure it's not . . ." Looking into Kate's eyes, he faltered.

"You mean, some mass hysteria cooked up by the fundamentalist community?"

"Well, it's just that . . . Dani's story is hard enough to swallow sometimes, but her behavior is even worse." He shrugged. "She's got a lot of emotional problems."

"Sure she does," agreed Kate. "All cult survivors do. You can't come through what these people have experienced and *not* have emotional problems. But that does *not* make them—us—liars."

Nathan shook his head. "I didn't necessarily think she was *lying*—"

"Hallucinating?"

"Hell, Kate, I don't know. You tell me."

Kate leaned forward in her chair, dropped her tone of voice, and said, "Nathan, if that woman is lying or hallucinating, then thousands of people from all over the country have been lying to all sorts of different therapists, law enforcement officers, and ministers. Or they've all had the exact same delusions. And I'm not talking about only kids. I'm talking about adult survivors, like Faith Daniels. Professional people. Responsible people."

Nathan shrugged. "Maybe it *is* kind of a . . . mass hysteria thing. They got the idea from TV or something." He avoided Kate's piercing eyes. He didn't want to offend her, but he had to say what he felt.

Kate shook her head vehemently. "Disparate stories began appearing in wildly different areas, from completely different sources, long before Giraldo Rivera ever heard about it."

"I don't know, Kate . . ." Nathan rubbed a hand over his eyes. "I don't figure how it is that this sort of thing could have been going on for years, maybe even *decades,* and law enforcement was completely deaf, dumb, and blind." With a shrug of his shoulders, he glanced away. He didn't want to get into a debate with this woman, but he had legitimate questions which deserved consideration. Besides, he knew that if he ever hoped to be with Dani again, he'd have to have some answers.

Kate was not daunted by Nathan's doubts. "It's a good point," she said agreeably. "The truth is, law enforcement officers really had no idea what to look for at a crime scene until recent years. If they came upon a mutilated body, surrounded by pentagrams and candles and upside-down crucifixes, they figured it was the result of some deranged mind. It didn't occur to them that all those things had symbolic significance."

She picked up the file and balanced it on her lap. "Technology had something to do with it, too. Until the widespread use of computers, there was no way that all these various departments from around the country could know that a case under investigation in their jurisdiction closely resembled one a thousand miles away. Now, with fax machines and FBI clearinghouses, there is a virtual flood of information on ritualistic crime in this country." She hefted the heavy file. "It's frightening."

Nathan nodded. It made sense. And maybe, then, so did Dani.

Kate leaned forward earnestly. "There are people who have spent years investigating these crimes who believe that some cults actually operate an underground crime network, running guns, drugs, and pornography." She gestured toward the file. "They have computers, too, you know."

God, it *was* frightening. Nathan looked at Kate. She was articulate and convincing. She seemed to have come to grips with the gruesome contents of the file—and with her own past. *She'd make a good cop,* he mused. "What I don't understand is how anyone can get other people to do this stuff."

She shrugged. "Three ways. Drugs. Mind control. Threats." She shook her head. "Cult members have families. I mean . . . would *you* talk?"

"But, Kate . . ." Nathan felt as if he were at sea without a life jacket, struggling to the surface for air. It would be so easy to simply swallow everything Kate was telling him, give in to paranoia, let the fear run his life, let it affect his decisions as a cop. He couldn't do that.

"You still have doubts, don't you?" she asked. She did not seem annoyed.

Nathan shifted in his seat. "It's just . . . I mean, if you want to know the truth . . . I'm not even sure at all about this Satan business. I mean, I sometimes have trouble even believing in God, to be perfectly frank. I can't believe there's some guy running around with horns and a pitchfork, telling these people to maim and murder."

But his doubts didn't seem to bother the patient woman. Kate said, "It doesn't matter whether or not *you* believe in Satan, Nathan. What *does* matter is that *they* believe in him." She gave him a shrewd glance. "And I can tell you that the devil—or evil, if you want to call it that—doesn't run around with horns and a pitchfork. He runs around with jeans and a Walkman. Or a suit and briefcase."

She gave him a moment to mull that over. "Nathan, what has Dani told you about a student she has, Adam Prescott?"

He gave her a sharp look. "Not much. Why?" The sudden change of subject was disconcerting.

"Well, he's very bright. Charismatic. Good-looking, too. I have knowledge that he's recruited members into a youth cult from kids who are into drugs and sex and heavy-duty parental rebellion. A few weeks ago, he quit coming to the meetings, but from what my informant tells me, he's still into satanism, and that worries me."

"So? What does that mean?" Her use of the police term *informant* made him uncomfortable.

"It means one of two things, both of them bad. One, he's

gotten too bizarre for this group, and he's gone solo, which could mean he's about to explode and do something violent and destructive, like kill his parents or somebody else. Two, he's found his way into an adult coven, which would be even worse."

Nathan swallowed. "Why? Why worse?"

"Because the most dangerous cults involve adult leaders who are able to order teen followers to commit their crimes for them."

"How on earth . . ."

"Just like the Army, Nathan. They recruit. They organize. They motivate."

A thought, unbidden, rose from the depths of his mind. *And they kill.*

Suddenly the room began to close in on Nathan. Every little fear he'd ever had—under-the-bed monsters as a kid, dark-alley fears as a rookie cop—all gathered about him like so many haunting spirits, taunting him.

Thunder growled, closer this time, and the lights flickered. The conversation had been so intense that Nathan had forgotten the approaching storm. He glanced away from Kate, his mind awhirl. He'd seen his share of bad people, but for the first time in Nathan's career, he faced the presence of *evil*.

He'd never believed it was possible. Not until now.

Chapter 25 ~~~~~~~~~~

As soon as Dani stepped into the living room of her house the Thursday afternoon after her trip to Austin, she felt it, an oppressive, gloom-clouded atmosphere. She'd been on a high during the drive home from Austin. The puzzle pieces were fitting together; her past was making sense; she was patching things up with her family. Like a powerful shot of adrenaline, the visit had energized her, given her new strength. She was ready to fight. It was almost a feeling of invincibility; after all, she had survived so much, surely she would survive this.

And then she walked through the door of her house in Maplewood. Thoreau's absence continued to leave a void in the house. Even worse was the painful memory of Nathan's last night with her. He had told her he was giving up on her, on them. Knowing that he wouldn't be dropping by late that evening after work made her feel suddenly vulnerable. Since the attack on Thoreau, she hadn't spent a night alone.

For alone she surely was. She could even hear the tiny *click* made by the den clock just before it chimed out the hour. To cover it, she turned on the TV, sorted through her mail, threw some clothes in the wash, made herself a sandwich, and opened a Coke. Anything to fill up those ticking minutes with noise and activity.

Finally she began a vigorous vacuuming, welcoming the noise and exertion. Over in the corner, against the wall, as if it had been swept back when the front door was opened, lay a white envelope.

For a long moment she stared at the envelope, fighting

down the old terror, stifling the urge to run. Slowly she picked it up, then tore into it so jaggedly that the envelope fell to the floor in tatters.

The message was typed on a plain piece of white paper:

> *Advzqd sgd Czqj Nmd cdrbdmchmf*
> *Sgd Vzsbglzm rddr zkk*
> *Sgdx eqnl sgd oqhdrsr cvdkkhmf*
> *Adknmf sn sgd mhfgs*

She'd been holding her breath, and she let it out in one big swoosh.

"This isn't fair," she whispered. "You're not playing by the rules."

For a long moment she stared at the note, but it remained incomprehensible.

She needed help.

She turned off the TV, left the washer running, gathered up her car keys, and went to see Kate.

As she had expected, she was greeted with a warm, affectionate hug, handed a plate full of melt-in-your-mouth brownies and a hot cup of tea, and settled onto the comfy sofa with breathless speed.

Kate was excited about the note, and ferreted out for Dani a book on word games. In it, they discovered the definition for *cryptogram*: "Cryptograms offer players a line or more of seemingly random letters, which, when deciphered with the correct key, translate into a word or phrase."

"The correct key," murmured Dani, dragging fretful fingers through her hair. As with the new locks on her doors, all Dani needed was *the correct key* to open up her life. The missing puzzle piece. The king on the chessboard.

She stared at the letters until they danced on the page. "How do we go about finding the correct key?" she asked Kate, her voice ringing with frustration.

"Two ways," answered her friend, munching on a brownie. "Elimination and repetition."

Drumming her fingers, Dani sipped her tea. "One word, *sgd*, appears four times," she commented absently.

"Then there's this other word," mused Kate. "Very similar—*sgdx*."

"Could it be an alphabet without vowels? Could the words be *sag* and *sagged*?" wondered Dani aloud, scribbling on a sheet of scratch paper.

Kate shook her head. "No. That doesn't figure because the first word in the message starts with an 'a.'" She pointed at the cryptogram. "Some of the words are capitalized. Proper names?"

"I don't think so," said Dani. "If that were so, then who would have a last name with only three letters? How could you decipher a name like *Nmd*?"

Kate rubbed her eyes. "Maybe they're abbreviations. Maybe *Nmd* stands for something like *Inc*."

"In that case," said Dani, "the first word in the company only has four letters, and all I can think of is *Ford*."

They looked at each other, then both said, "Nah."

Kate began to pace. "Surely the small words, and the repeated words, hold the key to the cryptogram. How many small words are there in the English language?"

Dani frowned. "Let's make a list. *A, and, the, of, to, on* . . ." Dani jotted down the ones she could think of offhand and Kate added a few. "Okay," she said. "Let's start with *and*." She wrote the letters *a-n-d* above the letters *s-g-d*.

"Then there's the word *sn*," pointed out Kate over her shoulder. "If the 's' was supposed to be an 'a', and the 'n' was suppose to be . . . No, because the 'g' in *sgd* was an 'n.'"

With a guttural cry of frustration, Dani jumped up from the sofa and pounded her fist into her hand. "Damn you!" she shouted. "I always hated word games and you probably know it!"

"Who are you talking to? Me?" asked Kate wryly.

Dani laughed. "I guess I've started thinking of my—what? Adversary? Enemy?" She sighed. "Anyway, I've started thinking of him as being, not just my secret past, but one individual—someone, ultimately, to be held accountable for it." She cocked her head at Kate. "Is that crazy?"

"Not at all. In fact, you may be right. And whoever he is, he's very clever."

In the silence that followed, Dani doodled on her pad. Giving intelligence and personality to her *enemy* (for that's what he was) was rather daunting.

Kate, as usual, seemed to read her mind. "Don't worry about it, dear. *We're* pretty smart and tough, ourselves, aren't we? Now, let's see if we can figure this thing out." She gestured toward the pad.

And as usual, Kate was right.

Picking up her pencil, Dani tried the word *the*. She wrote the letters *t-h-e* above the letters *s-g-d*, and right then, with an almost audible *click*, the key fit into the lock and the door swung wide open.

"You're a genius," said Kate when Dani was finished. She read aloud:

> *"Beware the Dark One descending.*
> *The Watchman sees all.*
> *They from the priest's dwelling*
> *Belong to the night."*

Kate's voice trailed away. "In all my work with satanic cults," she said quietly, "I've never encountered anything quite like this. What do you make of it?"

"Well, obviously they are all references to satanism. 'Dark One descending.' 'From the priest's dwelling.' 'Belong to the night.' All those phrases refer to satanism, as far as I can tell." Dani chewed the inside of her cheek.

"This is the first clear message, then, that a satanic cult is communicating with you."

"Well, I understood the passages from Dante's *Inferno*." Kate studied the note. "Are you going to show this to Nathan?"

"I don't know." Dani told her about the breakup with Nathan.

"How did you feel about that?" Kate refreshed her cup from a blue willow pattern teapot on a silver tray.

With a soft shrug, Dani said, "Like my heart was being torn out."

Kate grinned. "Good."

"Gee, thanks. Fat lot of sympathy I'll get from you."

"The fact is, you *felt*. Give it time. My guess is the nice, bewildered cop feels pretty much the same way. I suspect you two will meet in the middle somewhere when you least expect it."

Dani wanted to believe her, but if there was one thing her childhood had taught her, it was to always expect the worst. That way, you were never disappointed. If the best happened, well, then, it was a nice surprise.

After a time, Kate said, "Did you say that your foster parents went to prison for what they did to you?" Her mind had a way of jumping from point to point.

"That's what the lawyer told me. They and at least one of the others in the group."

"But he wouldn't tell you their names."

"They'd been blacked out in the files. I didn't figure it would do any good to ask."

"Never assume anything, Dani. Give the guy another call. Tell him a little about what has been happening to you. My guess is that he will relent."

Dani set down the plate of brownies. "I'm having a hard time learning to be assertive, especially when it is my own life. I mean, I'll stand up for a student any day."

Kate smiled. "Then think of that terrified little girl of twenty years ago as a child you encountered in your job. Do what you can to help her. Love her in just that way."

"You mean, don't think of her as *me*?"

"Not for a while."

Dani nodded. "I believe I can do that."

Kate leaned forward. "When you learn to love that little girl, Dani, you'll be well on your way to being healed."

"You're going to tell me that *then* I can love someone else, aren't you?"

"I'm going to tell you that you *should* love someone else then."

Dani sat back on the sofa, her cheeks burning. "I never thought of that."

"Even the Lone Ranger had Tonto, you know. To help him think of things like that. You can't go this one alone,

Dani. It's too dangerous—little ole Faith Daniels, all alone against a group of demented fanatics."

Why not? Dani thought bitterly. *It's all there was in the beginning.* But she didn't say it. She was feeling stubborn, resentful of Kate's comments. Kate, of all people, should understand. This was something she *had* to do alone.

Mulishly she wished she'd figured out the cryptogram without Kate's help.

The conversation brought the evening to an awkward, uneasy close, and soon Dani took her leave.

This time, when she walked through the door, her house was not only empty, it was dark and unnerving. She went through the rooms flicking on lights, and managed to find all sorts of excuses to stay up quite late, all the way to the end of the *David Letterman Show*.

It didn't make any difference. There was no friendly knock at the door, no welcoming hug, no chat over a late-night beer. Wearily she went to bed, leaving most of the lights still on. It took a long, long time for the bed to grow warm enough that she could sleep.

By the time last period rolled around the next day, Dani was bone-weary from the week's events. It was Friday, October 26—three weeks from the time she'd discovered the woman's body on the Palmer estate; almost one week from the day a man had confessed to Nathan Kendall to the murder of two other women.

How long would this cat-mouse game go on? she wondered irritably. If she must confront her tormentors, she wanted to get it over with.

Preoccupied with her thoughts, she returned from the rest room as the bell sounded to begin class, picked up her copy of the *Inferno,* and almost gasped. The book lay open to Canto Thirty-four, where a passage had been underlined: "Words would fail to tell me of my state. I was not dead or living."

She looked up, straight into Adam Prescott's eyes.

Never had she encountered more abject misery in the eyes of another soul. His appearance was disheveled, his manner dopey. His left hand was still bandaged. But it was his eyes that spoke out the passage from the *Inferno* with such clarity that suddenly Dani knew, without question, that it was Adam who had sent her each message.

Adam was the key, the final puzzle piece, the last king on the chessboard.

"Adam, I'd like to speak to you after class," she said, a little more loudly than was necessary. He glanced away from her, down at his desk, and didn't look up for the remainder of the period.

Dani struggled through the lesson, striving to hold her own scattered concentration, glancing nervously at the clock. How foolish not to speak to him before!

She'd been afraid. *Afraid*. What a little fool she'd been. Looking out at his bowed head from time to time, it was clear to her now that it was *he* who feared most.

He knew *what* to fear, *whom* to fear.

As the period drew to a close, Dani's mouth went dry, and her heart began a dull thudding in her ears. The answers to all her grief sat right there in the third row, and what had she done? Muddled through, squandering one clear warning signal after another.

Warning of *what*?

With a chill down her spine, she forced herself to face the fact that somebody, somewhere in this town, had deliberately cut off the boy's finger.

Was it the same person who had sliced off the breasts of two women, maybe three?

While the class worked at their desks on a homework assignment, Dani studied Adam's dark head and wrestled with her thoughts. What could she say to him that would induce him to break his fear-inspired vow of silence about the cult?

She thought about the earlier messages, the other passages from the *Inferno*. All of them had dealt with violence and mayhem; they'd been frightening. And she'd responded with fear.

But after Thoreau's ear was taken, after Adam lost the little finger on his left hand; then she had received the cryptogram, which read like . . . a warning.

But the passage today . . . this was a cry for help.

The bell rang. Dani nearly leapt to her feet from the shock of it. To her frustration, a student waylaid her with a question about the assignment, and to her dismay, she saw Adam elbow his way out the door.

"Excuse me. Just a moment." Breaking free from the student, Dani pushed past bewildered kids into the corridor. "*Adam!* Wait!" She spotted his tall form disappearing around the corner, toward the student parking lot.

Dani broke into a run.

Barreling past astonished faces, she sprinted down the slippery hallway and out the door, looking frantically back and forth. There he was, running for his car, jumping in. Bolting after him, Dani drew on all the strength she'd built up while running around the lake on the Palmer estate and reached the car door just as he was putting the spanking-new jet-black Thunderbird into gear.

"Stop!" she panted, clutching the car door. "I have to talk to you."

He looked at her with agonized eyes, then turned to look over his shoulder. "You can't!" he cried. "Leave me alone!"

"Adam." She grabbed his shoulder through the window. "For God's sake, you've got to tell me what's going on, before *we both get killed.*"

Through his shirt, she could feel him trembling. Throwing the car into reverse, he said through clenched teeth, "Come to my house after dark. My parents won't be there. Come through the alley. I'll leave the back door open. Wear a scarf or something."

Then he took off in a screech of tires.

Still breathing hard, Dani headed back into the building, thinking so furiously that when she encountered the same student still standing at her desk where she'd left him, waiting patiently for help with homework, Dani pulled a blank and couldn't even think of his name.

It wasn't until much later, as she cloaked herself in a dark coat and scarf, that Dani began to feel uncomfortable. Why had he asked her to come in through the alley? Why did he want her to cover up her appearance? For a moment, she hesitated, indecision paralyzing her. The moment didn't last long. Her desire for answers was too intense, too compelling.

She'd looked up his address in her files. A very prosperous neighborhood. His father owned a new-car dealership; his mother was a lawyer. Professional people. Country club set. She wondered what they thought of their only son's recent problems. She wondered if they cared.

The alleyway was broad and well lit. Discreet dumpsters hid unsightly garbage from view. Each home was surrounded by high fences in matching brick or expensive redwood. Everything was landscaped tastefully. Dani parked in the three-car drive behind the house, next to the black Thunderbird. A light came on automatically as she got out of her car. The garage door was closed.

Letting herself in through a latched gate in the fence, Dani walked around a curving flagstone walkway which circled a handsomely lit swimming pool. The sliding glass-paneled door was unlocked, as promised. Entering a massive den with beamed ceilings, rock hearth, and deep-pile white carpet, Dani called out, "Adam!"

The house was uncommonly quiet.

Instantly Dani was struck with an eerie feeling of unease. In a flash she saw her own vulnerability—how she'd fallen into a cleverly laid trap, a trap baited with a plea for her own pity. No one knew she was here. No one had seen her drive up. She was alone in this house with a disturbed young man who could very well be dangerous.

She turned and reached for the door. The thing to do was get out now.

But she couldn't.

There was something about the way he had looked at her in the parking lot—it *was* a cry for help! She had to see him, had to talk to him. This might very well be his—and her—last chance.

Emboldened, she crossed the den, heading for what appeared to be a kitchen around the corner, calling for Adam all the way. He was not to be found in the huge, sterile kitchen.

Across the hall, she saw a door. Timidly she knocked, then slowly pushed it open. Chaos greeted her eyes.

Heavy-metal-band posters wallpapered the room. Dirty clothing and leftover food littered the floor. The bed was unmade. Amid the clutter on the desk lay a dagger, the hilt of which was carved into a goat's head. She picked it up.

Dani thought she heard a sound. She whirled around, the dagger in her hand, fully expecting to see a furious Adam hulking in the doorway, but there was no one. Skin crawling, she threw down the dagger.

Compact discs lay scattered around the room. She picked them up, studying the titles. She'd never heard of the groups before, but they sounded hideous, with names like "Slayer," "Possessed," "Grave Digger," and "Lizzy Borden."

The closet door stood slightly ajar. Dani wondered what she would find if she searched it. She was halfway tempted to do so, but the compelling silence of the house called to her, like a ghost from the grave.

An overwhelming sense of dread draped itself over Dani like a shroud. Hurriedly she left the room. Back in the kitchen again, Dani spotted another door behind the refrigerator. Like the closet door, it stood slightly ajar. Heart pounding, Dani approached it.

Every thread of logic she had ever possessed screamed at her to get out. But, like a moth attracted to a deadly light bulb, she couldn't leave. She had to see what was behind the door.

With a trembling hand, she reached out gingerly and swung the door back.

A short flight of concrete steps led down to the garage floor. The kitchen light illuminated the steps, but not much else. There was a switch plate near the door with four light switches. Dani flicked one, and a light came on over the stove. Another illuminated the sink. The third shone down on a cabinet island.

The fourth switch threw the garage into bold bas-relief, burning each feature into Dani's brain forever: the neatly labeled tools on the pegboard, the lawn mower, the ski boat . . . and Adam's body, swinging gently to and fro from a ceiling rafter, his face alternately grimacing and frowning back and forth in the swaying light.

Chapter 26 ~~~~~~~~~

The call on Adam Prescott came while Nathan was having a hamburger at Kelly's with Seth. Nathan wrote down the address, and he and Seth gathered up their burgers and finished them in the car. Lord only knew when they'd get another chance to eat.

On the way, Nathan told Seth what he knew about Prescott, including the suspected cult involvement. He'd expected Seth to act skeptical, but he only nodded solemnly. "You hear a lot of stuff in the news about kids who get involved with violent cult stuff," mused Seth. "Remember that kid from Oklahoma . . . what was his name? Sean Sellers, who blew away his parents? And those kids who beat another boy to death with a baseball bat? They were all heavily into this cult business. It's scary, man. I'm just glad my kids are grown and drug-free, thank God."

Nathan nodded, wondering if he really wanted kids, after all, and pulled the sedan into one of the best neighborhoods in town, up to a sprawling house with a cluster of squad cars and an ambulance parked in front in the curved drive. Young Manny Garcia met them at the front door. "There's somebody here I think you'll want to talk to," he said excitedly.

"Where are the parents?"

"Gone to a convention in New York. Neighbors say they're gone a lot. They leave the kid home alone."

"Have they been contacted?"

"We're trying to reach 'em now."

Nathan followed Garcia through the entryway, past a

formal living room with a white baby grand piano and a spiral staircase, and into an enormous den with rugged beams and a stone hearth. A woman sat on the hearth wearing a dark coat and scarf over her hair, her back to Nathan, staring into the vacant fireplace. Manny headed toward her, and Nathan and Seth followed. There was something familiar about the woman . . .

Garcia touched her shoulder. She started, and looked up.

Nathan's mouth went dry. "Dani?"

Until that moment, her face had been a carefully controlled white mask, but when he said her name, the mask crumpled. She sprang to her feet and threw her arms around his neck.

"Oh, Nathan!" she sobbed. "It's all my fault." She was trembling. With an embarrassed, awkward glance at Seth's bemused face, Nathan embraced Dani, marveling again at how tiny she was, how vulnerable.

The scent of her hair made him dizzy.

He swallowed, collected himself, extricated himself from her arms, took her hands. "What are you doing here, Dani?" he asked gently.

"I found him." She rummaged in her bag for a tissue. Nathan looked over her head at Garcia, raised his eyebrows in question. Garcia nodded.

"Here. Sit down." He led her over to the couch and sat next to her, facing her. "I need to know why you were here in the first place. You're a schoolteacher. His parents are out of town . . ." He let the implication hang in the air between them.

For a moment, he thought the insinuation had made her angry, but she only nodded. "I know it looks bad. Adam told me to come. He told me his parents wouldn't be here, but I never stopped to think . . . I had to talk to him, Nathan."

Nathan sighed, squeezed her hand, got to his feet. "You sit here for a minute and get yourself together. I'm going to go look at the bo—at Adam. When I come back, I want you to tell me everything, okay?"

"Okay." She lifted her chin, which was still tremulous, and looked at him with blue eyes swimming with tears.

It cracked his heart. He turned away, somewhat brusquely. *I've got a job to do,* he thought. It occurred to him that he should turn the case over to Seth or call the lieutenant. He was too close to it.

In fact, under the circumstances, he would probably be removed from the case, anyway. But, for the time being, he was here. He would find out what he could. Garcia led him out to the garage. Seth followed. A patrol officer stayed behind with Dani.

The sadness of the scene drew them all up short for a moment. Nathan's heart filled with that old sense of gloomy inadequacy that he always felt in the presence of a young life cut short. It was the toughest part about law enforcement: finding dead kids. He could handle most anything else, with time, but the kids . . . the beat-up, wrecked-up, drugged-up, trussed-up kids . . . That always got to him and it always would.

"See this?" Seth pointed out one of the hands, hanging loosely at Adam's side. It was the one with the missing finger.

Nathan drew closer. "It looks like a binding mark."

"Got 'em on both wrists, which indicates to me that he was bound at one time or another."

Nathan gave him a level look. "Could he have bound himself first?"

"Anything's possible," said Seth. "It's what's *probable* that we need to consider."

"What are you saying?"

"Let's wait'll we get him cut down," said Seth, and Nathan nodded.

While they waited for the JP to arrive, Seth did his photography and Nathan assigned officers to secure the scene, collect evidence from the garage, deflect curious neighbors, and check the house for the possibility of a hiding intruder. After Sam Wilson arrived and checked the body, Seth finally nodded.

"Let's do it," said Nathan.

Seth, the tallest among them, cut the rope. Nathan and Garcia lowered the limp body to the floor. It was heavy, and stank from excrement released at the time of death. Still, it was a seventeen-year-old boy, whose life had once been full of promise. A mother's son. They laid him gently on the cold concrete.

Seth pulled the noose slightly back from the neck. "Just as I thought. See?"

Nathan and Garcia peered over his shoulder. The rope had made the expected burn mark in a slant from his chin up to his ears. But what Seth pointed out to them was *another* rope burn; this one straight around the neck, strangle fashion.

"There's something else," he said. "See this swelling here? There's a little bone in the neck that always breaks during strangulation, but not always from a hanging."

"Right," agreed Nathan. "I can't think of the name of it, but I know the one you mean."

Seth nodded. "Anyway, I think this swelling indicates that the bone was broken. Autopsy will tell for sure. In fact, I think autopsy will show that he asphyxiated, all right, but I think it happened *before* he swung."

"Murder, made to look like suicide?" said Nathan.

Seth shrugged. "I think we ought to look into it, don't you?"

They all turned expectantly to the JP, Sam Wilson, who'd been listening thoughtfully to their conversation. "I don't know, guys," he said. "Looks pretty clear-cut to me."

Nathan felt his neck beginning to stiffen. "What looks clear-cut?"

Wilson clasped his hands behind his back and rocked on his heels. "You got no sign of forced entry. You got no sign of struggle. You got a kid with a whole list of people who can tell you how screwed up he was. Hell, it looks like suicide to me. I see no reason to order an autopsy."

"*What?*" sputtered Nathan and Seth together. "Sam, if this were Dallas, there'd be an automatic autopsy," said Nathan. "They do postmortems on any unexplained or sudden deaths, especially on a kid this young."

Wilson puffed out his chest and said, "But this ain't Dallas, is it? It's up to me to order the autopsy, and I don't think one is required." He turned to leave.

"Wait." Seth's voice boomed in the cavernous garage. "What if we talked to the DA?"

"What if you did?" Wilson's face was reddening. "Only a district judge can overrule my decision."

"But what if the DA agreed with us?" persisted Seth. "Would you go along with it then?"

Wilson rocked on his heels some more, staring at his shoes. Finally he said, "Okay. Ask the DA. If she thinks an autopsy is needed, we'll do an autopsy. If she doesn't, we won't. Fair?"

The men nodded. "Fair," said Seth.

But Nathan had already turned away. Privately, to Seth, he said, "I want you to see about getting us a search warrant. Do me a favor first, though. Call up Kate McCall for me." He fished through his wallet for her card. "Here. Ask her to tell you what we need to be looking for around here as evidence of a ritual crime."

Seth blinked. "Are you kidding?"

Nathan sighed heavily. "God, I wish I was."

While Garcia spoke to the ambulance attendant, Nathan had one short, whispered conversation with Dani. Glancing toward the other officers, he said, "Didn't you say you came over to see Adam's parents because you were worried about him?"

"No. I said—"

"And you let yourself in the back door because he led you to believe they were expecting you, and you were told that most visitors used the back door, isn't that right?"

Dani's eyes widened.

Nathan murmured, "This case is complicated enough. I don't want to see you lose your job."

She stared at him, nodded. After a moment, she said, "It's true that I had no idea his parents were out of town."

With a cursory nod, he left her and went into the kitchen, where a weeping neighbor lady had made coffee. He poured some for himself and Dani and returned to the den, just as Seth left the ambulance attendant.

Nathan's stomach was queasy. He had just led a witness, which amounted to obstruction of justice. He could lose *his* job. But if Dani told the truth about Adam's cult involvement, about *her* involvement as well, she'd be fired so fast there wouldn't be time to pack her pencils. Maplewood was a small, peaceful town. Whispered rumors would run rampant.

Nathan gestured Dani over to the couch, flipped open his notebook, and asked her to tell him what had happened. Garcia also took notes.

Pressing her palms together, Dani looked at her hands. "Adam used to be a brilliant student," she said. "He had an IQ of 140, and he used to make straight A's. Last year, he went into a sharp decline, and had to be put in my remedial English class." She hesitated, rubbing her eyes. "Ever since school started this year, he's been more erratic in his performance, absent more often, and hostile toward his teachers. Last week, I noticed a dramatic change. He'd— had some sort of accident with his hand. He was depressed. He appeared to be on drugs. I decided to talk to . . . his parents about it—along with him, you understand."

Nathan gave her a reassuring smile.

"I caught up with him in the parking lot after school today and told him that I was coming by his house tonight. He told me to come in the back door." She swallowed. "I had no idea his parents were out of town."

"I thought you said earlier that you knew his parents weren't going to be here," said Garcia.

She didn't even blink. "I was so upset then. I must have gotten my words reversed."

Nathan kept his expression carefully neutral. "Why did you come on into the house?" continued Garcia.

"I called, and the door was open. I thought maybe he—they hadn't heard me."

"Why not? Was the TV on?"

"No. But . . . it's a big house."

"Okay. So then what happened?"

Nathan let out his pent-up breath slowly. Dani described going into the kitchen, finding Adam's room, seeing the door leading to the garage ajar. "By this time I knew something was wrong. It was obvious that the house was empty, but I had this feeling that something was *terribly* wrong. The way Adam's been lately, I had no idea what to expect."

When she got to the part about finding the body, a slow tear slid from the corner of her eye and down her cheek. It was all Nathan could do not to brush it away with his thumb.

Garcia asked, "Why did you say earlier that this was all your fault?"

"Because I had known for weeks that Adam was in some kind of trouble, but I waited too long to act on it." She curled her small hands into fists and beat them against her knees. "*Dammit!* If only I'd spoken to him sooner . . ."

"You can't blame yourself," Nathan said.

She got up and walked away from them, pacing back and forth. "I just can't understand why he killed himself. He told me to come. Why would he do that if—" She bit her lip.

"Do you have any idea what was bothering Adam?" prompted Garcia.

Dani stared into space, as if the men weren't there. "He was afraid," she whispered.

"Of what?" Nathan leaned forward sharply.

"That's what I came to find out," she said. "And I was too late."

At Nathan's request, Lilith Douglas came to the house to hear them out. Dani had already left, followed by a young rookie who'd been ordered to see to it that she got home safely and to check out her house before leaving her.

With Sam Wilson strutting along behind her, Lilith thoughtfully examined the scene of the hanging, Adam's pathetic body, then looked around his garish room without touching anything. After each had presented his case to her, she walked over to the sliding glass door which still stood ajar as Dani had found it and stared out at the pool, softly shimmering under its night-lights.

"I'm sorry, gentlemen," she said at last, turning apologetically toward Nathan. "I'm going to have to concur with Mr. Wilson." The pudgy little man gave them all a superior smile.

"Lilith! How can you say that?" Nathan demanded.

"I just don't see enough evidence to indicate homicide."

"But that's what the autopsy would show."

"The autopsy would not show anything conclusive, Nathan. Simply because there are two ligature marks on his neck—or even the broken bone—does not necessarily indicate homicide. He could have tried to hang himself from a prone position, say, underneath a table, and it didn't work. Or maybe it was too easy to chicken out that way."

Nathan shook his head.

"You've got a seriously disturbed young man—at the peak age, I might remind you, for suicide—who was becoming increasingly alienated from friends, teachers, and, I'm sure we will find, his parents. His room is a virtual monument to death. Unless you can come up with a clear suspect, Nathan, I see no reason to put his parents through the fear and agony of a homicide investigation."

For the third time in a month, Nathan tasted the sheer frustration of being alone with his doubts.

"What's going on, Bulldog?" asked Seth as Lilith drove away. Nathan was leaning into his hands against the fireplace mantel.

"That kid was dipping into some pretty wicked stuff," Nathan said, still preoccupied with worry over Dani. He wanted so much to talk to her, find out what *really* happened, but he couldn't. Not yet, anyway. If the lieutenant found out . . . "I'm afraid that whoever killed him might come after Dani."

"So you're pretty sure he was murdered."

"Aren't you?"

"Well, I usually like to go on my first impulses, but Lilith had a few good points."

Nathan told him about Kate and her comments that Adam

was dangerous; possibly even mixed up with an adult group. After a while, Seth nodded. "Well, then, I think it's time we went over that kid's room with a fine-tooth comb."

When they walked in the room, Seth let out a long, low whistle between his teeth. "Hey—ever notice how there are never any poor black kids involved in this shit?"

"What do they need it for?" teased Nathan. "They got gangs."

Seth traced a signal for "two points" in the air, and they got to work.

Adam Prescott had made very little effort to hide his involvement in satanism. Apparently he had little to fear from his parents. Maybe, thought Nathan grimly, it was the other way around.

Thumbtacked over his desk were a couple of ornate and intricate drawings depicting stylized versions of tortured images—Salvador Dali gone mad. Along with the hideous-looking band members pictured on the posters, and the gruesome music, Adam had preoccupied himself with all that was black about life: death, destruction, violence, and hatred. From an old *Life* magazine he'd torn photos of Nazi death camps and pinned them up over his bed. There were similar pictures of Hiroshima after the bomb, and the Jonestown mass deaths in Guyana.

Nathan felt claustrophobic. He tried to take a deep breath, but his lungs seemed unable to expand.

Seth pulled a cardboard box out of the closet and withdrew a long, black-hooded robe from it. Underneath the robe lay a *Satanic Bible* and a copy of *Necronomicon (Book of the Dead)*. Opening up the "Bible," Seth scanned a few pages, whistled again, and dumped it back into the box as if it had burned his hands.

Nathan found a lit textbook open to Dante's *Inferno*. A passage from Canto Thirty-four was underlined:

> *That emperor, who sways the realm of sorrow* . . .
> *Stood forth* . . . *Well from him*
> *May all our misery flow.*

Dani had said they were studying the *Inferno* in class. Nathan wondered if he should ask her about that passage. He was about to make a note of it when Seth chuckled, a macabre sound in their present surroundings. Nathan turned.

"I'll be damned," said Seth. "A name-the-baby book. This guy was *really* weird."

Nathan shook his head. The book, with its pleasant picture of a smiling baby, was too happy-looking for this place. He turned back to the desk. What had he been about to do?

"Kate said to check the refrigerator," said Seth. "Be right back." A few minutes later he came rushing back into the room. "You *won't believe this,* man. I found it at the back of the refrigerator." He held up a Tupperware container with a piece of adhesive on it that bore the legend "Adam's Jalapeños." Stepping into the room with a flourish, he removed the plastic lid.

Nathan drew near. "Dear Jesus. Is that what I think it is?"

Inside the container were four carefully stoppered glass vials filled with wine-red fluid.

The hamburger in Nathan's stomach congealed and rolled over. He could taste some of it at the back of his throat.

"Kate was right! I thought she was crazy," sputtered Seth. "She told me to look for this."

Dani had mentioned to Nathan that Adam was rumored to drink blood in front of his classmates. Could this be evidence of that? He swallowed nervously.

For a long moment, neither spoke. They'd never seen anything like it.

"Let's get it tested," Nathan heard himself saying in a high, hollow voice. "I want to find out if it's animal blood or . . ." His voice faltered. He stared into Seth's eyes, which were white all around the irises. "If this is human blood," continued Nathan, "then I want to know where it came from." The hamburger was a cold ball of clay in the pit of his stomach.

"Those cases have been solved, Bulldog," Seth said, but his conviction was weak.

"There's a connection between this room and those women and you know it."

Seth broke eye contact. "I don't know any such thing. I know this kid was fucked up. I know two women were murdered and the husband of one confessed to it. I know her blood was all over his car. I *don't* know that it had a goddamned thing to do with this fucked-up kid." His voice was rising.

"I want the blood tested."

"Fine. Have it tested. Even if it's human, and even if the type's the same as theirs, that does not, repeat, *does not* prove that it *came from those women*."

"For Christ's sake, Seth, this . . . vampire in Levi's . . . knew that Dani was on her way over here. He knew his folks were out of town. He told her to come in the back way. If that kid was murdered, then somebody else knew it, too! All I know for sure is that the kid's dead now and she's in danger and I can't do a good goddamn thing about it!" He was screaming and Seth's mouth was open and he had no idea how it had come to this. Ashamed of himself, he turned away.

Seth put one huge hand on his tense shoulder. "Get a grip, Bulldog."

He nodded. His stomach was roiling.

"Let's take this stuff into evidence," said Seth. "There's not much more we can do here tonight, especially with the parents still gone. We'll go back to the department, make out a report. This may not be an *official* homicide investigation, but I think there is sufficient doubt to warrant our handling the case for the time being, no matter what the JP or DA says about it."

Nathan turned back to Seth. "Sorry," was all he could muster.

"Don't worry about it. But I do think you're way too involved with this. Back off for a while. I'll take care of it."

Nathan nodded. For a time, they worked as a silent team, bagging the things from Adam's room they thought pertinent and making out evidence tags and filling out an evidence log. Moving mechanically, all Nathan could think about was Dani . . . Dani reporting the mutilated body at the Palmer

estate . . . Dani getting notes in her mailbox when women
were murdered . . . Dani's dog having his ear chopped off
while she slept in the other room . . . Dani coming here,
tonight, to meet with someone who kept a supply of blood in
his refrigerator.

Blood to drink?

As soon as Seth made his way out to the car with armfuls
of evidence to impound, Nathan bolted down the hall and
around corners, searching frantically until, at last, he shut
himself up into a room and emptied his stomach of its
turmoil.

If you want to keep your job, Sergeant, Lieutenant Ward
had said, *you'll stay away from that woman.*

What was his job really worth?

Flushing the toilet, Nathan bent over the sink, splashed
cool water on his face, and rinsed his mouth. The wall-to-
wall mirrors reflected a haggard, distraught man. He
splashed some more water over his face, took a few deep
breaths, arranged his expression into calmer lines, and
studied the image.

A perverse thought popped into his mind: *"Evil" is "live"
spelled backward.* He grimaced at himself.

How could Dani continue to *live* when there was so much
evil surrounding her?

Chapter 27 ～～～～～～

Dani shifted her weight in the seat of her car, snapped on the overhead light, and checked her watch. After midnight. Turning off the light, she rubbed a spot in the window next to her which had become fogged by her breath and looked out. Cold dark shadows moved underneath the trees, but she trusted the dogs. As long as no dogs barked, she figured she was alone. She made a cup of her hands and blew into them. The car was cold and cramped but she had nowhere else to go.

It didn't matter. No matter where she looked, whether she closed her eyes or opened them, she could still see Adam's body, swaying back and forth from shadow to light, his face, in death, filled with more sadness than she had ever seen during his brief life. All his swaggering bravado, then, had just been a bluff, a disguise for his own sadness.

Death knew no disguises.

But why? *Why?* The word beat a constant refrain in her mind. Why would he seem ready to see her, to talk to her, and then take his own life? It didn't make any sense.

With a sigh, Dani stretched her thin jacket closer over her body. The shock of finding Adam had electrified her, cleared the haze from her thinking. Seeing Nathan again had only clarified a decision that she'd made during the quiet confusion of sitting and waiting while police officers and emergency technicians examined the scene. Or maybe she'd made it sooner—maybe the day he walked out. It took something like this to drive it home.

Fool. She'd been a fool. Life was too, too short for her

kind of foolishness. With evil all around her, she'd rejected the one truly good thing that had happened to her since finding the woman's body at the Palmer estate. It seemed so very long ago, and yet it was only a few weeks.

Wasted time.

Time was too precious. She wasn't going to waste any more of it.

Bright light filled the car as another automobile topped the hill and shone its headlights into her sanctuary. She squinted into them. No way of telling.

The lights slowed, grew brighter, the rumble of an engine came to her. Her heart began to pound and she bit her lip. Dogs began to bark, some in loud bays, some in short yips, others in short spurts of warning.

The lights were blinding now. As the car turned and pulled in beside her, she shaded her eyes. A flood of dogs came bounding out from around the house, and she knew it was the right car because they were all wagging their tails. A little jolt of excitement shivered through her body. Shouldering her bag, she got out of her car and threaded her way through the dogs.

He was already out of the car, standing bewildered, absently patting first this dog's head, then that.

"What are you doing here?" Nathan asked.

She didn't speak, but pushed through the animals, slid her arms around his neck, pulled his head down, and kissed him, hard and long. He grasped her to him in a fierce embrace.

His voice, when he spoke, was rough. "God, I was sick with worry. I went by your house after work, and when you didn't answer . . ."

"Sh-sh-sh. Let's go in."

Arm in arm, they climbed the wooden steps of his front porch. He unlocked and held open the door for her. "Leave the dogs outside," she insisted. With a puzzled quirk of an eyebrow, he complied.

"Geez, it's cold in here," he said, once they were in the living room, and hurried over to the fireplace, where he built a strong crackling fire.

When he turned back to her, she stood naked before him.

He didn't touch her. It was as if he feared that she was so fragile she would shatter.

"Dani . . . what are you doing? Are you sure?" He tried to look her in the eye, but he couldn't prevent himself from staring down at her body, then back up.

She did not flinch at his gaze. Her heart clamored for her to say all the things in her mind: *I love you. I need you. I want you.* Yet some immensely frustrating perversity kept her from it. Instead she stood mute before him, offering herself to him as a precious gift, hoping that what she couldn't *say* just yet, she could *show*.

Tentatively he reached out a finger and traced a circle around the nipple of her right breast. The nipple stiffened. She caught his hand in hers, raised the fingers to her lips, and licked them.

She could feel him tremble.

She stepped forward, pushing his crisp hair back with her hand, tugging on it, pulling him into her. As she began to unbutton his shirt, she could feel goose bumps on his chest. He took off his holster and laid it aside. When he reached for his belt buckle, she stopped him. "Let me."

Pressing her breasts against him, she unfastened the belt buckle, unzipped the bulging pants, slipped her fingers underneath the waistband of his underwear, maneuvered them down over his hardness, and let pants and underwear fall.

All over, her hands massaged his body, the muscles in his back, his chest, his abdomen; his powerful erection. Nathan moaned.

She kissed him, his eyes and cheeks and forehead. She licked his lips. He crushed her to him, devouring her mouth, but she pulled away and began a series of tiny nipping bites, along his shoulders, over his chest, down his abdomen, to his straining member.

Nathan cried out, tangled his hands in her hair, pulled her head into him.

Pressing her hands firmly against his shoulders until he lay prostrate before the fire, she straddled him, arching her back until her firm round breasts pointed upward, and she worked him, sitting high on her knees, then plunging down the full shaft of him until his eyes rolled and his head lolled back, first slowly, then faster and faster as his head thrashed from side to side and he made guttural animal cries and then a shout, curling his head up into her breasts as his fierce heat spurted into her and his head fell back as though he were drugged.

After a time, she pulled gently away and stretched herself the full length of him, giggling as a kitten walked over her bare feet. He pulled her close. Eventually he said, "You are the most incredible, amazing, beautiful, exciting, *weird* woman I have ever known. I never know what to expect from you. I figured you'd be a basket case after what happened today."

"Let's just say it made me think."

"What about?"

She cuddled closer. "I don't want to talk about it yet."

"Okay." After another little silence, he chuckled.

"What?"

"I was thinking what Ward would say if he could see me now."

"Who's Ward?"

"My lieutenant. He told me to stay away from you."

She pushed up on one elbow, looking down at his face in the mellow half-light of the fire. "Why?"

"Your connection to these homicides, for one. It could compromise the investigation."

"Oh, Nathan, I'm sorry. I didn't know. I'd better leave—" She made to get up, but he held her fast.

"Oh, no. Not on your life. You're not going anywhere."

"I don't want to get you into trouble."

"You let me worry about that."

She settled back down in the crook of his arm.

"Dani, what brought you here tonight? I mean, what made you decide to . . ."

She thought for a moment. "I'm not sure," she said slowly. "When the officer left tonight, my house was so empty and strange. All I could think about was you. I couldn't *function* without seeing you." She sighed. "I don't remember one certain moment when I thought, 'This is what I'm going to do.' I just started putting some things in my tote and left and when I got here, it . . . it was like coming home."

He sat up, bent over her, and said, "Dani, I want this to *be* your home."

"What are you saying?"

He scratched his head. "I don't know. Maybe I'm proposing."

"*Maybe?*"

"Well, I . . . I don't want to be without you anymore. I can't hack it. That's all."

"Nathan . . ." Dani turned her head and studied the fire for a moment. He caught the warning in her tone and busied himself removing his shoes and pants. Then he reached for an afghan which was draped over the couch and settled it over them like a pup tent, but he didn't lie back down. He waited, watching her. From the shadowy corners, more cats crept closer to them.

"What?" he prompted. "What'd I do wrong now?"

"Nothing. It's just . . . I'm not ready yet to make any kind of commitment. There is still too much confusion in my life." Absently she stroked the gray cat who had curled up next to her.

"Look, I'm not trying to push you into anything. I know things are screwed up right now. I just don't want to be without you anymore, that's all."

Dani had never seen this man's face more naked and vulnerable. As a cop, he seemed always to have a sort of closed cynicism about him, an unfathomable quality that she'd often wondered about. She could see that he was taking a big risk with her. She wanted so much to be able to take that risk herself, but something still held her back, something indefinable.

More than anything, she wanted him to realize that she was giving everything she was capable of, and that, in time, she hoped to be able to give more. The words she wanted to say gathered in her throat and ached there. Finally she held out her arms again. For the briefest moment, he hesitated. Studying her face, he seemed somewhat satisfied by what he saw, then stretched out beside her, kissing her deeply and exploring her body with his hands.

She responded, furious with herself for her own limitations, yet eager to express her feelings with her body, wanting him to understand what she couldn't say aloud. His touch on her skin was feather-light and brought from her little inarticulate sounds of pleasure. At some point, she quit trying so hard and began concentrating on the delicious sensations his caresses aroused. Her body relaxed, grew languorous. His hands and lips traveled the length of her body, her toes and the insides of her knees, her thighs. Gently he spread her legs and crouched before her, his tongue a hot moist probe of her innermost treasure. At first, struck shy, she pulled away, pushing at his face, but he persisted, breaking down her resistance, her fight to maintain control.

Strange mewing cries filled the air, surprising Dani when she realized they were her own. Never had she known that her body could make her feel this way. She was caught in a whirlpool, slipping, sliding down a soft wet warm tunnel which she could no longer resist. As she began, almost against her will, to thrust against him, he gripped her buttocks in his strong hands and raised her to him. She tossed her head back and forth as honey flowed within her, building, building to an almost unbearable crest, too high . . . it was too much . . . stop, no, don't stop . . . don't stop . . . she was losing control, precious control, losing a part of herself, losing herself, losing . . . something broke loose within with a powerful overwhelming wrench and she wailed as he straddled her and thrust himself within her, catching her rhythm, pounding within her as her body contracted and released, contracted and released, until she could no longer tell where she began and he ended.

She wept.

Underneath the sheltering afghan, next to the warm

blazing fire, she wet his chest with her tears while he held her and stroked her hair.

"I never knew," was all she could say, and then, "Thank you."

"For what?"

"I don't know. For being patient, I guess." What could she say? He had shown her a taste of what it could mean if she took the plunge, risked all, and gave herself to him completely.

So this is what it means to make love, she thought. Because of her terrifying and confusing initiation into sex by her foster parents, Dani had never known what it was *supposed* to be like. And then in her teen years, those Dark Years, she'd put no more value on the sex act than she had on herself.

Eventually she had rejected men altogether, for the most part, never missing the intimacy, protecting herself, taking care not to get hurt anymore.

But here, sheltered and cherished by a man who obviously cared a great deal about her, who accepted her as she was, here she was learning that losing control was not always a bad thing, that giving in to the relationship did not have to be terrifying.

Was learning. Not had learned. It was an ongoing process, incomplete until she made a true commitment, until she spoke her words of love aloud and let them hang in the air between them for him to accept or brush away. It was going to take time.

The astounding thing was: he seemed willing to wait.

She was still marveling at that when, tangled in each other's arms, they fell asleep.

"Dani, I've told you and told you to fill out your scholarship form, or you won't be able to go to college and then we can't let you teach here anymore." Mr. Weams's smile was sly.

Dani was confused. "I thought you wanted Adam to get the scholarship."

His lips curled. "Adam's dead. Now it's your turn."

Dani opened her eyes. The fire was out, the room suffused by a soft golden glow. Something heavy pressed against her stomach. She raised her head. The fluffy gray cat blinked at her with large benign green eyes. She smiled and scratched its throat and was rewarded with a rumbling stomach massage.

For a moment, she held the disturbing image in her mind of Mr. Weams's sneaky smile and the words "*Adam's dead. Now it's your turn.*"

Like most of her dream-pictures, it wasn't pleasant.

Awkwardly she pushed herself into a sitting position. With a slight annoyed mew, the cat stalked off, tail up. A blanket had been added to the afghan, and Dani pulled it around her nakedness. She thought about her behavior the night before, and flushed hotly.

"I never saw anybody look so pretty first thing in the morning." Showered, dressed, and grinning like a kid at a carnival, Nathan stood before her with a cup of steaming coffee in his hand. "Or I should say, afternoon."

"What time is it?"

"Like I said. After noon."

"Oh, my God! I've got to get to work." She leapt up, fumbling at her blanket.

He tilted his head, watching her while she scrambled for her clothes. Taking a sip of coffee, he said, "Won't be too many kids there on a Saturday, will there?"

She stared at him, dropped her clothes, and mumbled, "Sometimes I wonder if I really *am* crazy."

"Crazy about me, I hope." He handed her his cup. "Hey, last night . . . you blew me away, lady."

"I don't know what got into me." She made a modest toga of the blanket.

"Whatever it was, I liked it." His eyes were warm and sincere. "I wanted you to know that it was, well, special."

"I bet you say that to all the girls." But she was pleased.

With a wink and a smile, he went to fetch a fresh cup of coffee.

Gathering up her tote and yesterday's clothes, she shut herself into a bathroom that was cluttered in a manly way but not unclean. The water was good and hot, so she helped herself to a shower, giving herself time to think before talking to Nathan again. She was still a little embarrassed about the night before, surprisingly modest about her nudity in front of him in the light of day. Silly, under the circumstances, but she was still getting used to the idea of total abandonment.

Pulling on a soft red sweater over jeans, she brushed her hair and her teeth and felt immeasurably better. She went in search of him and found him in the kitchen, frying up a couple of small steaks. The smell made her realize she was starving.

"Feel better?"

"Much." She went to him and he squeezed her to him with one arm, giving her a smack on the lips.

"I hope you're not the type to go running down the street at the sight of a little teensy-weensy bit of cholesterol," he said, dolloping milk and flour into the grease and stirring it into gravy.

"Only if I'm at the school cafeteria." As she began putting plates and silverware on the table, he pulled a pan of homemade biscuits out of the oven. "You say *I'm* surprising?" she teased.

He turned, one oven-mitted hand holding a wooden spoon. "Don't tell me you're going to be a female chauvinist pig and accuse me of not being able to cook?"

"Wouldn't dream of it."

His eyes alight, he smiled at her, and she busied herself with napkins, bewildered by the sudden rush of fear that gripped her. *This is what happiness is,* she thought. She couldn't trust it. She was too terrified of losing it.

He came up behind her, touched her shoulder. "What's the matter?"

"I don't know. I'm afraid to be happy, I guess."

He put his arms around her. "That comes from living in the future. The key to being happy is to live in the *now*. Seize the day!" He clowned with the spoon, twirling it like a baton. "Right now, things are great. Don't worry. Be happy." Releasing her, he began setting food on the table, whistling as he did so, tripping unconcernedly over cats and the "inside" dogs who hovered nearby, begging handouts.

The chicken-fried steak and cream gravy were the best Dani had ever eaten and she told him so. Still living in his "now," he was pleased, but she was beginning to slide into the past. Finally she said, "I can't stop thinking about Adam."

He nodded. "I know. But you just have to put it out of your mind. There wasn't anything you could have done, Dani."

"You don't understand." She told him everything, even fetching her teacher's manual from her tote and showing him the quote which had been underlined. "I'm ashamed that I feel almost worse about not getting information from him than I do about his death."

"It's not like the kid was all that lovable." Nathan shrugged. "That reminds me, there was a passage underlined in his copy of the *Inferno* in his room," Nathan told her. "Let me see if I can find it." While he searched through the pages of the book, Dani cleared the table. "This is a really boring poem, you know," he said with a grin. "Ah, here it is—the one about some emperor causing all the misery."

She read it.

"What do you make of it?"

Tapping the page with her finger, she said, "I've been doing a lot of reading on this ever since I started researching the meaning of my tattoo. These cults usually have a leader, called a High Priest or a High Priestess. Maybe Adam was referring to that." She handed him the cryptogram. "This is another message that was slipped into my mail slot the other day. Kate helped me figure it out."

He studied it. "What does it mean?"

"I'm guessing it's more references to the cult." She told him about her visit to Austin, and when she got to the part about her foster parents being sent to prison, he sat up ramrod straight. "Now we're getting somewhere," he said. "Give me their names and I'll run a check."

"I don't have their names. The lawyer wouldn't give them out."

"Don't worry about it. I can find out. What else have you got?"

Sponging off the table, she said, "Nothing specific. It's only an idea. I had this weird dream last night." She told him about it.

"So you think it's your turn to die. Makes sense."

She shook her head. "No. I think he was talking about the *scholarship*. I've been thinking about it again, after my principal made such a fuss for me to recommend Adam."

"For a *scholarship*?"

"The same one *I* got, as a matter of fact. You know, for promising students who don't necessarily have great grades." She shrugged. "It's probably nothing."

Nathan got up, helped stack the dishes. "No. What we've *got* is nothing. Two murdered women, a murdered kid—"

"*Murdered?*" Dani faced Nathan, sponge dripping, and read the look on his face. It said, *Whoops. I should have kept my big mouth shut.* "I thought he killed himself."

He turned away, ran water in the sink.

"*Nathan.*"

"I shouldn't be talking about this with you, Dani."

"So? According to your lieutenant, you shouldn't be talking to me at all. Please. I have to know."

He sighed. "We think Adam may have been murdered, and it was rigged up to look like suicide."

She stared at him, swallowed. "But why? *Why?*"

"Sit down." Nathan guided her to a chair, sat next to her. "Kate has been showing me some stuff, talking to me about this cult business. I think there may be something to it."

She tilted her head back, regarded him under her lashes. "I've been telling you that all along."

He flushed and went back to the sink. Her cheeks burned. Maybe *this* was why she couldn't seem to make a solid commitment. It was a matter of trust. He hadn't trusted her.

Maybe she hadn't trusted *him*.

Maybe she still didn't, not completely.

"Anyway," he said, splashing around with the dishes, "somebody didn't want Adam to talk to you."

"But how could anybody know?"

"I'm not sure. It could be the kid's been followed. Somebody might have seen the two of you in the parking lot. With a little . . . persuasion . . . I'm sure they were able to convince him to tell them you were coming." He pursed his lips. "Poor kid's days were numbered, anyway."

A pure, hot anger seized Dani with such sudden ferocity that she hurled an empty coffee cup across the room, where it smashed into the wall, sending shards of crockery and startled animals in a scatter.

"*What the hell, Dani!*"

Chest heaving, she shouted, "*It always comes back to me!*"

"That's not true. That boy was doomed long before you came into the picture. He was destroying himself."

Crestfallen, she looked down at her hands. "Why does he keep tormenting me? What does he want with me?"

"Who?"

"Him. *Him.*"

Drying his hands on a dish towel, Nathan came and stood before her. "Who do you mean? Tell me."

She sighed. "You'll think I'm crazy."

With a short, angry gesture, he balled up the towel and tossed it aside. "You wouldn't be here if I thought that."

She looked into his eyes and knew it was true. Gathering her courage, she said, "There's someone . . . I don't know who . . . but he hates me. He always has. All my life. He doesn't just want to kill me. He wants to torture me."

He regarded her seriously. "Who do you think it might be?"

"I don't know. Maybe my foster father, but I don't think so."

"Why not?"

"A feeling, that's all."

"Who else do you think it could be?"

Dani looked away from Nathan, into a place where no

one else could follow. Her voice grew quiet. "I don't know his name, but he is my enemy. He is the opposite of everything good that ever happened in my life, or ever will happen. He likes to play games. He knows it torments me, and it amuses him."

Her voice was a monotone, so quiet Nathan had to lean forward to hear her. "He is everything I have ever feared in my life, and he won't be happy until he destroys me."

Chapter 28 ～～～～～

Dani's face, as she talked about her "enemy," appeared to be in a hypnotic trance. Every time she went off the deep end like that, Nathan determined to yank her back into reality.

"Hey." He stood directly in front of her, forcing her to look up. "I'm not going to let anything happen to you. Nobody's going to destroy you as long as I'm around."

He thought she'd do something like sag against him, all relieved and happy to have someone take care of her. Instead, she laughed. It was a brittle, unconvincing laugh.

"Oh, Nathan," she said. "You're so naive."

"Naive? I'll have you know I've been called a lot of things in my time, lady, but *naive* isn't one of them."

"Well, where this subject is concerned, you are." Shaking her head, she picked up a broom and began sweeping up the shattered coffee cup. "You think you can just puff yourself all up, be the macho cop, and I'll be protected."

"I'm not talking about being macho—" he protested.

"Yes, you are. And I'm telling you that you are naive if you think that you, and you alone, can keep me from these people if they want to hurt me. You don't understand the power they have."

"Awww, you don't believe in all that 'Satan's power' mumbojumbo, do you?"

She looked up from the broom. "I believe in the power of fear. Cult members are bound together by it."

"Fear of what? Cops?"

229

"No. Fear of *each other*. From what I've read, some cults require not only a vow of loyalty, but a photograph of the new member, plus names and addresses of family members. If a member fails to obey the High Priest or Priestess, his family is in immediate danger."

Suddenly an unbidden image sprang into Nathan's mind: the terror-twisted face of Mac MacIntire in the county jail. *Just get my kids out of this town*, he'd said. *They'll find out I was talking to you*.

Kate McCall had said Mac was probably a fall guy for the cult, designated to assume the guilt for their crimes.

It was all starting to make sense, but more than anything in the world, Nathan didn't want it to. He'd've much rather had the questions than he would these particular answers.

Watching Dani sweep up and dispose of the cup, Nathan said, "All right. I'll bite. Let's play the 'suppose' game."

"The suppose game?"

"Yeah. Suppose there is a satanic cult in this area which is murdering women as part of a ritual sacrifice. Suppose the High Priest had a cult going back in California and your foster parents were members . . ." Nathan felt a quickening deep within, a signal that he was onto something. He'd felt it often when he discovered the one crucial piece of evidence that cracked a case. "Suppose they were using you in their rituals, and you ratted to the social worker . . . and the High Priest guy went to prison with your foster parents."

"Then he would have a motive to hate me. Revenge," said Dani, who was beginning to look excited herself. "Suppose he's been following me around all these years. Suppose . . ." Her face fell. "That makes no sense, Nathan. If the man wanted to kill me, he could have simply killed me whenever he got out of prison. It's been twenty years since all this happened. Why would he wait this long?"

"I don't know. Maybe he's still in prison. On the other hand, he'd have gotten out long ago. Especially if he was a good little boy."

Dani got them another cup of coffee and they sat down at

the table. "Maybe it took him this long to find me. I was adopted, my name was changed, we moved . . ."

"Still, a private investigator could have tracked you down in a couple of days."

"If he could afford to hire one."

Nathan leaned his elbows on the table. "Let's look at it from another angle. Why would he keep sending you all these little messages? Is that part of the game-playing?"

She shook her head. "I've thought about that. I no longer think it was him sending those messages. Now I'm pretty sure it was Adam."

"What for?"

"To warn me."

"All right. That seems logical. He was afraid to speak to you directly, so he tried to do it indirectly. But the notes didn't always make sense. I mean, he didn't tell you anything that could really help."

"I think he was going to," she said. "But they got to him first." She looked down into her cup.

Something flashed into the periphery of Nathan's mind, but he couldn't think exactly what it was. He frowned, but it was gone.

"Let me show you something." Dani headed for the den and Nathan followed her. From her voluminous tote bag she withdrew a fat file folder. "I wanted you to see this." She handed it to him. Nathan settled himself on the couch and began to read through its contents. When he got to the black drawings of the tiny, armless, mouthless child surrounded by huge hooded figures, he looked over at her where she sat opposite him, small in his oversized chair.

In many ways, she was a child-woman, desperate for love and security, but tough in many other, unexpected ways. There were other choices Dani could have made. She could have found refuge in insanity. She could have checked out through suicide. She could have run away. Instead, she'd come out fighting, facing the pain head-on, looking terror in the eye without blinking.

Nathan had thought he'd been attracted to Dani because

she was so fragile. Now he knew better. Now he knew that
he'd fallen in love with her courage.

With that knowledge came his own decision. He'd join in
the battle. He'd fight with her. Whatever price there was to
pay for that privilege, why, they'd pay it together.

"Okay. Here's the battle plan." Nathan had lit another
fire, and they were sitting cross-legged in front of it,
surrounded by various animal friends. Dani had a shoelace,
and she smiled as the kittens tumbled and frolicked over one
another, trying to get to it. There were only two now. The
white one had gone with the MacIntire children.

Nathan figured he'd get used to looking at her one of
these days, but it didn't seem as if it would be any time
soon. Especially not after last night. He'd never have
expected it of her. With effort, he focused his concentration
on the yellow legal pad in his lap. "I will get in touch with
that lawyer who handled your adoption and get the names of
the principals involved in your case—the ones who went to
jail."

"He might not want to give you the information."

"He will if I tell him it's part of an official police
investigation."

"Just the thought of *hearing* those names ties my stomach
up in knots." She cuddled a kitten.

"You can handle it."

"You think so?"

"I've got no doubt in the world. Okay. Your job is to
check out the scholarship angle."

"It's probably nothing. I mean, somebody who hates me
and wants to get revenge on me is not going to put me
through college."

"You just follow the lead where it takes you. Don't try to
out-logic it. Some things in an investigation often seem
completely unrelated, but they join together at the end."

She brightened. "Like a jigsaw puzzle!"

"Exactly. Now. I'll find out what's going on with the
inquiry into Adam Prescott's death. It's Seth's case, but

he'll tell me whatever I need to know." Nathan frowned again.

"What is it?"

"I don't know. There's something else that I should be remembering, but every time I try to, I blank out."

"Well, one thing I've learned about remembering is that you can't force it. It will come to you, probably when you least expect it."

"True. Next. Nobody knows you're with me—at least as far as we know, they don't. In any case, we'll move your car around back. It's dark there. Lots of trees. You go on to work as usual, but when you start home—or I should say, back here—take a roundabout route, go out of your way, and check the rearview mirror frequently."

"To make sure I'm not being followed."

"Exactly. I don't get home, as you know, until midnight or so. I want to know that you are safe."

"What do I do if I am being followed?"

"Either drive straight to the police department or go to a busy, public place and call me. If I'm not there, talk to Seth or Manny Garcia. They'll send a squad car around."

She nodded slowly, then said, "I'm going to need some more clothes and things, then. I only brought enough for one night."

"No problem. We'll take you to your house after dark and go in the back way. You pick up whatever you need and we'll return here."

She leaned her head back against the couch, and Nathan could see the lines of fatigue around her eyes. He'd seen that kind of emotional strain before, and he hoped for her sake that this whole thing would come to an end soon.

"One more thing."

She sighed wearily. "What?"

"Have you ever handled a shotgun before?"

She sat up straight. "What? No. Never."

"Well, you're going to learn. I want you to keep one loaded and within easy reach at all times while I'm gone. If anybody tries to come near this house, the dogs will give you plenty of warning so that you can be prepared."

"But Nathan! What if I shoot *you*?"

He pondered that for a moment.

"We'll arrange a signal. That way you'll always know it's me."

She nodded, looking doubtful and frightened. He hated the thought of her being alone, especially at night. In spite of what she had said, he couldn't shake the masculine idea that as long as he was around, she would be safe.

He reached for her and pulled her into his lap, cuddling her as she had done the kitten. More than anything else in the world, Nathan wanted to keep Dani safe.

Outside, shadows tiptoed around the corners of the house and gathered together to peer into the windows. Twilight. That dusky time of day when your eyes played tricks on you and everyday things looked sinister.

In Vietnam, he'd always been most frightened at dusk. The day seemed to crouch down then, and grow still, as if waiting to spring at some hapless grunt passing by through the elephant grass. The troops were always more jumpy then, as if they were under siege even if they weren't. Every quivering tree or hulking shadow became a sniper in their minds, ready to snuff out their lives with the oncoming dark.

In Vietnam, you never knew who the enemy was. He could smile in your face one day and lop a grenade in your lap the next.

A smiling enemy, gathering strength with encroaching shadows.

Nathan Kendall understood Dani's fear, could appreciate her "enemy"—who liked to play games, and who could wait patiently for twenty years for revenge.

Darkness crept over the windowsill and moved stealthily across the floor. Wrapped within the warm shelter of his arms, Dani shivered.

Chapter 29 ~~~~~~~~~~

Strange, thought Dani, how a school building seemed to draw life from its inhabitants, as if their restless energy was its own heartbeat, their breathless hallway cries its own oxygen. Within half an hour of the final bell, the school seemed to sigh its last breath, its walls collapsing into the vacuum created by the loss of its soul.

Within one hour of that last sigh, the building would be virtually bereft of life. Janitors took on the job of the mortician, cleaning up the body for public viewing.

Dani waited two hours.

Working alone in her room, catching up on paperwork (which she had sadly neglected in the confusion of recent events), she kept an eye on the clock, ears alert for footsteps or voices. When the grandfatherly janitor entered her room, push broom in hand, she smiled sweetly, made small talk, and asked would he mind terribly leaving the principal's office unlocked, so that she might leave some papers on Mr. Weams's desk before she left for the night? She vowed to lock the door behind her.

One advantage Dani had discovered to being pretty and young-looking was that elderly men always responded to her; they liked to hug her and look after her as if she were a valued granddaughter. It never occurred to them that she could possibly be deceitful. Of course, most of the time she wasn't.

School vandalism and theft hadn't reached the epidemic proportions in this small, conservative town that they had in urban areas, and the janitor was happy to do such a small favor for such a pretty little thing.

She waited.

The building held the stillness of death when she finally emerged from her room, clutching her tote a little too tightly to her body, walking a little too rapidly, her footsteps echoing with a *clickety-click* on the polished floors. The halls were festooned with ghoulish decorations, advertising a Drama Club-sponsored Halloween spookhouse. Lights burned at the ends of each corridor, but the hallways themselves had filled with shadows as dusk drew near outside, crowded closely by night.

She had wanted to be alone, but hadn't counted on the consequences of that aloneness. *Let's play the suppose game,* she thought grimly. *Suppose I'm not alone, after all. Suppose Adam's killer is waiting for me just behind that door.*

Stifling a shudder, she reached for the door to the principal's office and swung it open with as much bravado as she could muster.

It was empty.

Twilight slanted in from windows set high in the wall, revealing no bloodthirsty murderers, but only a long reception bar behind which were cluttered smaller desks for the school secretary and a couple of student assistants. Along one wall was a honeycomb of teachers' message boxes. Out of long habit, Dani withdrew some papers from hers and stuffed them into her tote. Adjacent to the message boxes was a door with a frosted window upon which was painted the word "Principal."

She tried the door. As promised, it was unlocked.

There were no windows. Dani was plunged into shadow. Nervously she flicked on the light. Every movement she made seemed to echo.

Now what?

Taking a shaky breath, Dani deposited her tote on one of the chairs facing the desk and, for want of any other direction, went over to the gray metal file cabinet behind the desk and pulled out the drawer marked "S."

She looked up "Scholarship." She looked up "Select Student."

It was that easy.

Removing the file, Dani sat at Weams's chair and studied the contents. Her recommendation for Jennifer Dawson was there. *So he didn't submit it, after all, the bastard*, Dani thought, then remembered with a strange feeling of relief that Adam Prescott was dead. He'd *have* to submit Jennifer's name now. The thought renewed Dani's hope. Thumbing through the pages, she finally came across a single sheet, describing the scholarship.

A sound.

It was only a barely discernible *click*, like that made when someone shuffles a stack of papers onto a desk to align them. A sound which would have been lost during the busy daysounds of a school building filled with life.

Now it echoed.

Dani raised her head. There, silhouetted against the frosted pane of glass, was the shadow-figure of someone standing just outside the door.

Like a deer caught in onrushing automobile headlights, Dani froze. Even her breathing stopped. For a moment, it seemed as if her very heart ceased beating.

The janitor?

No. He knew she was here. Why would he hover outside?

Night terrors from childhood flashed into her mind: the times when she was so frightened that she lay absolutely still, hoping that her bedroom intruders would think she was dead and go away.

Panic-stricken, she glanced around the room, looking for something, anything, she could use as a weapon.

Nothing.

The room filled with the echo of Dani's own heartbeats. She felt very faint.

The shadow moved away. A moment later came the soft *clunk* of the outer door closing.

Letting out pent-up breath, Dani began to tremble all

over. Her fingers were icy. *It was only the janitor, checking up on you,* she told herself.

So why hadn't he spoken?

He didn't want to bother you.

Yeah. Right.

Okay. If somebody wanted to kill you, he had a perfect opportunity. Don't be so paranoid.

Fumbling with the paper, she forced herself to continue reading. "The Select Student Scholarship is made possible by a grant from the Overman Foundation."

The Overman Foundation? What was that? She'd never heard of it. Maybe Nathan would know. Time to get out of here and find out.

Gathering papers together with shaking hands, Dani returned the file to the cabinet, picked up her tote, and stood for a long moment by the door, waiting. The tension was giving her a headache. Darkness gathered, gaining strength. She had to get out *now*.

Darkness was *his* strength.

With a burst of bravery, she snapped off the light and stepped into the outer office, remembering to lock the door behind her. There was barely enough light from the windows to show that she was alone.

Glancing at the message boxes on her way out, Dani halted, her heart once again hammering painfully in her chest.

There was a new message in her box.

Running like a wild thing before a predator, Dani fled the building and raced to the relative sanctuary of her car. Digging frantically through her tote, she finally located her car keys, then promptly dropped them. Panting, she struggled with the lock, climbed in, then peeled rubber out of the parking lot, driving as if demons were at her heels.

In her panic, she almost forgot Nathan's admonition to take a roundabout way to the cabin, but it was no problem to remember to check her rearview mirror. No one followed.

Ever thoughtful of Dani, Nathan had left all the lights in the cabin ablaze, and had laid a fire in the hearth which she had only to light. Surrounded by a swarm of happy pets, Dani collapsed on the couch and waited for her heart to return to a semblance of normal beating.

The animals soothed her. She stroked various eager heads until calm returned, then she withdrew the message from her tote. It was a passage from the Twenty-fourth Canto of the *Inferno:*

> *. . . already is the moon*
> *beneath our feet:*
> *the time permitted now*
> *Is short; and more, not seen,*
> *remains to see.*

Fear chilled her. She lit Nathan's fire.

Had Adam *not* been sending all the messages from the *Inferno*? Or had . . . whoever . . . learned of Adam's cryptic communications with Dani and adopted them as his own, adding them to the rules of the game which he made up as he went along?

Thinking of Adam reminded her of the cryptogram. She retrieved it from her bottomless tote bag and studied it.

> *Beware the Dark One descending.*
> *The Watchman sees all.*
> *They from the priest's dwelling*
> *Belong to the night.*

Dani had always assumed the message was a simple reference to satanic cults. Now she looked more closely. *Beware the Dark One descending.* Satan?

The Watchman sees all.

Who would that be? Were the Dark One and the Watchman one and the same? Did they refer to Satan, or to the High Priest?

They from the priest's dwelling belong to the night.

Cult members, right?

Why did she have this overpowering feeling that there was more to it than that?

Adam had been a very complex young man. *Nothing* he
ever did was simple.

Dani rubbed her eyes. She was tired and hungry and
discouraged and frightened. Her head ached with frustration. She needed nourishment.

Threading her way through dogs, cats, and kittens, she
went into the kitchen and opened the refrigerator. A bottle
of wine lay on its side next to a large glass bowl filled with
a scrumptious-looking salad. Plastic wrap was stretched
over the bowl. A note rested on the covering. She picked it
up.

*I made what Franz and Hans would call a real girlie-
meal for you. Love, Nathan.*

She laughed, and her heart filled with tenderness for this
considerate man. His reference to the macho weight-lifting
characters on *Saturday Night Live* was just what she needed
to ground her back to the real world.

She fixed herself a tray with a glass of wine and the salad
and carried it into the den, where she ate while watching
TV, a lonely-person habit she'd cultivated through the
years. Afterward she washed her dishes, poured herself
another glass of wine, and settled on the couch with the
affectionate gray cat. For a while, she made plans as to what
she could leave in the refrigerator for Nathan's lunch when
she went to work the next day while he slept from his
late-night shift.

It was nice, thinking about another person.

It was nice, being thought about by another person.

After a while she turned off the TV and went back to the
cryptogram. The phone rang, and as per Nathan's instructions, she let the answering machine get it. No one must
know she was here. It was Nathan. With a little thrill of
delight, she picked up the receiver.

"How ya doin', angel face?"

"All snuggy warm with a friendly gray cat."

"Agatha. She's nosy, but polite."

She giggled. "Agatha?"

"Yeah. As in Christie."

"You and your names."

"Wait 'til I start naming kids."

She smiled. It wasn't an unpleasant thought, having children with Nathan.

"You still there?"

"Absolutely. By the way, you were such a sweetie to leave me supper in the fridge."

"Hans and Franz would call me a girlie-man for doing it."

"I won't tell if you won't."

There was a happy pause. "Find out anything on the scholarship?" he asked.

"Oh, yes. I almost forgot." She hesitated. Should she tell him about her near encounter in the principal's office? No. Not yet. She didn't want to worry him on duty. "It's funded by something called the Overman Foundation."

"I've heard of that. Somewhere."

She waited while he turned it over in his mind.

"I must be gettin' senile in my old age. I keep forgetting everything. I'll check it out, anyway. Oh! I almost forgot, *again*."

"What?"

"What I've been meaning to tell you. Or ask you about, anyway . . . When we were going through stuff in Adam's room, Seth found a name-the-baby book. Like the one you have. It seemed real odd. What do you make of it?"

"A name-the-baby book?" Dani sat up straight. It was *there*—just out of reach. "I'm not sure . . ." Her voice trailed off.

"Well, think about it. We'll talk when I get home. No; I forgot you have to get up so early. Never mind. Go on to bed when you get ready and we'll talk about it in the morning. Wake me up."

"Then *you'll* be tired."

"Nah. I'll just go back to sleep after you leave." His voice dropped to an intimate tone. "In fact . . . wake me up real early, will you? Maybe we'll have time to play before you have to get ready for school."

"My, my, Grandma. What big teeth you have."

He chuckled, and suddenly Dani missed him very much. A disembodied voice over the phone wasn't enough.

"Well, I gotta go. You need me to pick up anything on my way home?"

It was such a domestic question that, for a moment, it threw Dani. She was so used to thinking for herself. What a luxury it would be for someone *else* to bring home milk, or whatever. "Can't think of anything," she said.

"Okay. Hey . . ."

"Yes?"

"I love you."

She swallowed, then mumbled, "Me, too."

It seemed to satisfy him. "Keep the doors locked," he said. "I should be home around midnight. If something keeps me, I'll phone. Otherwise, I'll give the signal before I come in the door."

"All right. I'll probably wait up, anyway."

"See you later, then."

They hung up, and for a long moment, Dani let the reverberations of his voice linger in her mind. Then she went back to the cryptogram.

A name-the-baby book.

Dani sat bolt upright. *Of course!*

In September, when she'd brought her name book to class, the kids had all had a ball, looking up their names, teasing one another, preening if the meaning was especially dignified or heroic, giggling if it was silly.

Adam. What had that meant? She strained to remember. Something about "man of the red earth."

That didn't appear in the cryptogram.

Yet he had a book like hers in his room.

She jumped up and paced the floor, cryptogram grasped in sweaty palms. Some of the words were capitalized, even though they were located in the middle of the sentence. She and Kate had commented on that but hadn't made anything of it.

Adam had constructed the cryptogram. She was sure of that. And he'd never made a careless move in his life.

Names. Dear God, they *had* to be names!

Wrestling with herself, she paced faster. Back and forth. Back and forth. The name book was at her house. She could pick it up after school. Or she could give Nathan a set of her keys and ask him to pick it up for her.

She'd have to wait until tomorrow.

She had the names! All she needed was the damn book. It would only take a few minutes to run over to her house and get it.

In a futile attempt to calm down, Dani switched on the television. Hopeless. She even took a hot shower, but it failed to relax her.

She couldn't wait. She would go mad.

Dressing hurriedly, Dani thought of calling Nathan, but she knew that he would only try and talk her out of it. Tell her to wait. She imagined a conversation with him:

You can't go back to that house, he would say. *They could be waiting there for you.*

But she'd had the locks on the doors changed, she'd say.

What difference does that make? he'd ask. *They could grab you outside.*

True.

She hesitated, impulse struggling against reason. *The time permitted now is short,* the note in her box had said.

Adam had given her the *key,* the last jigsaw puzzle piece. She'd had it in her possession for *days* and she'd squandered it. It might have even cost him his life.

How many more lives would be lost?

Standing in the middle of the living room, her gaze fell to the loaded shotgun, propped next to the front door. Nathan had shown her how to load and shoot it the day before and she'd done surprisingly well. Surprising to her, because she'd discovered that she enjoyed the feeling of power the weapon had given her.

They wouldn't expect her to be armed.

There was one more thing they wouldn't expect . . . for her to figure out their names and turn them in to the law.

A little thrill of excitement coursed through her, the adrenaline of a wild animal, closing in on its prey.

And they thought she was a little quivering bunny rabbit.

He thought she was, anyway. Her enemy who liked to quote from Dante.

He'd find out she had a few quotes of her own.

Dani had been warned that time was short. So she decided not to waste any more of it.

Already is the moon beneath our feet.

Slipping into her shoes, she wondered about that. A full moon was only a few days away, though gathering clouds hid its power from sight.

Her mind was racing, thoughts stumbling onto the heels of each other. Throwing on a jacket, she grabbed her tote and hesitated. Should she leave a note for Nathan?

Of course not. She'd be back in half an hour.

By the time he got home, she'd have all the answers he needed.

Dani sat for a long time in her locked car outside her house, the engine running, her foot on the brake, scouting the neighborhood and studying the front of the house for any signs of occupation or break-in. Nothing appeared to be out of order. Pulling back the hammer on the shotgun and cradling it close, she cut the ignition and withdrew slowly out of the car. Then she moved quickly for the front door and the sanctuary within.

The house was crypt-cold. She hurried through the living room, into the den, straight for the bookcase, and withdrew the book.

An interest, she'd told Nathan. His name meant "a gift, given of God." How true that had been.

She planned to take the book straight back to Nathan's, but standing there in front of the bookcase, she couldn't resist looking up the name "Prescott." Leaning the shotgun against the bookcase right beside her, she rifled through the book.

It meant *from the priest's dwelling.*

With a sharp intake of breath, Dani caught her lip between her teeth. She'd been *right!*

But she didn't know the other names to look up. She'd

have to read through all the meanings listed, and see what the names were that went with them.

Yet, compelled by a *need to know* that, for the time being superseded her fear, Dani found herself flipping through the pages, reading random selections.

Suddenly the words *watchman or guardian* seemed to leap out at her.

She read the name.

"*Oh, my God*," she whispered. "I've got to warn Nathan." Until now, it hadn't occurred to her that Nathan himself could be in terrible danger.

She headed for the phone, then hesitated. If she hurried, she might be able to find all the names. There might be more that Nathan would need to know.

Grabbing a sheet of paper, Dani sat down at the kitchen table, shotgun close to hand, and began scanning the book, front to back. After a few pages, she picked up the knack of it, and it went faster.

She found *belonging to the night* in the girl's section of the book, and stared at it long and hard.

No time to stop. She had to push on.

There it was: *dark one*.

Wait a minute . . . That *couldn't* be right. She'd have *known*, wouldn't she?

Hurrying, her head splitting from the strain, Dani thought for a while that she'd found all she was going to find when she discovered the name for *descender*.

She began to tremble. Pushing up from the chair, she reached for the phone. All she could think about was Nathan.

He wasn't in. Could they take a message?

"Tell him to call home as soon as possible," Dani said.

Leaving the book and the cryptogram on the table, she shoved the list of names into her tote, grabbed the shotgun, and hurried for the front door.

There she halted, and stared at the deceptively innocent sheet of paper resting on the floor. It had been slipped in the mail slot.

Slowly, horror crowding into her throat, Dani picked up

the note. It was another passage from the *Inferno*, this one from the fifth canto:

> . . . *Hinder not his way*
> *By destiny appointed; so 'tis will'd,*
> *Where will and power are one.*

Too late she sensed the presence behind her; too late she whirled, raising the shotgun; too late she felt the weapon being knocked upward; too late the gun went off with a powerful blast, blowing a hole in the ceiling, falling from her grasp; too late she felt the pressure of acrid-smelling cloth over her mouth, the painful grip of iron arms over hers; too late she fought not to breathe in the terrible sickening fumes soaking the cloth; too late she fought.

The last thing she heard was the ringing of the telephone. Too late. Too late.

Chapter 30 〜〜〜〜〜

Nathan waited impatiently for the answering machine to complete its recorded message, then he said, "Hi, babe, it's me." He smiled, awaiting Dani's voice on the pickup. Nothing happened.

"You wanted me to call, so here I am. Calling."

He waited some more.

"Okay, I guess you're in the bathroom or something. I'll be at my desk, oh, about another half hour. Call me back."

For about fifteen minutes, Nathan worked on a report, then glanced at his watch, frowned, studied the telephone. What was keeping her? Must be in the shower.

When the full half hour had passed, he called again, and again received his own impersonal voice.

His chest constricted in alarm. *Don't be paranoid,* he told himself. *Got to be a logical explanation. She's taking a bath or something.*

He waited fifteen more agonizing minutes.

When there was still no answer, Nathan grabbed his coat off the back of the chair and hurried out the door. He didn't even tell anyone where he was going. Along the way, he broke every traffic law in the book as his alarm escalated into panic.

She would not tell him to call as soon as possible unless something was wrong. And she wouldn't let his call go unnoticed unless something was *bad* wrong.

With a splay of gravel, Nathan skidded into the parking area in front of his house and bounded up the stairs, ignoring the ecstatic dogs. He rapped his knuckles on the door three times, then twice, then once, then let himself in.

Everything looked normal. The fire crackled cheerily. A wineglass with a little wine in it rested on the table by the couch.

"Dani?" he called, his voice a little loud with anxiety. When there was no answer, Nathan searched the whole house, then checked the back area. Her car was gone.

Why would she leave the house? She *knew* the danger.

Picking up the phone, Nathan called Dani's house, but all he got was *her* answering machine. Then he spotted the empty space by the door where he'd left the shotgun. *Dani,* he whispered, *what have you done?*

He drove straight to her house.

Her car was not in the drive. The lights were out, the doors locked. Growing more agitated by the moment, Nathan fidgeted on the porch, ringing the doorbell futilely. Just for the hell of it, he decided to check the windows.

In a rear bedroom, he found one with the glass broken out. There was no glass on the ground in front of the window, which meant it had been broken *inward,* and probably used to gain entrance to the house.

Nathan raised the window and climbed in. He felt an immediate sense of unease, and withdrew his revolver from its holster. Movi g cautiously, he went from room to room, turning on lights as he went.

Nothing had been disturbed in the house, neither did anything appear to have been stolen. And yet, standing in the middle of the den, Nathan felt an overwhelming sense of disaster.

He went into the kitchen. There, on the table, was the cryptogram Dani had showed him, and a book.

A name-the-baby book. Like the one Seth had found in Adam's room . . .

She *had* to have been here. There was no other way the cryptogram could have wound up on her kitchen table. Nathan took the book and the message and put them in his coat pocket. Then he went to the phone and called his house again. Still no response from Dani.

There were two messages on her answering machine. One was his own hang-up. The second got his attention:

"Ms. Daniels, this is Richard Miller. I have some more information on your adoption. It's been bothering me that I didn't tell you the whole thing before. I guess I was trying to protect you; or maybe lawyers are simply too used to secrecy. I don't know. Anyway, it's very important that we talk. Call me soon."

Nathan jotted down the phone number. He was intensely curious, but it was more important at the moment to track Dani down and make sure she was safe.

She had come and gone, apparently *after* calling him at the station. Maybe she was on her way back to the cabin right now. He headed for the front door, then froze. An ominous feeling of dread settled over him. Hand on his holster, he looked around. White powder and bits of plasterboard littered the carpet. Nathan looked up.

The hairs on the back of Nathan's neck bristled. He knew a close-range shotgun blast when he saw it.

Oh, God. One blast to the ceiling. No blood. No sign of the weapon, its user, or its intended target.

He hurried out the front door, locking it behind him.

All the way back to the cabin, Nathan grappled with his fear. Something terrible had happened to Dani. He *knew* it, and yet he didn't want to believe it. Not yet. Not till he had checked the cabin.

But the cabin was empty.

Collapsing on the couch, Nathan put his face in his hands. Tears of sheer frustration and panic prickled his lashes. He rubbed his eyes roughly and, elbows on knees, stared at the floor.

He had tried to protect her, and he had failed.

For the first time in his fourteen years as a cop, Nathan didn't know what to do or where to turn.

She was gone, and he had no earthly idea where to look for her.

He couldn't put out an APB on a grown woman who'd only been missing a couple of hours. Even the hole in Dani's ceiling was not necessarily evidence that a crime had been committed, especially since there was no blood or even signs of a struggle.

Somehow, they'd gotten to her. And he was emasculated, totally unable to protect her. A helpless shudder passed through Nathan's body.

"Goddammit. Goddammit. Goddammit," he murmured, rocking back and forth on his elbows, face buried in his hands. He thought about the woman in the morgue, whose breasts had been sliced off scalpel-clean, but whose vagina had been torn to pieces.

For a few moments, he gave into the panic, sobbing out his grief and frustration and helplessness. Sympathetic animals gathered around, offering mute comfort, and by sheer force of iron will, Nathan pulled himself together. He'd be no good to Dani like this.

Nathan wasn't much of a praying man, but for a long moment, he bowed his head, asking only direction and strength for himself and courage for Dani. Then he raised his head.

He had to think.

In the kitchen, he reached to the top of a cabinet and withdrew a bottle of Weller's whiskey. He took a strong shot. Then he sat down at the table. The whiskey burned his throat and warmed his belly. He took another shot, but only one. He had no intention of getting drunk.

One thing police work had taught him was the value of working together with other people as a unit, responding to crises as with a single mind, each depending on his own peculiar strengths and making up for his partner's weaknesses, and vice versa.

What Nathan needed was a team.

Dani had said that he, alone, would not be enough to fight. She was right.

Now that he was motivated and focused, Nathan was calm. He went straight for the phone, where he called in to the department to say that he would be checking out early, due to a family emergency. Then he sat down and began to assemble his team. He made a few more phone calls, put on a pot of coffee, gathered together some legal pads and pencils, and waited.

Kate McCall was the first one to arrive. She was all wrapped up in a complicated-looking poncho, and she carried a large, square Tupperware container in her arms.

"Homemade cinnamon rolls and cookies," she explained. "People think better when they're not hungry. Kitchen back here?" She brushed past a bemused Nathan and made her way to that room. "My goodness, you've got a regular menagerie, don't you?" Setting the container on the table, she leaned over to pat whichever heads were thrust to her. The sheltie, Joe Friday, held back in his usual shy way.

Nathan leaned against the kitchen counter and watched her. "If you don't mind," she said, "I'll make myself right at home." He had to smile. Unlike some men, Nathan didn't mind take-charge women, as long as they didn't insist on exhaustive power struggles over every little issue.

Miraculously Kate produced a serving platter he'd inherited from Roxanne and had forgotten he even had. In a jiffy she'd arranged her baked goodies attractively on the platter and had brewed up hot water for some herbal tea she'd brought along. "There's plenty, if you think anyone else would like some," she told him, then pushed past him again to lay the things out on the coffee table in the den.

Before he knew what had hit him, he was sipping coffee in front of the fire with Kate and her tea. The aroma from the rolls and cookies was wonderful, but he was afraid his nervous stomach would revolt even at the thought of eating just yet.

"I love this house," she said. "It's so masculine, yet still inviting to a woman. Comfortable. Dani said you built it with your own hands. You can feel that, in a house. It's a loving touch."

At the mention of Dani's name, Nathan's anxiety rushed in, like the huge tigers that bounded into a circus arena. Like the trainer, he could control that tiger, but he could never turn his back on it.

In a move that surprised him, Kate got up from the couch, came over to him, and took his hand in hers. "You're doing the right thing," she told him. "Just hang in there. We're going to find her."

She had a maternal presence about her, an earth-mother manner that was not altogether unpleasant. He squeezed her hand. "You sure about that?" he asked.

She squeezed back. "As sure as I am in the power of prayer." She returned to the couch.

There was a sharp knock at the door. Glancing out the window first, Nathan opened it. Seth Rollins stood on the porch. "You gotta do something about these attack dogs," drawled Seth. "They 'bout beat me to death with their waggin' tails."

For the first time that night, Nathan broke into a grin. It might not look like much, but he figured he'd assembled one hell of a team.

While Seth dove into Kate's tasty treats, Nathan told them everything, from the first day he'd met Dani and investigated her report of finding a mutilated woman's body at the Palmer estate, to Lieutenant Ward's order that he keep away from her, to his decision to shelter her, and why. He made no secret of the fact that he'd fallen in love with her—that wouldn't have been possible—but he gave them his professional assessment of the situation as well.

Though Kate knew most of the story, nearly all of it was new to Seth, and because of his esteem for Nathan, he gave it a respectful listening. When Nathan was finished, Kate asked to see the cryptogram and the name-the-baby book. He gave them to her.

Kate said, "I think I can assure you of one thing, Nathan, and that is that Dani is still alive. In fact, I can pretty well tell you how much time she's got left—and how much time we have to find her."

"How the hell can you do that?" asked Seth.

"Take a look at the calendar."

Nathan shook his head impatiently.

"The *date*," pressed Kate.

"Yeah, it's October thirtieth, so what?" asked Seth.

"Tomorrow is Halloween," she said.

Nathan felt that old familiar dread at his heels. Seth shrugged. "And next month is Thanksgiving. Big deal."

"It *is* a big deal," said Kate. "All Hallow's Eve is the high holy day to satanists, similar to the Christian Christmas. If anybody is twisted enough to make an actual sacrifice to Satan, he's going to do it at midnight on Halloween."

Nathan felt a small surge of hope. "So you think she's being held captive somewhere." An ugly thought, but so much better than that of her being dead already.

"That's right," Kate affirmed. "I think this whole thing has been leading up to Halloween. That means we've got . . ." She consulted her watch.

But Nathan already knew. "Less than twenty-four hours," he whispered.

Each person took on a task. Kate was to examine the cryptogram and name book and come up with the connection, plus lean on her "informants" in the underground cult world to see if she could find out what connection Adam had to this whole situation.

Seth was going to check out the Overman Foundation, and Nathan was to call the lawyer who had handled Dani's adoption, get the names of those involved, and run a check on them. They were all going to meet back at Nathan's house on noon the next day. If necessary, Seth was prepared to take off work that night and mount a full-fledged search. He also promised to contact other officers on the force who he knew were interested in ritualistic crime and who could be counted on to help, and to be discreet.

Nathan realized that Seth was taking career risks by helping him, especially since he served directly under the command of Lieutenant Ward. What they were doing could not be considered routine procedure in any department's book. There could be negative consequences—even forced early retirement, if it came to that. They could even be risking their lives. But Seth had brushed off those risks. It meant more to Nathan than he could express to his partner and friend. Not that Seth would have put up with a maudlin display of emotion in any event. As he left, Nathan shook his hand, looked him in the eye, and said a simple thanks. Everything else was unsaid, yet it was understood.

It was one of the good things about being a cop.

Because she was known as an anticult activist, Nathan felt it was safer for Kate to stay with him for the time being and she readily agreed. He welcomed her serene, quiet presence. Left alone, he'd have probably squandered valuable time just fretting about Dani. Instead, he let Kate press upon him one of her delicious rolls (though he declined the herb tea), and afterward, with a fresh cup of coffee in front of him, he called Richard Miller, Attorney-at-Law.

Though it was after one o'clock in the morning, it would only be eleven P.M. in California. Still late for an old man, but this was an emergency.

"Hello?" The voice was sleepy.

Nathan identified himself and explained his business. "I'm sorry to be calling so late, Mr. Miller, but the situation is urgent."

The voice, when it responded, was wide awake. "Of course. My God. I should have known something like this might happen eventually. What you're telling me has exactly the right theatrical touch."

"I beg your pardon?"

"Let me ask you something. How old are you?"

"Thirty-seven."

"Okay. That would have made you, what, in 1969?"

"I was sixteen."

"Hmmm. Well, you probably didn't pay much attention to the news then. You may not remember this. There's something I didn't tell Dani about her past—God knows I should have—but I'm going to tell you now." He paused. "The trial and adjudication of her case made national headlines."

"What?" Nathan sat forward in his chair. "And the Danielses never told her?"

"Her adoptive parents never knew. As the very young minor in question, her name was kept secret from the public. It was never revealed to the Danielses that the child they were adopting was the same one they'd been reading about in the paper."

Nathan sat in silence as the deep, dignified voice at the other end of the line went on. "Back in 1969, there was a Hollywood movie director who had made quite a name for himself making horror movies which dealt with the occult. A part of the film establishment back then diddled around with satanism. Anton LaVey, who founded the Church of Satan, often served as technical advisor on movies such as *Rosemary's Baby,* and this director was part of LaVey's circle for a while. His name was linked for a time with Jayne Mansfield, and he also knew Roman Polanski—you know, Sharon Tate's husband. In short, there was a whole scene in Hollywood, actors and directors and whatnot, who were interested in the occult and that sort of thing.

"This director made several big-time movies. Some you might have heard of. Let's see, there was *Devil's Dance*—remember that one?"

"Are you kidding? I saw that movie three times."

"And, um, *Lucifer's Talisman.* Oh, and *Master of the Moon.*"

"I remember all of those movies," said Nathan. "Big box-office for the high school set."

"Big box-office all around. Anyway, the director got so involved with the occult that he moved to San Francisco. At first, he joined LaVey's Church of Satan, but he was kicked out, and rumor had it that he was too bizarre even for them. LaVey took great stock on doing only what was legal and being legitimate. His so-called church tried to weed out all the lunatics from their membership."

"Isn't that something like the pot calling the kettle black?"

Miller chuckled. "Perhaps. But even LaVey could recognize when someone was too sick or twisted for his very public forum. He wouldn't tolerate it. Anyway, after that, this director dropped out of sight for a while. Everybody assumed he was in the planning stages of a real blockbuster. Well, it was a blockbuster, all right."

"What happened?"

"A little girl told her social worker that she'd been abused by her foster parents and others in a terrible manner, and from what she said and in the ensuing investigation, they were able to put together a rock-solid case that the director hadn't been making only horror movies, but also had a thriving business going on the side in child pornography."

"Dani."

"And a dozen other children. She probably doesn't remember, but there were other kids involved. The director had formed his own underground satanic church, and they were abusing children as part of some sick ritual and filming it. That was back before VCRs made duplication so easy, so he could command top dollar in porn terms for these films. They made him richer than Hollywood had."

Nathan let out a low whistle. "So when this became public . . ."

"Public like you wouldn't believe. The media went wild. Ms. Daniels's foster folks and the director all got stiff prison sentences. By the time they got out, the man's career in Hollywood was long finished. He couldn't make a driver's-ed film."

"What happened to him?"

"Disappeared. I tracked him for a while when I'd read that he got paroled, then I lost him. That was, oh, thirteen, fourteen years ago. I couldn't tell you where he is now."

"But you could tell me his name."

"I could, and I will. Gladly."

"Before you do, do you have any idea what became of Dani's foster parents?"

"After she called, I checked on that. When they got out of prison, they got back together again. Couple of years later, they burned to death in a house fire. Fire department determined arson caused the blaze. From what they could tell, the bodies had been bound and gagged, then doused with gasoline and set fire to—while still alive. The house burned down around them."

A chill possessed Nathan. He flexed icy fingers. "Better give me the director's name," he said. "I'll find him."

"I'll be glad to give you his name, but you know, of course, that he's probably living under an alias by now."

"True. But it's a start."

"All right. His name was Jonathon Bartholomew." He spelled it for Nathan.

Nathan's mind tumbled over itself with the implications of what the lawyer had told him. He had so much to do to unsnarl all the complications. He knew he could do it—experience told him that—but he didn't know if he could do it in one day.

Dani had so little time left.

Chapter 31 ~~~~~~~

Dani opened her eyes to a blackness so absolute it seemed for a moment that she hadn't opened them at all, but was still trapped in a dreamless entity which was not sleep, but an absence of being.

She brought her hand up to her face and groped around until she found it, rubbed her eyes, blinked, opened them wide. She was awake, then. Nausea lay pallid in her stomach. A piercing headache stabbed behind her eyes. For a moment, she closed them again and lay perfectly still, hoping to orient herself.

It felt as if she were lying on rough, cold concrete. There was no sound, nothing with which she could identify her surroundings. She may as well have been contained in a vacuum. Even after a period of time, her eyes did not adjust to the total darkness, and she struggled against a panicked thought that somehow the chemical they'd used to render her unconscious had blinded her.

They.

How did she know that her assailant had been more than one? Had she seen or heard something, something which teased the perimeters of her memory, something crucial she should now know? For a long time she lay still, striving in vain to remember. Perhaps it was an impression, nothing more.

The cold from the hard concrete seemed to seep into her soul. With it came a hopeless dread so profound it seemed wrenched from the very depths of her most terrorizing nightmares. Only there would be no waking from this.

She was already awake, and it hadn't ended.

Her teeth began to chatter. The blackness around her pressed against her with the finality of the grave.

Had they thrown her into some underground vault to die?

Dani pushed herself into a sitting position. She felt queasy and her head pounded with pain. She leaned her head against her knees and moaned softly.

It was the only sound in the room.

For a wild moment, Dani wondered if she was dead.

She shivered convulsively.

Something crawled up her jeans leg and it jolted her to action. She sprang to her feet, shaking her foot, gritting her teeth against the resulting onslaught from her stomach and her head, and took a stiff step forward, arms held straight out in front of her. Waving her arms back and forth, hoping to make contact with something, a door or piece of furniture or wall, Dani continued another couple of steps, then stumbled against something on the floor and fell forward, arms splayed out awkwardly in front of her.

She went down hard, her hands skidding on the concrete, her knees pressing against something heavy and soft. Panting, she felt around. An arm. Hair. Moving her hands like the blind reading braille, Dani at first denied to herself what she was feeling, until her hands touched something cold and wet and sticky.

Blood.

There was a body in the room with her.

Screams, torn from some inner nightmare of the soul, echoed from wall to wall; spine-chilling screams of horror unlike anything Hollywood could devise; screams of panic and misery swarmed around Dani, enveloping her, over-powering her; screams which didn't even seem to belong to her. But they did.

Because, no matter how long or how loud Dani screamed, there was no one, no one to hear them.

She was alone.

In the absence of light, sound, or movement, time ceased to exist. When Dani next became aware of herself, she was curled in the fetal position on the cold concrete, her back braced against a wall. She had no memory of getting there.

Like a wounded wild animal, Dani curled into herself, whimpered slightly, and waited to die.

Eventually, from somewhere disconnected from time and space, Dani became aware of a growing sensation of light. The light revealed nothing. It seemed only to exist in and unto itself, and it offered warmth, love, strength, and courage.

She did not know if it was a dream. All she knew was that she was not afraid of the light, even though she didn't understand it. She knew it was there to help her.

She sighed, and then she slept.

When next Dani opened her eyes, the nausea and headache were gone and her thoughts clear. She remembered the light but didn't know if it was a dream or hallucination or something . . . paranormal. All she knew was that the light held promise . . . hope. It was all she needed.

She got to her feet and groped around in the blackness as she had done before. This time, when she stumbled over the heavy soft object on the floor, she ground her teeth together and stepped over it, continuing on her way, feeling the darkness. Her hand touched something immovable, about waist-high, like a table. She felt her way around it and continued until she bumped into a shelf of some kind. Things fell to the floor with a clatter. She moved her hands along the shelf.

Her hand touched something round, smooth, and hard, like a ball. She rubbed her hands over it, then recoiled with a cry.

It was a human skull.

Forcing herself, she moved beyond the skull and continued to feel, until, to her great relief, she took hold of a large candle. Okay. It was a beginning. Where there were candles, there were bound to be matches, right? She continued her search.

She found them on a shelf high above the original shelf,

hidden behind some thick books. With trembling hands, she lit one, held it to the candle, then looked around her.

Although the wick was long and dry and burned with strength, the candle shed light only in the immediate vicinity. Gradually Dani came to understand why. The walls, floor, and ceiling of the room were painted black. There were no windows.

There was no doubt in her mind as to where she was. She had been in similar places many times, in her childhood.

Flashback demons possessed her, throwing at her an inner strobe-lit show of memories, of terror and pain and total, complete powerlessness, of being a little lamb surrounded by huge caped wolves. It was paralyzing.

It could have crippled her, but she refused to let it. Deliberately she blocked out the memories. Concentrating instead on the here and now, she decided that the control she *did* have wasn't much, but she wasn't bound or drugged, that was something; and at least she had a choice as to what she could do next. And what she had to do next was examine the body.

The flickering light of the candle jabbed back and forth in Dani's shaking hand, and her knees were so weak she had to hold on to the altar (for she knew that's what the waist-high table was, knew it without having to wonder) as she made her way back to the . . . thing . . . she'd stumbled over.

This time, she almost lost it again. This time, holding the candle high to shed as much light as possible below, she fought everything within her that told her to fling herself against the walls in a bloody frenzy of madness . . . because this time . . . she looked upon the body of the woman she had seen weeks before, half buried in the brush under the trees beside a small lake where she'd been running, on the Palmer estate.

Dani fancied that she could hear the blood rushing through her ears. Her arms and legs went numb and the candlelight seemed to dim. The room rocked.

She realized she was about to faint.

Quickly she set the candle down on the altar, crouched,

and put her head between her knees. She took deep shuddering breaths.

"I'm not crazy," she said over and over again. "I'm not crazy."

It couldn't be the same woman. There was no way. This woman was . . . whole. That woman would be, well, deteriorated by now. In fact, this woman didn't even smell dead.

Maybe she hadn't been dead that long.

Dani raised her head and peeked. The candle, still sitting on the altar, cast a golden circle of light on the woman's upper torso, showing the horribly mutilated breasts. In the flickering aura of the candle, it seemed, just for a moment, that the woman blinked her eyes, that maybe she even looked at Dani.

No. Don't think crazy thoughts.

Think logical thoughts.

Had this woman been recently murdered? If so, how could she look so remarkably like the woman from the estate? Forcing herself to look closer, Dani noticed something . . . unnatural . . . about the body. Not that she'd seen many other dead bodies in her life, but this one was . . . as if it had never possessed life at all.

Reaching out a trembling finger, Dani pressed the flesh on the woman's arm.

No. She pressed it again. Leaned closer. Took the candle from off the altar and held it over the face.

Dani's eyes widened and her mouth gaped open.

This was not a real woman at all. It was an extraordinarily real-looking dummy.

Like something from a horror movie.

Abruptly Dani stood up and plunked the candle down on the altar. Shaking her fist, she shrieked, "*You bastard!*"

Her voice, hoarse from her earlier screaming episode, came out as a harsh croak.

It explained everything—even the "body" she'd discovered at the age of fourteen. For a few moments, she felt exquisite, white-hot rage, a sense of violation, as if she had been psychologically raped.

The inner fire quickly burned itself out, and in the void was left fear. Had he followed her, then, all her life? Taunted her? Tormented her? Watched to see if she would go mad?

Was she some grand experiment?

Why? *Why?*

Because *he* . . . her nemesis, her enemy . . . was insane.

Not Dani.

It was a peculiar, bittersweet relief. On the one hand, there was an explanation for some of the traumatic events of Dani's life which had led others to doubt her sanity. It was a validation, as it were. An assurance that she hadn't been nuts. On the other hand, it meant that, clearly, her enemy had chosen now to close in for the kill.

Dani wondered how much time she had left.

Then she thought about Nathan. *No man is an island,* Donne had written, yet she had always considered herself one. It wasn't true. If she had only been willing to admit her own *need* for someone else, her own dependency . . . if she had only waited for him to help her . . . together, perhaps, they could have outwitted *him.*

Now she was a captive, God only knew where. Nathan was probably frantic, with no idea where to look.

"I love you, Nathan," she whispered.

It was one hell of a time to say it.

She found other candles and lit them all. Behind the altar, in glossy crimson against the black matte finish of the concrete wall, were the symbols Dani knew so well: lightning bolt, triangle, upside-down cross, triangle, and lightning bolt.

NATAS.

Satan.

She examined the articles on the shelves. One thick, leather-bound book caught her eye; embossed on the cover were the words *Book of Shadows.*

Under the glow of candlelight in this macabre room, Dani began to read. Soon, excitement quickened within her. *It was all here*. Names. Dates. Details of crimes committed in the Name of the Beast.

If she could get this book to Nathan; if he could turn it over to the FBI, crimes going back years could be solved, participants could be taken into custody all over the country.

She didn't read the whole thing, just flipped through the ponderous pages with its firm, meticulous handwriting. Then she placed it carefully back where she'd found it. She also straightened up the shelf she'd bumped into when the room was dark.

Then she combed every inch of the room, especially the corner stairway which led to a hatch in the ceiling. Though she realized there wasn't much point in it, she pushed against the hatch door with all her strength, but it wouldn't budge.

She stepped off the room's dimensions: about twenty-five feet square. The altar was roughly coffin-sized in length and width. Made of carved granite, it had an indentation in the middle, deepening at one end which funneled into a pottery pitcher placed underneath. Dani didn't want to think about what that was for.

Painted on the floor and encompassing the altar was a white circle. Within the circle was a pentagram. The altar rested at the center of the pentagram. Walking off the circle, she guessed it to be about nine feet in diameter.

Pondering the altar, Dani knew that there was no way the huge and heavy item could have been lowered through the hatch in the ceiling. The room then, must have been built around it. Because of the ceiling hatch and the concrete walls and floor, which felt slightly damp and smelled musty, she figured she was in a basement.

But a basement with a stone slab right in the middle of it?

She was weary of thinking and exploring. She sat cross-legged on the floor and leaned against the altar, staring at the "body." It had triggered such a psychic onslaught in her not once, but twice, that her sanity had almost been sacrificed on the altar of her own terror.

There was a scrabbling at the hatch door. Heart pounding, Dani scrambled to her feet. The door swung back, revealing a blinding shaft of light from above. Squinting, Dani shielded her eyes with her hand. Backlit, a black-robed form descended the stairway. The door dropped shut.

His face was almost hidden in the folds of the hooded cloak, but Dani didn't need to see it to know who it was. The cryptogram had told her that much, thanks to poor Adam. As the figure approached her, the sputtering candle-light, driven by the rush of air before the closing door, sent shadows jumping before and behind, playing a cruel trick on Dani's eyes, spooking away twenty years to reveal the ghost-figure who had chased her through countless night-mares.

She dodged behind the altar, placing it between her and this eerie, menacing . . . creature . . . who had left such a path of death and destruction in his wake.

He laughed, a soft, low chuckle.

Dani's skin crawled. She struggled to maintain control, clinging to the fragments of her torn courage like a thin coat on a screaming cold winter's night.

"I see you made yourself at home. Bring back any nostalgic memories?" He leaned forward against the altar. "How beautiful you are, my child. Like an angel. An angel named Faith." His modulated voice dripped like the phony blood on the fake body at Dani's feet. "You were the most beautiful of them all. My favorite, by far."

She spat in his face.

Slowly he reached up and wiped away the spittle. With a heavy sigh, he said, "You know, Lucifer was the most beloved of all God's angels. But he fell from grace, and went on to rule the world. You, too, have fallen from grace. Only, I'm afraid, you won't be ruling the world. That job is already taken."

"You're insane," she said.

He laughed again. "But *I* wasn't the one who got locked up in the loony bin, now was I?"

"Why did you do that to me? *Why?*"

"*Because you destroyed me, you little bitch! And I'm going to destroy you!*" His voice reverberated off the walls, striking Dani like a slap. She recoiled.

When he spoke again, his voice had calmed. "I've taken such pleasure in toying with you, watching you suffer, just as *I* suffered all those years in prison. I learned, though. I've been much more careful since then. Much more organized. Shall we say, I've . . . branched out. Although making movies was always my first love. I still keep my hand in. I just stay away from children."

"What about Adam?"

"Adam? I don't consider Adam a child. I'm talking about *little* children. Actually they aren't as easy to control as adults. Hard to believe, isn't it? But adults, I have found, will do *anything* for power, or money, or ambition."

"You killed him, didn't you?"

"Most disappointing. The boy developed a *conscience*, God knows where. Almost got past me, too. I thought he was smarter than that."

"What are you talking about?"

"He botched an assignment. He was ordered to bring us your dog and leave the ear on your pillow. Adam knew better than to disobey a direct command. Stupid little fool. He destroyed himself, really."

"So *you* cut off his little finger!"

"We must set an example of the consequences of disobedience."

Dani felt sick. More than ever, she blamed herself for Adam's death. He had saved Thoreau's life . . . for *her*. In the end, he had died for her.

And he had tried—oh, how he had tried—to warn her.

If only she'd deciphered the cryptogram sooner.

If only . . .

"By the way, don't expect your cop boyfriend to come riding in on his white horse to save you. I have . . . shall we say . . . sources within the police department who will see to it that he chases one red herring after another until it is too late."

Dani's heart chilled to ice. Her chest hurt. She could hardly breathe.

"If he tries to tell anybody about you, it will come to nothing, because your own history of instability will make it seem likely that you simply wandered off and disappeared. Coworkers will testify that you've been behaving peculiarly lately, have seemed distracted and upset by something. He, of course, will be so distraught that he will commit suicide."

Dani gasped.

"Stressed-out cops do it all the time. I think they call it . . . eating their gun? Such a disgusting term."

She tried to swallow. She couldn't. "They'll find me," she said in her throaty whisper.

"Never," he said. "A nice long bath in hydrochloric acid, sulphuric acid, and nitric acid will see to that. Remember the Wicked Witch in *The Wizard of Oz?* How she melted into nothing?" He chuckled gleefully. "You, my dear, will simply vanish without a trace. Just like that. But not before we have some fun first." He rubbed his hands together. "I've waited twenty long years for this."

He turned and headed toward the stairway. With a harsh, guttural cry, Dani flung herself onto his back, wrapping her legs around his waist and her arms around his neck, clawing his face with her fingernails.

With a black swirl of cloak, he swung back and smashed her against the wall, cracking her head. Still she clung to him, pummeling him with her fists, screaming her rage in almost inaudible whispers as her voice gave out.

Reaching over his shoulder, he grasped her by the hair in a powerful grasp and tore her off him. He flung her against the wall like a rag doll and gripped her throat.

Dani could see his eyes, burning black and empty, a void, his face contorted. Choking, she began to pass out. She kicked as hard as she could, but he was well swathed in the robe, and her legs were weakening.

"*You little slut,*" he hissed, his voice oily as a snake's. Still holding her by the throat, he cracked her head back again to the wall. She felt her legs go limp. "Don't you ever think you can defeat me. You didn't then, and you won't now. I'll destroy you. By the name of Lucifer, I'll destroy you."

He let her go, and she collapsed in a heap on the floor,

gagging for breath. She heard a sharp rap, then saw, out of the corner of her eyes, a flash of light, and then the hatch slammed shut.

The candles were still lit, but everything went black for Dani. She slumped to the floor. The last thing she saw was the mutilated body of the woman by the lake.

Chapter 32 ~~~~~~~~~~

The house was huge and had so many rooms Nathan lost count. From library to dining room to bedroom to more bedrooms, he searched, looking for Dani. He was certain that she had to be in this house. Finally, in one of the upstairs bedrooms, he found a closet. He knew he would find her in the closet. Slowly he opened the door. At first, he saw nothing but clothes. Then, off to the side and underneath the clothes, lay something crumpled beneath a blanket. He pulled back the blanket. It was Dani, dead.

Nathan sat bolt upright on the couch, sweating, his heart pounding. The fire had gone out and the afghan with which he'd covered himself no longer kept him warm. A shiver passed through his body.

Get a grip. It was not yet dawn. The house was still and quiet. Upstairs in his bed, Kate lay sleeping. Joe Friday, ever sensitive to atmosphere, crept close to Nathan and lay his head on the edge of the couch. Nathan stroked the little dog, a gesture soothing to both of them. A jealous Agatha sprang onto the couch and curled up close to Nathan.

He'd adopted Agatha and Joe Friday and all the other animals after coming upon them lost and wandering down roads and alleyways. He'd brought them home flea-bitten and scroungy and nervous, and had cleaned them up and fattened them up and made friends for life. He'd seen that same lost look in Dani's eyes, that first day. In a sense, he'd brought her home as well.

Now, in spite of all his loyal pets, the house seemed hopelessly empty without her. He leaned his head back

wearily, thinking, as always, about Dani. He'd seen a
movie once called *Steel Magnolias*, about a group of
Southern women. That title came to his mind as he thought
of her. On the surface, she seemed as soft, fragile, and
beautiful as a flower, but he knew she had a spine of steel.
He prayed that inner strength was sustaining her now.

It was that thought that propelled him up off the couch.
He'd only slept—sporadically at that—for a couple of
hours, but every minute he wasted was one minute less time
for Dani.

When Dani opened her eyes, her head was pounding, her
mouth cottony. She craved a drink of water. For some
reason, her wristwatch was gone, and she had no way of
knowing how long she'd been unconscious or what time it
was.

She needed to go to the bathroom, and her stomach
growled. The candles had burned alarmingly low. Staggering to her feet, she went round and blew a few of them out.
She dare not waste the light. The absolute darkness of that
black room would be too much to bear.

Dizziness sent a queasy feeling to her empty stomach,
and she sat down on the cold hard floor, leaning her head
back against the wall. With only a couple of candles
burning, the corners of the black room were plunged into
velvet shadow. The skull on the wall shelf glowed softly, its
eyeholes inpenetrable. From where Dani sat, the form on
the floor across the room looked very much like a real
corpse.

Never had she had more reason to go stark raving insane.

She shook her head painfully. No way. Not now. She'd
come too far. Yet, *he* had said she would never defeat him.
He had said he was going to destroy her.

Like the dying candlelight, her resolve began to flicker
and weaken. *Maybe he was right*. After all, how could she
fight? What could she do?

Her nose prickled and her eyes stung. *Don't cry, dammit*,
she thought, but a tear worked loose anyhow and crept

down her cheek. The truth was, she *couldn't* fight him alone.

"Oh, Nathan," she whispered. "I need you now. Please, please find me." Then she remembered the danger Nathan himself was in, and it was all she could do not to dissolve into utter despair.

For a moment, she wallowed in fear and self-pity, then she remembered the light she'd seen before. What had it been? She *could* have been unconscious, she *could* have been dreaming . . . On the other hand . . . the sensation she had received from the light had been overpowering. She'd been . . . enveloped . . . by a sense of love and protection. *If ever there was a God of peace and love and goodness,* she'd told Kate, *His spirit is present, right here, in this house.*

Could that same spirit have manifested itself to her *here*, in the presence of evil?

And if so, could she depend on . . . It . . . to help her now? To protect Nathan, and to lead him to her?

Which was greater, the power of love or the power of evil?

In all her life, Dani had never once depended on anybody or anything other than herself. Now she had no choice. Bowing her head, she whispered, "If You are there, and if You are listening, then, please, help us all . . ."

The noontime meeting at Nathan's cabin was discouraging. A computer check on Jonathon Bartholomew turned up zilch. After his parole, he seemed to have vanished. Kate reported to have had little luck with her "informants." Seth reported that the Overman Foundation had been started by a wealthy local citizen, Samuel Overman, some years before to benefit local charities. After his death, his daughter, Olivia Overman, had taken over the administration of the funds until her death fourteen years ago. Since she had no children, Seth was going to do some more digging to find out how the estate was being managed now.

"By the way, I called the school," interrupted Kate.

They stared at her. "What school?" asked Nathan.

"Dani's school. I told them she was ill and would need a substitute for a few days."

"*What'd you do that for?*" Nathan shouted.

"Would you rather they reported her missing to the police? I thought you wanted to keep this low-profile."

He looked at Seth, who nodded and said, "Under the circumstances, I think she's probably right. Otherwise you'd have her family down here, the media . . . Wherever she's being hidden now, they might be scared into moving her. We might never find her."

"Do you think we should call the FBI?" asked Kate.

"And report what?" said Seth reasonably. "We have no evidence whatsoever that she's been kidnapped or involved in any sort of federal crime."

"That's true. Then again," she added ominously, "there could be some officers involved."

"What are you talking about?" Nathan stared at her.

"Cops are only human, after all. Sometimes one is drawn into a cult. When that happens, the cult is kept abreast of every move the police make. They *never* get caught."

Nathan shook his head. "I can't believe that. These underground cults are involved in activities that are clearly illegal. I can't see a cop doing that."

"You never heard of a dirty cop or one who's gone bad?" asked Seth. "You never heard of one skimming off of drug busts or taking payoffs? C'mon, Bulldog."

The thought made Nathan sick to his stomach. "What's the world coming to?" he mumbled.

There was a long silence.

Finally Seth said, "So what do we do now?"

"Keep digging," said Nathan, and he couldn't keep from his mind a sudden and clear image of a grave.

In a dark corner, Dani was forced to relieve herself. The pungent odor of urine made her want to throw up, but she couldn't help it. This is what *he* had reduced her to. Still dripping, she pulled her panties and jeans back up, stepped over the puddle, and made her way to the opposite corner of the room.

She was famished. "What a wienie you are," she muttered. "Those poor starving children in Africa sometimes go days without eating, and here you are whimpering over a couple of lousy meals." She tried not to think about it.

The not thinking was the hardest part. The longer she stayed in her lonely prison, the more she thought about her foster parents, her dark and terrible years with them. The memories poured in like water crashing through a rain-weakened reservoir. The psychological strip-mining they had done on her had taken place over a period of years and encompassed far more than the horrors of the cult rituals.

The entire household had been completely devoid of love or kindness of any type whatsoever. Never had she received a tender touch or a soft word. Never had she been given a present. What toys she had were simply props to fool the caseworker. Anything which would be observed by the outside world—such as her clothes—were clean, neat, and presentable. But behind closed doors there resided only contempt, cruelty, and neglect.

She was not permitted to have friends. No one was ever allowed close enough to the family to guess their ugly secrets. She never attended parties or visited the homes of other children.

School was the only haven Dani had ever known; teachers the only kind adults in her life. She worked pitifully hard to please them, always the good girl, ever the perfect pupil. A smile or a pat from a teacher might have to last her for weeks as her only encouragement. She always stayed late, begging to clean the chalkboards or pick up trash—*anything* to avoid going back to the grim house of her foster parents. Painfully she remembered walking back as slowly as she could, lingering on street corners, dragging her feet, knowing she would be beaten for it (in places hidden by clothing so the caseworker wouldn't see), but doing it, anyway.

Summers and holidays were endless nightmares.

Weekend nights were unspeakable.

She shuddered, and was caught off guard by a wave of

homesickness for her *real* family, her adoptive family. They could never have guessed how desperately she needed their love, how dreadfully unworthy of it she had believed herself to be. Every negative behavior had been a test, her chance to prove to them just how much they were wasting their time.

What if she never saw her mother again? Why, *why* hadn't she told her on that last trip how very much she loved her? How grateful she was for giving her *life,* and love? And Daddy . . . too late. Too late.

Wasted time. It was *she,* Dani, who had wasted time.

How typically *human* of her not to realize it until it was too late.

As the day wore on, a sense of desperation began dogging Nathan's heels. Every lead he followed dead-ended. Every clock he passed seemed to loom at him with menacing hands.

At one point, he considered going to Lieutenant Ward with the whole story and taking his chances. Ward was a hard man to like, but as a cop, an easy one to respect. He was married to his job; consequently his focus on a case was laser-sharp. Maybe he would have an idea they hadn't thought of.

Then Nathan shook his head. The guy was too by-the-book. He'd make them wait several days before declaring Dani a missing person, and by then it would be too late.

His eyes were grainy and his head ached. Sitting at a traffic light, he heard a horn honking and barely turned his head. It was Seth, parked at a corner lot, gesturing wildly. When the light changed, he made a U-turn and pulled up next to Seth's car. He cranked down the window. "What gives?"

Seth was so excited that he could hardly get the words out. This was so uncharacteristic of him that Nathan found himself staring.

"Olivia Overman. Big stink in the family some years back. She fell in love with a younger guy nobody knew anything about. Whirlwind courtship. The whole bit. Over the family's objections, they got married. Few months later, Olivia croaks. Autopsy ruled natural causes but the family was *sure* she'd been murdered. Police wouldn't help, well, couldn't help them, really." His eyes were alight in his dark face.

"She left everything to the guy. The family contested the will, but they lost in court. He got it *all*. Set him up for life. Now he's a big shot, spending her money in style."

"Who is he?"

"You won't believe it."

"Try me."

"Okay . . . drumroll, please . . . Jordan Blake."

"The ChemCo guy?"

"One and the same."

"I don't believe it." Nathan shook his head. "No wonder I couldn't stand the pompous ass."

Seth grinned broadly. "What say we pay the guy a little visit? I already checked with his office. They say he's relaxing at home today, thank you very much."

"I suppose you know where it is."

"Follow me, kimosabe."

The Overman mansion could have been a movie set. Built on rolling green lawns in an imposing section of town, it had tall white columns, Tara-style, servants' quarters, and a separate garage that must have been a carriage house at one time. The entire estate was surrounded by a high wrought-iron fence, but the impressive gate was not locked. Nathan and Seth walked down a flagstone path winding beneath magnificent live-oak trees. A cloudy cold front was moving in and there was a distinct chill in the air.

A black maid in uniform answered the door. Seth glanced at Nathan, then showed his badge and asked to speak to Mr. Blake. "I almost said 'Master Blake,'" whispered Seth to Nathan as the maid showed them into a luxurious library with leather-bound books lining the walls. The room contained a fortune in paintings. Nathan wondered what kind of security Blake had.

A moment later, Blake entered the room, dressed in chinos and a thick handwoven sweater in rich autumn colors. "Nice sweater," mumbled Nathan as they shook hands.

"Isn't it, though? I bought it in Ireland."

Deep leather chairs scrunched as they sat. "What can I do for you, gentlemen?" asked Blake. Track lighting highlighted his wavy silver hair.

"We're investigating a missing person," said Nathan. "A high school English teacher named Faith Daniels. Do you know her?"

Blake's smooth smile was disturbed by a slight frown. "Let's see . . . I believe I did meet Ms. Daniels at a faculty event for the opening of a new library wing donated to the school by the Overman Foundation. A lovely girl, I thought. We discussed Dante's *Inferno*."

Nathan's body went cold. He couldn't speak.

Seth took over. "Have you seen Ms. Daniels recently, Mr. Blake?"

"No, I can't say that I have."

"We understand that the Overman Foundation grants scholarships known as the Select Student Scholarship. Is that correct?"

"Why, yes, as a matter of fact. We're very proud of that. The scholarship gives students a chance for an education who may have not lived up to their potential in high school."

Nathan found his voice. "Wasn't Dani, er, Faith, a recipient of that scholarship? That would have been . . . ten years ago."

Little crinkle lines appeared between Blake's brushed eyebrows. "Well, I'd have to check our records. I can't keep up with all the recipients."

"What about Adam Prescott?"

Blake shook his head sadly. "Tragic situation, wasn't it? We had only just received the recommendation on Adam from his principal when, unfortunately, he took his own life."

Nathan sighed inwardly. This was getting them nowhere. They couldn't make a clear connection between Blake and Dani at this point, and even if they could, he was too sly to slip into their net that easily. He stood up. "Mind if we take a look around?"

Blake's smile was polished. "Whatever for? Did you think Ms. Daniels might be *here*?"

"We're looking into everything," said Seth.

"Well . . . all right. I'll show you around myself."

Blake led the way, followed by Seth. Nathan trailed behind. There was the library, the dining room, and later, bedroom after bedroom, just like in his nightmare. It was all he could do not to check the closets.

Down in the massive kitchen, where a cook worked on a meal for one, Seth spotted a small corner door. "Where's that go?"

"That? Oh, the basement. I assure you, there are no bound and gagged schoolteachers down there." He chuckled. Seth and Nathan did not.

"If you don't mind, Mr. Blake . . ." Nathan persisted.

"You really want to see it?" He looked from one to the other. Seth nodded, glaring down from his formidable height.

They couldn't force him to show them the room. Not without a search warrant. And no judge in town would sign a warrant on this situation. Nathan's heart constricted.

With a shrug, Blake turned and, removing a key from his pocket, unlocked the door and snapped on a light from a switch plate just inside the door. Standing back, he gestured them toward the steps.

No way they would both wander down those steps with that guy holding the keys. Seth said, "You check it out. I'll wait."

Nathan nodded and descended the steps. He found discarded appliances, tools, expensive wines, and old furniture.

He did not, however, find Dani.

From time to time, Dani slept. There wasn't much else to do. Once, she got the *Book of Shadows* down and read some more of it. She didn't recognize any of the names listed but figured law enforcement might. She didn't hold the book very long, because she was afraid of getting caught with it.

As time wore on endlessly, she thought with increasing frequency about Nathan. If he had checked out her house, he'd have discovered the cryptogram and the name-the-baby book by now. Once he solved the puzzle, surely he'd be able to find her.

She worried, though, about some of the names she'd deciphered. If he hadn't found them out yet, he might blunder into a terrible trap.

If only she could have warned him.

If only . . .

Stop it!

She wondered if there was anything she could do, before they killed her, that could save Nathan.

On the way back to the cabin, this time with Seth following him, Nathan thought about a poem he'd read in a high school lit book. Something about the fog coming in on little cat feet. Only this time, it wasn't the fog. This time it was the dark, and it was coming in on the pads of a panther.

Kate flung open the door before they'd even gotten out of their cars.

"*I figured it out!*" she shouted. "Hurry."

The delectable aroma of homemade stew wafted out the door behind her. Nathan was surprised to find that he was ravenous. With Kate fluttering behind them, he and Seth headed directly for the kitchen.

"I broke the code," she said excitedly while they scooped stew into bowls. "Here." She shoved a piece of paper into Nathan's hand as he sat down at the table. He stared at the first line, written in her lavish scrawl:

> *Beware the Dark One descending.*
> *"Dark One" = Blake*
> *"Descender" = Jordan*

He looked up. "You were on target, Seth."

"Let me see."

"Just a minute." Nathan studied the other names on the rest of the page. Wordlessly he handed it over to Seth.

"No way," said Seth, glancing at the names. "This has to be a mistake."

"You want to see the name book?" asked Kate.

"No, I mean, the names are probably correct, it's just that, well, Adam *was* a nut, wasn't he? I mean, how accurate can the kid be? I can't believe this."

"For your own safety, you'd better," said Kate.

Nathan ate stew, but he'd lost the ability to taste it. "If this list *is* right," he said slowly, "then we can't trust *anybody,* can we?"

Seth stared at his stew. Finally he said, "I think I'll call home. Check on the wife. I'll be right back." He left to use the phone in the living room.

"It can't help but make you paranoid," said Kate sadly.

Dani found the dagger on the top shelf, hidden. It was the same dagger she'd seen in Adam's room, on his desk. At least, it looked like the same one. But how could that be? The police had taken it into evidence, hadn't they?

They had. She knew it.

So how had it wound up here?

You know how, she told herself. *You saw the list of names.*

Clambering down from the shelf, grateful for being such a lightweight that the shelves had held, she slipped the cold dagger blade carefully between her jeans and her skin and pulled her shirt down over the handle.

Then she stretched out on the floor to rest and wait.

"We know Jordan Blake is definitely involved, at least according to the cryptogram," said Seth. "We need to put him under surveillance.

"Best thing to do is split up," said Seth. "We'd keep in touch by radio."

"No good," said Kate. "They may have radios, too."

"Shit."

There was a gloomy silence.

"One good thing," said Seth finally. "I've found a few officers who're willing to help."

Nathan shifted uncomfortably in his seat. Kate was right. You couldn't help but be paranoid. He was afraid to trust *anybody* to help them at this point. "I've got another idea."

"Me, too," said Seth.

Seth and Nathan exchanged looks. "Could be a wild-goose chase," said Nathan.

"Nah," said Seth. "We're too damn good for that." He grinned.

For the first time that day, Nathan started to feel better.

The hatch door slammed back, jolting Dani awake. Before she could get her bearings in the semidarkness, something white floated down from the ceiling.

She blinked.

"Take your clothes off," called a disembodied voice, "and put that on."

The door slammed shut.

Stiffly she pushed herself up from the floor, taking care not to jab herself with the dagger, and made her way to the white heap on the floor. It was a long flowing gown, spotlessly white.

The white lamb, to be sacrificed to the black wolves.

It was starting.

Pulse throbbing painfully in her throat, Dani began to unbutton her blouse.

Mac MacIntire had lost weight since Nathan had seen him last. He was still being held without bail in the county jail for the mutilation murder of his wife and the unidentified woman.

As soon as the deputy left them alone in the same cramped office as before, Nathan grabbed the startled man by the throat and slammed him up against the wall. Mac's eyes bulged.

"We're gonna have us a little talk," snarled Nathan. With one arm pinning both the man's arms, he tightened his grip on Mac's throat. The smaller man choked.

"I know all about your shitty little cult activities, you insect. I know all about Jordan Blake and his games." Nathan pressed tighter. Mac gagged. "Now you *tell* me where the cult meets, or I swear to God you'll be wishin' you were in *their* hands instead of mine, you *got* that?"

Mac's eyes rolled back in his head.

Chapter 33 ⸯⸯⸯⸯⸯⸯⸯⸯⸯⸯⸯⸯⸯⸯ

Most of the candles had burned completely out by the time the hatch door opened again. Dani stood pressed against the opposite wall, dressed in the angelic gown, her hands hidden in its deep folds.

Someone came slowly down the steps, bearing more candles. Face hidden in the hood of the black gown, the person set out the candles and lit them.

Dani waited.

Turning toward Dani, the person said, "Take this. It will make it easier on you." It was a woman's voice. She held out a cup.

With a strike of her hand, Dani knocked the cup out of the woman's hand and lunged. The blade of the dagger met resistance. Grunting, she shoved, felt it plunge deep. The woman cried out. Her knees buckled. Hiking up her gown, Dani leapt past her and rushed headlong up the steep stairs.

Bright lights at the top of the stairs assaulted her eyes, rendering her blind for a moment. Still, she clambered upward, almost out, almost out. She could make out what looked like a laboratory. Stumbling, grappling, she reached the top of the stairs, almost out, when, from nowhere, she caught a glimpse of a boot swinging sharply in her direction, felt it crack against her chin, her head snapping backward, her arms pinwheeling, her feet scrambling, then she was falling, tumbling, heading downward, down into darkness.

ChemCo, Inc., was only decoratively lit at night, which worked to their advantage as Nathan and the others made their way from shadow to shadow, creeping with the stealth of a field mouse by moonlight. Cold wind-driven clouds rendered the night black-dark.

It was like a night raid in Vietnam. The fear was the same; but, in many ways, so was the training. That plus adrenaline gave them all the edge. Mac had told him to watch out for sentries. All it took was one false move and he'd been assured that Dani would be killed.

They were working in relays, moving silently from one perimeter to another. They'd been warned not to storm the place, and they'd taken the warning seriously.

Besides, there were only seven of them.

Standing in shadow, watching others slip silently around toward the shipping and receiving dock, Nathan could hear his own raspy breathing, feel his heart pounding a little too fast. He tried to control his almost overwhelming sense of urgency.

They had to move so slowly, and they had so little time left.

Chanting. Unholy singing. Shadowed faces by quivering candlelight. Dani opened her eyes to a familiar nightmare. She struggled to get up but she'd been tied down somehow, spread-eagled on the granite slab.

The gown had been removed.

Between her naked legs, she saw *him.*

"In the name of Satan, Lucifer, Belial, Leviathan, and all the demons, named and nameless, walkers in the velvet darkness, harken to us, O dim and shadowy things, wraith-like, twisted, half-seen creatures, glimpsed beyond the foggy veil of time and spaceless night."

Lifting a silver chalice over his head, his voice rang clear and melodic, just as she remembered it from so many nightmares ago. She was cold, miserable with her naked-ness. Each breath she took sent a stab of pain through her side, and her knee was throbbing almost worse than her head. She must have taken a real battering, going down those stairs. Lucky she didn't break her neck. Or was it? Perhaps that would have been more merciful. She glared at her nemesis, her enemy, with contempt. Just above his head, she could see the symbols for NATAS. Satan.

"Draw near, attend us on this night. Accept our most humble sacrifice. Take the blood of the life-force at its most exquisite moment, the moment of power, the moment of joy . . . the moment of death."

Her tormentor drank from the chalice, then passed it solemnly around the altar. Each robed figure drank from it in turn. Voices rose in an eerily enchanting harmony, monotonous and velvety in their unity. Leaning forward, he kissed her, his tongue probing deep into her mouth.

She bit down. Hard.

Gasping, he pulled away, but he didn't laugh. Instead, he slapped her so hard her head cracked to the other side. A white-hot pain shot down her neck. Her cheek stung. The chanting continued, louder, more frenzied.

Dani strained at her bindings. Above his right shoulder, she caught a glimpse of a blinking pinnacle of red light; a tiny dot not like the candles. She squinted at it. Then, sickened, she realized what it was.

They were filming her sacrifice.

Her enemy was watching her. Then he laughed, high and long.

"In the name of Satan, Lucifer, Belial, Leviathan, and all the demons, named and nameless, walkers in the velvet darkness, I take for myself this most glorious moment, even as I offer up this humble sacrifice."

With a dramatic sweep of his arms, he let drop his black hooded robe and stood before Dani, naked.

The voices rose with an added sense of urgency. Someone handed him the dagger—the dagger she'd found, she thought—and he began to climb up onto the altar, his body glowing from the candlelight, his erection hard and un-yielding. Like a living nightmare he crouched between her legs, the dagger in his left hand. His silver hair shone amber from the wavering shadow-light of the candles.

The chanting grew faster, faster. Mesmerizing. Hypno-tizing.

With the blade, he drew a careful circle around her left

breast. She felt a sting, and then a tickling on her side as blood dripped down. She ground her teeth together to keep him from having the satisfaction of seeing her cry for mercy.

At the sight of her blood, some of the cult members began swaying, as in a hypnotic trance. The chanting increased, grew louder.

Slowly, slowly, he drew a circle around her right breast.

She squeezed shut her eyes, swallowing hard to keep from whimpering. She felt him dip his fingers in the blood and write something on her stomach with it. Gooseflesh arose on her body, and the cuts on her breasts began hurting in earnest.

The voices rose, higher and higher, faster and faster, like a frenzied vocal orgasm.

She felt his hands between her legs, groping, spreading them so far apart she felt as if she were being ripped down the middle.

She opened her eyes. He was on his knees directly over her, his demonic eyes glinting, the dagger held in both hands over her heart.

Spellbound in the intensity of those otherworldly eyes, Dani realized that she was about to be raped at the point of death by the very devil himself.

To the beat of the chant, her brain drummed out its own refrain: *Help me. Please help me.*

There weren't that many sentries, after all, and Nathan learned that seven good men could accomplish a lot. They were able to subdue each surprised guard by a flash of a badge and a gun, a lightning gag, cuffs behind the back, and a trip to the squad cars, where they were locked in the back, behind the protective grille. They took the key from the pocket of the last guard and unlocked the door to the secret laboratory Blake had told him was used to develop new products.

Mac had said the hatch door leading to the secret basement was at the rear of the lab. Moving as quietly as possible, they rushed down the aisles, passing huge containers of phenalacetate, anhydras ammonia, and methaline.

Nathan wasn't a narcotics officer, but he knew what "new product" had been developed here: methamphetamines.

Speed.

No time to think about it now. He had to get to Dani *fast*. It was almost midnight.

The officers gathered around the hatch door set in the floor. Nathan squatted in front of it. Seth crouched behind him. The others clustered close by. All had their weapons drawn. Nathan held up three fingers, two, then one.

He flung open the door and tore down the first few steps in one fluid movement, took the stance, and shouted, "*Police!*"

Everything happened in a blur. The door slammed back, someone shouted "*Police!*" and for a split second the entire room froze.

"Drop it!"

She knew it was Nathan's voice but she couldn't believe it.

The dagger began to plunge down toward her, there was a booming sound, and her tormentor cried out, grabbed his arm, and rolled off the side of the altar. The dagger spun away as if in a slow-motion dream.

A movement caught Dani's eye. One of the cult members was reaching into his cloak, withdrawing something black that gleamed cold in the candlelight.

"*Nathan! He's got a gun!*" Though Dani screamed as loud as she could with her hoarse voice, she didn't know if he heard her.

Then an explosion went off so close to her ear that she was struck deaf.

Nathan tumbled to the floor.

A second *boom* went off, and the man with the gun fell backward.

Shouts and screams filled the air. There was an acrid smell.

Bright lights went on overhead, and Dani was blinded as well as deafened.

Where, please God, was Nathan?

Chaos erupted. Mixed with the shouting were scuffles, grunts, curses, and mass confusion. In a flash, she saw Seth's sad long face peering down at her. With his pocket knife, he freed her before she had time to realize what was happening.

"Get under the altar quick," he ordered, his voice almost a whisper. "It's the safest place in the room."

But she couldn't move. Her teeth were chattering and she felt light-headed. Without hesitation, he took her gently in his huge arms and placed her underneath the altar, pressed up against the stone slab. "Stay there," he ordered.

"*Seth! Get that one running up the stairs!*" someone hollered. Seth vanished, and Dani was alone in the midst of chaos, staring at her bruised and bleeding body as if it belonged to someone else. On her stomach, she made out the smeared insignia of her tattoo, written in blood. More blood drooled from her breast wounds and mingled with it.

Someone grabbed her wrist in a pincer grip and began to drag her across the floor. Too startled to cry out, Dani looked up—into the eyes of her enemy.

"*You can't defeat me. I told you that. Now I will destroy every last one of you.*" She saw him press a button on his wristwatch.

His wristwatch?

In the chaos of black robes, the screaming and shouting, the grunting and fighting and sounds of flesh hitting concrete, as she was being dragged by inches across the floor, Dani saw the man reaching out for something with his other, blood-drenched hand, reaching . . .

The dagger!

In the instant she spotted it, she dove for it, closed her fingers around it. The air filled with inhuman screams, hoarse, whispery screams, *her* screams, and she brought the dagger down with all the strength of twenty years of pent-up rage.

Too surprised to ward off the blow, he dodged instead, and the blade sank into his left shoulder.

The fingers of his good hand curled around her throat.

She clawed his eyes.

Bellowing, he let go. Possessed of demons of her own, beyond thinking or even *being* herself, Dani took both her hands, grasped the hilt of the dagger, and ripped it out of his flesh.

He screamed and ducked his head, his arms over his face. Still shrieking in hoarse ghostly whispers, Dani lifted the dagger over her head.

"Dani! No!"

She froze. Nathan reached for the dagger. He had to pry her fingers from it.

Then, while Jordan Blake whimpered in a heap in front of them, Nathan gathered Dani into his arms.

She said dully, "Why didn't you let me kill him?"

Some of the cult members had gotten away, scattering like cockroaches caught in the light, but Nathan figured they'd caught most of them.

If it hadn't been for Dani and Seth, he'd be dead. Her warning gave him time to duck and go into a protective roll. Seth's bullet removed all harm. Now the cult member who had drawn on him lay dead on the floor: Lieutenant Ward.

The district attorney, Lilith Douglas, sat sullenly in a corner, her black hood fallen back from her face. The High Priestess, Mac had told him. He hadn't believed it then, not even after seeing Adam's cryptogram. Now he was forced to.

Jordan Blake sat cuffed in another corner, closely guarded, his wounds bandaged with shreds of a black robe.

Dani lay on the altar, a black robe wrapped around her like a blanket. Her feet had been propped up on the pillow of another robe as added protection against shock. Though none of her injuries were serious, Nathan worried about the impact of the whole ordeal on her. The ambulance was on its way. Seth was asking her questions, and she was patiently, exhaustedly answering them. Over the officer's shoulder, Nathan blew her a kiss and headed toward the stairs for another look at the lab before the ambulance arrived. His own arm was wrapped up in a handkerchief, which would suffice for now, since he'd only been grazed. As he glanced at her, Dani caught his eye and crooked a finger at him. Nathan walked over and bent down.

"Closer," she whispered. He put his ear to her lips.

"I love you," she croaked.

Nathan pulled back and gazed into her eyes. Then he grinned and said, "It's about time you admitted it."

She smiled. Patting her cheek, he left her and began climbing the steep steps to the lab. Looking back at her now, so small and bruised and bleeding, Nathan wondered why he *hadn't* let her kill the bastard. Shaking his head, he climbed the stairs.

This speed lab was obviously a major operation, not like the usual "garage" labs found in small towns. Nathan had already made a call to the DEA.

He grinned. He couldn't help but gloat a little bit. After all, they were a big-time federal operation, and this had been going on right under their noses. Here he was, a small-town cop, and he'd made the bust. He loved it.

His glance fell over to a side shelf, and the grin froze on his face. There, nestled between two stainless-steel vats, was a clock. There was no hour hand on the clock, only a minute hand. Drilled into the face of the clock was a screw with wires attached to some batteries.

Nathan stepped quickly over to the clock. The wires behind it were connected to a tremblar device.

Most any soldier who'd been to Nam had a rough familiarity with explosives. A tremblar device was a simple wire loop with, in this case, a cotter pin dangling from the middle of it. If the pin touched the wire loop, it would set off the charge. This one had been so delicately constructed that there was only a one-eighth-inch leeway. The tremblar device was designed to be so sensitive that merely touching the clockface or any of the wires would set off the explosion.

Slowly, carefully, he leaned over. The wires could not be

cut. They were of the double collapsing relay type—which meant that no matter which wire you cut, the bomb would go off.

He would have to clear the building. Call the bomb squad.

Heart pounding, Nathan followed the wires leading from the clock. They were wired to a charge connected to a det, or detonator cord, which stretched over a deceptively innocent-looking small gray block of plastic explosives. The det cord stretched from that block of plastique around the corner of the cabinet to another, and from that one to another . . .

Nathan's heart clanged painfully against his rib cage, and his mouth turned to cotton. An explosion traveled more than 22,000 feet per second, so each charge would set off every other charge at virtually the same moment.

And all these flammable, explosive chemicals would blow this whole place to hell.

Nathan heard a tiny, almost imperceptible *click*.

The minute hand had moved. It pointed at the number eleven.

Five minutes.

Forget the bomb squad.

For a hysterical moment, he considered simply cutting the det cord from as far away from the tremblar device as he could trace it, but he was no explosives expert, and besides, how did he know Blake hadn't booby-trapped the det cord in some way?

He had no choice but to get this building cleared out. *Now*.

Hurrying with care to the door, Nathan said in a clear, loud voice: "We have to clear this building *immediately*. I have discovered an explosive device. Please be orderly but please hurry. When you get out of the building, get as far away as you can as quickly as you can. Please don't panic."

Everyone surged toward the door.

Everyone, that is, except Dani.

In the confusion of all the people rushing up the stairs, Nathan only had time to glimpse that Dani, instead of hurrying toward the stairway with everyone else, had pulled away from the protective grasp of one of the officers and headed for a shelf on the other side of the room, where she was reaching for something.

Nathan couldn't get down the stairs with everyone crowding up. Handcuffed suspects and cops alike were racing up the stairs and out of the laboratory. Frantically he tried to push against the tide. Through the chaos, he heard a high, demonic laugh, and spotted Jordan Blake breaking from the crowd and dodging *toward* the explosive device.

In a flying leap, Nathan brought him down in a hard tackle. Blake kicked and squirmed, fighting, in spite of the cuffs, to get away. Nathan gave him a good hard right cross on the jaw. Momentarily stunned, Blake allowed himself to be hauled to his feet and yanked away by Seth.

"Let's get out of here, man," yelled Seth.

"I've got to get Dani," Nathan said, pointing down to the basement, and bolted down the stairs.

Dani was kneeling on a bottom shelf, reaching over her head. Nathan raced over to her, grabbed her around the waist, and dragged her toward the door.

"Nathan! No! I've got to get the book. *Let me go!*"

"There isn't time! Come on!"

"The *book*. Nathan, it won't take a minute. I *have* to get it."

"We don't *have* a minute, Dani."

She broke free and dashed for the shelf. He caught her and they struggled.

"Dani! Have you lost your mind?"

"I've got to get that book!"

"There isn't time, dammit!"

There wasn't, and now he wondered if there was enough time for them to even make it out of the building.

Dragging her by the arm, he took the stairs two at a time. The black cloak she'd had wrapped around her had fallen off, but there was no time to worry about that. She was limping but he urged her to hurry in spite of it.

They sprinted through the speed lab, skidded around the corner, and ran across the shipping and receiving area. They just made it to the outside door when the building blew.

Chapter 34 ~~~~~~~~~~

The concussion of the blast blew them twenty scorching feet and sent them in a tumbling roll across the grounds. Dani landed in a wadded heap and lay there, thoroughly disoriented. She had no idea how she'd gotten there or what had happened to Nathan.

She felt powerful arms lifting her effortlessly. For a moment, she thought it was Nathan, but it was Seth, who jogged with her toward a squad car. "There'll be more explosions as the fire spreads," he panted. "Gotta get you out of here."

"Nathan?"

"I don't know, sugar. I didn't see him. I's concentrating on you."

Placing her gingerly in the front seat of the squad car, he jerked off his coat and wrapped it around her as if she were a child. To the officer driving, he said, "Get her out of here. Take her to the hospital."

"Right." The officer started to pull away.

"*No!*" she yelled, cranking down the window. The officer hit the brakes. "Seth! I can't leave without knowing what happened to Nathan. *Please.*"

For a moment he hesitated, studying her face, then he said, "Okay. Wait right here." To the officer he called, "Make her stay in the car."

The young man nodded, then touched the sleeve of her jacket. "You okay?" He looked so worried that, for a moment, she thought about how hideous she must appear.

A window-rattling blast caused them both to jump. A

297

spectacular fireball lit up the night and turned the clouds the color of blood.

On the police radio, Dani heard multiple emergency calls going out. Someone, apparently the fire chief, had ordered an immediate evacuation of the surrounding area. "Might be poisonous fumes," she heard.

Poison, hidden behind beauty. That was Jordan Blake, all right.

Blake. What had happened to *him*?

Where was Seth?

The young officer began to fidget. "I gotta get you out of here," he said apologetically. "It could be dangerous."

"No! Please."

"I'm sorry." He put the car in gear. She put her hand on the doorknob. He wrapped a gentle but firm hand around her arm. "I think you better stay put," he said, and drove rapidly away.

Helplessly she pressed her forehead against the cold car window, watching the flames of hell climb toward heaven.

Nathan came to, lying in the backseat of a squad car with what looked like fifty cops standing around looking worried. The air was filled with the screams of sirens.

It didn't do much for his headache.

He sat up and groaned. A cheer went up. Somebody slapped his shoulder and he lifted his head painfully. His neck muscles felt like steel rods. Fred Davis was grinning ear to ear. "Hell, Bulldog. Here we are working our butts off while you take a snooze in the backseat of a po-lice car."

The crowd parted for a tall, brown, familiar form. "Ain't you guys got nothin' better to do?" he growled. Most of them laughed softly and went on about their business after stopping by Nathan to congratulate him on some "first-rate police work."

He wondered how long he'd been out.

The first thing he said to Seth was "Dani?"

"Aw, geez, Loueez, you guys are monotonous. The first thing *she* said was *your* name. I wish you'd get married and put each other out of your misery."

Nathan grinned happily. "So she's okay, I gather?"

"Better'n you. I had a rookie take her to the hospital."

Nathan felt gingerly around on his head for lumps. "You got Jordan Blake locked up?"

Seth squirmed and looked away. Nathan sat up, wincing. "I hate to have to admit this, Bulldog, but the little weasel got away from me."

"Inside or outside the building?"

"Inside. I wasn't about to use up my valuable time chasing after him, either."

They could feel the heat from the burning building, even though they were parked a hundred yards from it. Nathan struggled to his feet, swayed, took hold of the roof of the car. A wave of nausea left him in a cold sweat. Seth peered at him. "Looks like you got a concussion, man. You need to go to the hospital yourself."

"Get on the radio," said Nathan to a nearby corporal, ignoring Seth. "Order a guard on Faith Daniels at all times."

Seth was incredulous. "A guard? Jesus, Bulldog. Ain't no way that dude could have gotten out of that building alive, at least not without one of us seeing him do it."

"I don't care."

"Look. *He* may have thought he was some kind of wizard, but *I* don't. I guarantee we'll turn up a set of his teeth somewhere in what's left of that building in a few days."

A third explosion rocked the car on its wheels.

Nathan wandered away from the car a few steps. "Where's my car?" he asked, trying not to look too bewildered.

Seth cursed under his breath. "Huh-uh. No way you're going to drive. Shit. I'll take you to the hospital myself. Goddamn. Do you realize how much trouble you are? Do you know I coulda got killed tonight? Biggest pain in the ass . . ."

And so he mumbled, all the way to the hospital.

"You can't go in there, Officer. Excuse me, Officer, but the doctor is working on her now. Sir—"

As soon as Dani heard the hubbub outside her curtained cubicle she knew it was Nathan. Her heart leapt within her. The curtains were yanked back and the startled doctor raised up from examining one of her breasts.

The accompanying nurse sputtered, "Well—you—you'll have to leave, sir!"

He pushed the doctor out of the way and knelt over her, cradling her head in his hands.

"Sergeant, please. You'll be able to see her in just a little while." The doctor was not pleased. Nathan put his face inches from hers and said, "I'll be right outside."

Then he stood up, grinned, and passed out cold, hitting the floor with a thud.

Doctors and nurses scrambled. Dani struggled to get up. Seth waved his arms over the whole lot and said, "It's okay. He's got a concussion but hell, with a head as hard as his, he'll be all right. Trust me on this."

Kate McCall insisted that Dani and Nathan have Thanksgiving dinner at her place. While her new black and white kitten—a gift from Nathan—cavorted at their feet, she put them both to work at the kitchen table, doing busywork, mostly, to stay out of her way.

It was the first time since Halloween that they'd really had the chance to sit down and discuss everything that had happened, to put in place the final pieces to the puzzle.

Lilith Douglas had pled out a light sentence in exchange for telling law enforcement everything she knew about Jordan Blake's cult and his various illegal activities. Since she was going to be disbarred, anyway, and her political career lay in ashes, the deal was accepted. Nathan shared some of her statement with Kate and Dani.

"It seems Blake—Jonathon Bartholomew—had a long time to put together his plans while in prison," he began. "All he needed was the funds, and when he met a rich, lonely spinster from Texas, he pursued her relentlessly, spending enough of the money he'd socked away right before leaving to serve his sentence to make her think that he was a contemporary of her class and not an ex-con on the make."

"Olivia Overman," said Kate.

"Right." He dropped one peeled potato in a bowl of water and reached for another. "The Overman Foundation provided a perfect screen for Blake's activities. Under the guise of charity, he was able to recruit most of his cult members directly out of college—the college they were attending, thanks to a Select Student Scholarship. By carefully selecting disenchanted young people, already rebellious, providing them with the first real opportunity of their lives, and seducing them with promises of fulfilled ambition, money, and power, it was easy to lead them, step by step, into the cult."

"That's the one thing I've always had a hard time understanding," said Dani, turning a potato over in her hands. "I don't see how someone can get people to do what he did. Not adults, anyway."

"It took time," said Nathan. "First, he taught them various 'relaxation techniques,' which involved listening to subliminal tapes. He presented himself as a mentor, someone genuinely concerned with their futures."

"Imagine how flattering that would be to a kid who'd known nothing but rejection from the adults in his life," mused Dani. "I can see it."

Nathan nodded. "In subtle ways, he led them into the doctrines of satanism, which is the total pursuit of self-gratification, pleasure, and ego enhancement. Gradually, as their loyalty to and dependence on him increased, he led them deeper and deeper into cult activities, until their consciences and defenses were broken down enough that they never stopped to consider the immorality or illegality of what they were doing." He plopped another potato into the water. "They trusted him implicitly."

"But how did he have access to them?" asked Dani.

"The scholarships had a stipulation. They were all for the same university."

"I didn't notice that when I was in the principal's office."

"You were in too big of a hurry, if you'll recall."

She nodded.

"Anyway, he already had student recruits on campus, and he kept a close watch on the new students with frequent visits to the campus. You he watched without making contact."

Dani shivered. "It still gives me the creeps, thinking I was being . . . watched . . . all those years."

"Then, after graduation—"

"Now I see it!" said Kate. "Because of his money and social position, he *was* able to set many of them up in various positions of business or community authority."

"Exactly. Lilith was even more special. He seduced her, made her his lover, took her into his thrall that way, and paid for her law school education. At any rate, once he had his core group of rabid followers, he was able to set up a nationwide network of underground crime, not only in drug distribution but in hard-core pornography. His ultimate plan was to eventually see his cult members in high political and legal spots, thus establishing his own 'legitimate' power base. Even his setting was carefully chosen. Nobody would ever think that someone from a small rural town in East Texas could operate in such big circles."

"I just can't figure out where I fit into all this," sighed Dani, fiddling with the pecans she was supposed to be chopping. She popped one in her mouth. "Nobody tried to recruit me for anything in college."

"Well, the guy was crazy. I mean, that's one thing you can't ever forget. He was certifiable. I think there's even a name for it, somebody was telling me. *Paranoid narcissism.* Taking self-love to a grandiose scale. Destroying whoever gets in your way. Anyway, once he found out where you were living, back in Austin when you were just hitting puberty, I think he set up that fake body as some kind of sick practical joke, and when you wound up in a mental institution because of it, he started making more serious plans for you. He knew he could use you someday. The scholarship and the local teaching job gave him a means of control over you. The only difference between you and his cult followers was that *you* didn't know."

She shuddered. "I wanted to throw up when I learned it

was Jordan Blake who got me my job at Maplewood High School. I'd sent out applications all over this area. I couldn't believe how fast they called." She pushed the pecans away. "But why do that to me again? Out at the Palmer estate?"

Nathan finished peeling his potatoes and reached for Dani's pecans, which he began chopping to smithereens. "Well, the thing Jonathon-Jordan failed to count on is that you can't make people toe the line, doing creepy, sinister, illegal things, for an entire lifetime. It's one thing when they're college age and hotheaded and eager for direction. It's another when they're in their thirties, settling down, finding their places in the real world."

Kate reached down and took the pecans away from Nathan. He gave her a sheepish grin. "The natives were restless, so to speak. Not as quick to obey his every command. He began to fear a leak."

"Like when he told me that somehow Adam had developed a conscience?"

"Right. I mean, what if they *all* did? Or just, say, the cop? Someone who could blow his whole operation sky-high?"

Kate rolled her eyes.

"Sorry. No pun intended. Anyway, I figure he was planning the first murder then, but he planted that body in your path so that you would make a false report, look nuts to the whole world, then maybe incur a little suspicion yourself when the real thing turned up."

Dani twinkled at Nathan. "But he didn't count on you and me, did he?"

"Hey, for a while there, I confess, I had my own doubts. You were acting pretty weird."

Kate said, "*That's* why he made no effort to destroy or hide the real bodies. He wanted the killings to be known, to be that much more of a weapon against his own cult members, more a way to control them and demonstrate his own power. With Lieutenant Ward's help, he could hide or destroy valuable evidence, and even plant someone like

MacIntire to take the fall. I mean, the man was untouch-
able."

"Right. The first murder was horrible enough, but the
woman was a drifter; no identity to anyone."

"She had an identity to me," interrupted Dani. She shook
her head. "It's one of those ironies of life, I guess. If you'd
been able to identify that first victim sooner than you did, I
would have recognized the name. Everything might have
fallen into place so much faster." She sighed. "I might have
even made the connection between Jordan Blake and
Jonathon Bartholomew."

Kate gave her a bewildered look. "What are you talking
about?"

Dani bowed her head. Nathan said, "That lawyer, Richard Miller, gave us a positive ID on the first victim. Her
name was Amanda Perkins. Dani knew her as 'Mandy'—
one of the children used by Blake and her foster parents
years ago in the kiddie porn ring."

"Oh, Dani. I don't know what to say." Kate squeezed her
shoulder.

"It was the tattoo," said Nathan. "I *knew* there was a
connection."

For a moment, they were silent. Then Nathan continued.
"Anyway, Amanda was unknown *here*. The cult never
expected one of their *own* to be next. Certainly Mac never
expected it. His wife didn't even know about his cult
activities. Then when he saw himself set up as the killer, he
knew good and damn well he'd better keep his mouth shut
or his kids would be next."

The room grew quiet, each thinking private thoughts too
sad, where the children were concerned, to express.

"Most of the cult members were surprised the night of the
first ritual murder," Nathan added. "After that, they were
terrified to realize that they were accomplices, and that if
any of them went to the police, at the very least they could
be arrested, and at the most, the same thing could happen to
them."

"Or to a loved one," whispered Dani.

"And that's what happened to poor Mac," said Kate.

Nathan nodded. "Poor bastard talked to Lieutenant Ward about it. He was the newest recruit. He hadn't gotten the full indoctrination. Blake had approached him mainly with a bribe—that's why their house was new and their furnishings so meager. Blake had set them up in that house. But the first murder jolted Mac so bad that, unfortunately, he believed the others were just as horrified as he was about it."

"Ward, of course, went straight to Blake," said Kate, cutting up the potatoes Nathan had peeled.

"We can only imagine what went on in that guy's mind when his own wife was next."

"Then, when he was told to take the blame for it or his kids would be next . . ." Kate's voice drifted off.

"Do you think the jury will be lenient?" asked Dani. "It seems unfair."

"I don't know, Dani. The guy didn't think it was unfair when he was overseeing the shipments of methamphetamines in pesticide containers from ChemCo's shipping and receiving dock all over the eastern half of the United States. The stuff moved from Alabama, through Tennessee, and on to the East Coast. Or when he moved into the new house Blake gave him."

She nodded, and stared out the window at the bleak, raw November day. Kate's herb garden looked dead, but she had assured Dani that new life lay hidden underneath the hard soil.

"He took Adam awfully young," she said sadly, still gazing out the cold window.

"Adam was already heavy into satanism when Blake recruited him. I think he admired you, though. At first, he took part in Blake's cruel tormenting of you because he still obeyed Blake without question. In fact, it was Adam who placed the dummy beside the lake that afternoon for you to find. It was Adam who stole your house key out of your bag and had a copy made before you'd even missed it."

"And Adam who took the theme papers I'd left by my chair."

"Probably."

"But he couldn't take Thoreau." Tears stung her lashes

and she looked down at her hands. It meant so much, having the big dog back home again. His lopsided grin often made her think of Adam. Nathan placed one big hand over both of hers and squeezed them. "It's all right. I think Adam may have redeemed himself by trying to help you figure out the puzzle."

"With the cryptogram," said Kate.

"Right. And, needless to say, Lilith Douglas went along with the JP on not ordering an autopsy because she knew good and well he'd been murdered. It's the same reason Ward kept squelching the investigation."

Dani sighed. "Once the dust settled from all this, it did occur to me that the Select Student Scholarship is now defunct, which means I can't recommend Jennifer Dawson for it. But I've been doing some digging. Maplewood Community College offers scholarships for single mothers as well as day care."

"What a great idea!" Kate beamed at her.

Nathan grinned. "I'm proud of you."

"No. Be proud of Jennifer."

"Here." Kate plunked down a bowl of salad greens in front of Dani and Nathan. "You guys make yourself useful."

They laughed and started tearing lettuce. After a moment, Dani said, "Well, I have to say I'm awfully glad I didn't kill anybody."

Kate said, "You're talking about the cult member you stabbed?"

"Yeah. I'd have done anything to get out of there, but, upon reflection, I have to say I'm glad one of the other cult members was a doctor."

"She wasn't hurt that bad," said Nathan. "That devil-worshipping doc had already sent her home by the time we got there. Didn't dare send her to a hospital, of course, because they report stab wounds to the police."

She met Nathan's gaze. "Of course, I wouldn't have minded so much finishing off Jordan Blake. I honestly don't think that would have preyed on my conscience too much."

Nathan shrugged. "You'd be surprised. Someday you'll be glad I stopped you."

She rolled her eyes.

"Besides," said Kate sarcastically, "the faithful lieutenant couldn't be everywhere at once." Then she asked, "What happened to all the other cult members? Some of the news was vague."

"We've rounded up all the local ones that Lilith knew about." Nathan avoided Dani's piercing glance.

"That's what haunts me," she said, forcing him to look at her. "You don't have any idea how far this network extends, what offshoots there may be in other states, or what crimes may be committed even yet by those offshoots. You should have let me get that *Book of Shadows*, Nathan."

The clever Jonathon Bartholomew alias Jordan Blake had apparently set more charges in the cult's basement gathering place as well, because it—with all incriminating evidence included—had been totally destroyed in the conflagration. Over and over again, Dani had gone over those final seconds in her mind's eye. She could almost *feel* that book in her hands. She glared at Nathan.

He didn't flinch. "I should have gotten you out of there. Which is just what I did."

She glanced back out the window. It was already getting to be an old argument. She figured it would come up again some other time.

But there was one thing they didn't talk about. She'd mentioned it once, before she was released from the hospital, but he refused to discuss it. As far as Nathan Kendall was concerned, the subject was closed. He was a logical man, and where logic failed, he chose to put it out of his mind.

But it would never be closed for her. Because the truth of the matter was that no trace of Jordan Blake, or Jonathon Bartholomew, or whoever he was—maybe Satan himself— no sign of him had ever been found in the burned-out wreckage of the ChemCo plant.

Dani stirred restlessly in her chair. It was supposed to be a day for giving thanks. Lord knew, Dani had much to be thankful for. Still, she couldn't seem to shake the tiny fingers of dread which occasionally clutched at her heart. Because as far as Dani was concerned, he could still be out there, plotting evil. Watching her.

It was the final step in her healing process, Kate had assured her, but sitting here in the cushioned pew of the church, Dani wasn't so sure. Liquid winter light streamed through the stained-glass windows, refracting into crimson, gold, and blue on the heads of the worshippers.

In spite of her chronic discomfort, perhaps even mild paranoia, about the possibility of Jordan Blake's reentry into her life (or one of his disciples in his place), Dani had made a recovery that seemed phenomenal to those who'd known her longest. Her nightmares, for one thing, had ended, almost as if *living* them had exorcised the final demons from her soul. Thus freed, she'd opened, as truly as a flower to the dawn, to life and all its possibilities.

Her family never completely understood what had caused the transformation; they were just thrilled to see it, and trusted her to make the most of it. Dani knew, though. Ironically it was a line from Dante's *Inferno* which expressed it best:

> *Know then, O waiting and compassionate soul*
> *that is to fear which has the power to harm*
> *and nothing else is fearful even in Hell.*

She'd learned that most of her little everyday fears were only dark figments of her own imagination, which would vanish when exposed to the light of scrutiny. Of her very real terrors, well, she had faced the enemy head-on; she had fought; and she had triumphed.

Facing and overcoming fear, Dani had learned, was a liberating experience. All she ever really had to fear was Jordan Blake. Once she had faced him down without flinching, she found that there was really nothing very frightening at all about something simple like falling in love.

Or getting married.

That was next on her check-off list of things not to waste time putting off ever again . . . but this had to come first.

Listening to the soft music, the muted voices of the choir, Dani squeezed Nathan's hand on one side and Kate's on the other. A sense of peace settled over her like a down comforter on a feather bed.

After all, she'd made it this far. There'd been times she almost cracked, almost didn't go on, but something always kept her going.

Another passage from Dante's powerful verse slipped into her mind. It came from the cantos on Paradise:

> *Here vigor fail'd the towering fantasy:*
> *But yet the will roll'd onward, like a wheel*
> *In even motion, by the love impell'd*
> *That moves the sun in heaven and all the stars.*

The pastor took his place at the podium. Dani's heart leapt into her throat.

"Today," he said, "we have a special guest. For the first time, she is going to share her story, in the hopes that it might help someone else who has ever . . . well . . . faced demons of his own." He gestured to Dani.

She rose and walked toward the pew, feeling hundreds of eyes peering at her back. At the podium, she turned.

The first thing she saw was Nathan and Kate, beaming at her. She felt a lump in her throat, cleared it, and thought, *It's time to give something back.*

Then, in a voice at first weak, then gaining in strength, she said, "Hi. My name is Faith Daniels . . . and I'm a survivor."